RAVE REVIEWS FOR CAROL CARSON!

"Ms. Carson has a writing voice all her own that is refreshingly different, warms the heart, and brings a smile to your face."

—*Rendezvous*

"Keep an eye on this budding writer. She has talent and imagination coupled with that delightful comic turn."

—*Romance Communications*

"You won't want to miss this one."

—*CompuServe Romance Reviews* on *Family Man*

"It's well worth the buggy ride."

—*Romantic Times* on *Family Man*

"Carol Carson is a deft voice at telling a rollicking romantic tale. *Bad Company* will tickle your funny bone."

—*Affaire de Coeur*

Carol Carson "breaks into the romance scene with a fresh and amusing plot line [and] gives readers a new name to add to their keeper shelves."

—*Heartland Critiques* on *Bad Company*

"Carol Carson's warm sense of humor will keep you smiling."

—Debra Dier, author of *Saint's Temptation*

A POINTED DISCUSSION

"That isn't what I think it is, is it?"

"Yes, Mr. Sullivan, it most c-certainly is." Despite being cold enough to make a snowman shiver, Nora-Leigh felt in control for the first time since she'd met this handsome yet arrogant man. It was most gratifying. "It's a knife—a very long, very sharp knife. It's my grandfather's actually and a very nice one it is, too. Don't you think?" She emphasized her point by moving the flat of the blade a trifle closer to his backside and pushing the point hard against his personal parts, though not enough to cut the cloth. It was just to grab his attention. She got it.

He gave her a frank stare of bemusement and, if she wasn't mistaken, a slight nod of admiration, then carefully stood up, his hands loose at his sides. Water lapped at his ankles, his clothes pressed flat against his body. His mouth quirked upward in a slight grin and this time she was certain the look he gave her was one of begrudging respect. "Well, Miss Dillon. I may not have wanted you along on this crazy quest, but I'll give you credit: you are far better prepared for danger than I expected."

Shivering and stiff with cold, Nora-Leigh took Clay's proffered hand and rose awkwardly to her feet. "I try."

Much to her surprise, Clay clutched her shoulder with one hand and captured her chin with the other. He touched his warm lips to her chilled ones with a short, sweet, gentle kiss. "Well done, Miss Dillon."

FORTUNE'S Treasure

Carol Carson

LEISURE BOOKS NEW YORK CITY

Dedicated with love to my daughter, Corey,
my son, Patrick,
my daughter-in-law, Samantha,
and the most recent joy in my life, my grandson, Jesse.
You are special, wonderful treasures I keep close to my
heart, even when you are far away.

A LEISURE BOOK®

December 2000

Published by

Dorchester Publishing Co., Inc.
276 Fifth Avenue
New York, NY 10001

ISBN 0-8439-4806-X

The name "Leisure Books" and the stylized "L" with design are trademarks of Dorchester Publishing Co., Inc.

Printed in the United States of America.

Visit us on the web at www.dorchesterpub.com.

Chapter One

Steamboat Bend, Montana
Spring, 1886

I hate children.

Nora-Leigh Dillon winced when the horrible notion crossed her mind as she stood in the sunny schoolyard watching her students play their silly games. She rolled her eyes heavenward and prayed that God would forgive her for the terrible, selfish thought. Because it wasn't true. Well, not entirely true. She simply hated teaching, and children were an unfortunate aspect of the teaching profession. It seemed as if each day she spent in the classroom, life passed her by, and her dreams drifted away like the feathery wisps off a cottonwood tree.

Day in, day out, year in, year out, her life grew more tedious: teaching the children, advising them, guiding them. She'd begun teaching when she was just a girl and

9

after six years, she was weary of the monotony. She longed for a life of her own.

From beneath the brim of her straw hat, she looked out over the sun-dappled schoolyard at her brood, an even dozen boys and girls, playing, laughing, and chasing each other. She wondered if something was missing inside of her. Some maternal, loving female part such as her mother, Elsa, possessed. Her mother adored teaching, and adored children. She reminded her daughter often about her love of children. Nora-Leigh wondered if that was her mother's subtle way of complaining that she had no grandchildren to love and adore. As if grandchildren were in the realm of possibility. She scoffed at the foolish idea.

When Elsa's eyesight had begun to fail, Nora-Leigh had reluctantly taken over the teaching duties in Steamboat Bend. Of course, the fact that no one else in town offered to become the school's teacher had a little something to do with her decision. Few people in the small farming and ranching community could read and write. Even if they had possessed the skills, few had the time or inclination to take up the position. No, it had been up to her.

Nora-Leigh sighed and folded her arms over her chest. She leaned her head back against the unpainted wall of the clapboard school while still keeping an eye on her students. She felt no maternal joy when wiping a dripping nose, or reminding fourteen-year-old Jake Forrest that spitting wasn't done in the presence of ladies. She didn't feel much like a mother or a teacher when she scraped manure off a pair of small booted feet before the child brought the stench into the schoolroom for everyone to share. Some days she felt so stifled she could scream. But then, once in a while, when a child grasped a difficult equation or discovered a love of reading, it all seemed worthwhile.

Most of the time, though, she felt bored and incomplete. And she worried that she was somehow poisoning their fertile young minds with her wish to be anywhere else but in that suffocating classroom.

How she'd envied Mary Lou Anderson when she'd married at sixteen—the same age Nora-Leigh had begun teaching—and moved to Denver, or when Jack Mitchell graduated from her classroom and traveled to San Francisco to become a journalist at a well-known newspaper.

"Miss Dillon!"

Nora-Leigh glanced up from beneath her bonnet to see a whirlwind of a little girl running toward her. Her yellow gingham-checked skirt flew about her ankles, showing off the blue satin trim and white lace ruffle of her pantalets. Despite the mud in the schoolyard, her boots shone as if recently polished. Nora-Leigh took a deep, fortifying breath.

"Miss Dillon! Sherman is looking cross-eyed at me," seven-year-old Amanda Hartson whined in a louder than usual voice. She dashed right up to Nora-Leigh and tugged on the front of her skirt. Expectation lit the girl's frowning freckled face. Amanda was the daughter of the richest man in town—a man who made his fortune in gold mining and who along with his arrogant wife spoiled little Amanda near to death with a wardrobe full of frilly dresses, and a cart and pony of her very own.

If the little girl didn't complain to her at least once an hour, it meant she was absent from class. Nora-Leigh counted to ten before replying. "Just ignore Sherman, Amanda. He will stop if you don't give him any undue attention. Perhaps you should feel fortunate that he isn't biting your arm this time. Don't you still have teeth marks from yesterday?"

Her tiny mouth gaped in a surprised "Oh," and her eyes widened. She nodded without further comment as if she'd given it serious thought. Then she ran off, seemingly satisfied with the advice.

Did all schoolteachers have the irresistible urge to throw their McGuffey's Readers out the window, break all the children's slates into pieces, lock the doors, and run off without a backward glance? Oh, how wicked and selfish she sounded.

Thank God, school would be out for the year in four days.

Four days. Four *long* days.

Nora-Leigh was already daydreaming about how she would spend her summer: searching for treasure, panning for gold, discovering unknown possibilities. It was her one true ambition. This year she would find a long-lost treasure, make a fortune, and travel the world to see all the wondrous sights she'd read about.

Nora-Leigh glanced at the timepiece pinned to the front of her bodice. Outdoor recess was over. She hated to go indoors, not only because she had to resume teaching but also because this was the first sunny day all week. She trudged across the schoolyard and rang the bell to get the children inside. She heaved a heartfelt sigh. Four days. . . . How many hours was that, she wondered as she stepped into the small single room. She now had a mathematical problem for the older children to solve this afternoon. Of course, they had to work on geography first—and that was Nora-Leigh's favorite subject.

After school, Nora-Leigh, as exhilarated about her freedom as any of her charges, rushed home and changed into trousers and one of her grandfather's chambray shirts. She stuffed her hair up beneath a dingy old straw gardening hat and grabbed a shovel, then ran off feeling much like a guilty child avoiding chores.

She had been digging only fifteen minutes when an abrupt rustling in the trees behind her startled her so badly that she lost her balance and stumbled forward. With a screech, she fell into the shallow hole she'd been so diligently digging. She tumbled head over heels and landed on her hands and knees. Her shovel followed her in and landed with a plop, tossing up a clod of mud that splattered her face and neck. Mud squished between her fingers and splashed on her trousers. Unfortunately, it had been raining for two straight days and only today had the sun come out.

"Damnation!" She felt she could get away with the unladylike vulgarity since she was alone. Besides, she rather liked the sound of it on her lips. "Damnation!"

Feeling as foolish as a dumb milk cow, she scrambled out of the hole. When she heard the same rustling again, she ducked beneath the drooping branches of a spreading fir tree. Squatting on her dirty knees, she prayed that the dead needles would soften any sound she inadvertently made. What would her students think if they found their teacher covered in mud and digging a hole in the middle of nowhere?

The sun scarcely reached through the thick branches, and the tree blanketed the area beneath it in a gloomy gray. The death-like quiet gave Nora-Leigh a sense of isolation. Her heart thudded in her throat as she strained to hear the sound again. She brushed her sweaty, blister-covered palms against the twill fabric of her trouser legs and waited. The pungent evergreen scent of the towering fir tree tickled her nose.

For what seemed like long, agonizing minutes she sat there anticipating the worst—Indians in war paint, although they hadn't had anything to go on the warpath about in a good many years; most had been marched away to reservations. Or rabid wolves, a pack of them with sharp fangs dripping blood, ready to tear out her throat. But when was the last time a pack of wolves attacked a human?

Or more likely, as rational thought coursed through her befuddled brain, it was Billy Seth Torrence. That boy'd had a crush on her since they'd been thirteen years old and in the schoolroom together. And although now physically an adult, Billy Seth wasn't quite normal in the head. He'd followed her around Steamboat Bend for ten years like her shadow, making calf eyes and bestowing slobbery kisses on her whenever he caught her unawares.

The boy—she guessed she should call him a man even though she still thought of him as a boy—didn't know the meaning of the word "no," or he chose to go deaf whenever she blurted it in his elephant-sized ear. Everyone, including her own granny who never said a bad word about anyone, said he had the biggest ears in Steamboat Bend. The men who sat in the town square and did nothing but gossip and gripe said other parts of his anatomy were oversized as well. She could only imagine. She tried not to think about Billy Seth's oversized *parts*, however, because her face turned red, which gave away her wayward thoughts and made those gossipy old men hoot with laughter. They thought of her as that eccentric spinster woman, Nora-Leigh Dillon.

She chanced a quick peek through the emerald-green tree branches, then breathed a deep sigh of relief. It turned out to be nothing at all like she'd imagined. She hadn't known how she would begin to explain the digging to her students or their parents, or even her own family, but it was just a man. Still, this was a stranger to Steamboat Bend, and one could never be too careful.

He was tall and wide-shouldered. He sauntered along the path in a confident manner, pulling a plodding dapple gray horse behind him. He wasn't even trying to be quiet. He started to whistle a merry song dreadfully out of tune, and as loud as you please.

"Hey there, woman," he called out, momentarily stopping his whistling. "You might as well crawl out of there." His voice rippled with challenge. "I can smell you beneath that tree."

Smell me? How could he smell me? She knew she didn't smell bad. She had bathed just last night with her favorite French-milled lavender soap she bought from the general store. Why, Franklin Homer himself told her it came over on a boat all the way from Paris, France. Franklin pronounced it "Paree." She'd even shampooed her hair with it. Twice.

Nora-Leigh stood still and didn't so much as blink. Maybe he was bluffing.

He wasn't. When a strong arm reached through the branches, snaked around her waist, and hauled her unceremoniously onto her feet, she yelped. No. She hollered like a branded yearling calf. He immediately let loose, and she fell onto her posterior. Not that it mattered, since her trousers were already muddy. Still, falling on one's backside in front of a man was humiliating. And a fine-looking man at that. Not that she really noticed or was interested in that sort of thing. Not at her advanced age. She was long past that.

She looked up at the sound of his deep laughter, ungracious from a family member but downright rude coming from a complete stranger. He returned the stare. Nora-Leigh was taken aback a bit when she saw that he wore a black patch over his right eye, and that a glimmer of humor sparkled from his left. He had a thick sable-brown mustache that covered his lips but did nothing to disguise the grin that covered his face.

"That wasn't nice," she complained, even though she knew she sounded like Amanda Hartson on one of her most irritatingly petulant days. She stood and swiped ineffectually at her bottom.

Watching her brush at the seat of her pants, he chuckled as if he couldn't help himself. "Good God, but you're a muddy mess. I'd give you a hand but you'd probably slap me. Should I apologize for laughing?"

She frowned. "No, I don't think that's necessary, but I don't smell, sir. And how did you know I was a woman, anyway?"

"I didn't say you smelled *bad*. As for knowing you were a woman, well, I never smelled a man that smelled so sweet." His voice, no longer challenging but smooth as warmed molasses, could, as Granny would say, coax the birds from the trees. "But nor have I known a woman that was quite so dirty. Pardon my familiarity, but you've got a glob of mud here." He reached over and brushed at the tip of her nose. "You do smell purty, though, just like some purple flowers I once saw on an island in the South China Sea."

She rolled her eyes. "What a simpleton you must think me."

His dark brows rose. "Why?"

"You've never been to an island in the South China Sea—or anywhere else so exotic, for that matter."

His lips turned up in an amused grin, displaying dimples in both cheeks. "And how would you know that?"

"Look at you." Her glance swept up and down his rangy frame, taking in the worn black boots, the well-washed chambray shirt, and the denim trousers that clung to his hips and thighs like a second skin. He even wore a red neckerchief tied in a careless knot around his throat. "Although you're clean, you're either a cowboy or a miner or my name isn't . . . well, that's neither here nor there. I'm not trying to be rude, sir, but I consider myself a good judge of people. And unless I'm badly mistaken, you've never set foot anywhere east of the Mississippi, and certainly not in some port of call in the South China Sea."

One hand rested on his hip as he peered into her face with that unfathomable pewter-colored eye. "Is that so?"

"Yes, well . . ." He made her feel oddly uncomfortable

16

with that knowing grin and that single twinkling eye. "I should be on my way."

He bent to retrieve her shovel. Handing it to her, he said, "Don't forget this, darlin'."

"I'm not your darling, Mister—"

"Sullivan," he supplied. "Clay Sullivan. But you're someone's darling, aren't you now?"

"No, absolutely not." Flustered and completely at a loss for something else to say, Nora-Leigh backed up and, yes indeed, fell right back into the hole.

The stranger dropped to his knees and peeked at her, that all-knowing smile dimpling his cheeks once again. "Are you all right, miss?"

When she nodded, he held out his hand and effortlessly hauled her to her feet. "So this is how you got so muddy. What are you trying to do? Dig all the way to China?"

Nora-Leigh began walking back toward town, away from this insulting man. "No, sir, I'm not."

He stepped in line with her and walked beside her. "Well, it won't work."

"What won't work?"

"Digging your way to China. When I was eight years old I tried. All I got for my hard work was blisters on my hands and a reprimand from my Pa."

Nora-Leigh stopped and glanced at his face. "I'm hardly eight years old anymore."

He stopped also. "No, ma'am." He glanced at her mud-stained shirt and trousers in one all-encompassing gaze. "You most certainly are not."

She didn't understand why he made her so uncomfortable. No man had ever looked at her in quite the same manner. She started forward again, and he did the same. "I'm Steamboat Bend's schoolteacher."

"A science experiment, then?"

"What?" she asked, confused and anxious to be away from this unfathomable man. It was almost as if he knew

17

her innermost thoughts. She found it most disconcerting.

"What are you digging for?"

"That is my business."

He hooted with laughter. "You're a prickly one, Miss Schoolmarm."

God, how she hated that word. It sounded almost as bad as "spinster." In her mind, it was as interchangeable as her own name. Schoolmarm, spinster, Nora-Leigh Dillon. Steamboat Bend's only single woman, and stuck there until they put her in her grave. Out here the men outnumbered the women at least five to one, but no one wanted her. Except, of course, Billy Seth Torrence.

"Miss?"

They were on the edge of town, near the first crossroads of homes and businesses. Without a good-bye, she abruptly turned the corner to the right and left him standing there calling after her. She ran most of the way home.

"Nellie, I believe I've found the one. Come take a look."

Nora-Leigh set down the book she'd been trying to read and stood. She might as well give up—she'd read the same page at least five times. It appeared Granny wasn't about to let her get any reading done. She crossed the room to stand beside her diminutive grandmother . . . again. Just to placate her, Nora-Leigh glanced out the window at the dusty street.

Nothing new ever passed their home on the main thoroughfare; she saw the same neighbors pulling wagons loaded with bags of seed and planting equipment, familiar men on foot and on horseback, and boisterous miners in the streets and staggering out of the saloons. Steamboat Bend, Montana, was as dull as boiled cabbage, and about as pleasing to the nose. Nora-Leigh heaved a sigh.

Granny swatted her arm as she held the faded blue flower-sprigged curtain aside. She pointed her pudgy index finger so Nora-Leigh couldn't help but see the man she was pointing out.

Granny leaned close and pushed her nose up against the parlor window. The glass immediately fogged over.

Nora-Leigh shook her head. Praise the heavens, Granny still had most of her sensibilities, but her sight was puny at best, even with the help of the spectacles that clung to her button nose.

She waggled her finger at a man sitting astride a huge, dapple-gray horse in front of the livery. The horse and rider looked appallingly familiar, though his back was to her so all Nora-Leigh could see was the man nodding his head as he leaned on the pommel and talked with the livery owner, Slim Jim Walken. Surprised that Granny even recognized the gender of the stranger, Nora-Leigh took a closer look. He sat confidently in the saddle, lean and weathered, his hat clutched in one large hand. The parched wind tousled his overlong chocolate-brown hair.

Nora-Leigh leaned forward as the man turned his head. There was a rather obvious difference between this man and any others. A black leather patch covered his right eye. She again noticed the thick mustache that he brushed absentmindedly with his thumb and forefinger. Aside from the eye patch, though, he looked little different from any of the half-dozen other men Granny had thought looked like promising husband material and had been pointing out to her for the past hour. Unfortunately, Nora-Leigh knew this man. They'd met under rather embarrassing circumstances just yesterday. That could only be Clay Sullivan of the mischievous grin, dimpled cheeks, and rude manner.

"Well proportioned, if I do say so myself. A good, honest face, too."

"Oh? And how can you tell that, Granny?"

"Because his eyes are set wide apart. That's a good sign, means he's trustworthy. You need a man who's trustworthy. Course, my own eyes aren't what they used to be. What do you see?"

Nora-Leigh paused a moment and pretended to take a closer look. She brought her gaze around to Granny's beloved face. "He has a nice hat."

A disapproving frown flitted across her grandmother's lined features as she dropped the curtain back into place. "Humph."

"And if I'm not mistaken, that's a birdcage strapped to the back of his mule."

Granny's eyes widened, her jaw dropped, and she stepped up and took another look. "Humph."

"Humph yourself. I think it's time you and Mother stopped meddling in my life. I don't wish to marry. That man or any other."

Granny pulled on one of Nora-Leigh's curls. "In a pig's eye. Every woman wants to marry."

Nora-Leigh knew she was lying when she answered, "I don't."

"In all my born days, gal. What's wrong with you?"

Nora-Leigh cocked her head to one side. "I want to travel around the world. I want to go adventuring, and see new things, and . . . well, seek my fortune."

"Phooey. You can seek your fortune right here in Steamboat Bend. Actually, right there across the way. I'd wager that's a man who could set your blood to boiling and make it an adventure in the bargain."

Nora-Leigh couldn't help but smile. "Granny, what a thing to say."

"Honey, you're not getting any younger."

Nora-Leigh wrapped an arm around her grandmother's stooped, shawl-covered shoulders and gave her an affectionate squeeze. "I love you, but you sound just like Mother. Come and sit down. Let's have tea ready for her when she gets home from visiting with Auntie Sarah, and just forget all this silly talk of marriage."

"It's not silly."

Nora-Leigh barely managed not to roll her eyes as she helped Granny to the sofa. "Where's Gramps?" she called over her shoulder as she headed for the kitchen.

Granny gave an unladylike snort. "That old man. He's outside puttering in his garden. Why, he hasn't grown a vegetable worth putting up in forty years. I don't know why he thinks he can start now. Montana just doesn't have the good rich soil for gardening, not like they do back East."

Nora-Leigh stuck her head around the corner. "But I thought you loved Steamboat Bend."

"I do, honey, I do. It's just that you can't grow anything here but rocks and fanciful legends."

Nora-Leigh wrapped her arms around her waist and sighed, then leaned against the doorframe. "Oh, Granny, that's just what I love about Montana—the folk tales, the superstitions, the Indian lore. It's all so interesting, except that I never get out of Steamboat Bend and it's about as exciting as watching grass grow."

Granny shook her head, her mouth set in a thin line. "You and your grandpa—two peas in a pod. If it weren't for his rheumtiz, I believe he'd take you up on that adventuring, prospecting for gold, or finding lost treasure or some such nonsense."

Nora-Leigh grinned. "What fun that would be."

Granny grinned back. "You know you're giving your mother gray hairs with the things you do—riding that bicycle all over town and wearing men's trousers. Why, when you cut off all your pretty hair, I thought Elsa was going to swoon."

"Mother can be such a stick-in-the-mud sometimes. She needs to be more modern. Modern women are cutting their hair."

"And you're a modern woman, huh?"

"Yes."

"Go make the tea, dearie," Granny said, then motioned Nora-Leigh closer. When she bent down, Granny whispered, "I love your short hair. I might even cut my own, but don't you dare tell that ole stick-in-the-mud."

Nora-Leigh smiled and gave Granny a gentle hug. "Thank you, Granny. I think I'll go change and ride my bicycle down to meet Mother, and then walk her back home."

"Oh, *that* will delight the poor woman," Granny muttered. "She so loves to hear about you riding that contraption around town in your trousers for all and sundry to see."

Nora-Leigh winked at her grandmother. "I know."

Clay Sullivan tossed his hat on his head and headed his horse toward the boardinghouse that the liveryman suggested was a good place to stay. He'd stated that the food was good and plentiful, and the widow woman who owned the place was pretty and welcoming to bachelors. That last was said with a wink and a knowing grin. The boardinghouse was definitely worth a look.

Before he set out of town again, he needed a place to stay where he could chart his maps. The thought of a nice hot soak in a real tub sounded good, too. He'd camped just outside of town last night to clear his head and focus on his new undertaking. He'd cleaned up in a cold stream.

Once he was settled, he could ask around town about the legendary lost gold shipment that had brought him to Steamboat Bend in the first place. He knew the old-timers loved a good yarn, and this one was as good as any.

Unless he found someone who had either worked on the *Far West* river boat or had been on the freight wagon that was carting the shipment, he doubted it would be found so many years after the fact. But the Army was paying him cash money to search for the missing gold, and he would get paid regardless. Of course, it didn't hurt that if he found the gold he would get a percentage, and that little chunk of change would make a nice downpayment on the cattle ranch he planned to start. This was his last assignment for the Army. Their guns were no longer needed in the West as the Indians were mostly quiet on the reservations, and the railroads were bringing in settlers by the carload.

He walked his horse past the schoolhouse and, with a smile turning up his mouth, recalled meeting the schoolmarm yesterday. What a corker she was. He was surprised the good townsfolk allowed such an odd upstart to mold the minds of their precious offspring.

A woman took a hesitant step off the porch of the house next to the school and cocked her head as if listening to the sounds around her. She was older than Clay, and yet he found her uncommonly attractive and somewhat familiar. Coal-black hair laced with streaks of silver surrounded an unlined ivory complexion and a tentative smile. She walked out onto the porch and didn't even squint against the late afternoon sun.

"Howdy, ma'am."

She waved a friendly greeting in his direction. Despite the fact that she was old enough to be his mother, he found himself staring at the handsome woman.

His stallion, Jolly, sensed his lack of attention. The horse shied, sidestepping and prancing, his hooves kicking up dust and dirt. Losing a stirrup, Clay found it took all his concentration just to keep his seat. By the time Jolly quieted, the damned horse had proceeded to step right into the path of a two-wheeled contraption that Clay had seen only recently in his travels.

Its rider swerved the newfangled machine to avoid collision, hit a hole in the road, and tumbled ass-over-teakettle into the dirt.

The older woman screeched as the conveyance and the boy on it cartwheeled in a confusion of arms, legs, churning wheels, and a wholly enlightened vocabulary.

"What the devil!" Clay vaulted from his mount and rushed over. He crouched down and grasped the young man's slender arm. Pulling him to a sitting position, he asked, "Are you all right?"

The youngster stood, jerking his arm from Clay's grasp. He dusted off the seat of his trousers and stared up at him with a clear, disarming gaze. Dust coated his face from forehead to obstinate chin. "You should watch where you're going, Mr. Sullivan."

Clay opened his mouth to speak when he recognized her. Long, black-velvet eyelashes and large, almond-shaped hazel eyes. His gaze lowered to discover a familiar button nose, parted pink lips. He couldn't help himself as his eyes drifted even lower to full breasts pushing against a man's chambray shirt. The schoolmarm. A woman, all right, with a smallish waist and rounded hips that no trousers could ever hope to disguise. His hand burned where he'd touched her arm. He swallowed . . . hard. He dropped his hand to his side.

"You. Again!" Clay swallowed again and found himself repeating his question of yesterday. "Are you all right?" He brought his gaze back to her fetching face. She stared right back at him.

She started to brush off the front of her dirty shirt, but when she saw him watching her, she stopped, her hand poised in mid air. Instead she pointed a finger at herself. "Of course it's me. I could have been killed."

By this time the older woman had found her way into the street. She took the girl by the shoulders, and in a strange manner that Clay found perplexing, her hands mapped the younger woman from head to toe. "Are you all right, Nellie?"

"I'm fine, really. Will everyone please stop asking me that?"

"You gave me quite a fright," she said.

24

"Me too, ma'am."

The young woman turned and stabbed Clay in the chest with a well-placed finger. "You weren't watching where you were going."

"That's a fact. I caught a glimpse of this handsome woman here and plumb lost my head." He tipped his hat to the dark-haired woman. "Sorry, ma'am."

The younger of the two placed both hands on her hips. From eyes that could freeze boiling water in less than a minute, she again stung him with her indignant gaze. "I think you owe me an apology, too."

"I apologize . . . Nellie." He couldn't help but see the agonized expression that crossed her face at his use of the name. She most definitely wasn't a Nellie, he thought. Nellies were sweet-natured and compliant, not like this girl who was as prickly as a desert cactus. He bent forward and fingered one of the short curls that poked out from beneath the ugly hat. The tips barely grazed the curve of her chin. He knew it was personal and a question a gentleman would never ask, but he couldn't stop himself; the woman brought out the rascal in him. "Who scalped your hair, Nellie?"

She slapped his hand away. "That's none of your business, and it's Miss Dillon to you, sir."

"Nora-Leigh, where are your manners?"

Nora-Leigh. Now, that name most definitely suited her.

The older woman offered her hand to Clay, but her eyes didn't seem to be focusing on him.

Clay felt like kicking himself. He realized belatedly that the woman was blind, or at least partially sightless. Talk about that, he was a blind fool for not noticing sooner!

The older woman spoke. "I'm Elsa Dillon, and if you haven't guessed as much already, this hoydenish girl is my daughter."

He gently took her hand. "Pleased, ma'am. Clay Sullivan." He turned toward the woman's outspoken daughter and said, "Why, Miss Dillon, so good to see you again."

Her rosy mouth turned down at the corners, and she gave him a grudging nod. "Mr. Sullivan."

"You've met?"

"Briefly," Nora-Leigh and Clay said simultaneously.

"And what are you doing in Steamboat Bend, sir?" Mrs. Dillon asked.

Clay wasn't sure how to reply to the question without sounding impolite or unfriendly. Even though the Army employed him as a civilian scout, their policy was to keep a low profile if possible. But Steamboat Bend wasn't overly big, and his business was sure to be known before long. Still, some cards should be played close to the vest. Going after lost gold shipments for the federal government was undoubtedly one of them. And his military superiors wouldn't want everyone and their long-lost uncle heading out to the Crow Reservation with a shovel and a pick, digging up trouble between the Indians and the civilians. That was why Ethan had suggested the damned pirate disguise. Clay normally wouldn't wear the dad-blamed eye patch; he certainly didn't need it.

"A business venture," he finally replied. He picked up Jolly's reins and waited, watching Nellie as she bent over——good God, but those trousers fit her in an interesting way—and righted her bicycle. "Those two-wheeled contraptions are something, all right."

Mrs. Dillon shook her head. "Dangerous is what they are. I'm sorry about the accident."

"No harm done."

She glanced in the direction of her daughter and gave the girl an unmistakable look of displeasure. "This time."

"Mother, your tea will be cold by the time we get home." Nora-Leigh mounted the bicycle, stretching her trousers enticingly across her rounded backside. Clay had a difficult time yanking his gaze away.

With one foot on the ground and one on a pedal, Nora-Leigh cleared her throat when she caught him staring. He jerked his head away from ogling at her fetching behind and instead captured the young woman's blushing gaze. Her eyes grew large and liquid before she glanced away from his unwavering stare of interest. Subtlety had never been his game. "Sorry about the accident. You're sure you're all right?"

"Right as rain." Somehow it didn't sound as if she meant it. She took the bicycle for a turn in front of the school. "It seems to be all right," she called out.

Clay couldn't take his eyes off her. Long legs pumped the pedals, the wheels turned, and her rump hitched rhythmically back and forth. Back and Forth. Back and forth. His mind reeled.

"She's a handful, that one," her mother said for his ears only.

Clay shot Mrs. Dillon a glance. Curiously, she was smiling at him. It was a good thing she couldn't see him ogling her daughter. She'd probably have him arrested. At the moment, though, even if his life depended on it, Clay couldn't have disagreed with her. He'd enjoy a *couple* handfuls himself.

"You know, Mr. Sullivan," she whispered with a twinkling in her opaque eyes, "I can't see at all in the distance, but I do have limited vision up close. Not well enough to read a book, mind you, but well enough to read faces—and yours is speaking volumes."

Slightly embarrassed, he jerked his gaze away from Nora-Leigh's enticing backside and grinned at her mother. "Pardon me, ma'am."

She patted his arm. "Perhaps it was ungentlemanly to stare, but it was also unladylike of me to comment about it and embarrass you in such a fashion. I just couldn't seem to help myself, though. Nora-Leigh is a beautiful young woman when you take the time to look past her eccentricities."

"I'm sure she is," he agreed, "but I deserved to be put in my place." It didn't matter what he thought of the woman. He had a job to do for which he could claim a tidy sum of money if he accomplished it on schedule. He didn't have the patience or the inclination to court independent-minded schoolmarms who dressed like boys and acted as if they didn't care that they were scandalizing their own family and the entire community as well.

Nora-Leigh had circled around and returned, then dismounted. She took her mother's arm and guided her to the side of the road. "We really must be going, Mother."

Clay watched her maneuver her bicycle contraption and deftly hold on to her mother's arm at the same time as they walked down the street. No, he had no time for girls like that. He shook his head. What a corker! He'd do well to steer clear of that one.

Chapter Two

As she set the table for supper, Nora-Leigh found herself staring out the window but not noticing the view. She couldn't stop thinking about the stranger she'd run into. Or maybe she should call him the one that ran into her.

Clay Sullivan.

The thick, brushy mustache that hid his upper lip. That one soft, laughing, silver-gray eye. Even now she blushed as she recalled his awestruck gaze the moment he recognized her—both as a female and from their previous encounter outside of town.

Then she recalled his arrogance. His ungentlemanly stare. His so-called business venture in Steamboat Bend. He was no doubt a reckless gambler or a fast-drawing gunslinger. Or a nefarious land-grabber searching for gold. He might represent a railroad baron from back East and was even now buying up all the valuable property in Steamboat Bend to lay down tracks and take over the town.

Nora-Leigh laughed out loud. Her wayward thoughts and overactive imagination were going to get her in trouble again. There was no valuable land in Steamboat Bend. The Northern Pacific steamed through the dusty little town and seldom stopped; no one exciting arrived, and no one boring wished to leave. And there was no gold to be found in the nearby creeks and rivers. She'd looked. Diligently. On many occasions.

With a fingernail she scratched off a bit of dried food from the tine of a fork, then placed it beside her plate. Washing dishes was one of her chores, but she seldom gave it much effort, and, unfortunately, it often showed. She had more interesting things to concentrate on—like listening to Gramps tell tales of his river-boating days.

How wonderfully dangerous and exciting it all sounded. To be able to travel wherever one wanted. It was a dream that Nora-Leigh had coveted since she was six years old.

Lost in thought, Nora-Leigh didn't realize she was no longer alone until she heard a raspy chuckle from the back door. Startled, she glanced up.

"Daydreaming again, Nellie girl?" Gramps asked. He stood just inside the door, a grin splitting his weathered face. A dimple danced in either cheek as his lips twitched in amusement.

She hadn't even heard the squeak of the hinge that always needed oiling or the slam of the door that never quite closed correctly. She returned his wry grin. "Caught in the act."

He patted her shoulder as he passed behind her. "Nothing wrong with daydreams. So long as you're living a good life while you're dreaming. I've for certain had my share."

"Of dreams?"

"You just betcha. I always wanted to run away to try my luck with a pickaxe or a gold pan, and then come home with my chest pushed out a-braggin' to my friends and family about my wondrous find."

Nora-Leigh shook her head. "I can't imagine you leaving Granny like that."

"Neither could I, honey. I expect that's why I never did it."

He plopped down onto a wooden kitchen chair and groaned as he jerked off his dusty, care-worn boots. Then he stood and went to stand beside Nora-Leigh. Lifting her chin, he stared into her face. He smelled of freshly turned earth and his favorite cherry pipe tobacco. Bits of dirt still clung to the rolled-up sleeves of his shirt. "So what are your daydreams about, honey?"

"I doubt they differ much from yours." At his surprised expression, she continued, "No, I don't want to pan for gold, but I'd like to travel and see the world a little bit, maybe even have some adventures someday. I know I'm a disappointment to Mother."

His expression turned somber. "You could never be a disappointment to her or your grandmother and me."

"Sometimes I embarrass her . . . but I don't think I'm cut out for teaching, Gramps. Honestly, some days I don't think I even like children."

The dimples in his cheeks deepened as he chuckled. "Of course you do."

"Mother would like me to marry and give her a passel of grandchildren."

"We all would like that."

"If I had been a boy, things would have been different."

Gramps snorted, then brushed a kiss across her cheek. "You'd have made a terrible boy, unless," he said with a sly twinkle in his eye, "you like boys who are pretty, and curved in all the wrong places."

Nora-Leigh threw her arms around his barrel chest and strong back. The rough tweed of his shirt caressed her cheek. "You're a big fibber, but I love you all the same."

31

"And I love you, Nellie girl." He stepped to the dry sink and began pumping water to wash up for supper. He stood in his stockinged feet shaking his head; then a chuckle slipped from his lips. "A boy. Ha! That's a good one."

Granny walked into the room and sat down at the table. She eyed Nora-Leigh and her husband with a quizzical expression. "What are you two busybodies up to? Anything an old lady like myself might be interested in?"

"You're not old, Clarissa," crooned Nora-Leigh's grandfather.

Here he goes again, she thought, trying her best not to grin. She pretended to turn her attention to the bubbling pot simmering on the stove. A flirt from the tip of his nose to the tips of his toes, Gramps could sweet-talk any woman, no matter her age. Even after all these years together, Granny wasn't immune, nor did she try to be. She enjoyed his banter as much as anyone.

"If I'm not old, then what am I?"

"You're a plum, Mrs. Spooner, ripe for the picking and just the way I like all my ladies."

Granny gave an unladylike snort. "Pipe down, you old codger. There aren't any other women in your life."

Gramps leaned back against the cupboard, drying his face and hands. He took his own sweet time, then held up both hands in a submissive gesture, waving the white towel above his head. "What do you mean? Women surround me. Why, between you and Elsa and Nellie here, I've got my hands full." He turned to Nora-Leigh and caught her eye, then winked at her. "Besides, I like the odds. I truly do."

Nora-Leigh caught the expression on Granny's face and burst out laughing. Gramps joined in. Granny looked as surprised as someone caught in the outhouse with the door open. She crossed her arms over her thin chest and tried to give Gramps a mean expression. Tried, but failed.

Soon she too was chortling like a lovestruck turtledove.

"I just never know what's gonna come out of that mouth of yours, Devin Spooner. I swear."

Bill Terrell squinted against the blinding glare of the noonday sun, then turned his bearded face up to the sky for the first time in three months. He inhaled a long breath. Behind closed lids, his eyes burned with white-hot heat. His ragged blue uniform was dirty and stained, his body stank, and his skin itched from innumerable flea-bites. His gut seethed with hatred, a bitter snapping that sizzled like a panful of rancid bacon.

Busted down from corporal to private in the United States Army, he rode away from Fort Keogh without leave on a stolen, spavined mare that would be lucky to last fifty miles. Terrell headed southwest and didn't look back.

He ruminated over the last three months he'd spent in the fort's jail while Clay Sullivan walked around a free man. In his mind there was no justice in that, and he planned on remedying the situation as soon as he tracked the man down.

Terrell had lost his rank, three months' wages, and his pride in one fell swoop when that conniving Sullivan had had him arrested for neglect of duty and stealing from the Army. Hell, the service paid so damned little, what choice did he have? He couldn't live the life he wanted on what measly earnings the Army doled out.

Well, now he had his life back, but Clay Sullivan would pay. Terrell would track him down like the cold-blooded animal Sullivan was. He'd kill him, slowly, painfully, any way that he could devise, just so Sullivan suffered as he had suffered every day for ninety days in that dark, cold cell with no blanket and little food, and no self-respect.

That Indian-loving, no-account Sullivan would pay with his worthless life.

From the general-store owner, a thin and gossipy, surprisingly young man named Franklin Homer, Clay received the break he'd been seeking. Homer told him about a retired old-timer who lived right here in Steamboat Bend and used to be an engineer on the steamboats that traveled the riverways throughout the Dakota and Montana territories. Homer even believed he'd heard tell that the old man's experiences included work on the *Far West*.

After settling his horse and mule at the livery and himself at Mrs. Shay's boardinghouse, Clay couldn't contain his excitement. He washed up, changed into his disguise, and walked to the riverman's house, despite it being the supper hour and being near to starving himself. He ignored the stares, grinning to himself. After all, he was a stranger in a small town and he suspected the eye patch and his odd style of dress warranted speculation.

When Clay came to the described house, he stood on the front walk and caught himself admiring the cozy home. It reminded him of the house he'd grown up in back in Ohio. The white picket fence, the wrap-around porch, the wooden swing. Long-forgotten memories of playing with his four brothers and his sister, Belinda, in just such a yard danced through his mind. He found himself smiling as he opened the gate and moved up the walkway.

The swing swayed lazily in the early evening breeze. A painted wooden bench, chipped and faded, sat beneath a lace-covered window. He sat down on the bench as he pictured his own mother sitting there, a work-worn apron tied snugly about her waist. A bowl cradled in her lap as she snapped beans or shucked sweet corn. Her brown eyes crinkling at the corners when she spotted Clay or one of his siblings. Funny that such a homely thing as a simple bench could remind him of his youth.

He shook off the sentimental thoughts and knocked on the door. From inside, he heard laughter. One voice was a deep masculine baritone, and the others were women's soft, yet enticingly female, full-hearted tones. Clay listened, his head cocked to one side. He liked nothing better than the sound of a woman's voice, particularly a woman's gentle laughter.

The door suddenly opened. Clay straightened when he recognized Mrs. Dillon in the doorway, an expectant look on her attractive features.

He removed his hat, smiled, and smoothed back his damp, unruly hair. "Ma'am, it's Clay Sullivan."

Her unseeing yet tender eyes twinkled when she recognized his name. "Why, Mr. Sullivan, how nice to meet you again so soon."

"Ma'am, it's good to see you again, too. I apologize for arriving at this hour and disturbing your supper." He hesitated, then glanced over her shoulder. "I think I may even have the wrong house. Are you acquainted with an older gentleman, a retired riverman by the name of Devin Spooner?"

"You've got the right house, sir. That would be my father."

She smiled and patted his arm, then took him by the elbow and escorted him past a shadowy parlor and a small bedroom into the kitchen, where an older woman stood in front of the stove wiping her hands on a towel and a weathered gentleman sat at the table. Their faces were creased with deep lines, which bespoke many years of life and laughter, and they were still chuckling when he entered the room. They glanced up and gave him welcoming smiles.

The hoydenish daughter—Nora-Leigh of the enticing backside—looked up at him just as she was about to set

35

a steaming bowl on the table. All traces of laughter disappeared from her face, replaced by a frown of recognition. Dressed in a gown of copper fabric that buttoned up high to her neck and glistened like raindrops, she looked soft and round in all the right places.

Her curly hair, loose and free-flowing about her face, fell just below her ears in waves of thick, amber-streaked shades of honey. For an observant man, he was surprised he didn't remember the distinctive color, but then, both times he'd seen her she'd been wearing a god-awful man's hat. Her eyes, eyes he was quite certain he would never forget, shone with an inner glow. This girl, who quite obviously didn't know her own sensual appeal, exuded a passion and fire he longed to be burned by. It took all his willpower to tear his gaze away.

Nora-Leigh couldn't believe her eyes. Clay Sullivan stood in the entrance to the kitchen looking perfectly comfortable and as at home as if he walked into their kitchen every day of the week. An angelic smile tipped up the corners of his mouth.

Her mother held his arm as if they'd been friends for years. "Dad, Mother, this is Mr. Clay Sullivan. He's come to see you, Dad," her mother said, before turning her beaming face to the intruder. "Have you had your supper, Mr. Sullivan?"

"No, ma'am, I haven't," he replied, shaking his head, "but I sure don't want to impose on your kind hospitality."

Nora-Leigh stared at Clay. She would have sworn that when she saw him before, his eye patch covered his right eye. Now it covered his left. It was very odd. His dark hair, uncombed and unfashionably long, glimmered with droplets as if he'd washed up in a hurry and it hadn't had a chance to dry.

He'd changed into incongruous clothes, too. Instead of dressing in denim pants and a chambray or flannel shirt as did most of the men in Steamboat Bend, he wore an old-fashioned snowy-white shirt with billowing sleeves, tight cuffs, and a loosely tied string at the neck. She noticed how he wore his trousers tucked inside knee-high black boots. They were black, tight-fitting trousers that hugged his hips and his, oh my . . . A heated flush worked its way up Nora-Leigh's neck. She pulled her gaze back to his face. A gold hoop glimmered in the lobe of his left ear and a gold coin dangled from a pendant around his neck. Goodness, but he looked just like a photograph of a pirate Nora-Leigh had once seen in a book she'd borrowed from the lending library.

Her mother and grandparents didn't seem to notice his odd attire, or good manners kept them from saying anything.

Gramps stood, a smile of welcome on his face. "No imposition, son." He leaned across the table and held out his weathered hand. "Devin Spooner. Pull up a chair and eat. You look hungry enough to eat every last hen in the henhouse, and the eggs for dessert."

"No argument there." Clay shook her grandfather's hand and eyed the food set on the table. She could almost see his mouth water as he gazed at the sliced ham, the steaming cornbread, the crock of yellow, creamy butter, and the peas and onions in white sauce. It had been a long day. Even her own mouth watered.

Clay pulled out a chair for her mother and waited until she seated herself, then wasted little time in sitting down and making himself comfortable as Granny filled a plate to overflowing for him. Nora-Leigh noted with a bit of pique that he didn't pull out a chair for her or wait for her to be seated. Muttering to herself, she sat down and frowned at him, but Clay didn't even bother to glance in her direction.

"Thank you for the invitation," he said, pulling his

chair forward. "I can't tell you when I last ate a good home-cooked meal."

"We get company so rarely, it's always a pleasure," her mother said.

"It surely is," Granny reiterated, a mile-wide smile wreathing her face. She stared at Clay like a hawk hovering high over a mouse, just waiting to swoop down and have him for dinner. It was as plain as Auntie Sarah's bread pudding that Granny thought this man would be good marriage material.

Nora-Leigh's mother smiled mischievously as she added, "How do you know it's going to be a *good* home-cooked meal, Mr. Sullivan?" Apparently, Granny wasn't the only conniving, and none too subtle, matchmaker in the house.

Nora-Leigh could have wept.

Clay looked stunned for a moment. Then he waggled his brows as a grin spread across his face. "A jest," he said, nodding in understanding. "Still and all, this is real kind of you, feeding a stranger like myself. I do appreciate it."

"No one's a stranger in these parts, Mr. Sullivan," Granny pronounced as she dished up a plate of food for Gramps. Nora-Leigh helped herself, as did her mother.

Nora-Leigh watched Clay as he watched her mother as unobtrusively as he could. He seemed amazed how her blindness didn't seem to hinder her abilities. Nora-Leigh guessed she was used to her mother's ways after so many years. To a person not acquainted with blindness, however, it probably was fascinating.

"Don't get many visitors to Steamboat Bend?" Clay asked.

"We get lots of visitors, sir, but none of them are strangers to Gramps," Nora-Leigh said, glancing at her grandfather with an affectionate grin.

"Well, some are stranger than others." Gramps hooted with laughter, and Granny joined in.

Clay managed a grim smile. He placed his fork on his plate and leaned forward on his elbows. "I expect you're wondering what I wanted to see you about."

"We're all as curious as the proverbial cat, but we can wait until after we've eaten, I reckon. Good manners and all."

"No need, Mr. Spooner. It's easy enough to explain. I'm a bit of a treasure-seeker, a fortune hunter if you will. I've traveled many places all over the world searching for riches—jewels, gems, gold, and the like."

"Oh?" Nora-Leigh questioned.

Eyes set wide apart. Granny said that meant an honest, trustworthy person. Horsefeathers! Nora-Leigh spent enough hours in the classroom to know when someone was lying, and Mr. Sullivan was in the midst of a whopper. She knew he was a scoundrel from the moment she first laid eyes on him. No one could trust a man who smiled so much or bore such a self-assured expression on his handsome face. Besides, his eyes weren't all that wide apart.

Of course she could only see the one.

A trickle of sweat dribbled down Clay's spine. *Traveled all over the world! What a lie!* As he sat there eating these generous people's food, the devil was no doubt plotting how to get him into hell.

This pirate getup was not an effective disguise. He felt like a fool in the billowing blouse and tight trousers. He was glad he hadn't let Ethan talk him into wearing the red sash and sword at his side. He fingered the gold hoop in his ear. The earring was obviously too much, and besides, it had hurt like hell when Ethan had pierced the lobe three days ago. Even now, scorching heat emanated from the wound. What had he been thinking?

What he knew about piracy he could tick off on the fingers of one hand. Damn that blasted younger brother of his! Ethan had put the fool notion in his head. He thought it would be a hoot if Clay pulled off the clever disguise, and Clay agreed. Who would question a pirate seeking treasure? Who but Nora-Leigh Dillon. And of course she would; he was miles from an ocean.

He had the distinct feeling that he'd crossed over an invisible line and Nora-Leigh saw him for exactly what he was. An impostor. He knew the instant he walked into the room that she suspected something. He could read her thoughts as though they were printed on her forehead. She would make a lousy poker player. Still, he wasn't much better himself, and he had the feeling that he'd backed himself into a corner.

He'd best do some fast talking or he'd find himself in a heap of trouble, not only with the Army but also with this family. "I'm here to talk to you about your experiences on the *Far West* during the Indian uprisings."

"Now, those were interesting days. Eh, Clarissa?"

His wife nodded. "More than this old lady wanted, that's for certain. When I wasn't fretting about Devin's hide, I was praying for his soul. Now that the Indians are all on the reservation, I don't worry so much."

"I hate to be the one to tell you, but not all of the Indians are on the reservation, ma'am. Some of them are renegades hiding out high in the hills and mountains living a fairly quiet existence. But some are convinced that they will eventually get their old life back."

"How would you know that?" Nora-Leigh asked.

His fork stopped halfway to his mouth. She was quick, all right. He carefully set his fork to the side of his plate and said to her grandmother, "That's just the rumors I've heard hereabouts. I don't reckon they have the heart for any mischief, though. Those bureaucrats in Washington won't allow it. If the Indians did do something out of line, they'd have the Army all over them like shi—" He cleared his throat, as Gramps chuckled.

When Nora-Leigh glanced at her grandfather, he ducked his head and pretended to be inspecting the solitary pea left on his plate.

Clay wished he could do the same. "Anyway, as I was saying, the Army would be all over those Indians like ants at a church social."

"That's good to know," Mrs. Dillon said. "We haven't lived here all that long, but long enough to be wary."

"How long have you folks been in Steamboat Bend?"

"About eight years," Mr. Spooner offered. "I fell in love with the wide-open Montana sky while steaming up and down the Missouri and the Yellowstone. Weren't many settlers then, just the Indians and the Army chasing them to hell and back. Oh, there were always a few mountain men and miners around, but they mostly lived and worked farther west in the territory.

"When I retired I talked Clarissa into coming out here to settle, but she wouldn't do it unless Elsa and Nellie came along." He patted his daughter's hand. "They were a little harder to convince."

"Now, Dad, I had a good teaching position in Missouri." Elsa turned her attention to Clay and smiled. "It was just that I was a widow. My husband died in 'seventy after lingering a long while with war injuries. I had a little girl to support, so I began teaching. After doing that for so many years, I didn't want to come out here to the Montana territory and find myself with no way to support us. Of course, by that time Nellie was in her teens."

Clay grinned at Nora-Leigh. "And now your little girl is all grown up—and she's the teacher."

"Yes, and she does a wonderful job. When my eyesight began to fail, she took right up where I left off, even though she had a different dream for herself."

Grandma Spooner snorted. "Phooey. All Nellie needs

41

is a good man to look after her." She turned her bespectacled attention toward Clay and eyed him closely. "Are you married, Mr. Sullivan?"

"Granny!"

"No, ma'am, I'm not married." Clay tried not to smile. Nora-Leigh looked so humiliated that Clay took pity on her and changed the subject back to what he wanted to discuss anyway. "Mr. Spooner, were you on the *Far West* back in 'seventy-six when they were ferrying supplies upriver to the Seventh Cavalry?"

"Yes, sir, I was. Now, them was frightening times."

Clay leaned forward. "Did you know about the gold shipment that the captain was supposed to have buried?"

The old man paused. "I sure did. I even drew up a map at the time so we could go back and retrieve that gold."

"Gramps!" Nora-Leigh's face radiated excitement. "You never told me that before."

"Why, Nellie girl, you'd have been digging for it yourself and no doubt getting into all sorts of trouble. Anyway, that's a far trek from here . . . and now it's on Crow land."

Clay couldn't contain himself. Nora-Leigh was just too ripe a target for him to ignore. "So that wasn't what you were digging for yesterday?"

All eyes fell on Nora-Leigh. She turned a delightful shade of pink, frowning all the while at Clay. "James Whitney's father, Stephen, told me when he walked his boy to school yesterday that a stagecoach overturned a few years back and that several of the people were afraid they'd be robbed. They buried their jewels and money and hoped to come back later to retrieve them." She looked sheepishly around the table. "He said they never went back. Something about a misunderstanding with the driver . . . but Mr. Whitney said he knew exactly where it was buried."

Mr. Spooner smacked the table with the flat of his hand, then shook a finger at Nora-Leigh. "Mind you, Nellie, these folks in Steamboat Bend have got nothing better to do than gossip. I'm surprised that Whitney and his cronies weren't hiding behind a tree just watching you and laughing their backsides off. If Whitney was so darn certain where that loot was, why wasn't he digging it up himself?"

"Golly. I never thought of that."

"That's one silly legend that has been circling round-about Steamboat Bend forever, and I doubt very much that it's true."

During her grandfather's tirade Nora-Leigh's face turned from bright red to pale as paste. Mrs. Dillon patted her daughter's hand. "I'm sure they weren't watching you or you would have noticed, but really, dear, you have to quit believing everything everyone says to you. You're much too gullible."

Clay almost laughed. Gullible? Nora-Leigh hadn't believed a single thing he'd said since they met. "I didn't see anyone, Nora-Leigh, if it makes you feel any better."

"It doesn't."

Cursed woman. He changed the subject back. "Mr. Spooner, I'll pay you for the use of that map."

"It should be mine," Nora-Leigh said.

"Now wait a minute, both you young folks."

"How much?" Clay asked.

"I never thought to sell it," Mr. Spooner said.

"I'll pay top dollar."

"Gramps! You can't think about selling it to a stranger."

"I haven't said I would or I wouldn't. If it's where I recall, it's on Indian land anyway, so I don't rightly know if it belongs to them or the Army." The old man grinned. "Mr. Sullivan, did you have a figure in mind?"

"Whatever you think it's worth."

He snorted. "I believe it's worthless. I'd bet my last dollar that someone dug it up years ago."

Clay refused to let the opportunity slip away, granddaughter or no. "You set the price, sir, and I'll pay. It's my loss if it's not there."

"You can have it for nothing. I just have one stipulation."

"What's that?"

"You see, Nora-Leigh's been working hard teaching those kids and she deserves a bit of a respite." He sat back in his chair and tucked both hands beneath his armpits. With a slight glint in his eye, he leaned forward and continued, "And she's been hankering for an adventure. You can just as well take her along with you."

"Dad! It's not proper!"

"Devin! It's not safe!"

Both of the older women at the table looked at the elderly gentleman like he was as dumb as a fence post. His daughter in particular looked like she wanted to wring his neck. Nora-Leigh showed clear amazement in her eyes.

"It doesn't matter, ladies," Clay replied. "I can't do that."

"Why not?" Nora-Leigh asked.

"I'm not taking any woman along with me."

"You can't have the map without taking me."

"I *won't* take you."

"Then you can't have the map, Mr. Sullivan," Nora-Leigh stated.

"Now, Nellie," cautioned her grandmother. "He does make a strong case. This is no time for you to be traipsing around the countryside. I'm not sure the hostiles aren't still up in the hills."

"I'll be perfectly safe"—Nora Leigh glanced at Clay—"with Mr. Sullivan. You wouldn't let anything happen to me, now would you?"

"Of course not."

"See?"

"That's not the point," Clay said. "You won't *be* with me."

"I agree with Mr. Sullivan, dear," Nora-Leigh's mother added. "Besides, you'd be unchaperoned."

Nora-Leigh jumped to her feet, startling everyone at the table. Clay tried to contain the grin that threatened to turn his lips upward. By God, she was a spitfire.

Pacing between the stove and the table, she gestured with flinging arms and hands. "This may be my last chance!"

"For what?" asked her grandmother with a perplexed look on her face. "You're a young gal."

"I am not all that young."

"Now don't get riled, but tarnation, Nellie girl, none of us are."

"You don't understand. I'm going to be an old maid—what am I saying? I'm *already* an old maid. An old maid schoolteacher with no prospects, no suitors, and no chance of ever leaving Steamboat Bend. If I don't take this chance, I may never get the opportunity again. Don't you see?"

Clay watched her closely as she glanced at her mother to gauge her reaction to her words. Elsa frowned, lines forming between her brows. "I don't understand. Opportunity to do what, dear?"

"Explore, adventure, spread my wings, get out of Steamboat Bend for a while."

"Before you get your knickers in a bunch about having this all-fired big adventure," Clay said, "let me ask you a few questions, Miss Dillon."

"All right." She stopped beside his chair, folded her arms, and with a contrary stare dared him to talk her out of it. "Go ahead."

"Have you ever slept in the open before?" Clay asked. "With only the stars for a blanket?"

"Yes. When we came west, I slept in the wagon at night."

"That's not quite the same thing. Can you cook over an open fire?"

"Yes. I've never done it by myself, but I know I could if I had to. Besides, you can do it, can't you?"

"I'm asking the questions here. Do you ride anything besides that bicycle contraption?"

"Like a horse?"

Clay snorted. "Uh, yeah, like a horse. You know—four legs, a mane, a tail, long nose, kind of tallish, comes in all colors and—"

"They make a neighing sound," she finished for him.

Clay snorted again, but laughter threatened to override his sober expression.

"I believe I know what a horse is, Mr. Sullivan."

"But can you ride one?" When she didn't answer, he forged on. "What would you do if you saw an Indian? Scream? Swoon? Faint dead away? Could you defend yourself with a gun or a knife if need be?"

"I can take care of myself."

He doubted it. This little hellion needed a caretaker.

Clay looked away from Nora-Leigh and glanced around the table. The elder Spooners and Mrs. Dillon hadn't contributed to the conversation for some time. They sat by, listening and watching with looks of astonishment on the women's faces, and one of amusement on Nora-Leigh's grandfather's face. Apparently, no one was about to intervene.

"Anything you can do, I can learn," she said. Her chin lifted at a stubborn angle. "And do as well, probably."

What should have been a normal conversation between adults seemed to have dwindled to a childish argument between Nora-Leigh and him. It was up to Clay to convince her and her family that this idea was madness.

"We'd be sleeping together, you know. Just the two of us, all alone in the wilderness." He lifted his eyebrows suggestively. "We might have to keep each other warm at night."

Nora-Leigh's mother gasped, understanding his unspoken statement. He hated to look at her and see the shock on her face. He was sorry for having had to go so far, but he couldn't stop now. Even though her face was the color of parchment, he drove his last nail into the coffin. He stared at Nora-Leigh. "Do you see what I'm saying, Miss Dillon?"

"Not exactly," she murmured, an uncertain frown puckering her brow.

"Do I have to be blunt?"

Nora-Leigh's mother leaned toward her daughter and whispered in her ear. Nora-Leigh's eyes widened. Her mouth gaped like a fish gasping for air.

Then with a decided crack, her jaw snapped shut. Her eyes danced with belligerence as she stared back at Clay. "I'll have to borrow Gramps's hunting knife." She paused, never taking her gaze from him. "Just in case any varmints crawl into my blankets at night."

She stood and with a deliberate movement pushed her chair up to the table. Then she smoothed the front of her dress with both hands. "Mr. Sullivan, I'll be ready to leave in three days."

This time, it was his jaw that dropped.

Chapter Three

Early the next morning, Clay sauntered from his room at the boardinghouse and headed toward Franklin Homer's general store to buy supplies. He hoped the brisk morning air would refresh his muddled brain. He generally thought of himself as a calm, disciplined, practical man, even analytical at times. However, after spending a few hours at the confounding, slapdash Spooner and Dillon household, he'd spent the rest of the night tossing and turning in his narrow bed. What little sleep he managed was consumed with dreams of a saucy woman chasing him on a two-wheeled contraption, running him down, and beating him over the head with a wooden spoon. And then straddling him and kissing him senseless.

He woke with a pounding headache, and an unmerciful hardness in his nether parts. How in God's name had he been hoodwinked into taking the bewitching Nora-Leigh Dillon along to find the lost Custer gold shipment?

Had he agreed to take her? He still wasn't certain. He

remembered leaving the Spooner home, bone-tired and confused about the particulars. He needed that map, though, and that was a fact. And he would do whatever it took to get it, even if it meant escorting the little school-marm on her so-called big adventure. But she didn't know the meaning of the word if she thought traipsing through rough country on horseback would be an adventure.

While riding as a civilian scout with the Army he'd learned several things, the foremost being that if something could go wrong, it would.

First, the weather never cooperated. In the service, you slept in cold, drenching rain or by day slogged in ankle-high mud. You ate dust and grasshoppers along with your beans and bacon. Or you couldn't sleep at night for the heat. Very few days could be called accommodating, especially on the plains. There the wind blew cease-lessly. In the summer, the sun beat down in a relentless continuity that could drive you crazy, and in the winter, snow piled up faster than you could holler howdy. Adventure? Ha!

As he walked to the store, curious townsfolk eyed him with suspicion. A few of the braver young boys even asked him outright if he was a pirate. Soon grown men were walking with him and questioning him, too. By the time he stopped in front of the general store, a crowd had gathered around him, peppering him with questions he had no earthly idea how to answer.

All during the time he bought supplies and for the rest of the day, he evaded questions point-blank, dodged others like bullets, and sometimes outright lied. He wanted to go back to the fort, tail between his legs, and forget the whole damned assignment. He wouldn't do it, though. Cursing Ethan and his goldarned stupid disguise, he lied his way through the day until at last he wasn't sure of his own name, much less what fabrications he'd told. Thank

God most of these people knew less about pirating than he did.

Devin Spooner sought him out in the late afternoon and escorted him to Early's, the nearest, and only, drinking establishment in Steamboat Bend. They ordered two glasses of beer and took them to a table in the middle of the room. Except for four card players intent on a game of poker and one lone drunk holding up the bar and forcing the barkeep to listen to his prattle, the place was empty.

"Well, son, have you changed your mind?"

Clay looked across the scarred table at the old man. His rheumy eyes twinkled with mischief and good humor. Clay suspected the man's granddaughter took after him. The mischief part anyway, with an equal dose of feistiness and a singled-mindedness that would put the fear of God in a lesser man. Clay had never crumbled beneath a challenge before and he wasn't about to start now. "No, sir. I need that map and I'll pay the price, whatever the cost."

"Even if that cost includes escorting my granddaughter?"

"If that's what it takes. I won't say I like it much."

"Can't blame you any."

Clay eyed the old man. "You trust me?"

"Yep."

"Why?"

"Oh, I don't know." Deep in thought, he looked across the room at the table of poker players, then turned back to Clay. His furrowed brow, creased with deep lines and leathered from the sun, smoothed out when he replied, "I'm a purty good judge of character, I think, and though I know you're no more a pirate than I am . . ."

Clay winced.

"I reckon you'll cherish my Nellie as I do."

Cherish. Interesting choice of words. One that made

Clay a bit uncomfortable. He recrossed his boots as he stroked his mustache. It sounded way too much like a wedding vow. He didn't want to find himself at the wrong end of a shotgun when he brought Nora-Leigh home. "I'll look after her, if that's what you mean. She won't come to harm. Do you want credentials?"

"Nope. If you say she won't come to harm, that's good enough for me," Devin replied.

"What about her reputation? Would anyone marry her after she did this?" Clay asked, seeking a way out, any way out.

"No one's wanted to marry her yet, I'm sorry to say. I don't see this changing anything."

Damn. Clay shrugged his shoulders. Well, he'd given it his best shot. Being a pragmatic man, he'd just do the best he could with an impossible situation. Maybe if he made it hard enough for the girl, she'd change her mind.

Devin slapped Clay on the shoulder. "How about another beer and then we'll go home and have a taste of Clarissa's fine cooking again."

"I wouldn't want to impose two nights in a row, Mr. Spooner."

"Call me Devin. If you're going to be spending the next few weeks with my granddaughter, we ought to be on friendlier terms."

Later, at the dinner table, Clay still found himself searching for a way out. He didn't need a woman tagging along with him. She'd just slow him down. He looked across the table at her. And she'd be one helluva distraction.

Searching for any excuse, however lame, Clay blurted out the first thing that came to mind. "Nora-Leigh, don't you need to stay here in town to take care of your mother and grandparents?"

He looked around the table at the astonished faces. He had definitely wedged his polished black boot in his mouth this time. He swiveled toward Mrs. Dillon and touched her hand, grasping for a bit of redemption. "No insult intended, ma'am."

"None taken, sir," Nora-Leigh's mother replied, but her taut facial expression indicated otherwise. Her tone turned decidedly icy when she spoke again. "Though I may not see well enough to teach, I'm not in my dotage yet, Mr. Sullivan. I take quite good care of myself, thank you very much. Once again, I do believe you've overstepped the intricate boundaries of etiquette, but I'll attempt to forgive you . . . again. You are, however, trying my patience and my goodwill."

"Yes, ma'am, I see that I am." A distinctive warmth worked its way beneath his collar and heated his face. The last time Clay remembered blushing he'd been wearing short pants and hiding behind his mother's skirts. For someone who'd spent a lifetime dealing with cocky first lieutenants, and who could guide a platoon of men at midnight on a moonless night, he found himself floundering and nearly speechless. Women—they left him bewildered and tongue-tied.

"Dammit all, Sullivan." This time Nora-Leigh's grandfather sounded affronted as well. "I'm insulted even if you ain't, Elsa. And furthermore—"

"Aren't, Dad," Elsa said, interrupting him.

"Ain't, aren't, I don't give a hoot 'bout what's properlike." He stared at Clay. "Now, Mr. Sullivan, you best—"

This time his wife interrupted him. "Don't get all het up, dear."

"But we ain't decrepit, Clarissa, and I, for one—"

"Aren't, Dad."

"Can't a man just once finish a sentence around here?" he hollered, his face flushed. He glared once again at Clay, then gazed with irritation at his daughter, who, of course, couldn't see his frowning features.

Clay needed to defuse the situation and get the con-

versation back to where it belonged: discussion of the
map. But not tonight. He wasn't prepared for any more
battling or lying. As he stood up, three pairs of disapproving eyes stared at him. For some unknown reason,
Nora-Leigh seemed to be the only one not frowning. She
did stare at him, however, as if he'd grown a third eye in
the middle of his forehead.

A part of his personality urged him to wink at her, but
with her grandfather watching him like a coiled rattlesnake, he refrained. "I left my manners on the boat, er, I
mean ship. I haven't been around real ladies much of
late." At least that was the truth. It was about the only
thing he could honestly claim at this point.

"Fiddlesticks," Nora-Leigh said. "There's no ship or
schooner or even a leaking rowboat."

"Nellie!"

"No, Mrs. Dillon, let your daughter have her say. I'd
be curious as to what she's thinking. After all, if we're
going to spend the next few weeks together, she has a
right to question me."

"Sir," Nora-Leigh's grandfather said. "I have a few
more questions myself before you get my map and escort
Nellie on this big adventure."

Clay glanced at him and saw his eyes sparkle with
amusement. What was the old man about? On the one
hand, it seemed he wanted Clay to take his virginal granddaughter on a possibly dangerous trek; on the other,
maybe the old geezer had to act the part of the father
looking out for her welfare and reputation. In the same
position, Clay wasn't certain what he'd do, but he sure
as hell wouldn't find it humorous. Maybe Spooner's mind
was slipping.

Clay's eye watered and he blinked away the moisture.
Seeing with one eye was as annoying as arguing with a
mule. A headache throbbed at his temple, and his neck
ached from corkscrewing his head halfway around his

body every time he looked at someone. Clay reached up to adjust the damned patch when he realized he'd put it on the wrong eye. Lord, what next?

"What's with that pirate getup anyway?" Nora-Leigh asked, startling him. He lowered his hand to his lap and forced a smile. Her tone suggested she wasn't buying any explanation, plausible or otherwise, that he might choose to give her.

Clay winced, praying for celestial intervention. A bolt of lightning? A clap of thunder? His mother had warned him about lying. He squirmed in his seat. His *seeing* eye leaked like a rusty tin can. Beneath his breath, he cursed the damnable eye patch, wiped off the tears, and took a fortifying breath. "I don't know what you mean."

"If you were a pirate, then I'm Grover Cleveland."

"Nora-Leigh," her mother scolded, "now you're being rude."

"I just wish to know what our Mr. Sullivan is doing dressed like that."

Nora-Leigh's grandmother smiled at Clay. "He's a sailor," she stated. "Very fetching, too, I might add. I particularly like the fit of your trousers, young man."

"Mother!" Elsa yelped. "Is that anything to say?"

He'd purchased them in a hurry with no thought to size. They were too small, too snug, and displayed every muscle, every tendon, every last thing from waist to calf. Everything. Clay couldn't decide if he should be insulted or humbled. Either way, he was one hundred percent embarrassed. He mumbled a thank-you.

"A sailor, Mr. Sullivan?" Nora-Leigh's mother asked. Thank goodness the woman was near-blind. Elsa had no idea that her mother was speaking about the way his trousers displayed his male anatomy. Her head tilted, her expression questioning.

"Yes, ma'am," he said in a strangled whisper. He clung to his dignity, what little was left of it, and pushed aside his chair, turning to go. "Much as I'd like to stay, I believe I'll take my leave now." He noticed Nora-Leigh's frown of displeasure, her grandfather's smirk as he perused Clay's too-snug trousers, and her grandmother's roving eye as she admired them. The old woman had no shame.

"Mr. Spooner, I promise to answer any questions you have tomorrow." He covered his mouth and gave a jaw-cracking yawn. "If you all don't mind, it's been a long day and I need to find my bunk. Good night to you."

"I'll walk you to the door, Mr. Sullivan," Nora-Leigh said, her voice tight with incrimination.

Clay could hardly wait to have her alone.

"Good night, ma'am," he said to Elsa Dillon, patting her on the shoulder. She covered his hand by way of reply.

"Thanks for supper."

"It was a pleasure, honestly, Mr. Sullivan."

He said his good-byes, and Nora-Leigh led the way to the front door. At the threshold she stopped, then abruptly swiveled to stare up into his face. The darkened room, bathed only in the narrow light emanating from the kitchen, cocooned the two of them in the cozy atmosphere. Her fragrance, soft and sweet as a bouquet of wildflowers, wafted over him. Her honey-colored hair shimmered in the low illumination. One escaped curl danced at her jaw line and tickled her cheek. He repressed the urge to twist its length around his finger and pull her close.

Nora-Leigh cocked her head and thrust out her chin. The full, moist lips that so attracted him were now pursed tight against any inclination he might have had in that particular direction.

While she unknowingly attracted and enticed him with her looks and heavenly scent, she was as prickly and dangerous as a porcupine in her behavior. He knew better than to come too close and get those quills stuck in his stubborn hide. With a smile threatening to turn up the corners of his mouth, he waited for her to speak and give him a set-down.

"I'm excited about our adventure together, Mr. Sullivan."

Surprised by her calm voice, he nodded his head. "So am I, Miss Dillon."

"But no amount of bullying, authoritarian—"

"Authoritarian?"

"Dictatorial—"

"Dictatorial? Why, Nellie, you really are a teacher."

"Don't call me that."

He clasped her stubborn chin with his callused fingers, relishing the feel of her petal-soft skin. He bent down and kissed her tawny cheek. "Miss Dillon, I know a few big words myself, and I gotta say I look forward to our *association*."

He winked, then slid by her and pulled the door shut behind him, but not before he heard a salty vulgarity worthy of any sailor pass through her rosy lips.

By the light of the lantern beside her bed, Nora-Leigh studied her grandfather's map, drawn on the back of a bill of lading. The edges of the water-spotted paper were frayed and torn and weathered by time. The map was almost wholly incomprehensible.

The river, a double line of snaking turns, wasn't identified by name. The landmarks were unremarkable trees and rocky outcroppings, which in this part of the country were as numerous as cattle droppings. No indications of distance were given. It seemed as if the map had been drawn to deliberately befuddle anyone trying to follow it. Nora-Leigh yawned, stretching her legs and wiggling her toes. She snuggled beneath the covers, then carefully set the map on the table beside her. She smiled. It was a good thing grandfather had found his calling on a steamboat, because he was no cartographer. Still, maybe she could ask him what he recalled about the area when he made up the map.

Excitement thrummed through her veins. Her heart quickened with anticipation. Even her skin tingled. She simply couldn't wait to begin her adventure.

Despite having to put up with Clay Sullivan's arrogant manner and high-handed ideas, she couldn't wait.

"How come you never learned to ride?" Clay asked. He stood next to the porch, hatless, watching Nora-Leigh as she descended the steps.

The afternoon sun flickered in his dark hair, where burnished streaks of gold glinted from the many hours he'd spent outdoors. With his hands on his buckskin-clad hips, legs wide apart, he looked strong and handsome and wholly in charge of the situation. He loosely held the reins of a small spotted horse, saddled and ready to ride.

When she didn't immediately respond, Clay's mouth beneath the thick mustache quirked upward in a knowing smile. "I thought everyone rode," he said.

"Not everyone." Nora-Leigh shaded her eyes and stared up at him. She waited for his teasing rebuttal.

"Everyone who lives west of the Mississippi does."

Just minutes before, he'd come to the door of her home and ordered her to change into trousers or something suitable for riding, and meet him outside. She'd just returned from school, tired, and had been thinking about taking a short nap. She disliked his imperious manner but was so dumbfounded by his blatant demand, she couldn't come up with a ready reply, witty or otherwise. Now she stood in front of him dressed in her grandfather's clothes and weather-beaten hat ready for whatever Clay wanted. Within reason.

"I never needed to before," she said defensively, moving to her left so the sun didn't shine in her eyes when she looked up at him. It wasn't as if she disliked horses or feared them, she had just never had the opportunity to ride. She liked her bicycle better, and it didn't require feeding or grooming. And it didn't require any other paraphernalia like a saddle and bridle.

"I believe I've spent more time on a horse than off."

"Oh? Even on your ship?"

The line of his mouth thinned and his smile disappeared. "I meant when I wasn't on the water, of course."

"Of course."

He was a terrible liar, but she'd give him credit. He recovered quickly. He would be hard to catch in an out-and-out lie, but Nora-Leigh had little doubt she could do it.

"Now what can you tell me about this little beauty?"

Nora-Leigh glanced at the horse. Its eyes were closed, a back leg cocked. A very pretty horse with a speckled coat, it stood very still—not even a twitch or a switch of its tail. "Is it alive?"

He chuckled. "*She* is very much alive, just napping."

Nora-Leigh stepped up and patted the beast's neck. She didn't even budge. "This is the horse I have to ride?"

"Not only ride, but groom, feed, and otherwise take care of. This is your horse, Gingersnap. Ginger for short, or so her last owner said."

Nora-Leigh couldn't contain her surprise. "You bought me a horse?"

He snorted. "Hell, no. Your grandfather bought her." He gently led the horse up to Nora-Leigh. "Get a leg up." When she hesitated, he asked in a daring voice, "Are you afraid, Miss Dillon?"

"No, Mr. Sullivan, I'm not afraid. Of anything." With that, she lifted her foot to step up onto the stirrup. It was a little higher than she anticipated. She missed on the first two tries. On her third attempt, Clay palmed her bottom and boosted her up into the saddle. The feel of his wide, warm hand against her trouser-clad backside so startled her, she almost tumbled over onto the other side of the horse, who was as startled as Nora-Leigh herself.

Laughing beneath his breath, Clay caught her around the waist before she fell off the animal, then held her until she settled comfortably in the saddle. Only when she quit squirming did he take his arm away. "Next time, either ask for help or find a step or a big stone to stand on. You're a mite short on one end to jump into the saddle all by yourself, even on a small horse like Gingersnap here."

"You might have told me before."

"You might have asked for help."

"You are no gentleman."

He grinned. "Never claimed I was."

"Is this the kind of treatment I can expect after we leave?"

"You can expect much worse." He placed one hand on his hip as he stared at her. Even though she sat astride the horse, they were nearly eye to eye. Although he wasn't exactly glaring at her, his face contained no warmth, just a cool composure. "I'll admit it. I don't want you along; you'll just slow me down. I'm only taking you because it appears you come with the map. If I could figure out a way to shake you, believe me, I would. And it wouldn't bother me in the least."

"Well, you're completely honest about that, aren't you? You're not planning on leaving me somewhere?"

"Humph, that's a good suggestion. I'll give it some thought." Above his lips his thick mustache twitched. With his thumb and forefinger he brushed the edges in a downward motion. Nora-Leigh watched, wondering what he would look like without it and without the eye patch. She had a feeling he would be even more handsome, and undoubtedly, more cocksure.

"Are you ready for your lessons now?"

She couldn't take her eyes off his parted lips. The tip of his tongue just grazed the corner of his mouth. "Lessons?" she asked, unable to look away. "What lessons?"

Clay shook his head. "Damn," he muttered beneath his breath. "Riding lessons, Miss Dillon. Have you forgotten already?"

Shaken by her schoolgirl fascination with his mouth, lips, and tongue, Nora-Leigh at last found her voice. "No, no, I'm ready."

"All right. Let me shorten the stirrups so you don't fall off before we even begin." Clay clasped her calf in the palm of his hand. Nora-Leigh jumped, scaring the poor mare, who snorted and skittered. She pranced sideways and barely missed trampling Clay's feet.

Somehow the faux pirate kept hold of the reins and stepped out of the way. "Relax, for God's sake. Just let your leg hang down."

Relax? With the heat of his palm penetrating the cloth of her trousers and sending sensitive tremors up her thigh to parts better left unmentioned? How could she possibly relax?

She glanced at his frowning face, which looked undaunted by their close proximity. With single-minded composure he adjusted one stirrup, then moved to the other side of the horse to adjust the other. She couldn't see without falling off the horse, but from where she perched above him she felt his warm hand and long fingers whenever he touched her leg.

"Now stand up," he said, stepping away.

"In the stirrups?"

"Yes." He sighed with obvious male exasperation.

Awkwardly, Nora-Leigh stuck her booted feet into the stirrups and stood up. She glanced at Clay, whose gaze followed the length of her legs up to the juncture of her thighs. Without warning, he leaned forward and placed his hand on the saddle between her legs.

"Hey, remove your damned hand!" Without thinking, Nora-Leigh plopped back down in the saddle and sat on that same damned hand. Clay's large male hand. His large, warm, male—unmoving, thank God—hand.

Clay cleared his throat. Glancing up into her face, he said, "I believe you need to stand up for me to do that, Nora-Leigh."

As fast as a dog could wink, she complied. Embarrassed as could be but determined to brazen out the awkward situation, she waited for Clay to move his hand away.

In a voice hoarse with pent-up laughter, he said, "That seems about the right length for your stirrups."

Nora-Leigh refused to meet his eyes. She waited until she could look at him without blushing. By gosh, if she was going on this trip, she'd best learn to get over her embarrassment at the slightest little thing. And this was most certainly not life and death. After all, they'd soon be living together—eating, sleeping, washing up. Nora-Leigh straightened. She hadn't thought of that until just this minute. Bathing could be difficult. Oh, well, she'd cross that bridge, or more likely that creek, when she came to it.

Right now she needed to learn to ride a horse.

She sat up straight and turned her head to look at Clay. He grinned back, his one gray eye sparkling. His eye patch lay slightly askew against his bronzed cheekbone, giving her the merest glimpse beneath. Was that eye movement in the shadowy recesses? Surely not. The lowering afternoon sun was surely playing tricks with the play of light on his face. She squinted a bit to get a better view when he suddenly turned away from her and adjusted the patch. When he looked at her again, the fabric covered his eye completely.

"You ready to continue?" he asked.

"I am."

"Scared?"

"No."

His brows rose a fraction, but he said nothing more about it. "The saddle horn," he said, tapping the knob in front of her, "is not for hanging on to."

Why not? It was just the right size for her fist. Both fists, actually. "What's it used for then?"

"Cowboys use it. But as I don't reckon you'll be roping any steers in the future, it doesn't matter."

"I guess not."

"Now place your reins in your hand like this." He demonstrated with one hand and then watched as Nora-Leigh held them the same way. The thick leather felt awkward twined around her fingers. She didn't see how she could possibly steer the horse. "That's good," Clay continued. "You always hold them in one hand, not one in each or you'll look like a dude for sure and end up riding around all day in circles."

"All right."

"Gingersnap is a gentle mare who will do whatever you tell her to, but you got to know what to say and when, and I'm not talking about using that lovely mouth of yours."

"Oh?" *Lovely mouth of mine?* What did he mean by that?

"That's right. You'll guide her with your knees." He placed his hand on her leg and squeezed. "Did you feel that?"

Was he mad? Of course she felt it. Warmth radiated up and down her leg. He squeezed again. Involuntarily, Nora-Leigh squeezed her thighs together and the previously napping Gingersnap showed signs of life. She lifted her head and stared at Nora-Leigh. Nora-Leigh dropped the reins, and as they fell they slapped the side of Ginger's neck. The horse took off as though a pack of hunting hounds were nipping at her heels.

Eyes wide open, Nora-Leigh screamed for help and hung on to the saddle horn with both hands clutched tight.

Behind her, she could hear Clay cussing a blue streak. That and the beat of her heart were the only sounds she heard as she flew through town. She held on for dear life and prayed no one in Steamboat Bend would notice.

Who was she kidding? Nothing in Steamboat Bend went unnoticed, and nothing Nora-Leigh Dillon did went unremarked upon. She continued screaming until all she saw on either side of her were the trees and scrubby brush on the outskirts of town.

Clay wanted to throw back his head and laugh outright. Instead he hurriedly sought his own mount. The faithful horse fell into a gallop before he'd fully settled himself into the saddle.

Naively he'd thought teaching Nora-Leigh to ride was going to be as easy as walking across the street to greet a friend. Ha! He watched as the dust churned beneath Gingersnap's racing hooves. If luck was with him at all—and when had it ever been?—that danged woman would fall and break her neck and he'd be done with her for good. A twisted ankle or a broken arm would at least keep her in Steamboat Bend and out of his hair. Anything that would keep her away from him would be fine.

He raced out of town after the bellowing woman, half hoping a little accident would befall her. He considered the notion that at times he could be an uncaring, contemptible bastard. That this time involved Nora-Leigh bothered him more than he cared to think about.

It bothered him even more when he found Gingersnap without Nora-Leigh.

Chapter Four

Clay found the horse with its sides heaving and head hanging low. The winded mare stood off the beaten path shaded beneath the low branches of a willow tree. Sweat glistened on her torso, and the reins dangled between her front legs. Clay saw no sign of Nora-Leigh.

Be careful what you wish for. He cursed his previous ill thoughts about the young woman. He might not want her accompanying him, but he hadn't wished her any real harm. Swallowing hard against the fear convulsing his stomach, he scanned the ground on either side of the narrow road. He couldn't have passed without seeing her, could he? *Unless she'd been thrown wide of the dirt road.* Cursing aloud, he ripped off his damned eye patch and stuffed it in his trouser pocket.

Jolly pranced as Clay climbed down. He brushed the stallion's sweat-soaked neck. "We'll run later, boy. Right now I got to find that woman. Can't have her granddaddy after my hide. Besides, if she's broke her neck, he's liable to kill me."

He thought he heard something. He turned toward the sound. There it was again—an unmistakable human groan, faint but definite. It echoed just off to the far side of the willow tree where Gingersnap stood beneath its sheltering branches.

Clay scrambled down a rock-strewn embankment, then waded across a creek of inch-deep clear water. There lay Nora-Leigh sprawled on the other side, face down and unmoving. His heart thudded in his chest as he crouched beside her. He touched her neck with shaking fingers. Thank God. Beneath his thumb the pulse throbbed at a shallow rate. He saw no cuts or bruises, no blood, no outward sign of injury. Her legs or arms weren't bent in an unnatural position, yet she lay as still as a statue.

In all his years as an Army scout, he'd never been more frightened. He'd never examined a woman for injury before, but he didn't stop to think about convention. His hand trembled as he ran it along both sides of her narrow rib cage, then down her fragile neck and back. Through the flannel material of her shirt and the twill of her trousers, he felt his way over every delicate bone and vertebra and down each slender leg before easing her over onto her back. She moaned when he moved her, and he released the breath he just then realized he'd been holding. Her eyes fluttered but stayed closed, hiding her physical condition from his seeking gaze. With her face the color of a cold campfire, she looked like death. Clay's mouth felt as dry as ashes. He couldn't swallow past the lump in his throat. His breath came ragged and fast.

"Nora-Leigh?" he whispered. He clasped the back of her head and lifted her head gently onto his knee so he could peer into her ashen features. "Nell, honey? Can you hear me?"

Her beautiful hazel eyes fluttered, then opened, blinking several times. She stared at him with a frown that made him want to whoop with pure pleasure. It was a look he recognized after knowing her for a mere two days: extreme irritation coupled with female contrariness.

"Who are you calling honey?" she complained in a husky growl.

He couldn't have been happier, yet couldn't seem to find his voice. He found himself grinning like the town drunk.

As she tried to sit up, Clay placed his arm around her shoulder and steadied her in a sitting position. She stared at him, her eyes glazed.

"Do you hurt anywhere?"

She gave a startled laugh, then said, "Ask me where it doesn't hurt."

He smiled. He'd expected her to give him holy hell. Her good humor surprised him, particularly when she surely must be in considerable pain. "That's understandable. You took quite a tumble. How's your vision?"

She stared at him, then squinted her eyes. She chewed on her bottom lip before saying, "I think I'm seeing double. I see two of your pretty eyes."

Damn. He'd forgotten to replace the confounded eye patch. He looked aside as he reached into his pocket and fished out the durn thing. He tied it around his head. When he looked back at Nora-Leigh, she stared at him, blinking fast and obviously trying to focus on his face. Had she said he had pretty eyes? She *must* be delirious.

"I think there's something else wrong with my vision. Everything looks grayish, almost dark."

"It's late, the sun's about to set."

"Thank goodness. You know what else, Mr. Sullivan?"

"What's that, Miss Dillon?"

"I think I need a few more lessons before I try gallop-

ing on my trusty steed. When she ran beneath the tree
branches, I forgot to duck."

Clay stifled the laughter that sprang to his lips. One
had to admire her spunk and her sense of humor. "I
reckon it's a good notion to keep the galloping to a minimum for now."

"By the way, is Gingersnap all right?"

"She's fine."

"One other thing, Mr. Sullivan."

"We really ought to be going." Clay stood up, then
helped Nora-Leigh to her feet. She wobbled against him,
and he wound up back on the ground holding her in his
lap.

"Mr. Sullivan?"

"Yes?"

"This is highly inappropriate."

"Yep."

"But I guess I am a bit faint and I feel kind of light-
headed, the way I do after I drink a glass of Gran's home-
made dandelion wine."

Clay pulled her up against his chest, enclosing her in
a loose hug. He brushed a damp strand of mussed hair
from her forehead. He stared into her eyes, still glassy,
but beautiful and beckoning. The greenish brown color
looked almost emerald in the fading twilight. "Better?"
he asked.

"Yes," she murmured.

Without thinking about what he was about to do, he
kissed her brow. She smiled up at him and whispered,
"Thank you." Then her eyes rolled back in her head, and
within the circle of his embrace, she fainted dead away.

Warmth surrounded Nora-Leigh like a heavy woolen
blanket. An agreeable scent with citrus overtones drifted
up her nose. Her body bounced ever so slightly as if she
were riding in a badly sprung wagon. She opened her eyes

to total darkness. As she regained her senses and her sight, she realized that Clay held her in his arms as he walked back toward town. What she smelled must be his shaving soap, for it seemed to come from his neck and face.

He held the reins of the horses as they followed along behind him. He seemed oblivious to her weight or the fact that she was now awake and staring at him. Feeling safe and secure in his arms, Nora-Leigh had the unbelievable desire to snuggle up against his chest. One of his hands was wrapped tight against her ribs just beneath her breasts . . . uncomfortably close, she noted. Her heartbeat kicked up a notch as she peeked at the span of his fingers spread along her ribs. His other hand held her beneath her thighs where no man had ever touched her before.

The whole concept of being held this close to a man disconcerted Nora-Leigh, but she found it comforting at the same time. She'd have to analyze that later. Strength emanated from his body all the way from his wide shoulders down to his hard-muscled legs. His strides, long and measured, continued without pause.

From this close she saw that his chin was covered with a day-old lightly colored beard, a surprising contrast to his dark hair and mustache. His one silvery eye twinkled in the gloaming as he hummed the same song she'd heard the first time she'd seen him. It was out of tune. Apparently, the man couldn't carry a note even if it were placed in an empty egg basket.

"What happened?" she asked.

He stopped and looked down at her. An impish grin turned the corners of his mouth upward. "You, my dear woman, swooned."

"How is that possible?"

"Your body relaxed in the comfort of my strong arms, oxygen bid a fond farewell to your brain, and—"

"I don't need a science lesson." Just when she thought

he might be somewhat agreeable, he had to go and act like a . . . well, like a man, domineering and know-it-all. "Put me down right now."

Instead, his arms tightened around her and his grin turned into an insolent smirk. "Are you sure, Miss A-B-Cs? You might be wobbly on your feet, and you wouldn't want to faint again. I might not catch you this time."

He was insufferable. "I'll take my chances."

Clay continued walking, not even looking at her anymore. "It isn't far, and I don't mind."

Nora-Leigh wriggled, but it was apparent by the way his arms twined around her in a superior and most inappropriate way that he wasn't about to let her down. "Mr. Sullivan, *I* mind. I do not want the townsfolk seeing me like this."

"I'd prefer to carry you."

"I'd prefer to walk."

"But I'm bigger and stronger," he answered in an arrogant tone. Nora-Leigh wanted to kill him. Instead she reached up and yanked on his ear as hard as she could.

He yelped and dropped her to her feet. As he rubbed his reddening ear, he muttered, "You are one hellishly stubborn woman."

"And you, sir," Nora-Leigh replied, setting off toward town at a hasty pace, "are equally so." She glanced over her shoulder and smiled. Clay stood in the middle of the road, frowning as he kneaded the edge of his ear. When he looked at her, she continued, "I think we will do all right together once I learn how to ride a horse."

"Two mule-headed people like us? How d'you figure?"

"I shall have the map, and you need it to locate your gold." She wasn't about to tell him the map would be as helpful as a broken compass. "You have the experience of traveling on the prairie, and I will get my adventure."

"I fail to see how being stubborn affects any of that."

"You see, you're doing it again."

She shrugged her shoulders and marched off down the road. Men! How could they be so wooden-headed? His stubbornness was as obvious as the nose on his handsome face.

One day after giving Nora-Leigh a riding lesson that left him with a pounding headache, a bruised shin, and a head jammed full of her so-called practical criticism, Clay met with her grandfather on the back porch of his home. He sat on the top step with his back against a pillar while Devin sat in a rocking chair. Clay watched as he filled his pipe in a methodical way he must have perfected over a number of years.

Inside, the women cleaned up the supper dishes. A warm, amber glow shone from the curtained windows in squares of light on the porch floor. Clay watched as the women's shadows crisscrossed in that light, making oddly shaped patterns. Occasionally Clay heard a drift of feminine laughter or muted conversation. He glanced at Devin. The old man puffed on his pipe as he stared out into the coming night, seemingly lost in thought.

Tomorrow would see Clay and Nora-Leigh off. She on her adventure, and he in search of Custer's lost payroll. Clay had resigned himself to the task of escorting the unconventional woman, and if nothing else, the trip would undoubtedly prove interesting. It had been a long while since he'd spent time with a woman, any woman, be it an Army wife, a painted strumpet, or the women in his own family.

"Well, son, how's she doing?"

"She's aggravating, opinionated, headstrong, and as stubborn as a mule."

Devin smirked as he set his pipe on the table beside him. "I believe I already knew that about Nellie. What I wanted to know is, how's she doing with the riding?"

"Ah." Clay shrugged. "I reckon she'll have a sore backside for the first few days, but she and the mare are starting to speak the same language."

Devin gave Clay a lopsided grin. "Poor horse didn't stand a chance, did she?"

Clay smiled back. "Nope."

"What about you?"

Did he stand a chance against Nora-Leigh's cheerful optimism? He doubted it. "Me?"

"How are *you* holding up?"

"Most of the time, that girl is like a boil on my backside." He shook his head. "And my ears are ringing from all her strange ramblings and carrying on. It must be the teacher in her. One minute she's as calm as a horse trough, then she's riding herd on me, but I expect we'll make do. Somehow or other."

Clay awaited a reply, but when one wasn't forthcoming, he sat back and admired the stunning Montana sunset.

"And will you return her in a virginal state?"

Clay nearly toppled off the porch. "God, I hope so," he replied without thinking, then realized what he'd said. It was too late to retrieve it. Seemed he always put his foot in his mouth with this durned family. "Begging your pardon, Mr. Spooner—"

"Devin, son." He cocked his head to the side and continued, "If yore gonna be spending the next few days and nights"—he eyed Clay with a decided glimmer—"in the company of my granddaughter, you can at least remember to call me Devin."

"Devin." Clay repeated, shaking his head and once again leaning his back against the porch pillar. "If she ever kept her thoughts to herself, I might find her appealing. But as it is, I don't believe you have a thing to worry about. That girl couldn't keep her mouth shut long enough for anyone to steal a kiss, let alone work up to anything more."

Devin heaved a gloomy sigh and picked up his pipe again. He touched a twisted piece of straw to the candle burning beside him and relit the bowl. Several puffs of the fragrant cherry tobacco wafted across the porch. "That's kinda what I figured."

Clay frowned. He must be reading him wrong, but Devin sounded sorely disappointed that his granddaughter would retain her virginity while in Clay's care.

If he lived to be an old man, Clay would never understand this strange family.

Gray smoke curled into the night sky and disappeared among the twinkling stars and stray wispy clouds. The waning moon, a curve of silvery light, hung high above Blue Buffalo's head. Wrapped in a worn blanket to ward off the chill of the evening, he gazed into the dying campfire. Thoughts about his long life, now nearing its end, swirled through his head. How he knew for certain that he would die soon, he couldn't say, but he had little doubt that this would be his last season on earth.

Soon his soul would find its place within his tribe, the Mountain Crow, with family and friends, and with his beloved first wife, Cattail Blossom. They were gone from earth but not forgotten. Never forgotten and never far from Blue Buffalo's thoughts.

He lived with regrets. Far too many. But none concerned the way he had lived his life. Among his people he hadn't been liked, for he could be a heartless man— cold at times and cruelly savage, even to his own family. But because of his skill and bravery as a hunter and warrior, his bad humor had been tolerated. Among his enemies he had been hated and feared.

Now he was simply an old man.

With bones that ached and muscles that creaked and complained, it took him longer each sunrise to crawl from his blankets and face the day. How his Crow father would mock him if he were to see his arrogant son move at such a snail's pace. His eyesight was poor, his hearing all but gone, but his memories were still as bright and sparkling as morning dew on a blade of grass. But to pick up his bow and sight down the length of an arrow and actually spot his target, much less hit it, was impossible. Even now he couldn't hear his enemies if they were hiding in the grass no more than a stone's throw away.

Unfortunately, he could hear the snoring of the miner sleeping on the other side of the fire. A friend of long standing, Nat Arbogast slept the deep slumber of the innocent and the pure of heart. His snoring, Nat's only true fault, could wake a bear in the depth of winter hibernation.

In Nat's company, Blue Buffalo slept little, but he did not mind. It was at times like this that he wondered if any of his family lived. He would never find out.

He had refused to be herded like a domesticated farm animal onto the reservation lands and forced to adapt to the white man's culture. He wouldn't even travel the short distance to visit, even though he knew exactly where they were. So be it. He'd chosen his life. They'd chosen theirs. He was not sorry about his decision. He was a wanderer and a hunter, not a farmer, and he would be until he took his last dying breath.

Last night, in between stretches of Nat's snoring, Blue Buffalo slept. He dreamed of a small dog, sun-streaked in color, and her pup. One moment they were following his back trail, then they dissolved into a beautiful white woman, dressed in man's clothing, who held the hand of a boy child. They followed in the path of Blue Buffalo and Nat as they traveled and hunted. For days on end the woman asked questions about everything from the Indian way of life to the names of the plants they passed, until Blue Buffalo felt that his ears would overflow like a raging river and his head would burst, so full was it crammed with her incessant flow of words. Although he spoke the English tongue, he still had difficulty understanding her.

Then one day without warning the woman and child had vanished like a puff of smoke. All around him silence reigned. Strangely, he found he missed the talkative woman and her boy.

He didn't know what the dream meant—that was for a medicine man to interpret—but he knew that his and Nat's lives would sometime in the future be forever altered. He lifted his gaze once more to the endless night sky. Who could say whether the change would be good or bad?

On his way to the Spooner-Dillon residence, Clay encountered a well-dressed man with a face like an aging coonhound and a body like a hog ready for the slaughterhouse. He rushed up to Clay. With a beefy hand he pulled him away from the street and into a quiet alley. "Mr. Sullivan?"

Clay had his gun halfway out of the holster before he caught the frightened, though determined, look on the older man's overweight face. Still wary, Clay replaced the pistol and answered, "Yes?"

"The pirate, Clay Sullivan?" he said, red-faced and puffing to catch his breath, his double chin wiggling and his pendulous jowls waggling.

"I'm Clay Sullivan."

"Mayor Hannibal Boardman, sir."

Clay could hardly believe his eyes when the man actually bowed. He bit back the sarcastic retort that popped into his head. "Pleased to make your acquaintance. What can I do for you?"

Boardman glanced at Clay's hip. "Where's your cutlass?"

It took a moment for Clay to realize the meaning of the question. He struggled not to grin when he said, "It's a little awkward here in town, so it's packed away."

"Ah. Your sword, too?"

Clay nodded.

"I've read about your exploits on the high seas."

"You did?" Clay couldn't have been more astounded if he'd told him that the circus was coming to Steamboat Bend and they wanted Clay to tame the lions.

The wattle beneath the mayor's multiple chins brushed against the collar of his stiffly starched, pristine white shirt as he replied, "I believe it was in the *Helena Herald*."

Ethan's work, no doubt. That boy would plant a story just to irritate him. Clay couldn't wait to hear about his own infamous exploits. "When did you read this?"

"Oh, it must have been in the last six months or so."

"What did it say exactly?"

The mayor cleared his throat and began to speak as if he stood at the town square podium giving his Fourth of July patriotic speech. "That you boarded a Spanish ship, or was it a British ship? No matter. You and your fellow murdering pirates—no offense—"

"None taken."

"—killed ten men in a bloody battle and made away with a hundred pounds of the queen's gold bullion. Before you left, you set fire to the ship and sank it."

How Clay wished he had a hundred pounds of gold. Then he wouldn't have to be on this foolish mission or listen to men like the mayor, although this little tale was somewhat amusing. "Killed ten men?"

"In cold blood. With sabers, cutlasses, and pistols."

"You don't say? A saber, huh? Any survivors?"

"Only one. He recounted his tale for a paper back East, then the Helena newspaper picked it up."

"Did the newspaper mention me by name?"

The mayor nodded vigorously. "Yes, indeed, sir. Clay Sullivan. They called you the Bloody Scourge of the Atlantic."

"Bloody Scourge, huh?"

The mayor's ruddy face paled. "Of course, I'm no one to say how a man should behave—"

"That's a fact."

The mayor took a deep breath, then continued. "But I hope you plan on taking better care of our schoolteacher than that. She's a treasure we can't afford to lose."

"That wasn't the impression I got."

"What do you mean by that?"

"She thinks her prospects for marriage are about as likely as getting struck by lightning."

"I wasn't referring to her getting married. That wouldn't do at all. We don't want to lose our teacher. As you may know, they are as scarce as hen's teeth out here. We just want you to bring her back in one piece."

Clay forced down a spark of anger that made him want to strangle the pompous ass. "So it's not Nora-Leigh that you're worried about. It's simply the precious position."

Clay leaned toward the man. The mayor's eyes widened, but he stood fast. Clay hated to admit it, but he had to give Boardman credit for standing his ground against Clay's obvious anger. "I'm thinking of making the woman a pirate, too, teaching her how to become as bloodthirsty as I am. The Bloody Scourgess of the Atlantic. What do you think of that?"

"Humph." The politician gave him a peeved look. "I think that Devin Spooner is making a terrible mistake by allowing you anywhere near his granddaughter."

"That so?"

"Yes, indeed. I'm only speaking to you now because I am paid to be the spokesperson for the interests of Steamboat Bend."

"And those interests are that I bring back your precious schoolteacher in one piece. Am I reading you right?"

"Partially. We also feel it's only fair that if anything should befall Miss Dillon, we would be compensated."

"We?"

"The citizens of Steamboat Bend. You appear to be a wealthy man, Mr. Sullivan, and although I'm not sure what your interests are here, I have a good idea. Still, I guess that's none of my business, but as a killer pirate you must know about monetary matters."

Clay snorted. "Get to the point, Mr. Mayor."

"We want our money up front, before you leave."

Clay threw back his head and laughed. God, what a muddle he'd made of this pirate business. If it wasn't so asinine and insanely stupid, he might even get more than a chuckle from it. But he wanted to punch the mayor right in his arrogant, self-righteous face. Instead he bit down on his irritation and jammed his hands in his pockets. "There is no money now, there's not going to be any money in the future, and you and your cronies wouldn't be getting their grubby hands on it if there was. I'll tell you one thing, though. The next time I decide to go pillaging and pirating, you'll be the first to know. You and the citizens of your fair city can tag along. Who knows? Since you're so anxious to get your hands on my gold, you just might like murdering to get it."

The mayor's jowls dropped and he sputtered ineffectually without saying a word.

"I'll bring back your teacher, I promise you that, but you sure as hell don't deserve her."

"Now, wait a minute, I'm not sure you understand my meaning here."

"Your damned meaning is clear, all right. Just tell your friends that I carry a gun, as well as a knife, and I'm not a bad shot with a rifle. I'll be back with your prized teacher. Now get your sorry ass out of my face."

The mayor waddled away, giving quick backward glances every few steps as if he expected Clay to pull out a bloodied cutlass and slash him to bits.

Clay wanted to kick the man's retreating butt. The

mayor had shown him one thing, though. Steamboat Bend
didn't appreciate Nora-Leigh as a good woman, but only
saw her as their eccentric teacher. In this backwater town,
another teacher, good or bad, would be impossible to find.

Nora-Leigh glanced out her bedroom window and shook
her head at the sight before her. By twos and threes, children and adults appeared like silent wraiths in the pre-
dawn semidarkness and were milling about in the yard.

Frowning, she turned to toss the last of her clothing
and personal items into her grandfather's worn leather
satchel.

If she had her way, she and Clay would have left
Steamboat Bend by now with no one the wiser and no
one asking impertinent questions. But somehow—she
saw her grandfather's hand in this—the schoolchildren
had found out she was leaving. And her mother, bless her
misguided heart, seemed to have helped with this gathering. Nora-Leigh had little doubt that there would be a
grand sendoff.

So now here they all were on her doorstep, a dozen
noisy children and their parents. She noticed the adults
wore similar expressions of misgiving. Some even wore
expressions of longing. Many of the boys sat cross-legged
on the steps or the damp ground, and the younger girls
giggled as they sat dangling their short legs on the porch
swing while their curls bounced in unison. The older girls
watched the older boys. The older boys watched the older
girls but pretended they didn't. Most of the parents stood
in the yard talking quietly among themselves.

When she pushed aside the curtains and looked outside
again, everyone was munching her mother's tasty oatmeal
muffins and drinking her special cinnamon-spiced hot tea.

Oh, sweet Lord. Nora-Leigh wanted to tiptoe out the
back door and disappear like the morning mist. Instead,
she donned her practiced teacher-knows-best smile along

with her twill trousers, flannel shirt, and knee-high boots. She tucked the well-worn map inside her boots along with a long, wicked-looking knife. Then she made up her bed with special care. It would be a while before she did the familiar, homely task again. She took a look around her bedroom, then gave the quilt one last loving pat.

She carefully pinned her hair into a staid bun, hoping to achieve a confident, above-reproach schoolmarm look, then grabbed up her packed satchel and glanced in the mirror. It confirmed her previous opinion. She looked young and inept, and as frightened as a rabbit trapped in a wolf's den. Although she wanted to go more than she could say, she'd never been away from her family for any length of time. Still, this was part and parcel of the adventuring experience. Despite that thought, she proceeded outside with quaking knees, her heart thundering and a forced smile on her face.

Looking piratical in his open-throated white shirt and shiny black boots, Clay caught her eye as soon as she stepped onto the porch. Behind him, the sun was just coming up and added to his swashbuckling appearance. With one thumb tucked into his belt, he stood talking in his usual confident manner to Henrietta and Bert Lahr and their two boys, Jack and Jamie. If she wasn't mistaken, he winked at her before turning back to hear something Bert was saying. Since he only had one eye to wink with, it was hard to say for sure.

Her grandmother and grandfather stood in the yard talking to her most demanding student, Amanda Hartson, and her nanny, the famous and beloved Elizabeth. Nora-Leigh didn't know the poor young woman's last name, but she pitied her for having to put up with the child. However, according to Amanda, Elizabeth was a model of decorum and etiquette who knew everything. *Elizabeth says a lady should always carry a parasol to keep her face from freckling. Elizabeth says refinement comes from playing the pianoforte or the violin or singing a lovely melody. Elizabeth says a young lady should be seen and not heard.* From what Nora-Leigh could tell, Amanda seldom took the last piece of advice to heart.

Amanda's father, the well-known and respected gold baron, Hershall Hartson, was of course nowhere to be seen. And far be it from the girl's mother to make an appearance. That would surely be below her station. According to Amanda, her mother thought Steamboat Bend was "much too provincial." She preferred Chicago or New York. Nora-Leigh couldn't help rolling her eyes as she moved out into the yard. She would not miss Amanda Hartson the least bit.

In the street, Clay's dapple gray stallion—Jolly Roger, Nora-Leigh believed Clay called him—looked overwhelmingly large but he stood alert and quiet, saddled and ready to ride. He seemed not to notice the mare that pranced next to him or the cantankerous-looking pack mule piled high with provisions.

Nora-Leigh's eyes widened in disbelief when she spied a glossy black crow, the size of a small dog, perched atop the mule's back. His piercing onyx eyes assessed her as well, and he didn't like what he saw. If a crow could look arrogant, this one did. His wings fluttered as if he were about to take flight and attack her. Nora-Leigh got ready to duck. Instead, his wings settled back against his body and she relaxed. Somewhat.

"Why, Nora-Leigh, I understand you're about to undertake a holiday," Amy Sue Lederer gushed as she took Nora's chilled hand into her own. She beamed at Nora-Leigh as she continued. "And on a pirate ship. How exciting."

What had her mother told this woman? That Nora-Leigh had taken up piracy as a hobby? Or was it her grandmother or her grandfather spreading rumors? God only knew.

Amy Sue lived in the large house next to theirs, and she claimed she was a widow though rumor had it that in her day she'd been quite a loose woman. She had "spent time"—this was said only in a whisper and never in mixed company—in a brothel in the red-light district in Denver. Nora-Leigh found those rumors difficult to believe, however. The woman was eighty if she was a day, toothless, square-jawed as any man, and homely as sin. Judging by her looks, she had never been a beauty, and her figure could easily be compared to a beanpole. And her breath could knock over a bull at ten paces. Still, she was always pleasant and she meant well.

Nora-Leigh smiled at her but kept one eye on the crow. It looked back at her with a threatening glare. Nora kept on walking until she found her mother passing out muffins.

"Mother?" she pulled her aside and whispered. "Where did you tell Amy Sue I was going?"

"Why, dear, I told her you were taking a sea voyage for your health. It seemed fitting with Clay and all."

"And what exactly did you tell her was wrong with me?"

"I wasn't specific. I think I mentioned female problems."

"Female problems?"

"Female problems?" came an echo over Nora-Leigh's shoulder. There stood Clay with a questioning glare on his face. "If there's something ailing you, I'm not about to take you with me."

"There's nothing wrong with my health." She grabbed Clay's arm and pulled him close so she could hiss in his ear. "Mother is trying to keep the gossip down about us traveling together. Her not very nice idea was to say I needed the fresh sea air to cure me."

"And that's supposed to *stop* the rumors about you and me?"

"Mother seems to think so."

Clay leaned closer. His warm breath tickled her ear, sending gooseflesh up and down her arms. "Your mother will be right soon enough."

"What?" Nora's heart fluttered.

"I ride hard, eating up the miles quickly. You'll be breathing my trail dust all day. It doesn't make for a tasty supper. Unless I'm dead wrong, you'll be ailing soon enough."

Nora-Leigh stiffened her back and drew away. "I'm made of sterner stuff than you seem to think."

His brows rose in a doubtful expression. "We'll see."

That sounded like a challenge.

Chapter Five

Clay stepped up on to a tree stump, put two fingers to his mouth and whistled loud enough to wake even the residents of the Steamboat Bend cemetery. The crowd of townsfolk who were gathered around him quieted and turned their attention to him.

He waited, assessing his audience, then placed his hands on his hips. He strove for a confident arrogance, jutting out his chin and cocking his head in what he hoped was a pirate-like pose.

"As many of you may already know," he began, "I'm a pirate. I've sailed all over the world searching for treasure. I came to Steamboat Bend because I hear tell there's gold near your fair town."

He paused for effect. This seems to be working, he thought. Every eye was on him. "But I don't abide interference and I give no quarter. In other words, don't follow me. Don't even think about it."

He caught the eye of Mayor Boardman and winked.

The good mayor's face blanched. "Your mayor will tell you I don't take captives, and I don't leave witnesses. Now, mind you, ordinarily I'm a good-natured man. Just don't make me mad. I've been known to disembowel people for attempting to cross me."

He glanced at Nora-Leigh. Horror and disbelief were upon her face, and it was all he could do to keep a straight face. He gave the crowd a cocky grin. "But you people have nothing to worry about, 'cause I know you won't get me riled. And I promise to bring back your sweet little schoolteacher unharmed—leastways, not by my hand."

He hopped down and wandered among the crowd, waiting for Nora to say her goodbyes.

Nora-Leigh's hopes of a quiet departure had evaporated with the morning mist. She had no idea what a tearful send-off it would be. Her mother sobbed. Her grandmother wept. Even her usually stoic and sometimes starchy grandfather wiped tears from his cheeks. Everyone—from the mayor, who seemed to avoid Clay, to the undertaker to her youngest student—carried on as though Nora-Leigh were never going to be heard from again.

She understood their concern, but soon grew tired of hearing such things as "be careful" or "watch out for other pirates" or storms, or sharks, or whatever the person speaking feared most. Why couldn't any of them just wish her a good time? The mayor's wife suggested that she write a journal. That seemed like good advice. No one said, however, that they would see her soon. It was a bit disconcerting.

"Wear a hat," suggested Amanda Hartson's nanny, Elizabeth. Nora-Leigh thanked her for the thoughtful suggestion. Not that it would help her freckles any. They popped out whether she wore a hat or not. Just being outside made them appear on her face like unwanted weeds in the vegetable patch.

Her head swam with the last-minute advice and wisdom from the townsfolk, to say nothing about just trying to recall all of the riding instructions she'd received from Clay.

After getting a boost from her grandfather and carefully stepping into the stirrups, she was ready for the journey.

Atop the mare and eager to begin, she glanced around the yard looking for Clay. Then she looked down—way down. It was an unbelievably long way to the ground, particularly if one was falling. No matter what, she most definitely wasn't comfortable with this business of horseback riding. Not one little bit. She wasn't sure that she even liked the tall, unpredictable creatures. And she wondered at the good sense of Clay riding a male horse. Didn't stallions harbor amorous intentions toward mares like the one she rode? The whole idea couldn't help but be a disaster—and it would most likely be hers.

She didn't like the look of the pack mule either. Cantankerous didn't begin to describe his overall bearing or the way his eyes watched her. She had a feeling he would be giving her trouble. And that was no parrot that Clay owned. He was a crow from his shiny black feathers to his large, sturdy beak. The bird, too, eyed Nora-Leigh with evil intent. He just sat on top of the pack mule, watching, wary, making her more uncomfortable by the minute. She wished Clay would hurry up so they could leave.

She stared across the people-filled yard as Clay worked his way toward his waiting horse. Suddenly she felt a tug on her boot. Before she knew what was happening, she hurtled off Ginger and into the strong arms of a man who proceeded to kiss her with boyish enthusiasm. It could only be Billy Seth Torrence.

"Billy Seth! Let me go!" she managed to say between sloppy, wet, puppy-like kisses. The overall effect wasn't much different from the way a dog says hello with his tongue. All over her face. Yet he held her so tight she couldn't breathe.

"You cain't go, Nellie," he stated in a near sob. Tears coursed down his sad face at the same time that one large hand slid down Nora-Leigh's back and cupped her backside. She reached behind her and grabbed his fingers, pulling his hand away. "I thought you and me was gonna get harnessed up together."

Nora-Leigh's eyes widened. Where would he get such a confounded notion?

He thrust against her, his tongue washing her face. That better not be what she thought it was pressed up against her thigh. Disgust filled her. She struggled against his hold, but he wouldn't relinquish his death-like grip on her. Instead, if anything, he pulled her tighter against his straining body. My goodness, the men in Steamboat Bend were right. Big ears equaled big . . . well, bigger *other parts* as well. That *other part* was making its forceful self known. And Billy Seth refused to remove his chest-crushing hold on her. Her lungs ached for air as she desperately tried to wriggle out of his hold.

"Billy Seth, l-let go of m-me. I c-can't breathe."

"I cain't let you go. I love you too bad."

"What a touching sight, Miss Dillon. I didn't realize you had a beau."

Nora-Leigh glanced up to see Clay just beyond Billy Seth's shoulder with his hands on his hips, a piratical smirk turning up his lips.

"I don't," she hissed, gasping for breath. "Do s-something."

Clay threw back his head and laughed. Loudly. The audacious nerve of the man. She was getting her face scrubbed by a randy simpleton and was close to passing out, and Clay found the situation uproarious.

"Please," she mouthed, begging him with watering eyes.

With the back of his hand, Billy Seth wiped the tears from his face. "I always wanted you, Nellie. Most 'specially betwixt the sheets."

Nora-Leigh saw stars before her eyes. Her knees wobbled.

"Uh, Billy Seth, is it?" Clay tapped her eager suitor on his shoulder. "If you don't let our little schoolmarm here go soon, I reckon she won't have the breath to warm anyone's sheets."

"Wha'?" Billy Seth leaned back to scrutinize Nora-Leigh. He scrunched up his face, stuck out his chin, and studiously stared at her face. He must have recognized the about-to-faint look on her features because he stepped away, but not before he lasciviously rubbed up against her thigh. There was no mistaking his intent. Without a backward glance, he sauntered away as if nothing untoward had occurred.

If she weren't trying to breathe and stand upright at the same time, she would have hauled off and kicked him but good. The nincompoop. Then she would have done the same thing to Clay.

Nora-Leigh's knees buckled when air burst into her throbbing lungs. Clay grabbed her elbow to steady her, then handed her his handkerchief. She wiped the spittle from her face. "You waited long enough," she gasped.

"It was worth every minute," he whispered, "just to see you squirm in that young man's loving embrace."

"You have a strange sense of humor."

He pulled her close and stared into her face, his gray eye twinkling. He'd never looked more devil-may-care than at that moment. "So I've been told."

"I'm fine. You may release me now."

"Why, honey, I reckon I'll just hold on to you a minute more," he drawled. "We'll give the good people of Steamboat Bend one more thing to gossip about, aside from your lovesick beau's passionate good-bye."

"He's not my beau any more than I'm your honey."

"You sure you want to leave? You could still settle down and marry. Have a passel of kids with Billy Seth." He grinned. "He really, really likes you."

"I'm not particularly fond of children. And let go of me."

He frowned. "You like kids. You're a teacher."

"Just because I'm a teacher doesn't mean I like children."

"All women like kids. Just wait until you have some of your own."

"I don't think so. I'm not having any children, and I'm *not* marrying Billy Seth Torrence." She beckoned Clay near so she could talk without being overheard. "He's not right in the head."

"No," he gasped, wide-eyed.

"Yes, it's true. I heard tell that his mother dropped him on his head when he was a babe. Besides, it's just an infatuation he has with me."

"He's quite taken with you, all right, but then I reckon I could work up an infatuation for you myself." He moved his head so close that Nora-Leigh could feel his breath against her neck. Like the gentle flutter of a butterfly wing, his tongue brushed along the lobe of her ear. A shiver skittered down her spine and gooseflesh rose on her arms. Her knees weakened again and his hold tightened.

Nora-Leigh looked up into his presumptuous, mocking face. "You will say or do anything, won't you, just to keep me from going?"

He looked at her, openly amused that she'd caught on. "Yep."

"You won't even deny it?"

"Nope."

"Well, it won't work. I have my grandfather's map. I'm going, and that's that."

88

He caught her ear with his teeth and gave it a gentle tug. Nora-Leigh, without much success, tried to ignore the hot flare of desire that tore through her body. She swallowed hard. "Are you purposely setting out to ruin my reputation?"

"What do you think?" he asked in a husky whisper. "I've done every damn thing I can think of to dissuade you from coming with me but you are as cursedly stubborn as a bull calf. If I kissed you right here and now with all your family and neighbors watching, do you suppose that'd do the trick?"

She glanced around. The townsfolk were all watching with avid expressions on their faces, but no one seemed inclined to stop him. It was as if he'd mesmerized them as well.

If I kissed you right here and now. What did he mean by that? Billy Seth had just kissed her and hardly anyone batted an eye. Of course, that was Billy Seth, not Clay.

He didn't give Nora-Leigh enough time to reply. He molded the contours of his lean, hard body against her, then placed one hand in the hollow of her back, effectively holding her against him. He clasped his other hand to the back of her head. The heat of his body enshrouded her as he bent his head and stared at her, daring her to say something, to deny him. When she didn't, his lips grazed hers. His thick mustache, soft as a kitten's ear, tickled her upper lip. She smiled and waited, her eyes fluttering shut.

She expected a gentle kiss, a gentlemanly kiss. She was wrong. There was no gentleness about it.

He kissed her like she'd never been kissed before. The action was eager and bold, hungry and persuasive, and overwhelmingly male. Rough and untamed in its intensity. She couldn't explain why, but she found Clay's kiss enthralling, thrilling, and exhilarating beyond belief. And she loved every minute: The way he smelled like leather

89

and early morning air; the way he tasted—just a hint of his morning coffee; the way he held her—snug against his broad chest and taut stomach, his thighs brushing against her own. His lips were unexpectedly silken yet firm. Her heart pounded, blood pouring through her veins, and her body melted against Clay like candle wax.

His lips still locked to hers, Clay turned her head just enough to force her mouth open with his tongue; then he proceeded to make love to her mouth. It was heavenly. Because his insistent lips demanded a response, Nora-Leigh willingly gave him one. She shivered with wanting as her tongue danced with his, then drew it into her mouth as he had hers.

He jerked away from her, his broad shoulders heaving, his breath ragged. The mocking, amused look on his face had disappeared. His cheeks were flushed. His smoky-colored eye blazing, he asked in a gruff voice, "What the hell do you think you're doing?"

"Returning your kiss," she answered in a breathy voice she hardly recognized as her own.

"Are you out of your mind? That was no kiss you gave me. That was one hotly righteous request for me to do what should have been done to you a long time ago." He sounded peevish. "You oughta get yourself hitched before you burst into flames and take some poor unsuspecting sodbuster along with you."

"I quite liked it," she answered in all honesty. She patted her own heated cheeks and watched his eye widen with disbelief.

"You what?"

"I liked your kiss. I'm no expert, of course. But it seems you kiss very well. Made my heart kind of do a little jig inside my chest. I thought I could feel the blood actually coursing through my body. It was most exciting. A very enlightening lesson."

"An enlightening lesson, huh? Let me tell you something, little lady. Kisses like that lead to more, a whole helluva lot more."

"Oh, I could have stopped anytime."

He frowned. "I doubt that."

She nodded, sure of herself. She was a teacher, always in control. Well, maybe not always. Her control may have slipped a bit when Clay kissed her. But that was something she would never admit. "Certainly I could have stopped. I did, didn't I?"

"No, ma'am. I did."

She ignored him. "It's like teaching a child to read. You teach them to read one word at a time, then a phrase, and before long, they're reading whole sentences. Isn't that what you're trying to do? That was just your way of teaching me. One little kiss to warn me not to come with you, that you're a scoundrel whom I should avoid. Next time it'll be something more. Each time something more until I've run off screaming like an untried schoolgirl. Well, it's not going to happen. Roll up your sleeves, Mr. Sullivan. You're going to have a fight on your hands."

The phrase that exploded from his lips, if nothing else from the scandalous conversation, singed the ears of the entire population of Steamboat Bend. Two women, one the Methodist minister's wife, fainted. Mothers covered the ears of their children. At least five people, all elderly gentlemen, who stood close enough to hear, hooted like they'd been on a two-day bender.

To say the least, Nora-Leigh found it a somewhat troubling beginning to her adventure, but nothing—not even a heated, bone-melting kiss from Clay—would deter her now. They were on their way.

As they rode, Clay thought. At the first contact of their lips, he had experienced Nora-Leigh's searingly hot vitality, her exuberant love of life. And it had been totally unexpected in a simple kiss. Simple? Sinful was more like

91

it. With that first touch, the shock of her lips sent a hornets' nest buzzing inside him, nearly buckling his knees. Right in the head or not, Billy Seth Torrence was right about one thing. Feeling like a lecherous billy goat, even Clay wanted Nora-Leigh betwixt his sheets.

This was going to be the absolute worst, the longest, the most agonizing undertaking in Clay's entire life. Five miles from town and his blood had yet to cool down. Worse, he didn't see it happening anytime soon, and he couldn't blame it on any blazing spring weather. Clouds shadowed the sky. Unless he was sadly mistaken, before sunset, rain would make this day a soggy, uncomfortable mess.

He couldn't stop the memory of Nora-Leigh's mouth— the taste, soft, sweet, and inviting. Even when he had forced his tongue halfway down her throat, she hadn't shuddered or pulled away. Her honeyed mouth had pulled him inside and he was like to never leave.

Holy hell. By all that was right, he should just turn around and forget this entire misbegotten business.

Jolly Roger, sensing his discomfort, pranced toward Nora-Leigh's mare, keeping her off balance as well. Clay watched the girl concentrate on controlling the horse. She caught her lower lip between her teeth, and a frown of determination etched itself between her brows. He grew shivery all over just thinking about those sharp little teeth and what they might do to his bewitched body.

He drew a deep breath and let it out slowly, but he couldn't tear his gaze away. Her grandfather's misshapen hat had fallen off her head but clung to her slender neck by its string. Shadows fell across her whiskey-colored hair, sending waving glimmers of light around her head. Her artless, wide-eyed, innocent gaze took in everything. Every tree, every bush, every rock outcropping. Every small creature that skittered across her path. Oddly enough, he envied her at that moment.

Her damnable kiss would plague him until his dying day. He shook his head. How could such a guileless, small package hide the hot-blooded woman inside? Phew! What a trip this would be.

He looked away and tried reminding himself that the money he recovered would buy his freedom, his ranch, and his long sought escape from the relentless boredom of army life. He needed to stay focused, restrain himself, and forget the bewitching creature beside him. But he couldn't seem to help himself. Like a revolving carousel, his gaze unerringly came back to Nora-Leigh.

"Mr. Sullivan?"

Clay looked away from her face and stared ahead. He pulled his hat low on his forehead. "Yes, Miss Dillon?"

"What are the names of your animals?"

"My stallion is named Jolly Roger, Jolly for short. The mule's name is Stubborn; I reckon I don't have to tell you why. And the crow's name is Calico Jack."

"Very pirate-like."

He wasn't about to tell her that his stallion's name was only Jolly and the crow had been just plain Jack at first. "Guess so."

"How many days do you think before we get there?"

"You got the map," he reminded her. "If you showed it to me, I reckon I could guess."

"We're following the Bighorn."

"Yep."

"To the juncture of the Little Bighorn."

"Right so far."

"How long will that be?"

"It depends."

"Why are you being so difficult? You're worse than the boys in my classroom."

"That bad? Why don't you just sit back and enjoy your grandfather's bribe on this so-called adventure of yours."

She pulled up on her reins, stopped Ginger, and turned

to stare at him. "My grandfather didn't bribe you."

"No? You're with me; I didn't want you with me. What else would you expect would have convinced me, Miss Schoolmarm, if not a bribe?"

"You may call me Nora-Leigh, Mr. Sullivan. I prefer to think of it as a payment for the use of the map."

"A payment," he repeated in an overdone, high-pitched imitation of her voice. "I'll call you sweetheart, honey, Miss Schoolmarm, any damn thing I want to—"

"The bane of your existence. The burr under your saddle. As much trouble as a motherless calf."

"What?"

"I'm just trying to help."

"How's that?"

"I'm telling you all of the names and phrases for me that are a botheration to you. There's a good one. Botheration."

"Miss Dillon, would you kindly shut up?"

"Yes, sir."

The little darling actually smiled, which riled him even further. It took him a moment to recall what it was he had meant to say. "Anyway, you have no recourse but to keep your sweet ass planted in that saddle and follow me. I know this land, and by now you must be long lost."

At his vulgarity, her chin came up. "I most certainly am not. If I wanted to go home, and I don't," she said, looking at him with her stubborn chin raised a notch further, "all I have to do is turn Gingersnap around and follow the river home."

He snorted derisively. "The big *if* being *if* you could turn Gingersnap around. You ride that mare like a greenhorn straight off the train from Boston."

"I thought I was doing quite well, considering."

"Well, you haven't fallen off again."

"That's right."

" 'Course, all we've done is walk. Let's wait 'til tonight

and see what your ass has to say about that."

"You're very rude."

"I never said I wasn't."

"No, you didn't."

Clay shook his head. He could insult her. He could be crude and obscene. He could kiss her senseless. But there was just no unsettling or deterring her. Yet. Tonight, though, after eight to ten hours in the saddle, just might be her undoing. Clay smiled to himself.

Three hours later, Nora-Leigh found herself squirming in the saddle, attempting without avail to find a comfortable position. She had no idea the confounded contraption perched on the back of a horse could grow so hard in such a short time. After all, the beast's back was curved, as was the saddle. It really should have been more comfortable than it was.

Clay stopped the horses but once, and without a word of explanation climbed down. He disappeared behind a large boulder. She didn't have to be told what he was doing. Blushing profusely, she heard the splashing plainly enough. Well, what did she expect? There weren't any outhouses about. When he returned, still adjusting his trousers, he quirked an eyebrow at her. She shook her head. Even if she had to answer nature's call, under no conditions would she do it when he might be privy to the nature of her business. She could wait until they stopped for some other reason. And she would be much more discreet.

Clay hadn't spoken to her since she'd told him he was rude. Every time she started a conversation, he answered in grunts or one-word replies. She had since given up talking and simply enjoyed the landscape, adjusting to Ginger's uneven walk. With each step, her bottom teetered like a rocking chair, rolling from side to side rather than front to back. Could one's buttocks bruise? She supposed a good whacking would do it, but was simply riding on a horse enough?

"I've had the feeling that someone's been tailing us since we left town." Clay surprised her by speaking. He looked around, then back over his shoulder.

Nora-Leigh glanced over her shoulder as well. She'd noticed his preoccupation, and this was perhaps the third time in the last fifteen minutes that he'd checked their back trail. Still, she saw nothing but overcast skies above the river cliffs, and just behind them, a thicket of willows. On either side of their horses stretched endless clumps of shrubby prairie sagebrush. She couldn't help wondering if his worry was for his own safety or for hers. She wanted to believe he was a gentleman who bore concern for her well-being, but, taking in his concentrated frown, there was little doubt about his feelings toward her. He was no gentleman. That fiery kiss before they left had proved that. But she'd always dreamed of exotic travels . . . and no ill-humored, hot-blooded scoundrel could take away the joy she felt about this first adventure.

Ever optimistic, she tried deflecting his worry. "You're just imagining it, I expect."

He snorted. "I never imagine anything."

She didn't doubt that for a minute. He was the most unimaginative person she'd ever met, except maybe in his ability to spark hers. That he could do easily enough.

He turned toward her, the saddle leather protesting beneath his weight. One eyebrow rose in question. "Do you know, by chance, if your jealous beau is following us?"

It was Nora-Leigh's turn to snort. "I've told you. Billy Seth isn't my beau. He wouldn't know how to be jealous, nor would he be able to follow. Besides, how would *I* know if anyone was trailing us? You're supposed to be the expert."

There was a pause. "How come?"

"How come what?"

"How come you don't have another beau? What about the other single men in town besides Billy Seth?"

"I told you, that boy doesn't have all his faculties."

"He seemed to have all his other parts, though." Clay grinned. "He was a pitiful sight, that's for sure, but he was damned sorry to see you go."

"He didn't even notice when we left."

"Sure, he did. He even told me he'd wait for you." He lifted his eyebrows suggestively. "No matter what."

"You are such a storyteller, Mr. Sullivan."

"You still haven't answered my question."

"I've already forgotten. Which one was that?"

"Why no other men have been begging for your hand in marriage."

"Have you taken a good look at me? In case you haven't noticed, the folks in town think I'm a bit eccentric. Good enough to teach their children but crazy all the same. I ride a bicycle. I wear men's trousers. I can't play the piano. I can't sing. I can't tat or embroider or sew a straight stitch. I wear my hair too short. I go outside without a bonnet. And besides everything else, I'm a terrible cook."

"Yeah, but women are scarce around these parts. Even homely ones can fetch a husband."

At her raised eyebrow, he hurried to add, "Not that you're homely. Why, they even—wait a doggone minute." Clay pulled back on his reins so quickly his stallion bucked. He controlled his horse, but not before Gingersnap shied away. Clay reached over, grabbed the mare's bridle, and pulled her to an abrupt halt. He stared at Nora-Leigh, his pewter-gray eye wide with disbelief. "You can't cook?"

Nora-Leigh glanced away. "Isn't this lovely country? Why, I never imagined it would look like this. I wasn't paying that much attention when we first came to Montana. I guess I was just so excited about traveling. Of course, I was a young girl then. Youngsters seldom notice their surroundings. They are always more worried about themselves, leaving their friends behind, the things they know and are familiar with. Why, I guess—"

"You can't cook," he said, repeating himself. "Why, Miss Dillon," he said, his voice thick with sarcasm. "Back when I asked you if you were fit for the trail, you told me you could do anything as well or better than I could. And it just so happens I'm not a bad cook."

Oh, dear. How was she going to get herself out of this jam? "Well, I, that is, I—"

"Lied to me?"

"No, no, I would never do that."

He leaned closer, so they were almost nose to nose. "What would you call it then? You must have a fancy name for it in that high-falutin' teacher's brain of yours."

"Hmm. Well, there is prevaricate."

He nodded. "That's a mouthful, all right."

"Equivocate."

"Now, there's a teacherly word if I ever heard one. Does it mean lie?"

"Pretty close. Then there's quibble, fib, stretch the truth . . . um, I'm sure there are more," she said.

"Stretching the truth sounds close. . . . But I'd say lie fits the bill as perfectly as my damned hat fits my head."

"What about *your* lies?"

"Like what?"

"Like you're a pirate who's sailed the seven seas, or been to the Spice Islands or wherever it was you said you'd been. I may not be a cook, but neither are you a pirate."

"Like yourself, I have perhaps prevaricated. However. Though I may not be a *good* pirate," he said with a smile, "I am a pirate. Whereas you are neither a cook nor a good cook."

"Prove to me you're a pirate."

"How?"

Suddenly an arrow whistled through the air and thudded into a tree not two feet above Clay's head. Before Nora-Leigh could even think about what to do, Clay pulled her from the saddle and tossed her to the ground. The air whooshed from her lungs as Clay's heavy body covered her own. Both horses reared and raced off.

Chapter Six

"Are you all right?" Nora-Leigh whispered in a shaky voice.

"Of course I'm all right," Clay answered. "You?"

"I'm scared senseless, and my heart is beating like a drum. But other than being squashed by your considerable weight, I'm fine." She lowered her voice. "Are we in danger, Mr. Sullivan?"

She heard the disgust in his voice. "If that's who I think it is, we're not. But we're not moving until I'm damn sure."

Nora-Leigh couldn't keep the shock from her voice. "You mean someone you know would shoot at you?"

"Without a second thought." He rose to his elbows and twisted his head around to look where the arrow had come from. "Don't move a muscle until my say-so."

With her face pressed against the ground and her nose mere inches from a scrub willow, Nora-Leigh licked her dry, cracked lips. Her heart fluttered madly in her chest as she regarded Clay. His single penetrating eye blinked, then widened. Fury danced in its dark gray depths. In one quick movement, he leapt to his feet, his right hand poised above the ominous-looking gun tied at his thigh.

With his free arm, he reached out and yanked Nora-Leigh to her feet. He held her quaking hand enclosed in his grasp, then gave her fingers an encouraging squeeze. She welcomed the gesture of reassurance and pressed up against his side. Never in her life had she been so frightened as when that arrow whizzed by her head and smacked into the tree trunk. She would recall the noise for the rest of her life. She still half expected a tribe of screaming Indians to pour over the hillside and attack them.

Clay seemed to understand. He stood close to her, his strength giving her a small measure of courage. However, he didn't take his gaze off the Indian or the white man who now stood a stone's throw away near the curve of the creek. Their expressions were wary, their weapons at the ready. But despite that, they didn't appear ominous, just prepared. The white man held a shotgun cradled in the curve of his arm, but he didn't seem in a hurry to use it. And if Nora-Leigh wasn't mistaken, he was smiling beneath his thick, tangled, yellowish-gray beard.

She watched as Clay clenched his gloved hand into a fist. Then he visibly shook it out, relaxing the fingers. "Dammit, Blue Buffalo, you could have killed either one of us. I have a few good years left and am partial to my skin."

"You know him?" whispered Nora-Leigh.

"Like the back of my hand."

"I did not hit you," the Indian answered in slow, measured English. "I sent the arrow above you because my arm is weak and my eyesight poor." He separated from his companion, paced forward, and jerked the arrow from

101

the tree. After studying it a moment, he replaced it in a beaded quiver slung over his shoulder.

"Why did you shoot the damn thing at all?" Clay asked.

Blue Buffalo gave them a pointed look. "To let you know I was here."

"Couldn't you just say hello like normal folks?" Clay released a long-drawn-out sigh and visibly relaxed. Then he pointed to where the arrow had struck. "And you didn't miss by all that much. What are you thinking? If you can't see straight, you might hit us by mistake."

"No mistake. The wind carries the arrow for me so it will not strike you. If it was your time, then maybe, but it is not your time."

Clay screwed his mouth into a frown and shook his head.

"It is the way," Blue Buffalo replied inscrutably.

Nora-Leigh's heart was only just resuming its normal rhythm, but she couldn't resist a question. "Where did you learn to speak English so well?"

Surprising her, Clay answered for him. "He's picked it up here and there. From me mostly, I reckon, and the missionaries probably had a hand in it, too."

Blue Buffalo gave a snort of disdain. "Pah."

"Mr. Blue Buffalo," Nora-Leigh said, "you are quite an interesting man."

The Indian nodded in agreement.

"What do you think, Mr. Sullivan?" Nora asked.

"I'm sure Blue Buffalo thinks himself very interesting. Now, could you possibly be quiet for half a second? You're going to insult the man if you're not careful. And you," he said, pointing his finger at Blue Buffalo, "can take your Indian mumbo-jumbo right on up into the hills. And take your old pal with you."

"We will stay and eat with you."

"I don't rightly think so."

Blue Buffalo glanced at Nora-Leigh and nodded his

head. "The look in the woman's eyes is an invitation to stay and eat a meal with you."

"You're mistaken; that look in her eyes is not an invitation. I reckon it's fright or, knowing her, curiosity." Clay glared at Nora-Leigh as if he could read her inner thoughts.

She shrugged her shoulders. She had no idea how the Indian knew it, but she *did* want to talk with him. She'd never get a better opportunity to learn more about the world outside of Steamboat Bend. The man's bronzed, lined face bespoke many years of hard living. Now that her fear had abated, she even had little doubt that he would be a more amiable dinner companion than Clay, whose sole intent seemed to be to infuriate her.

Clay spoke again. "That look only means she's never seen a Crow Indian as old as you are."

"I am old, that is true . . . but wise. And hungry. And this woman was in my dream vision one moon ago. Is she your wife?"

"Hell, no."

Nora-Leigh gave Clay what she hoped was a withering look. He had answered the question with a little too much enthusiasm for her vanity to gracefully accept.

"Where do you go with her?"

"None of your damn business. Kill yourself a rabbit, Blue Buffalo. Make it two and we'll join *you* for the noon meal."

Blue Buffalo peered at Clay. "Tell me, scout, when did you lose your eye?"

"Makes you look like a goldarned pirate," added the Crow's companion with a grin.

Clay didn't reply.

Nora-Leigh tore her gaze away from Blue Buffalo long enough to look at the Indian's friend. His snowy-white hair hung down past his shoulders in two wild, unkempt braids. His months-old, perhaps years-old, yellowed beard

103

lay long and scraggly against a cadaverous chest. Squint
lines spiked out from his deep-set dark eyes. She noted
his height, short for a man and nearly the same as her
own. He wore a store-bought green flannel shirt, badly in
need of washing and mending and missing all of its buttons, and dirty, gray, fleabitten long johns. Buckskin leggings and a breechcloth covered his scrawny legs and thin
flanks. His brown hat made her old worn one look new.
The torn leggings were stained with what could only be
blood and heaven knew what else. She had a feeling that
close up he would not smell overly fresh. Still, he smiled
at her and Clay in a friendly, welcoming fashion.

"What is this word 'pirate'?" Blue Buffalo asked.

"First things first." Clay gestured at the Indian's bow.
"You gonna attack me again?"

"I did not attack you," the Indian rejoined. "You are a
friend. I have no wish to harm you."

"All right." Clay rubbed Nora-Leigh's back and pulled
her forward. "Then I suppose there should be introduc-
tions. This is Nora-Leigh Dillon. Blue Buffalo."

"Nice to meet you, Mr. Blue Buffalo."

"Uh, Nora-Leigh . . ." Clay began, then shook his head
and rolled his eye heavenward. "Oh, never mind." Nora
ignored him.

"We will eat together?" the Crow asked.

"I'll hunt us up something," offered Blue Buffalo's
friend. The old man walked forward with slow arthritic
steps, then held out a liver-spotted hand to Clay. When it
was accepted and shaken, he grinned. Several teeth were
missing, and the rest were as discolored as his beard. Still,
he seemed a free spirit with a natural affability and an
easy grin. "Nat Arbogast. I may be older than our mutual
friend here, but my eyes are still as sharp as they were
when I was a youngun. I'll be back with grub before hell
can scorch a feather." He tipped his filthy hat to Nora-

Leigh. "Nice to meet you, ma'am. It ain't often we see a woman, eh, Blue?"

"No," the Indian replied, studying Nora-Leigh, his eyes roaming from her hat to the tips of her boots. She didn't mind. He didn't stare at her like the men she knew in Steamboat Bend where their eyes stopped at her bosom or, if her back was turned, her backside. He seemed more curious about her clothes.

The man named Nat waved as he crossed the creek, then disappeared beyond a line of timbers.

"You have not answered any of my questions, scout."

Clay snorted. "What's your hurry?"

"I have lived a long life. Who knows how much longer I will live? I wish to take much wisdom with me into the next world."

Clay laughed. "Blue, you'll outlive us all."

With a fatalistic expression on his lined features, the Crow shrugged his shoulders. "Who can tell?"

"Who, indeed?" Clay turned to Nora-Leigh and swatted her on the bottom. "Well, Miss Dillon, you might as well give yourself a rest. You'll thank me later."

Feeling her face flush, she jabbed him in the ribs. He grunted, not seeming in the least bit displeased by her annoyed reaction, then grinned at her. Tapping the end of her nose with his gloved finger, he said, "And, Nora-Leigh . . ."

"What?"

"You best keep that god-awful hat on your head. That there nose will be as red as a rooster's comb if you don't."

"Thank you for the advice, sir. Is there anything else?"

He placed two fingers in his mouth and whistled. Within seconds his stallion came trotting up from out of nowhere. Gingersnap followed at a leisurely pace. Nora-Leigh couldn't have been more surprised. For a pirate, who supposedly spent his time on the water, he certainly had a way with horses. She would confront that preposterous story of his as soon as the right opportunity arose.

"Might as well make yourself useful. Walk these four-legged creatures down to the river and water them. Refill the canteens and look for a good place to make camp. I'm gonna chat with Blue Buffalo a minute. Then I'll meet up with you."

She pointed at the pack mule, who hadn't even run off when the Indian had shot at them. "What about him?"

"I'll take care of ol' Stubborn, there. He isn't partial to people." With that, he turned and moved toward his Indian friend.

A good place to make camp? Thinking of Clay's request, Nora-Leigh glanced around at the prairie surrounding her. Every square inch looked much the same. Scrub willows or tall sagebrush, each plant was a tiny, twisted tree. There were clumps of juniper, and serviceberries and chokecherries. High bluffs rose on either side of the river. The earth was bare and brown where animals had grazed it clean. What would a good place look like? But she hated to ask another stupid question, so she just gathered the trailing reins of their horses and began walking toward the river.

She turned to take another glance at Clay and Blue Buffalo, and was annoyed at what she found. They were both staring at her bottom. She whipped her head around before they saw the heat that infused her cheeks and stalked off.

"She is a handsome woman, scout."

Clay agreed. "Yeah, but she's a chatterbox—"

"What is this 'chat-ter-box.' "

"She can talk the bark off a tree." He mimicked a moving mouth with his fingers. "Yap, yap, yap. I'd as soon listen to my own thoughts."

Clay followed Blue Buffalo's interested gaze as the Indian glanced once more at the girl's retreating backside.

The fabric of her grandfather's threadbare trousers clung to her buttocks like a second skin, and with each step she took, each delectable curve swayed in a distinctly engrossing manner.

All right, so she had a few good qualities.

"She will give you many fine, healthy children."

"Oh, no, you've got the wrong idea. She and I, we . . . that is, we don't work together . . ." He remembered all too well the way her kiss made him feel. Hot, lusty, weak in the knees.

All right, so sometimes they worked together. "We don't agree on anything."

"You don't need to agree," Blue Buffalo answered. "You only need to share her blankets. The agreeing will come later."

"We won't be sharing any damn blankets, not on this journey, or anytime in the future. This is honest-to-God work I'm doing for the Army, Blue Buffalo. I had no choice but to bring her along. It's a long story, but you're mistaken if you think she appeals to me." He caught one last glimpse of Nora's head before she disappeared behind a rise. Her hair shimmered in waves of golden wheat despite the cloudy day. He recalled her almond-shaped eyes, the color changing with her mood, and the dark sweep of her lashes.

All right, so she appealed to him. That didn't mean he was going to do anything about it.

"She tempts you, but you are not man enough to admit it."

Clay bridled at the affront and opened his mouth to protest. Blue Buffalo held up his hand to stop Clay's objection before he could get a word out. "When the moment is right, you will know what to do with her."

Clay snorted. "I already know what to do: steer clear of her."

Blue Buffalo nodded knowingly. "Not an easy thing to do."

"Hell, she doesn't even fancy kids." Clay grabbed the mule's bridle and pulled his head up. Left on its own, the stubborn beast would likely eat so much it would be unable to waddle, much less walk, after the noon repast. Clay pulled the mule along as he started toward the river. Blue Buffalo followed alongside.

"She likes them," Blue Buffalo stated. He continued as if it were an indisputable fact. "All women love children."

"That's what I thought, but she says she doesn't. She even told me she doesn't want any younguns of her own."

"From a big, strong warrior like you?" Blue Buffalo grinned. "She would want yours."

Clay felt heat stealing up his neck. "Why, Blue Buffalo, you've made a joke and embarrassed my sensitive soul."

He chuckled. "Not me. It is the woman. She has stolen your heart. You do not know it yet."

"Can we change the damn subject?"

"If that is what you wish."

"Yeah. Now tell me, what're you doing traveling with a white man? You've been a loner for so long, I thought you didn't like people . . . let alone white men."

Blue Buffalo smiled an all-knowing smile. "When our paths cross, we hunt together. He is a good companion and an old friend. He is a good man, too. When we part ways, I go my way and he searches for the yellow rocks in the rivers and streambeds."

"A gold miner, eh? That would explain the crippled knees and hands. You and he should be natural enemies, though."

Blue Buffalo cocked his head to the side in serious consideration. "At one time, maybe, but now we are both old men. No longer warriors."

"I guess not."

"A hard life he has chosen, but why? I have asked the

question before to him, but he has no answers that I can comprehend."

"He's just got gold fever, I expect." Clay spotted Nora-Leigh walking up and down the stream bank, her hands on her hips, a perplexed frown on her face. He couldn't help but grin. The woman was as useless on the trail as an organ grinder's pet monkey would be. If only he could get his hands on her grandpa's map, he might be able to persuade her to go back. He used to be pretty good at persuasion.

"What happened to your eye?" Blue Buffalo asked.

Clay grinned, then lifted the eye patch. "Not a thing."

Blue Buffalo gazed at Clay like he'd lost his mind. "Why cover it, then? It makes no sense. You need both of your eyes."

"Don't I know it. It started out as a disguise—a dumb one, albeit—so the folks in Steamboat Bend wouldn't question too much who I'm working for. The Army doesn't want anyone to know what I'm up to. Who would associate a pirate with the Army, right? But when I'm sure no one is following me, I'll take it off."

"When I leave you and the woman, I will check your back trail for you."

"Thanks, I appreciate it."

Clay released Stubborn to make his way into the water. He and Blue Buffalo sat down on the high bank of the Bighorn while the mule drank. Pulling his legs up and resting his wrists on his knees, Clay watched the clear river flow by and wondered what Blue Buffalo was thinking. Was he remembering times when his people wandered this land free from the white man's greed and disease, from the constant influx of settlers and miners? Did he recall better times with his family? They were questions better left unasked. Though he and the Crow had known each other for almost ten years, Clay knew little personal information about him. On the range, no grown man, white or Indian, wanted his personal thoughts and desires spoken aloud or questioned by another. That was why it annoyed him that Blue Buffalo knew more about how Clay felt toward Nora-Leigh than he preferred. But the Crow was wrong, anyway. There was no future for Clay and Nora-Leigh. Despite his attraction to her, they were too different.

She was too headstrong. He was too independent.

She was too chatty. He preferred to keep his thoughts to himself.

She wanted adventure. He wanted a permanent home and a family. He found it sad yet amusing how very different they were.

Even now she was making her way toward him, her stride deliberate, her frown firmly in place.

Nat Arbogast returned from the opposite direction with three fat rabbits and saved Clay from having to listen to any more of her incessant prattle. The midday meal would be a good one.

He and Nat gutted and skinned the animals while Nora-Leigh and Blue Buffalo talked. From what Clay overheard, she did most of the talking, bombarding the poor man with questions about everything from his clothing to his age. He politely answered them all in his usual slow, enigmatic way. He didn't even seem to mind her impolite curiosity. At one time, he heard them laugh together. He realized with a start that he'd never heard Nora-Leigh laugh before. The sound of it startled Clay. He stared at her in wonder. The sound of her laughter was uncommonly sweet and tender.

When they all sat down to eat, Blue Buffalo leaned close to Clay and whispered, "If you do not wish to marry this woman, I would like to make her my next wife."

Clay couldn't contain his shock. "Are you crazy?"

"In this town that you talked of earlier, she has family whom I could trade with?"

"You're kidding. Right?"

"I only will let you guess at my intentions, scout," he said with a significant lifting of his brow. "In the meantime, think of her value to you."

"I doubt I'll have time," Clay said, unable to keep the irritation from his voice. Her value? To him? Her value was a map she kept well hidden from him. That was the extent of her worth.

"Mr. Sullivan?"

On the opposite side of the fire, Nora-Leigh sat on the ground cross-legged, her hair mussed, her hazel eyes wide with excitement. "Mr. Blue Buffalo tells me that he's known you for a very long time, so long he can't even count the moons."

"Yeah?"

Her mouth thinned into a tight-lipped smile. "I explained piracy to him, and he maintains that you're no pirate, that you've always been an Army scout. A pony soldier, he calls you. Is that true?"

"We'll talk about this later when we're alone."

"Are you putting me off?"

"Call it what you want, but I don't aim to discuss this here and now."

She glared at him. He thought he heard a chuckle from Blue Buffalo, but when he looked in his direction, the man sat as serene and still as a puddle of muddy water.

After they ate, Nat and Blue Buffalo left them, but not before giving a promise to keep an eye out for anyone following Clay.

He helped Nora-Leigh mount Gingersnap and they trotted off again, following the path of the Bighorn. Clay knew the gold had been left somewhere near where the Little Bighorn joined the Bighorn, and he hoped to make it there by nightfall.

Clay didn't know women well. And he'd had no idea what it entailed to travel with one. They did not make their destination by nightfall.

111

*   *   *

"We'll halt here for the night."

Though Nora-Leigh threw Clay a grateful, tired smile, he couldn't help but be annoyed. They were still a long, hard ride from the juncture of the two rivers he'd hoped to make their first day out. And yet he almost felt sorry for his riding companion. Almost. Her clothes were covered in dust and hung like Monday's laundry from her weary body. Her eyelids drooped and her shoulders sagged. Her nose was pink with sunburn and new freckles dotted her reddened cheekbones. He doubted she would stay awake to eat, much less fix herself a plate. The only thing keeping her on Gingersnap's back was the saddle.

He dismounted and lifted her off the mare. When her knees collapsed, as he knew they would, he held her upright until she stood on her own. Pressed close, he shivered. Even after spending so many hours on a horse, her feminine scent was still strong and sweet, and it enticed him. He had to restrain himself from pulling her closer against his chest and burying his nose in the fresh lavender of her mussed honey-colored hair.

"Do your business, then meet me upstream a ways when you're done," he ordered. His voice was harsher than he'd intended.

From wide eyes, she glanced up at him, obviously stung. Suddenly sorry, he wanted to take her sweet, pliable body into his arms and tell her he wasn't angry with her. That he could never be angry with her. He wanted to kiss her, again and again, and then again. He wanted to lay her down in the grass and make leisurely love to her. Instead, he stomped off to leave her some privacy.

He took the horses and mule with him. "I'll be within hollerin' distance," he called over his shoulder as he escaped.

Releasing the animals to find their own way down the bank, he scrambled down the steep incline and squatted in ankle-deep water. Cupping his fingers, he brought the cool snowmelt to his mouth several times until he'd quenched his thirst. Then he soaked his kerchief, whipped the darn patch from his head, and wiped grime from his neck and face.

Next, he rubbed his eyes. After a day of using only one of them, they were taking their own sweet time working with each other again. For probably the fiftieth time in three days, he cussed his brother, Ethan, for suggesting the damnably foolish disguise. Anything else would have been better. A musician passing through town. A gambler with a pocketful of someone else's money. Even a miner with gold fever. Those disguises would have been simpler. And then he could have seen where the hell he was going instead of swiveling his head like a child's top whenever he wanted to look behind him. Worse, for some confounded reason—probably because he wasn't blind—he could never remember which eye he was supposed to have lost.

He sank back against the rocky bluff and took a deep breath, enjoying the view and the quiet of the end of a long day. Here, the river was no more than a stone's throw across. On the other side, wild pink rose bushes vined together in an overgrown, prickly tangle. He'd wager that Nora-Leigh, when she arrived, would spot those flowers and wade across the stream just to pluck a blossom. He could envision her tucking it into her hair where the placement behind her soft shell of an ear, to say nothing of the scent, would drive him to do something he'd regret later. He stood up and brushed off the seat of his trousers.

He started up the bank, then heard her calling his name.

"Down here," he hollered back. He spotted her face bearing a wan smile.

Chapter Seven

Nora-Leigh glanced down the steep embankment. She could just make out the top of Clay's dark head. He looked up and beckoned her to come down. She smiled, raising her hand to wave and, without watching her feet, stepped slightly forward. It was a mistake. Her boots slipped on the loose dirt. With a screech of fright trapped in her throat, she rolled down the hill and slammed into Clay's body. She heard the breath rush from his lungs with a resounding gasp as he too toppled over, pulling her with him.

Nora-Leigh clutched Clay's shirt collar. She held on for dear life, but the fabric gave way with a ripping sound, and his shirt tore down the front nearly to his waist. She clutched his neck then, and held on with both hands as they tumbled into the icy water. The frigid temperature stole Nora-Leigh's breath away. When they came to a stop in the middle of the creek, they lay in several inches of bone-chilling water. Clay's considerable weight lay atop her.

Water drenched Nora-Leigh's clothes, soaking her to the skin. Her hair clung to her face and neck in thick, frosty strands. Water poured into the top of her boots, dousing her socks and sending shivers up her spine.

Clay lifted his head, turned to the side, and spat out a stream of water. As he swiveled back to face Nora-Leigh, a droplet fell from his chin onto her face. Beads of moisture sparkled on his thick black eyelashes. Up this close, she saw that his mustache wasn't dark brown as she remembered, but golden, and it, too, shimmered with amber highlights. His torn shirt clung to his body, outlining pebbled nipples. A mass of dark hair spread across his muscled chest and narrowed down his taut belly.

"Are you all right?" he asked.

"I th-think s-so," she stammered.

"Seems as if I'm always asking you that."

Nora-Leigh's teeth began chattering. Although Clay lay atop her, no heat emanated from his body to warm hers. He wasn't shivering, though, nor did he seem the least bit uncomfortable with their intimate positions.

"Not to be blunt, Miss Dillon, but has anyone ever told you that you're a mite clumsy?"

"I n-never thought I was be-before I m-met you."

"Somehow I can believe that. You're even beginning to make me feel like a bumbling idiot."

"I do apolo-g-gize, Mr. Sullivan, but it was an accident."

"Stop with the Mr. Sullivan, will ya? Just call me Clay."

"All right, but I—"

He waved his hand in a dismissive gesture. "You know you're starting to turn blue, but," he continued, grinning gleefully, "I believe I prefer you in this position."

She failed to see any humor in their situation. "I m-might never thaw out."

He tossed back his head and hooted with laughter. "I know of a few ways."

"I'm sure you d-do," she snapped.

"I could move." He sat up on his heels, his weight above her, his hands on his hips, but he didn't allow her to get up. He slanted her a sly grin. "A gentleman would."

"A gentleman would, but of course we've already d-determined that you're no g-gentleman. And at the moment I don't feel m-much like a l-lady either."

"A very soggy lady maybe."

"Yes, very soggy."

"And cold," he added.

"Yes, very c-cold."

"Where does that leave us?"

"You will surely find this hard to believe, but *clearly* I have the edge here," Nora-Leigh said.

Clay's grin widened. "How d'you figure? As I see it, I'm on top and that puts me *clearly* in charge."

"Mr. Sullivan?"

"What, Miss Dillon?"

"Are you numb from the cold water? Can you feel anything?"

He smirked. "I'm kinda wet."

"Anything else?"

"What d'you mean?"

"I mean this." She stuck a lethal blade—she'd kept it in her now water-logged boot for protection—point first between Clay's widespread legs. He didn't budge. She pushed upward, watching the expression on his face. When the blade became evident, he jumped, his knees almost clearing the streambed. His eyes widened; his grin disappeared.

He swallowed loud enough for Nora-Leigh, and even the horses standing nearby, to hear. She glanced around.

The mule drinking from the creek lifted his head, water dripping from his snout. The crow, who'd been giving her a menacing glare from the branch of a tree overhead, flapped his wings but didn't fly off. He continued threatening Nora-Leigh with his beady-eyed black stare, though. Watching the bird, she half expected it to fly down and grab the knife from her hand.

More gratified by the fact than a lady ought to be, Nora-Leigh noticed that she had Clay flustered. His face was pale, and his lips thinned. He bent his head forward to look between his legs, then lifted his hands away from his body. "That isn't what I think it is, is it?"

"Yes, Mr. Sullivan, it most c-certainly is." Despite being cold enough to make a snowman shiver, she felt in control for the first time since she'd met this arrogant man. It was most gratifying. "It's a knife—a very long, very sharp knife. It's my grandfather's, actually, and a very nice one it is, too. Don't you think?" She emphasized her point by moving the blade a trifle closer to his backside and pushing the point hard against his personal parts, though not enough to cut the cloth. It was just to grab his attention. She got it.

He straightened, then gave her a frank stare of bemusement and, if she wasn't mistaken, a slight nod of admiration. "Be careful, will you?"

"*You* better be careful, Mr. Sullivan. I've never handled a blade this big."

"Now, just take it easy."

"If you don't get off me this instant, I may have to geld you. I could be wrong, but that would make you even less the gentleman that you proclaim you aren't."

He obliged. He carefully stood up, his hands loose at his sides. The water lapped at his ankles, and his clothes pressed flat against his body. His mouth quirked upward in a slight grin, and this time she was certain the look he gave her was one of begrudging respect. "You are clumsy, Miss Dillon, and I sure as hell don't want you here, but I'll give you credit. You are better prepared for danger than I expected."

Shivering and stiff with cold, Nora-Leigh took Clay's proffered hand and rose awkwardly to her feet. "I try."

Much to her surprise, Clay clutched her shoulder with one hand and captured her chin with the other. He touched his warm lips to her chilled ones with a short, sweet, gentle kiss. A gentleman's kiss. "Well done, Miss Dillon," he whispered in a silky voice. His breath feathered against her cheek. "You learned to defend yourself right nicely. I suspect your grandpa would be proud of his little Nellie right about now."

As quickly as he'd pulled her to him, he released her, then stepped away. He walked down the center of the creek studying the bank as if seeking the easiest spot to climb out.

"Mr. Sullivan?"

He glanced over his shoulder. "What now?"

"You've misplaced your eye patch."

He reached up and touched his face, then swore long and loud. He swung around quickly, so Nora-Leigh couldn't read his expression. The man was an incorrigible liar. And caught at it.

Wickedly pleased, she grinned. "You have two matched, quite lovely gray eyes. They seem to be in fine working order. I believe I'd find a new physician if I were you. You've been sorely misdiagnosed. I expect even the best pirates need both their eyes to plunder, pillage, and maraud the seven seas. Don't you think?"

"All right, all right," he said, throwing up his hands. "I'll tell you everything you need to know—tonight. Including why I'm wearing a disguise."

After changing into a dry buckskin shirt, and not bothering with the eye patch, Clay started a small campfire.

Not that he'd thought he could pull off the disguise forever, but he had been hoping for more than a few days.
If nothing else, it would have kept her from questioning
him too closely about his true mission. But that chance
was gone now.

He glanced at her wan face as she sat cross-legged
across the fire from him, dry at last in an oversized gray
flannel shirt and her grandfather's trousers. She'd covered
her sagging shoulders with a blanket that she clutched
about her. Her endearingly small stockinged feet stuck out
beneath the edge of the blanket. One elbow rested on her
knee with her palm propping up her chin. Her plate of
food sat untouched by her side. An oily film covered the
leftover coffee in a tin cup resting against her knee. Her
eyelids drooped like a flag on a still day, and dark cres-
cents lingered beneath her eyes.

He looked around at the wet clothes she'd strewn about
on the low-lying brush and shrubs. They waved in the
evening breeze, slowly drying. Off to the west, a bank of
gray clouds glowered in the sky. If he wasn't mistaken,
they'd have rain within an hour. Her carefully placed
clothes would be soaked all over again, if not blown away
by the wind.

They were in for a miserable night. But then, he suspected Nora-Leigh was already miserable. He hoped.
Maybe then she'd turn back.

She caught him staring at her and blinked several times,
wincing as her chin came off her palm. "Is something
wrong?"

"I was going to ask you the same thing."

"Why?" she asked softly.

"How are you feeling?"

"Fine."

"You're lying."

Her chin tilted and her eyes widened, but she didn't
reply.

119

"Your butt's not sore?"

"No."

"Your back?"

"No."

"Darlin', you're a terrible liar."

She leaned toward him, her gaze defiant. "Why do you keep asking me questions when you don't believe anything I say?"

"You're just saying what you think I want to hear. Not the truth. You don't want me to know how really awful you feel."

With a stubborn glint in her eyes that Clay was just beginning to recognize, Nora-Leigh's head tilted to the side. "That's not quite true."

"Ha." Clay leaned back against his saddle and laced his hands behind his head. He closed his eyes and took his time replying. "Your back aches like you've been bent over a washboard for ten straight hours scrubbing clothes. Your ass is so damn sore it feels like the worst bruise you've ever had in your life. Just sitting on the ground hurts, and the thought of climbing back onto that horse again makes you want to weep. Your face is sunburned, and your lips are dry and chapped. And unless you're a better horseman than I'm giving you credit for, the palms of your hands are covered with painful blisters."

He cocked open an eye and stole a glance at her. Her own eyelids were closed, but he thought the grimace on her face spoke volumes. "And now you're thinking, 'This is just the first day. How am I going to last another?' So, Miss Schoolmarm, how close am I?"

She didn't answer. He heard a light snuffling sound from across the campfire and opened his eyes. God, he hadn't made her cry, had he? Horrified, he sat up. He wanted her to want to return, but . . .

"Nora-Leigh?"

Clay found his weary traveling companion sound

asleep, her chin on her chest, her hands resting in her lap. She was even gently snoring. He stepped around the campfire, then knelt beside her. He took her hand in his. He was right. Several blisters covered the palm. They would break tomorrow and her palms would be as painfully sore as her backside.

Mesmerized, he watched her sleep. Her breath eased in and out of her parted lips in a slow, deep rhythm. He could just make out the ivory edges of her sharp little teeth. His breath caught in his throat as he envisioned those teeth nipping at his body in the throes of passionate lovemaking. My God, what was he thinking? She was asleep, and he was half aroused. He reached out to touch her, but then caught himself. Still, she was asleep. Where was the harm? With a snarl, he shook his head. *You randy old goat*, he berated himself. *Since when have I started molesting sleeping virgins?*

The blanket fell from her shoulders. He lifted the corner and started to wrap it around her again, but his hand grazed her collarbone and the side of her slender neck. He felt the pulse of her blood. He drifted the fingertips of one hand across the fullness of a breast, then yanked his hand away. What a fool. With startling clarity, he realized that her defiant, can-do attitude hid a delicate bone structure and a far too frail, achingly soft body. She looked too innocent, too fragile, and despite the knife she carried in her boot, too trusting by far. It took all his willpower not to take her in his arms.

Something in the vicinity of Clay's heart ripped open. He squeezed his eyes shut. During the last eight hours, the little vixen had wedged herself into his soul. In the next few weeks it would take an Old Testament miracle to release her from his thoughts, to say nothing about his fear for her safety and well-being.

He wondered, not for the first time, what he'd gotten himself into for the sake of a damn stash of missing gold.

With a shake of his head, he reminded himself of the one thing he should never forget: his questionable future as a cattle rancher. That always reminded him of his goals.

Since bad weather was coming, Clay built a lean-to a safe distance from the river. Made of oilskins and hardy sticks, the tepee-like construction was designed to keep the rain out but was scarcely big enough to sleep one full-sized adult, much less two. He hadn't planned this excursion with two in mind.

Shaking his head, he dragged his and Nora's saddle and gear inside and arranged the small space for sleep. He finished off her plate of cold bacon, biscuits, and congealed gravy, never wanting food to go to waste. He cleaned up and stored as much as possible beneath the lean-to, then hobbled the horses and the mule, knowing the noise of the coming spring storm would likely startle them into running off.

Jack could fend for himself, Clay thought, but then remembered from past experience that the pea-brained crow hated thunderstorms and would hide anywhere he could. He hoped the bird found shelter before the storm hit. Stupid bird.

Going over and fetching her, Clay carried Nora-Leigh into the lean-to and laid her down without disturbing her. Jealous of her unwakable state, he lay down himself and wrapped both their blankets around the two of them for warmth. They lay very close together, enough that Nora-Leigh's small body heated his blood and aroused his senses. Her breath, sweet and enticing, tickled his cheek. Despite her riding in the saddle all day, he could still smell those purple flowers she said she had in her soap. He sighed, then laid his head on his curled arm and watched her sleep, knowing he'd get little sleep himself before the rain started, and none after.

*　　*　　*

Drowsy but not fully awake, Nora-Leigh heard rain. She opened her eyes to see that Clay had built a lean-to to shelter them, and indeed, outside it was raining quite hard. As she lay there she was startled into full wakefulness by a loud clap of thunder.

She tried to roll over but couldn't. Beneath the blankets, one of Clay's arms rested across her waist, his fingers buried beneath the hem of her shirt and the lace of her chemise. His warm touch grazed the bare skin along her ribs, setting off a tingle of awareness. One of his legs was splayed across both of hers, effectively pinning her in place. His scratchy day-old growth of beard pressed against her shoulder, and his soft, even breath tickled her neck.

She couldn't believe how Clay slept on, despite the noise of the storm. As her eyes adjusted to the darkness, she examined her trailmate. Never in her life had she been this close to a man, close enough to actually touch the black beard darkening his face, to see the crescent shape and each separate hair of his thick brows, the fine texture and bronze color of his skin. She was also surprised by how clean he smelled. Apparently he'd taken advantage of their time in the creek earlier.

She marveled at the novelty of her situation. Beside her, Clay slept silently, his breath hardly a whisper as it slipped through his parted lips. He was so quiet it was hard to believe he slept at all. Her grandfather snored so loud that everyone in the house heard his rumbling.

As she watched, his eyes fluttered open. He blinked several times, then mumbled, "Hi," his voice thick with sleep. His fingers along her waist flexed, sending a flicker of excitement along her bare flesh. He seemed unaware of the movement. "I fell asleep."

"You sound surprised."

"Didn't think I'd be able to with your sweet little . . . that is, what with you . . . oh, damnation, never mind."

He paused as he glanced around. "It's raining."

"Yes," she agreed. "Quite hard, but it's nice and dry in here."

Clay yawned, his jaw cracking loudly. It seemed he realized then how close they were to each other. With obvious deliberation, he rubbed his thumb along her bare skin just above the waist of her trousers, staring at her face as if waiting for a reaction.

Nora-Leigh simply lifted his hand away and placed it beside him. His drowsy eyes brightened, and he grinned. He sat up, his head scraping the roof of the tent. He ducked as he reached for his boots, then seemed to think better of it and leaned back against a saddle, draping his hands over his bent knees.

The thunder clapped again, and lightning slashed across the sky. Clay stuck his head out the opening, then pulled it quickly inside and shook droplets from his hair. "The horses are a mite skittish, but a little rain won't hurt 'em none. How about you? Does the rain make you skittish?"

"Not at all," Nora-Leigh said as she pulled herself to a sitting position. They sat knee to knee; he hunched over a bit to accommodate his height. With so little room, they had little choice but to sit close to each other. Nora-Leigh found she didn't mind. She drew an odd comfort from his close proximity in the tight space. "I actually like thunderstorms."

"Do *I* make you skittish?"

"No. Should you?"

One thick black brow rose in disbelief. He gave a little chuckle. "Guess not. At least not the way you handled that blade this afternoon. So, how is this fine adventure after one day?"

"I love it. I do," she said when she saw a look of disbelief cross Clay's features. She brushed the hair from her eyes and leaned forward. Placing her hand on his forearm, she continued, "Seeing Blue Buffalo and talking

124

with him and his friend Nat; being able to see the country. It's all so beautiful, isn't it?"

"Yeah," he said, smiling. "I reckon it is."

"Did you see that mountain goat?"

He nodded, his expression puzzled.

"And I thought I saw a cat of some kind. And the deer and rabbits and so much other wildlife. I wished I had one of those photographic machines so I could get pictures and take them back for Mother and Granny and Gramps. Of course, Mother couldn't see them, but I could tell her what's on them and she'd be thrilled to hear about what I'm seeing and doing."

"I reckon they would appreciate knowing what their little girl is getting up to."

"They surely would. Why? Is that supposed to mean something?"

"Not a thing." He shook his head with a little too much vigor. "By the way, you didn't get the map wet, did you?"

"No, Mr. Sullivan, I wrapped it in waxed paper before we left. It's perfectly safe."

"Clay, honey. Call me Clay. When you call me Mr. Sullivan, I think you must be talking to my pa. Besides, Mr. Sullivan sounds a mite too formal for bed partners."

"We won't always sleep this way," she informed him.

"Yeah, too bad," he said wistfully, a slight grin tugging at his lips. "It sure is a pleasure waking up in the middle of the night with a warm woman in my arms. A warm, willing woman would be even better."

"Mr. Sullivan, are you still trying to embarrass me?"

"Clay," he said, a twinge of impatience overcoming him. "Is it working?"

"No."

"What about all your aches and pains?"

Nora-Leigh grinned. "What aches and pains?" she asked playfully.

Clay snorted. He opened up his mouth to reply when

thunder resounded so loudly that the ground shook. His jaw snapped shut; then he cocked his head to the side as he listened to the sounds from outside the tent. Above the sound of the rain, she heard one of the horses squeal; it had to be Gingersnap. Then the mule brayed, just before lightning lit up the night sky.

The flap of the lean-to suddenly tore open and a black and yellow visage appeared. Scared witless, Nora-Leigh screamed. She fought to catch her breath as she backed away from the frightening presence. It felt as if someone had stolen the breath from her lungs. Her vision dimmed. In her mad scramble to get away, she tripped and fell against Clay. Flabbergasted, she heard a deep rumble of laughter from deep in his throat and close to her ear.

"Where's my knife?" Nora-Leigh burst out. "Get your gun! Shoot it! Clay?" Her voice rose with terror. "Shoot it!"

Chapter Eight

Nora-Leigh plopped into Clay's lap, quivering like a plucked fiddle string. Her whole body shook. He tilted her jaw but couldn't make out her features in the darkness. He wasn't sure what she thought had entered the tent, but it was obvious that its sudden appearance scared the stuffing out of her. Clutching his shirt, she buried her face against Clay's chest. "I can't look."

When a black shape flew into the tent, Nora-Leigh screamed. Clay was sure as shootin' that her sudden howl robbed five years of his life. Only much later did his heart slow to its normal rhythm. The rain continued, at a slower pace, and it sounded as if the thunder and lightning were beginning to diminish and move off toward the east. Thank the good Lord.

"It's just Jack," Clay whispered in a muted tone. "The crow. He's afraid of thunder, and he's trying to get away from it."

She was over the edge, though. "No, no, no, that's no

bird. I saw it. It has devil eyes and curved horns and a big, black cape. If it's not a demon, it's an evil spirit. I know it is. I can't look at it; it might turn me into one of its own. We've got to get out of here. *Now*."

Clay wrapped his arms around her and held her close. "No, honey, it's not. It's just the crow." But she didn't believe him. The fear and near-hysteria in her voice chilled him to the marrow. Her chin trembled like she was about to cry. *Please, don't,* he thought. Crying women made him feel helpless, confused and, for some unknown reason, guilty as sin. Even when he damn sure knew it wasn't his fault, the sight of a grown woman's tears would inevitably bring him to his knees. And he'd be apologizing and falling all over himself like an idiot in an effort to quell the weeping. God save him from hysterical women.

Nora-Leigh burrowed against him, hiding her face in his neck. Her breasts molded against the wall of his chest. The purple flower scent he was beginning to associate only with her assailed his senses. Tender as a butterfly's wings, her lips moved beneath his ear. He jumped, nearly leaping out of his socks.

"What are you doing?" he croaked. Her lips weren't the only body parts moving in this tent. His own sprang to life with a vengeance. He glared at the black shape perched in the corner. This was entirely the bird's fault.

Calico Jack chose that moment to flap his wings and caw. Nora-Leigh screeched again. Her grip on Clay tightened, nearly strangling him.

"Nora-Leigh, honey, if you'll just relax your grip on me, I'll light a lantern and you can see for yourself there's nothing to be afraid of." *Except me, because if you don't get off my lap and stop blowing in my ear, I can't be responsible for what happens next.*

"I'm not a-afraid."

Dear God. The whispered words swept along Clay's

neck and sent shivers of delightful expectation coursing through his veins. Gooseflesh popped up on his arms. He squeezed his eyes shut, then released a long sigh. He rolled his shoulders trying to relax. Nothing seemed to help.

"Of course you're not afraid." *But I sure as hell am.*

He placed a restraining hand on the fingers clutching his collar. Slowly she unfolded her arms from his neck, but instead of completely releasing him she placed her hands on his face. With the tips of her fingers she stroked his lips, then brushed his mustache with the pad of her thumb. She ran her hand along his cheekbones, then up and over his closed eyelids. He swallowed hard. "Nora-Leigh, what the hell are you doing?"

No healthy red-blooded man should have to endure holding a sweet young woman in his lap and do nothing more than embrace her. Her touch set off sparks of desire that even the rain couldn't extinguish.

"It really is my crow," he repeated, feeling his patience dwindling and his arousal multiplying with each passing moment. Frustration made his voice gruff. "Just turn around and take a look."

Her fingers danced along his face like they were searching for something, touching, moving, driving him crazy. He couldn't take the tension one second longer. He did the one thing he damn well shouldn't, the one thing guaranteed to take her mind off the crow. It was the one thing he'd wanted to do since he carried her to bed last night: He kissed her.

Nora-Leigh started when Clay's lips found her mouth. His kiss was as unexpected as waking up in the night had been, his heavy body pressed against her own. His sable hair swung forward to trail over the back of her hands. The thick, cool strands tantalized her with their satin texture. Like a man in pain, he moaned. The hard length of his arousal pressed against her bottom.

Clay's heated lips stole her breath and swept every other thought from her head. Beneath her palm, a muscle in his jaw clenched.

She waited expectantly for him to deepen the kiss, but it didn't happen. He lifted his mouth and drew back. Just a hair's breadth separated them. His ragged breath mingled with her own. He leaned close and nipped at her lower lip, then pulled it into his mouth. Her heart skipped a beat. Her stomach fluttered. Her senses whirled.

He released her lip, but not before his tongue bathed the heated flesh. He sighed into her mouth. "Honey, I'm about as agitated as a jackrabbit right now. Have you calmed down yet?"

"No . . . yes . . . I don't know."

"God, I hope so. Sit tight. Keep your eyes closed if it helps. I'm just going to reach over here." Carefully he leaned around her and grabbed the lantern from his pile of gear. "And light this lamp."

He had it going before she knew it. It lit every square inch of the lean-to. Slowly she turned around and looked at the shelter opening. She stared in disbelief. As Clay had tried to tell her, it was just his crow that had entered the tent and scared her so. It stood at attention, staring nastily back.

At the time, the apparition had seemed much larger, menacing and demon-like. Its eyes had appeared yellow to her, but as she looked at the bird now, they were black as coal and quite small. Calico Jack stood just inside the tent, his beady eyes trained on her, his black feathers fluffed. In the golden glow of the lantern light, water beads glistened on his wings and head. He looked no more like the devil than the lantern at her feet.

Nora-Leigh turned back to Clay. "It's your crow," she said, stating the obvious.

He gave her a tired smile. "I tried to tell you, but you weren't inclined to listen."

Nora-Leigh shook her head, then peered down at her clasped hands. She wished she could touch him again, borrow a little of his courage. "I feel so foolish."

With gentle fingers, Clay swept the loose hair at Nora-Leigh's temple away from her face. He lifted her chin. His pewter-gray eyes peered into hers. "Don't. Just forget about it."

Their eyes locked. Nora-Leigh studied Clay's features. Something intangible, something Nora-Leigh couldn't define, passed between them. Stillness blanketed the tent. A soft hiss of breath escaped Clay's mouth. He blinked, then turned away. He lowered the flame on the lantern until only a dim glow softened the night. "It's time we got some sleep," he said in a hoarse voice.

"Yes," she agreed, scrambling off Clay's lap, still embarrassed by her near-hysterical actions.

"Don't worry about Jack. We've known each other a long time. He's harmless, I promise you."

"I won't," Nora-Leigh said. She lay down and pulled the blanket up to her chin, as far from Clay as she could get, facing away from his knowing eyes.

She heard the rustle of his clothes and felt the tug on the blanket as he lay down himself. "As soon as Jack realizes the thunder has passed, he'll skedaddle on out of here, so don't fret none if you hear him."

"I won't."

"Good night, then."

"Just one more thing, Mr. Sullivan." A question had popped into her head.

"Huh?"

"If you kissed me before to try to dissuade me from accompanying you, why did you kiss me this time?"

His answer came immediately, in a matter-of-fact, no-nonsense tone. "To take your mind off your fear."

"Oh."

"Did it work?" Clay asked.

"Yes. Yes, it did." She swallowed the knot of disappointment lodged in her throat. "That's the only reason?"

"Yes."

"I just wondered." What did she expect? Only simpleminded men like Billy Seth Torrence wanted to kiss her. Obviously, she appealed to one sort of man: a simpleton.

"Don't you be getting any ideas, Miss Dillon," he added, a touch of humor in his voice.

"I wouldn't dream of it." No schoolgirl fantasies of marriage, family, or a man who loved her madly would ever enter Nora-Leigh Dillon's sensible head again. She was much too prudent, much too realistic, and much too down-to-earth for that—or she would become so. No man would ever kiss her because he was attracted to her and simply wanted to show her how much she meant to him.

She squeezed her lids tight against the threat of tears at the back of her eyes. They weren't really tears, she admonished herself. Sensible women didn't cry over such things. This trip was the adventure she wanted, and nothing more. It was high time she remembered that.

After what seemed an eternity, Clay heard Nora-Leigh's even breathing. He rolled toward her and gently eased her onto her back so he could gaze at her while she slept. He hadn't missed the way she had lain down facing away from him, or the hitch in her voice when he told her his kiss meant nothing.

He'd lied about the kiss. Lied like a dog. And it had about killed him to hurt her, because the kiss meant so much more to him. He wanted to give back to her what she gave to him, but knew it was wrong to take advantage of her vulnerability. Still, he craved her passion—the way she looked at him with such wanting, such energy and honesty in her lovely gray-green eyes.

Hungrily he stared at her and drank his fill. She looked so lovely in the glow from the lantern. The honey-gold light couldn't take the pink from her cheeks and nose, and her hair was tousled and begged for his touch. Never again would he think of long hair as sexy. Shortish hair that curled around a woman's ears, tickled her chin, and caressed her cheeks like a lover's touch would forever remind him of Nora-Leigh's spirit and vitality.

He brushed her flushed cheek with his thumb. In her sleep her mouth quirked up in a sweet smile, and she turned toward his thumb. He ran it along the fullness of her lower lip. Whether her cheeks were red from the sun or from his kisses, he couldn't say. Just touching her face, he wanted badly to make love to her. The implications of his nearly irresistible desire troubled him more than he could say, but still the ache in his groin refused to go away. He reminded himself that it was just want, not need; just lust, not love. This was just his body's way of reminding him that he was a male who'd gone too long without a woman.

Clay knew he could take her easily. She was ripe with wanting, and unless he was reading her wrong, she was falling in love with him. He hoped he was reading her wrong and that it was just admiration he occasionally glimpsed in her gaze.

Damn her silly, reckless hide. Damn her for making him care. He took her hand in his and rubbed his thumb gently across the palm. It was some time before he fell into a restless, uneasy sleep, his fingers entwined with hers.

Bill Terrell squatted in the lee of a rocky outcropping, his knees to his chest, his poncho and the brim of his hat protecting him from the worst of the torrential downpour. His raging thoughts centered on one man. Clay Sullivan.

From Fort Keogh, he'd followed the man's trail up the

Yellowstone, then down the Bighorn to Steamboat Bend, a one-horse town with friendly, talkative folks. They'd been more than eager to discuss Clay Sullivan, the one-eyed pirate. While Bill knew nothing about Clay ever having been a pirate, or how he'd lost his eye, from their description, he knew he was on the right track. Of course, the fact that Clay had taken off with the town's precious schoolmarm surprised Terrell. Sullivan had always been a loner who liked to travel light and move quickly. His days as a scout had taught him the trail well. But Clay wasn't expecting to be tracked, so he hadn't bothered to hide his back trail. And until this rain, he'd been as easy to follow as the river.

Terrell scratched his bearded face and cussed aloud. Sullivan was like a thorn in his thumb that wouldn't budge, becoming more inflamed and painful with each passing day. Even when Terrell had stopped in Steamboat Bend, he couldn't sleep, couldn't eat, and couldn't even get excited about paying a two-bit whore for a fifteen-minute romp. Not until he killed Clay Sullivan would he rest easy.

Still and all, things were looking up. The stolen mare that he thought wouldn't last fifty miles was proving to be an excellent mount. Unlike Bill, whose guts felt like they were eating at him from the inside out, she seemed to thrive on the trail. She'd gained weight and picked up her pace with each day that passed.

It wouldn't be long now. The woman would slow Sullivan down. Victory was almost in Bill's grasp. He dozed off thinking of the many ways he would torture the bastard before he finally killed him.

Nora-Leigh opened her eyes, blinking the sleep from them, thankful she was alone in the tent. She ran a hand through her matted hair and frowned. She touched her face, tight and hot with sunburn. Today she would wear her hat on her head, not strung around her neck to dangle uselessly down her back. As she fingered her chapped lips, she recalled Clay's gentle kiss, the draw of his mouth on her own. Then she remembered it meant nothing to him. A meaningless kiss that signified *absolutely nothing*.

Stop it, she scolded herself. She didn't want a man's kisses anyway. She wanted an adventure and she was getting it. Still, getting frightened by that stupid crow had been silly. She wished she could take back the inappropriate reaction and show a little more backbone. Jumping into Clay's lap and whimpering like a lost child hadn't scored any points with him, that was for sure.

God, how her muscles ached. A stiffness and soreness new to her body made her feel as old as Gramps. She tossed off the blanket, sat up, and groaned. This was her adventure, she reminded herself. It would take a few days of riding to get used to everything, especially the wide horse beneath her very tender bottom. She found her boots and yanked them on.

On her hands and knees, she rummaged around in her bag until she found her hairbrush. She grabbed it and crawled out of the lean-to. She squinted as the morning greeted her with a bright cheerfulness she didn't quite share. Nearby, Clay squatted in front of a small fire, his back to her. A buckskin shirt was stretched taut across his wide shoulders and broad back. Capable as ever, he looked at ease and natural with a fork in one hand and a steaming cup of coffee in the other.

The smell of the brewing coffee and frying bacon lingered in the crisp air. Nora-Leigh's stomach growled. Clay glanced over his shoulder.

"Hungry?" he asked.

She stood up, stretched, and without meaning to, groaned aloud.

Clay grinned at her, then turned back to the pan of sizzling bacon. "A little stiff this morning, are we?"

"No," she lied.

"Ha," he muttered. "Did you hear Calico Jack fly off after the storm passed?"

"No, I slept fine."

"Good."

She wandered over to the fire and sat down to brush her hair. "Where is he now?"

"Oh, he's fine and dandy. He'll fly off to do whatever it is crows do, then he'll rejoin me whenever he wants company."

"Wasn't he supposed to be your pirate's parrot?"

"Nah." He gave her a lopsided grin as he sipped his coffee. "But it made you wonder, didn't it? Jack latched on to me a few years back and has followed me from hell to breakfast ever since. He pretty much sticks around during the day, then disappears at night. He's not much of a talker, takes anything bright and shiny he can steal, and will swipe the food right off your plate when you're not looking. But what the hell, he's company."

"How do you know he's a he?"

Clay's brow shot up in surprise. "Damn. You know, I don't know that for sure. Maybe he's a she and I should be calling her Jill instead."

Nora-Leigh noted that he'd discarded the eye patch for good. She couldn't resist commenting. "No more pirate disguise?"

His smile turned into laughter. "I only wanted to bamboozle the folks in Steamboat Bend, so they wouldn't speculate on what I was doing in their fair town. I never intended to let it go on forever. Hell, have you ever tried seeing with one eye? It's nigh impossible."

"Bamboozle?" she asked.

The brush snarled in a particularly thick length of hair and Nora-Leigh muttered an imprecation beneath her breath. Clay rose to his feet and took a step toward her, his arm extended, his fingers reaching out to her. She

136

glanced up and caught his smoldering stare. He stopped, and his hand drew into a tight fist. He shook his head and abruptly swung around. She heard him grunt, then say something beneath his breath that sounded like "damn crazy fool." With stiff, angry movements, he forked the bacon out of the frying pan and tossed it onto a tin plate beside the fire. One thin slice missed the plate. He plucked it off the ground and stuffed it in his mouth.

"Eat up," he ordered. "I'd like to hit the trail before dusk sets in."

"It's barely sunrise."

"Exactly," he grumbled. "Get a move on."

He stomped off to saddle the horses. Nora-Leigh wondered what had suddenly happened to his good mood. And what had that hot stare been about? She didn't wait to contemplate it, however. She grabbed her bacon and bit off a savory piece. The rest she nibbled as she went in search of a private spot to relieve herself. Thankfully, Clay was busy dismantling the lean-to and folding up the blankets, and he didn't question her.

Conversation stopped for the rest of the day. Every time she attempted to talk with Clay, he gave her a grumbled one-word reply or ignored her altogether. She contented herself with observing the beautiful, wild Montana country with its hilly, soft green and brown landscape and abundant wildlife.

They followed the meandering course of the Bighorn River, stopping only to let the horses drink and Clay attend to personal matters. She found it incomprehensible that he had so little concern for her sensibilities that he always allowed her to listen to him "water the bushes." He didn't seem in the least bothered as he returned, buttoning up his trousers. He'd tilt his head in a questioning glance at her, and each time she'd give him a negative response.

Though he seemed quite comfortable with making do

137

in the out of doors, Nora-Leigh wasn't so relaxed about it, especially with Clay close at hand and within hearing distance. She doubted she would ever be able to just hop off her horse, dash behind a bush or a boulder, and drop her trousers as did Clay.

Of course, she had yet to master dismounting without nearly falling on her backside. Only recently had she become accustomed to Gingersnap's uneven gait and begun to feel comfortable in the saddle. No, *comfortable* wasn't the right word. She was only now becoming tolerant of the feel of the saddle. Her bottom felt as if she'd been given twenty whacks with the flat side of a frying pan. With a fervent prayer, she hoped that soon she would develop calluses or learn to move as one with the horse—as Clay did seemingly without effort.

Suddenly he pulled up on his reins and stopped. Trained to follow his lead, Gingersnap stopped when Clay's stallion did. Clay pushed his hat to the back of his head and stared at Nora-Leigh.

Concerned, Nora-Leigh looked about her for danger. "What is it?" she whispered.

"When was the last time you bathed?"

She sat up straighter and stared at him. Now what was he talking about? "That's very personal."

"When?" he insisted.

"I haven't actually had a bath since we left," she admitted. "I've been washing up every day, though, and I did have a slight dunking in the creek . . . if you recall."

"I can still smell you."

Nora-Leigh's cheeks burned. "I'm sorry. I'll bathe more thoroughly tonight."

"No, you misunderstand my meaning." He leaned his forearm on the saddle horn and squinted, then pointed a finger at her. "That purple flower smell is making me crazy." He shook his finger at her, emphasizing his point. "Stop washing with that damned soap."

He gave her one last pointed glare, then spurred his horse and set off at a gallop, kicking up mud clods left and right. The mule tied to Clay's saddle brayed in discontent but, since he had little choice, followed. His shorter legs churned and his whinny echoed off the low hills. Clay didn't look back.

Nora-Leigh sat a moment, her mouth hanging open, her mind a blank. Frowning, she stared after his retreating figure. Before she lost sight of him, though, she kicked Gingersnap into a slow trot. Following at a safe distance, she tried to comprehend what he'd just said.

Stop washing with that damned soap.

It was the only soap she'd brought. If she didn't use it, she wouldn't be able to wash at all. What did he expect her to do? Not wash at all? Most of the time, the man was a complete puzzle to her. Moody and unpredictable, he baffled her with his behavior. And they said women were hard to understand! Most of the women Nora-Leigh knew couldn't hold a candle to Clay Sullivan.

She moved along the river's edge for at least thirty minutes before she caught up, but she could always hear the stallion's hooves ahead of her. By the time she did catch him, the sun was low on the western horizon. Clay had unsaddled his horse and unpacked the mule. Both animals were hobbled and grazing nearby. Clay was nowhere to be seen.

Nora-Leigh gingerly climbed off Gingersnap. By now she knew enough to hold on to the saddle until she had her legs steady beneath her. Gingersnap, bless her soul, stood still. As Clay had instructed her early in their riding lessons, she removed the saddle, then wiped Ginger's sweaty hide down with the saddle blanket. She removed the bridle, all the while talking to her in a soothing voice. Ginger didn't need hobbling. She wouldn't leave Clay's stallion's side. Nora-Leigh detected a romance in the making.

No longer afraid of the huge animal, Nora-Leigh enjoyed her company. The mare didn't criticize or berate her. She did as Nora-Leigh wanted and never complained. Most horses, she soon discovered, were much better behaved than children. And some, like Gingershap, were more likable.

She gave Ginger one last pat of affection and went looking for Clay. Looking down a steep embankment, she found him squatting at the river's edge. He wore no shirt. As if he'd just washed up, sparkling drops of water clung to his bronzed back and glistened in his dark hair. He looked up as though he heard her or sensed her watching him. Soap covered the lower half of his face.

"Be careful," he warned, pointing up the side of the muddy bank to where she stood. "The rain left the ground soft and a mite unstable."

He turned around, his hands busy, his head bent over the water.

Because she hadn't quite heard the last of what he said, she took a step forward. "What?"

"Careful!" he hollered. "The bank is liable to give way if you get too close."

Which, of course, it did.

Chapter Nine

The precarious ground collapsed beneath her feet and Nora-Leigh pitched forward. Her arms flew up and her legs slid out from under her. She rapidly descended the embankment on the palms of her hands and the seat of her pants. The single thought in her head as she slipped down the incline through the mud and muck was, *Oh, no, not again!* She prayed she wouldn't slide into Clay.

But, of course, she did.

She crashed into him and knocked him over.

"Yeow!" he hollered. His arm flew out. His legs slid forward. Splat! He sprawled on his butt at the river's edge. Mud squirted from beneath him like a fountain of slimy brown rain, then showered down upon his shoulders and head. A sticky mire of dark silt oozed out beneath the seat of his trousers.

He cursed Nora-Leigh's ancestry at length. Waving a grubby hand at her, he growled, "God almighty. To think I called you clumsy before."

141

Nora-Leigh slid to a stop, gasping for air. She landed on her bottom not two feet away from Clay. Fortunately, she wasn't in the mud. Horrified by her blunder, she stared at his face.

The right side of Clay's mustache was missing.

"I thought you fancied your mustache."

"I did. I was shaving the rest of my face."

A thin stream of blood trickled down the side of his chin and plopped without a sound into the river.

"Oh, no, Clay." Nora-Leigh sucked in a breath, then pointed to his face. "You've cut yourself."

"The hell you say." With the back of his hand he scrubbed at his face, only making matters worse by spreading mud all over his features.

She scrambled to his side, knelt, and lightly stroked the ragged cut. The gash began beneath his nose on the left side and ran down to the corner of his mouth. He pushed her hand away, splashed water on his face erasing most of the mud, then gingerly probed the wound with his thumb. He ran a cautious finger along what was left of his mustache. He wore a baffled expression. Nora-Leigh couldn't tell if he was just annoyed or truly angry.

Clay reached up the bank and snagged his saddlebag. He rummaged inside until he pulled out a triangular shard of broken mirror. He stared at his face, turning his head from side to side. His frown vanished, and a wry grin began to turn up the corners of his mouth. As if it didn't hurt, he brushed the blood away, though in one deep spot above his lip it continued to bleed. He seemed not to notice.

Appalled, Nora-Leigh looked over his shoulder into the mirror as well. As if the mustache felt odd, Clay kept touching his face, his fingers rubbing his partially denuded lip. He quirked his mouth from side to side.

"What d'you think?" he asked as he turned to Nora-Leigh. He tossed the mirror on the ground.

She stared at him. His sparkling gray eyes twinkled with . . . amusement? Surely he didn't find this funny.

"I've ruined your face," she moaned.

He gave her a genuine smile of amusement. "I doubt it."

"But I cut you."

"I cut myself."

"Yes, but it was my fault, and now you'll have a horrible scar."

"Horrible, huh?" He chuckled. "Believe me, I've got a few others. D'you want to see them?"

"But they're not on your face!" She couldn't keep the anguish from her voice, which only seemed to amuse him all the more.

Laughing, he brushed the last of the blood from his face. "I don't think it'll hurt my handsome face much."

"I'm really so very sorry. Do you think you need stitches?"

"What do you think I am?" Clay said, sounding truly affronted. "A damned embroidered pillowcase? Hell, no, I don't need stitches."

"But it looks deep."

"I'll live. It's a shaving cut."

"But what will you do now?"

He shrugged his shoulders. "I reckon I'll shave the rest of it off. Elsewise I'd probably fall off Jolly."

"Fall off your horse?"

"Yeah, I'd be lopsided. That'd make me fall off for sure."

Stunned, Nora-Leigh stared at Clay. What was he talking about? He was an excellent horseman. Nothing short of a lasso could pull him off his mount.

He looked at Nora-Leigh, then gave a bark of laughter, and she realized he was kidding. Playfully she splashed water at him, hitting his bare chest and face. A few drops caught his half-mustache. She watched in fascination as he licked at the droplets with the tip of his tongue. His tongue swept across his upper lip. He shook his head. "Strange," he murmured.

"Have you had it a long time?" she asked. Guilt bit at her conscience. Did he regard his mustache as an important facet of his masculinity? She knew her adolescent male students always seemed inordinately proud when they first developed whiskers. Even when they couldn't grow a full beard, they carried on about the few sparse hairs sprouting on their chins as if their pending manhood was just waiting around the corner.

"Since before I came West."

"It'll grow back."

"I don't know," he said, shaking his head and staring down at the river flowing beside him. "Maybe once you shave it all off, that's it. I'll be as fresh-faced as a newborn."

"I don't think that's the way it works," Nora-Leigh stated. Surely he knew that.

He glanced at her and she caught his grin.

"I'm joshing, Nora-Leigh."

"Oh." She studied his features. "I think you'll look very nice without it."

He rubbed a thoughtful finger across his lip. "Nice, huh?"

"Yes indeed. Nice."

"Guess we'll just have to find out." He reached for the razor, rinsed it off, and proceeded to shave the hair from the other side of his lip. Nora-Leigh watched in fascination. With one hand he pulled his skin taut, first one way, then the other. His chin jutted forward. The muscles in his arm flexed and bunched. She watched as water fell from his face, clung to his chest a moment, and then slid down his taut belly. Nora-Leigh glanced up and was chagrined to find him watching her, his eyes dark and serious. He lowered his hands to his side.

"Done," he pronounced.

"My goodness," Nora-Leigh said, taken aback by the difference in his appearance. "You're a beautiful man."

He choked, then cleared his throat as if embarrassed by her honestly spoken statement. "God, I hope not."

"No, I mean it." She ran her index finger along the bare flesh beneath his nose. Cool and smooth beneath her fingertips, the flesh quivered slightly. Clay stilled. His breath slowed, and she heard him swallow.

He cleared his throat. "You're the one who's beautiful, Nora-Leigh. But please stop touching me. I can't be responsible for what might happen."

She wrenched her hand away and, rising to her feet, stumbled backward. Clay reached out and clasped her hand to steady her. She opened her mouth to reply and found his laughing gaze upon her. "Did I scare you?"

"No," she lied.

"I didn't mean to this time, I really didn't. But we've got a long trip ahead of us. I'll admit I'm drawn to you." He shook his head. "I can't explain it, but there it is, plain as that button nose of yours."

Nora-Leigh didn't hear much of anything after the word *beautiful.* "You think I'm beautiful?"

He frowned. "Hell, yes. Isn't that what I just said?"

"I don't know."

"You are, believe me, but I promised your grandfather I'd deliver you back to him in approximately the same condition that you left in. You'd do well to keep your distance from me. I'll do my best to keep mine, and maybe we won't go borrowing trouble. I can't afford to forget my duty."

"Duty?" His duty to her grandfather? Nora-Leigh didn't understand. "Other than to Gramps, what duty do you have?"

"Never you mind. Just try to keep away from me," he

145

said, back to his usual disagreeable self. "Is that perfectly clear?"

"I understand."

"You do? 'Cause I sure as hell don't want you going back with a babe in your belly."

Appalled, Nora-Leigh gazed at him. At first she found the notion horrifying, but then the thought of holding Clay's child in her arms didn't seem so bad after all. But she couldn't let him know that. "Mr. Sullivan, we're in agreement on that, then. That's the very *last* thing I want."

"Well, damn. You don't have to sound so disgusted by the notion of having my baby," he grumbled. He rose to his feet, turned, and took a disgruntled look at the back of his muddied buckskin trousers. He reached in his saddlebag and found a towel. Wiping his face, he said, "At least we understand our situation, then."

"Oh, yes," Nora-Leigh agreed. For some unknown reason she found herself fighting tears. "We don't want to make a baby just because you find me a little attractive. That would surely ruin your plans for the future."

"Right," he answered. "Yours as well. It's tough to go adventuring when . . . Why don't you go start supper? I'm starved. I'll be up to help as soon as I scrub the mud off me and my clothes."

Why did it seem he gave her a compliment with one hand, then took it away with the other? Why did it bother her anyway? Why was she forced to remind herself, time and again, that it didn't matter?

Nora-Leigh trudged away, confounded, confused, and hurt. She began gathering sticks and small branches for the fire. As she stacked them, she realized she had nothing with which to start a fire. She headed back to the river. Clay was prepared for any circumstance, and he carried lucifers in his saddlebags. She would just get them herself while he cleaned up.

*   *   *

Without the mustache covering his lip, Clay felt naked. It made him feel as if he were walking around undressed, which at the moment he was. When he landed in the river, mud had found its way into every orifice of his body. He had to remove his clothing just to wash away the muck. Even his long johns had been saturated with gooey mud.

Again he fingered his upper lip, not quite used to the feel of the bare skin there. True, he could always grow a new one, but the guilty look that sprang to Nora-Leigh's face every time she caught him feeling his upper lip made him think twice about it. It might be worth leaving it clean-shaven to keep her mindful of this . . . of its danger.

He needed to keep on his toes. The desire stirring up in him would be his, as well as her, undoing if they weren't careful. She had to understand that. Just the thought of her having a baby prompted thoughts of home and hearth. His ranch. His family. His baby. Nora-Leigh's baby.

Damn. He couldn't allow his thoughts to wander in that particular direction. The time was wrong. The place was wrong. The woman was wrong. Right?

Clay stood, naked as the day he was born, ankle-deep in the river, bending over slightly to rinse out his long johns. Nora-Leigh dashed for cover. She ducked behind a cottonwood tree, clutching it with both hands, then peeked around the trunk. Clay hadn't heard her. In fact, he was whistling.

Limned by the setting sun behind him, every aspect of his anatomy was outlined in sharp, crisp detail. Dark-skinned and powerfully built, he called to mind a photograph Nora-Leigh once saw in a picture book. The photo had been of a Greek marble sculpture of a nude man—tall, proud, and noble—with a broad chest, narrow waist, long, well-developed legs, and absolutely no doubt about his gender. At the time, Nora-Leigh couldn't tear her fascinated gaze away from the picture even though it produced a blush that burned her face. She felt the same now with this flesh-and-blood man who so resembled the statue.

Nora-Leigh flushed from her hairline right down to the tips of her toes as she stared at Clay. She knew it was wrong. She shouldn't look at him in all his glorious, naked splendor. She should run in the opposite direction. But she didn't.

Dark hair covered his heavily muscled thighs and calves. His naked buttocks flexed every time he wrung the water from his long johns. With each movement, his bronzed flesh rippled, his overwhelming presence compelled her to watch. A shudder ran the length of her. Her pulse quickened. Deliciously wicked thoughts flashed through her mind. The worst of which was that she wished he'd turn around so she could see his front.

Over his shoulder, Clay glanced up at the bank. Nora-Leigh quickly pulled back her head. She held her breath, and he continued whistling. When she braved another look, he was already wearing a clean pair of buckskin trousers and was pulling a shirt on over his head.

Nora-Leigh tiptoed away, her heart racing, her face feverish. A grin was firmly planted on her lips.

What would Elsa Dillon think of her naughty, wayward daughter now? And wouldn't Granny be jealous? Nora-Leigh could scarcely contain her amusement.

Nora kept her distance as she and Clay worked to put together the supper meal. Every time he so much as moved toward her, she about-faced and practically ran in the opposite direction.

He was happy to see that she didn't seem as weary or travel-worn as yesterday, despite the fair pace he'd set today. But her cheeks were still rosy in spite of the hat she'd worn. He noticed, but refrained from commenting upon, her muddy trousers. The fabric clung to her buttocks like a second skin, outlining a fetching backside just the right size for two male palms to cradle. *Stop it*, he chastised himself. He was an Army scout. A man in a man's world, for God's sake. *Stop thinking about things you can't have.*

Many times he'd gone months without a woman and hardly given it a second thought. He wasn't a lusty man by nature, or so he used to think. But now with Nora-Leigh constantly underfoot and smelling like some exotic—or was that erotic?—flower, he couldn't keep his thoughts from straying into forbidden territory for five minutes.

She sat down across the fire from him and, leaning forward, began slicing a peeled spud into the frying pan. He sat opposite her and simultaneously dropped onion slices in with the potatoes.

She glanced up, colored like a schoolgirl, and dropped her eyes to the potato in her hand. She continued cutting, dropping the slices into the grease to mingle with Clay's onions.

"What's wrong?" he barked.

"Not a thing," she barked right back, taking him by surprise by the ferocity in her voice.

Clay poked at the fire. "Then why won't you look me in the eye? Do I look so bad without the soup strainer?"

Her lips twitched. "Not at all," she said, clutching tightly the potato in her hand.

"Look at me," he ordered. "Now."

Obediently, she lifted her head, but their eyes clashed for a fraction of a second. Her lips turned up in a wary smile. Her blush deepened to a dark, rosy hue; then she dropped the remains of the spud in the skillet and placed the knife on the ground beside her. When she buried her face in her hands, Clay was completely taken aback. *Please, God, not tears.*

Her slight body shook. Then a giggle bubbled up and burst from her pursed lips. Her laughter built slowly, then gushed forth like a geyser.

"What is so damn funny?" Clay growled.

She lifted her head, and waved her hand because she couldn't speak through her giddiness. Tears leaked from the corners of her shimmering eyes. She looked at him, bit her lower lip, and broke into another gale of giggling.

"Can't you let me in on the joke?"

She gave her head a negative shake.

Never before had Clay heard Nora-Leigh laugh in such an uninhibited manner. Much to his amazement, he found it highly arousing. He began to wonder if she—say, belched—would he also find that stimulating? Probably, he thought dismally. His thoughts remained on her, arousingly so.

Her giggles died enough for her to speak. "I spied on you."

"When?"

"Before. In the river."

"You watched me bathe?" A grown man didn't blush, Clay reminded himself as his face flushed with heat. "What did you see?" What a stupid question. What did he think she saw on a naked man? "Why?"

Nora-Leigh ducked her head as a giggle escaped her lips.

All right. Grown men did blush, Clay admitted. They also became heavily aroused when certain thoughts entered their heads. Thoughts of young women watching them as they bathed bare-ass naked. Thoughts of young women bathing *with them* bare-ass naked. Thoughts Clay was having right now.

"Nora-Leigh," he managed. He shifted his weight to a more forgiving position. "That wasn't a very ladylike thing to do." He sounded like a parson preaching to the congregation. But he didn't give a damn that she had spied on him. He was surprisingly pleased.

"I know." She sounded unrepentant.

"Well?"

"It's not very gentlemanly of you to say so."

He snorted. "You're no lady for watching."

"I know," she repeated. Though she had it lowered, her face was as red and heated as his felt. He thought he still detected a slight grin, though.

Before they burned and became inedible, and while he still had a few of his faculties functioning, Clay lifted the damned potatoes and onions from the fire and set the pan aside. "Are you the least bit sorry?"

"No."

He shook his head. "I know I shouldn't ask this. I'll probably be kicking my butt from here to Helena when you answer, but why were you laughing?"

"I've never seen a naked man before. Only in books."

"Where the hell did you get a book with pictures of naked men, for God's sake?"

"Not real men," she added quickly. "Statues. Greek statues made of marble."

Clay felt something like relief. She wasn't *that* liberal. "And you thought real men looked that way?"

"You do." She lifted her head and clasped her hands beneath her chin. Despite her obvious embarrassment, she met his gaze. Admiration and longing glowed in the depths of her liquid eyes.

"And that's funny?"

"No. What was funny was seeing you rinsing out your muddy long johns and not wearing a stitch of clothes while you did it."

"That isn't funny. I had mud in places that men don't speak about in front of ladies."

Nora-Leigh giggled.

Clay smiled. "But I'd bet that stubborn mule of mine that you've got mud in the same places."

"What?" Nora-Leigh jumped to her feet and brushed at the back of her trousers. She grimaced when her hand came away covered in dirt.

"See?" Clay said, unable and unwilling to stop gloating. A deep rumble of laughter erupted from his throat. "Now who's laughing?

"If you want to wash off real quick-like before we eat, go ahead. I promise not to look."

"Thank you. I'll hurry," she said, scampering off.

"Of course," he called after her, "I don't always keep my promises."

Clay could have sworn he heard a distinct unladylike vulgarity pass Nora-Leigh's sweet lips.

"I'm a little bit afraid," came a small voice from out of the shadowy darkness. The fire, burned down to a few red embers, gave off enough heat but little light. Clay couldn't see Nora-Leigh clearly even though she lay fairly close. She continued in an apologetic tone: "I guess I'm scared most of making a ninny of myself again the way I did last night when your pet crow entered the tent."

Ah-ha! So the impish sprite wasn't quite as confident about living in the rough as she pretended. Clay hid his smile from her. He lay no more than two feet away from her slender body. He heard her shallow breathing. He knew each and every time she shifted beneath her blanket.

Wolves prowled nearby; that's what they'd been discussing. Their haunting howls broke the still of the night, but Clay knew they wouldn't venture close even if she didn't. Nothing could hurt her with him so near. He wouldn't let it. His hand was never far from a weapon, be it the shotgun by his side, the knife in his boot, or the pistol beneath the saddle he used as a pillow. But he wasn't about to tell her that. Let her squirm a bit. She deserved a comeuppance after watching him bathe in the nude.

"What do you want me to do, Miss Dillon?"

"I don't know."

"Tell you a bedtime story?" he asked in a voice rife with sarcasm.

"No, I don't think that's necessary." After a slight pause, she added, "But you could kiss me good night."

Clay nearly choked on his saliva, but managed to blurt out, "Why don't you go to sleep?"

"Just a good-night kiss?"

"No."

"Why not?"

"Nora-Leigh." His body temperature rose along with his voice. "I'm warning you."

"You don't have to kiss me on the mouth like you did before."

Not on the mouth? Prurient thoughts of kissing her elsewhere jumped to life at the many possibilities presented by that not-so-simple statement. "No. I don't think so."

Her blanket rustled and he saw her turn her body toward him. Her flowery, entirely too enticing fragrance tickled his senses. By the light of a waning moon, he saw her rise up on an elbow and bend over his chest. He couldn't draw in air. Her warm breath caressed his face as her satin, petal-soft lips grazed his cheek. The innocent touch electrified his traitorous body.

"Good night, Clay," she whispered. "Pleasant dreams." She rolled away from him, and soon her even breathing told him she'd fallen asleep.

He pulled the blanket up to her chin and pressed a kiss to her forehead. "Good night, Nora-Leigh." He reached between them and entwined their fingers.

Staring up into the star-filled sky, he wondered how this woman managed to wedge her way inside his every daytime thought and his every nighttime dream.

He released a long sigh and shook his head. It would be a long while before he found the comfort of slumber himself.

"You aren't partial to women, are you?"

Clay pulled back on the reins and stopped Jolly. He stared at Nora-Leigh as Gingersnap slowed alongside his stallion. Now what had prompted that fool question?

"Of course I like women. Why?"

"Why what?"

The woman could drive him crazy with all her confounded questions. "Why would you ask such a damned foolish thing?"

"So it's just me that you don't like."

"I like you well enough." Well enough to get a rooster in his trousers every time he got a whiff of her sense-stealing scent. Was that well enough?

"Then why wouldn't you kiss me last night?"

He glared at her. He didn't like talking about things like this. It wasn't . . . well, it wasn't manly, dammit. "I like to do the kissing, the starting, and the finishing up. I don't appreciate being told by a sassy schoolmarm who doesn't know north from south when I should kiss a woman." He glanced skyward for the bolt of lightning that was going to strike him down for that big, fat lie. He liked kissing and a whole lot more, and he didn't care who started the process.

"Is that all, Mr. Sullivan?"

"Yeah, that's all there is to it."

"I keep forgetting that you're no gentleman."

"I don't know why."

"Me either, since you remind me of the fact often enough."

"Damn right I do." With that, he kicked his stallion into a gallop. Over the rough terrain they flew, and know-

ing the jarring pace he'd set, Clay guessed Nora-Leigh's
tender rear end wouldn't last twenty minutes. He felt only
slight remorse, but if she didn't stop asking personal questions, he was going to do more than kiss her. A whole
helluva lot more. And the only way to save her butt
seemed to be by sacrificing it.

Nora-Leigh pulled back on the reins. Blowing for air,
Gingersnap complied, stopping. The horse's head
drooped, its sides heaving. After a few short minutes, the
mare caught its breath and lowered its head to nibble on
the high grass. Nora-Leigh closed her eyes and rested her
aching head against Ginger's warm, glistening neck.

She would only stop a minute. She couldn't take the
pain anymore. Her bottom felt as if on fire. Her back
ached, her neck was cramped, and her stomach was
growling like a bear after a winter of hibernation. Her
head felt as though she'd been kicked by that stubborn
mule.

She didn't much care if Clay rode off without her by
this point. If she got left behind, or if she was eaten by
a mountain lion, it'd all be the same to her. She could
hear Jolly's hoofbeats as Clay continued on. Fine. Let him
go. She had to get off this horse.

Chapter Ten

Nora-Leigh glanced up to see Clay looking at her over his shoulder. He'd come back for her, and now he beckoned with a wave of his hand, slowing his stallion to a moderate walk. Nora-Leigh urged Gingersnap forward to move alongside his mount. Grateful for the measured pace, Nora-Leigh closed her eyes and rolled her shoulders to flex the tightness in her stiff back and neck muscles. She opened her eyes, then turned her head to find Clay watching her with a speculative glint in his eyes. His gaze darted away when their eyes met.

"I'm going to ride up the trail a few miles and scout around," he stated, staring straight ahead.

Nora-Leigh studied the worn path but saw nothing unusual. Clay had told her on their first day out that this was an old Indian trail. Since then, she'd kept her eyes peeled for artifacts, such as arrowheads or beads, which would verify his statement. So far, nothing. For some reason, some part of her wanted to catch him in a lie, to trip him up.

"Just keep the river in sight," he said, "and you won't get lost. I'll be back in an hour or so."

Without waiting for her reply, he dismounted, untied the pack mule, and retied it to Nora-Leigh's mare.

Obviously preoccupied, Clay moved next to her, fiddling with the knot of the reins. "Since you'll be walking at a slower pace, it'll be easier to keep Stubborn with you."

With startling clarity, it occurred to her what Clay was saying. Her stomach clenched. She chewed her lower lip as she stared at his busy hands, then at his face.

"Is something wrong?" she asked.

Clay glanced up at her; then his eyes narrowed. He looked off into the distance. Removing his hat, he scratched his head. With a deliberate movement, he replaced the hat after smoothing back his rumpled hair. "I told you before, I thought we'd been followed. Almost since we left Steamboat Bend. I've still got that gut feeling. And not just followed, mind you, but damn well good and tracked. I'm gonna leave a sign or two that I can check when we go back that way. Then I'll know for sure."

"Ah, very clever of you. For a pirate, that is."

His serious expression diminished for the moment as he gave her a sheepish grin and a nod of concession.

Nora-Leigh leaned down and patted Gingersnap's neck. Through lowered eyelashes, she glanced at Clay. "Should I be worried?"

His grin disappeared. "Nah, I'm just being cautious."

His voice was too calm and casual, too self-assured, for Nora-Leigh to believe him. Was he lying to keep her from worrying? Or was there another reason? "Do you know why anyone would follow you?"

He remounted his stallion. "What makes you think it's me they want? Could be you."

She gave him a mocking smile. "I wasn't the one who came to Steamboat Bend dressed in an outlandish disguise. I wasn't the one asking all kinds of personal questions. I wasn't the one searching for gold."

He gave a sarcastic snort.

"I have nothing to hide," Nora-Leigh reminded him. "While you apparently do."

He scowled at her, his eyes dark and insolent. "Do you think I'd purposely put you in jeopardy?"

She shook her head. "Not on purpose, maybe, but some men will do anything to get what they want, especially the type who all they want is money."

"So you think I'm one of those kinds of men," Clay said, spacing his words evenly. "I'll do whatever it takes to get what I want, no matter the consequences?"

"I don't know you well enough to say," she said. She wondered why she'd taken such a supercilious tone. Even to herself she sounded like a reserved and prissy schoolmarm. She hated that and wanted to take the words back, but it was too late. She could see by the look on Clay's face that she'd hurt his feelings. Being a man, of course, he would never admit it. He would simply take a nasty tone in return.

"Dammit, Nora-Leigh. Your granddad trusted me with your safety. That should be good enough for you."

"It should," she sneered. Why didn't she apologize to him?

Clay shook his head. "I've had about enough insults from you for one day." He kicked his stallion and called out over his shoulder, "I'll be back. Try to stay out of trouble."

"I will."

"I doubt it," he hollered, "but try anyway." Then he disappeared down the trail in a cloud of dust.

She hadn't deliberately insulted him. It just seemed that whenever they tried to hold a rational conversation, it turned into an unpleasant debate that made one or both of them angry. She doubted they could ever get along without clashing. They were just too different.

Nora took one last look around. The shadow of the Bighorn Mountains fell across the valley they were crossing, giving it a beauty she had never seen before. It lifted her sagging spirits.

With renewed enthusiasm, she nudged Gingersnap lightly with her heels. The mare started forward but stopped suddenly when the mule dug in his hind legs and refused to budge. Over her shoulder, Nora-Leigh glared at the recalcitrant beast. "Giddyap, mule."

Stubborn as his name, he refused to move. She kicked Gingersnap again, but as soon as the mare stepped forward, the confounded mule stepped backward. Gingersnap looked at Nora-Leigh as if to say, "I'm trying."

"I know," Nora-Leigh agreed.

Kicking her foot out of the stirrup, Nora-Leigh swung her leg over the saddle and hopped to the ground. She walked back to the mule and stared at the stubborn animal. "What's wrong with you? You never give Clay any trouble."

As she reached for his bridle, he answered by trying to nip her. She jumped out of his way. "You ungrateful wretch! Who do you think feeds and waters you? All right, so it's usually Clay, but you should be grateful to me, too."

He thanked her by stepping on her foot and biting her on the wrist.

"Oww!"

Nora-Leigh gave the beast a scathing look before she limped over to a fallen log and sat down. Luckily, he hadn't broken the skin on her wrist, thanks to the padding from her shirt and jacket. She pulled off her boot. Her throbbing foot was already beginning to swell. Suddenly she realized the foolishness of her move: She wouldn't be able to put her boot back on, and she would play hell trying to ride in stockinged feet.

Of course, that was even if the mule cooperated. She looked over at Stubborn, who bared his teeth and brayed, kicking out his back legs.

No. She wasn't going anywhere. Well, Clay had said he would come back to her. He would just have to come back a little farther was all. Maybe he wouldn't even notice that she hadn't moved. Were there any distinguishing landmarks nearby? She glanced around. Not that she could tell. But as she thought of Clay's eyes and the way he'd tracked the country around him as they rode she felt secure. Nothing got by him.

But could she hope he wouldn't notice that she hadn't moved? When hell froze over, thought Nora-Leigh, thinking of one of her granddad's favorite sayings.

A cold, light rain began to fall a short time later. Surprisingly, the mule didn't balk when Nora-Leigh led him and Gingersnap to cover beneath the canopy of a nearby copse of cottonwood trees.

She leaned her back against one of the thicker tree trunks and, pulling up her trouser leg, examined her swollen foot. Grimacing, she slipped off her sock. The top and sides of her foot were a brilliant shade of purple, and the foot was twice its normal size. Her ankle, too, had swollen to nearly the size of her calf. She doubted any bones were broken, though. The pain was minimal unless she put her weight on it, but it was unquestionably bruised. Colorful, too. Mixed in with the purple were bright red and a lovely shade of burgundy. Nora-Leigh had a dress the very same color. Clay, undoubtedly, would be amused by her latest mishap. Especially because this time it didn't involve him. She smiled to herself. He would appreciate the humor of the situation. Or, on second thought, he might not.

Thrill to the most sensual, adventure-filled Historical Romances on the market today...
FROM  LEISURE BOOKS

As a home subscriber to the Leisure Historical Romance Book Club, you'll enjoy the best in today's BRAND-NEW Historical Romance fiction. For over twenty-five years, Leisure Books has brought you the award-winning, high-quality authors you know and love to read. Each Leisure Historical Romance will sweep you away to a world of high adventure...and intimate romance. Discover for yourself all the passion and excitement millions of readers thrill to each and every month.

SAVE AT LEAST *$5.00* EACH TIME YOU BUY!

Each month, the Leisure Historical Romance Book Club brings you four brand-new titles from Leisure Books, America's foremost publisher of Historical Romances. EACH PACKAGE WILL SAVE YOU AT LEAST $5.00 FROM THE BOOKSTORE PRICE! And you'll never miss a new title with our convenient home delivery service.

Here's how we do it. Each package will carry a 10-DAY EXAMINATION privilege. At the end of that time, if you decide to keep your books, simply pay the low invoice price of $16.96 ($17.75 US in Canada), no shipping or handling charges added*. HOME DELIVERY IS ALWAYS FREE*. With today's top Historical Romance novels selling for $5.99 and higher, our price SAVES YOU AT LEAST $5.00 with each shipment.

AND YOUR FIRST FOUR-BOOK SHIPMENT IS TOTALLY FREE!*

IT'S A BARGAIN YOU CAN'T BEAT! A Super $21.96 Value!

LEISURE BOOKS A Division of Dorchester Publishing Co., Inc.

GET YOUR 4 FREE* BOOKS NOW—
A $21.96 VALUE!

Mail the Free* Book
Certificate
Today!

4 FREE* BOOKS 🌹 A $21.96 VALUE

Free Books Certificate

YES! I want to subscribe to the Leisure Historical Romance Book Club. Please send me my 4 FREE* BOOKS. Then each month I'll receive the four newest Leisure Historical Romance selections to Preview for 10 days. If I decide to keep them, I will pay the Special Member's Only discounted price of just $4.24 each, a total of $16.96 ($17.75 US in Canada). This is a SAVINGS OF AT LEAST $5.00 off the bookstore price. There are no shipping, handling, or other charges*. There is no minimum number of books I must buy and I may cancel the program at any time. In any case, the 4 FREE* BOOKS are mine to keep—A BIG $21.96 Value!

*In Canada, add $5.00 shipping and handling per order for first shipment. For all subsequent shipments to Canada, the cost of membership is $17.75 US, which includes $7.75 shipping and handling per month.[All payments must be made in US dollars]

Name _____

Address _____

City _____

State _____ *Country* _____ *Zip* _____

Telephone _____

Signature _____

If under 18, Parent or Guardian must sign. Terms, prices and conditions subject to change. Subscription subject to acceptance. Leisure Books reserves the right to reject any order or cancel any subscription.

(Tear Here and Mail Your FREE* Book Card Today!)

Get Four Books Totally
F R E E* —
A $21.96 Value!

PLEASE RUSH
MY FOUR FREE*
BOOKS TO ME
RIGHT AWAY!

Leisure Historical Romance Book Club
P.O. Box 6613
Edison, NJ 08818-6613

AFFIX
STAMP
HERE

She would now slow him down more, and he already was anxious to be free of her.

Clay. The man confounded her at every turn. He could be so warm and tender. She remembered how his arms felt around her when she'd been terrified by his crow. He'd been warm, protective, strong. His lips had caressed hers so gently. He'd made her feel safe and right somehow. Then, as changeable as the weather, he'd grown cold and indifferent, almost as if he were another man. She thought he liked her, even admired her at times. But more often than not, he made her feel like the eccentric, spinster schoolmarm she was—unwanted, unwelcome, and unloved. A woman men were willing to let teach the town's children, but not to give them youngsters of their own.

The sky darkened to pitch-black, and the rain fell in sheets. Gingersnap and Stubborn hung their heads as the precipitation dripped from their coats. Nora Leigh stood up, hobbled over to them, and removed their gear. No animal, two-legged or four, was going anywhere in this weather. A flash of lightning underscored that dismal thought. She prayed that Clay would find them before nightfall.

He didn't.

As the day grew shorter and darker, Nora-Leigh watched for his return. The rain grew steadily worse, so she wrapped herself in an oversized oilskin raincoat and waited. She chewed a slice of beef jerky and ate a tin of peaches for supper.

She shivered with each blast of icy rain that pelted her face, for she had no way to make a campfire—even if she could find any dry wood. She had all the food; Clay had the lucifers to start a fire. She had the oilskins; Clay had the weapons. At least, if worse came to worst, she did have Gramps's knife tucked into her boot.

Surprisingly, she wasn't frightened, even when Jack flew out of the branches overhead and landed at her feet.

161

As she sat watching him, he waddled close to her horse's legs and tucked his wings back against his body. He settled beneath the edge of her coat, out of the miserable weather.

"Coward," she commented. "Do you show up only when it rains?"

He cawed in reply.

She certainly had a way with animals, she thought.

She wedged her empty canteen between two rocks and watched as the rain filled it with fresh water. Who had said she didn't have the grit or savvy for outdoor life? She glanced at her going-away present from Gramps. A bright and shiny brand-new compass. She faced due east, away from the wind and rain. The animals kept their rumps to the west also. And people called them dumb animals. Ha! Nora-Leigh surprised herself with her bit of whimsy. Considering her circumstances, she was holding up well. Still, she prayed Clay would find her soon.

"Hello the camp!"

Startled, Nora-Leigh looked up. Her gaze darted left and right, but she could see nothing through the pouring rain and the darkness of night. Her heart pounded and her head spun. With a trembling hand, she pulled her knife from inside her boot. Rising to a crouch, she held the blade concealed next to her leg.

A man, dripping rain and shivering as badly as she, stepped into her limited range of vision.

He removed his scraggly hat. Rain poured off its brim. "Nat Arbogast, ma'am. Remember me?"

"Yes." Nora-Leigh released a partial sigh of relief. "Yes, I do. How are you, Mr. Arbogast?"

"Call me Nat." He grinned, showing several empty spaces where teeth should have been. "I'm wet and cold. Same as you, I reckon."

He stood several yards away, twisting the brim of his battered, dirt-brown, moth-eaten hat, obviously waiting for an invitation to join her. Water dripped off his two long white braids and yellowed beard. Thinning hair covered a nearly bald pate spattered with raindrops. He was dressed half in white man's clothing and half in Indian attire. He was nearly her own height, much thinner and much, much older, so he probably wasn't a real threat to her, but she wavered, unsure of herself. She didn't know what to make of him. What would Clay do? Of course, Clay was confident about everything he did. This wouldn't cause him a moment's hesitation.

"I got the makings for a fire," he stated, watching her closely but not coming any nearer. "I know you don't know me at all and you oughta be cautious 'round strangers, particularly men, but I swear on my saintly mama's grave, I'm harmless as an ole hound dog."

"I'm sorry," Nora-Leigh said. "It's rude of me to be so nervous."

He shifted from one foot to the other. "I understand, missy. I surely do."

"I suppose I shouldn't admit it, but you can see the way of things for yourself. I could lie and say that Mr. Sullivan is off hunting or some such thing. Of course, that would be highly preposterous—"

"Preposterous?"

"Unlikely, sir. That would be unlikely considering the inclement weather—"

"Inclement weather?" he queried, his left brow quirked.

"The rain. But as you can see, I'm alone. Mr. Sullivan and I got separated, and I don't know where he is.

"Under ordinary circumstances I consider myself a very good judge of character," Nora-Leigh stated. "But I'm out of my natural sphere of knowledge here. You must think me highly rude and uncommonly inconsiderate."

"Not at all," he said agreeably, considering the way he shivered and shook with the cold and the rain. "You can never be too careful. In fact, I got to tell you, this ole

163

trail is well traveled, 'specially as you get closer to Fort Custer. Did you know you're on reservation land? I'm surprised you ain't seen no one else. You been right lucky that someone less friendly than myself hasn't chanced upon you."

"We're on reservation land? I never even thought of that. Please, Mr. Arbogast," she said, beckoning with a wave of her hand as she made up her mind. "Join me."

Nat took a wide step around the mule who had been eyeing him suspiciously since he stepped beneath the cottonwood tree. He sat down cross-legged across from Nora-Leigh. To her delighted surprise, he began to pull pieces of wood from inside his coat, his shirt and trouser pockets, even from the pack he carried over one stooped shoulder. He stacked them neatly between them. Before long, he had a little blaze going. He kept adding firewood until she soon felt its soothing warmth and welcomed the comforting light. Their bodies and the overhanging tree limbs kept out most of the windswept rain, so the fire had a chance to burn without problems.

When he saw her amazed expression, he chuckled. Rubbing his hands above the fire, he said, "I saw this storm brewing. I've been caught in the rain before when there wasn't a dry stick to be had, and I don't much cotton to sleeping on the cold, wet ground. Not after so many years of doing just that. My weary bones are stiff enough as it is. So I gathered up some wood in preparation."

Nora-Leigh shook her head. "I'm still new to the outdoor living experience."

" 'Outdoor living experience,' " he repeated, grinning. "You have quite a way with words, missy. I promise it won't take you long to remember to provision yourself once you've spent one long, wet, miserable night."

"Yes. From now on, that will be one aspect I shan't forget."

"No, ma'am. Who's your companion there?" He

pointed to the crow whose beak and one black eye peeked out from behind Nora-Leigh's jacket.

She laughed. "That's Mr. Sullivan's pet crow, Calico Jack."

"Calico Jack, eh?" His head cocked to the side as he stared at the crow; then he shook his head. "Strange pet. Now, missy, about Clay Sullivan."

Nora-Leigh gave him a hopeful look. "You didn't happen to see any sign of him before the rain set in, did you?"

"Nah, sorry to say I didn't. If you don't mind my askin', how'd you two get separated?"

"Clay rode forward a ways to scout around. He said he thought we were being followed. He left the pack mule with me so he wouldn't be slowed down by him. First I couldn't get the mule to so much as budge, then the darn fool creature stepped on my foot and bit my arm. My foot swelled up like a bullfrog, and I couldn't ride, much less walk. So I decided to just stay put where I was and let Clay find me. Or so I thought. He should have been back long before now. I just hope nothing has happened to him."

Nat glanced at her foot and shook his head. He made as if to pick it up. "May I?"

With a gentleness that belied his scruffy exterior, he examined Nora-Leigh's tender foot, turning it one way and then the other, squeezing and gingerly pressing the tips of his fingers against the tender flesh. "Nothing's broken, just badly bruised, far as I can tell, but that damned—pardon my ripe language, missy—that mule did a bang-up job. Right colorful."

Nora-Leigh stared at the bare foot, just now warming up next to the fire. "Yes, isn't it?"

"Still and all, I wouldn't be worrying about Clay Sullivan, missy."

"Why is that?"

"Blue Buffalo says he's the best the Army's got."

"The best what?"

"Why, the best scout, missy. The best durn scout they got."

Nora-Leigh couldn't believe her ears. "Mr. Sullivan is an *Army* scout?"

"Yes, ma'am."

She repeated herself. "He's with the Army?"

Nat chuckled. "He's a civilian with the Army. Not Army regular."

"But he's on Army business?"

"Can't say for certain myself, but I reckon he is."

"That scoundrel never told me any such thing."

Nat cocked a bushy white brow and his mouth twisted into a thin line. "Not to pry into your personal business, but what did he tell you he was doing out here?"

"It's rather a long story, Mr. Arbogast." Nora-Leigh couldn't keep the anger from her voice.

"I reckon he had his reasons."

"Oh, I'm sure he did, all right." The lying, conniving, thieving skunk! Wait until she saw him again. He would get such an earful that his ears would burn. No, on second thought, Nora-Leigh decided to keep the information to herself. It might prove useful later on. When he tried to tell her more of his tall tales. From here on out, Nora-Leigh Dillon wasn't going to be the gullible young thing Mr. Sullivan presumed her to be.

"He's a good man."

"Mr. Arbogast—"

"Nat," he reminded her.

"Nat, you don't need to champion our Mr. Sullivan. He's quite good at that himself."

"Champion?"

"It means to stand up for, to defend."

"Ah. I got to tell you, missy, your way of palaverin'

leaves me confounded half the time and just plumb bamboozled the rest."

"Sorry, I'm a schoolteacher. I guess it comes naturally."

"Ah. That explains it. Never learned to read, myself. Write neither. Can't cypher very good neither. Never took the time."

Nora-Leigh smiled. "Well, Mr. Arbogast, you've got the time now."

He grinned back, understanding. "Reckon I do. Even have me a teacher all to my ownself."

"Yes, indeed you do."

Nora-Leigh spent the rest of the night beginning to teach Nat how to read. She had a book with her—one she'd hoped would help her acclimate herself to travel in the West. It was one of Beadle's dime novels called *Bob Woolf, the Border Ruffian: or, The Girl Dead-Shot*. Nora-Leigh particularly enjoyed the story because the heroine, Hurricane Nell—her own mother called Nora-Leigh Nellie—also dressed in men's clothing. Besides, Hurricane Nell could handle any situation. Nora-Leigh much admired the heroine.

And soon, Nat admired her also.

Nora-Leigh was Clay's responsibility. He didn't need to remind himself. Guilt bit deep into his uneasy thoughts.

He'd made hard promises to her granddad, to her mother, and to Nora-Leigh herself. He promised to keep her safe, and, dammit, she would have been if he hadn't tried to get the jump on whoever was following him.

He had no doubt about it now. He'd circled back and caught sure signs of a single shod horse, and when he rode forward he'd found evidence of a small campfire. Heat still emanated from the dying coals. That was before the cold rain set in. Despite pulling up his collar, water now dripped off the brim of his hat and ran down his neck, soaking his shirt and bringing gooseflesh to his chilled skin.

He prayed that Nora-Leigh was safe and out of the worst of the rain. Right now, it fell lightly. That wouldn't last, though. He could just make out a bank of scuttling clouds, dark as pitch, off to the west. Behind this light rain would come a good old-fashioned thunderstorm, just like the one that had scared Nora-Leigh the other night. Just their darned luck. One could travel for days in eastern Montana and never see a drop of rain. In the last forty-eight hours they'd suffered through two gully-washers.

Did Nora-Leigh see the bank of gray, roiling clouds off to the west? Was she making preparations to get out of the worst of the coming storm? God, he hoped so. Still, if they didn't meet up soon, he'd play hell finding her in the dark of night and the driving rain.

He kept on—his head down, rain pouring off his hat brim—inching northwest. He couldn't see or hear the river in the dark and the driving rain. He prayed Jolly's good sense would tell him when they were near the river and he wouldn't step off a steep bank and drown them both.

Clay worried, something he'd never done in his entire life. It was an emotion he didn't know how to deal with. His stomach churned with acid. His heart pounded inside his chest. His mind whirled with thoughts of Nora-Leigh. He couldn't stop remembering little, seemingly insignificant things about her. Her pert, sunburned nose. How her laughing hazel eyes sparkled with delight and wonder. How her proud chin popped up like a jack-in-the-box when a stubborn thought entered her head or determination drove her to speak her mind. How she drove him crazy with her questions. And at the same time drove him crazy with wanting her.

He couldn't lose her.

Not now, when he was just beginning to know her.

Not now, when he was just beginning to like her.

Not now, when he was just beginning to love her.

Oh, why had he left her? For those very reasons.

Going any farther in the pelting rain was a foolish, chancy proposition. Clay couldn't judge direction or distance. He couldn't see ordinarily recognizable landmarks. And he was passably certain he wasn't on the old Indian trail anymore. Still, he and Jolly miserably trudged on: Clay feverish and shivering with the onset of illness, the stallion loyally obeying his master. If anything happened to Nora-Leigh, Clay would never forgive himself. He refused to quit searching until he found her or dropped dead trying.

With his chin tucked into his chest and his head bent low, he never saw the man hiding in the tree above him as he passed. Nor did he hear him as he vaulted from a low overhanging branch.

The ground slammed into Clay, forcing the air from his lungs, jolting his bones. He kicked out and rolled to his side. Clear of his horse's hooves, he gasped for breath. Stinging rain battered his face. He shook his head to clear it, but a sharp kick to his temple further dulled his dazed senses. Darkness filled the edges of his vision. As consciousness fled, Clay's only thought was of Nora-Leigh. *Please, let her be all right.*

Chapter Eleven

Clay sensed heat not only on his exposed flesh but throughout his aching body. It was an intense fieriness unlike any he'd ever experienced. First, he felt as if he were roasting on an open spit, then chills tore through his shaking limbs. Between bouts of hot and cold, a vise gripped his chest with hard, unrelenting talons.

Perspiration beaded his torso, face, and neck. What felt like cactus thorns scraped his throat every time he swallowed. His head throbbed, and nausea threatened to spill the meager contents of his stomach.

He tried to open his eyes but they fluttered ineffectually against a layer of cloth tied round his head. He could see nothing but shadows, indistinct images that flickered across his dimmed eyesight. His vision slowly began to clear. As sunlight filtered through the fabric, he realized it was full daylight. He must have been unconscious throughout the night, at least eight to ten hours.

Clay struggled to sit up, only to discover that he lay

flat on his back, his wrists and ankles bound with strips
of leather that were firmly tied to stakes hammered deep
into the ground. He did have one thing to be thankful for,
he thought dismally. It was no longer raining. That was
a two-edged sword, however, because he would have
killed for water to ease his parched, scratchy throat.

Clay heard heavy footsteps approach. He waited,
clenching his teeth.

"Sullivan, 'bout time you woke."

As if to get his attention, the man kicked Clay in the
hip, not severely but enough for Clay to know the man
meant business. As if Clay couldn't have guessed: He lay
staked out in the open minus his boots and stripped to the
waist.

"I was afraid I mighta knocked you upside the head a
tad too hard, but it appears your noggin is good and solid.
I didn't want to kill you . . . yet, that is. Where's your
purty travelin' companion?"

Clay swallowed hard. "I'm alone."

"That's a damned lie," he said in a mocking tone. He
then gave a bark of laughter. "Well, maybe not. I reckon
you're alone right now."

"Who . . . ?" Clay coughed. "Who are you?" His words
came out grating, rasping against his raw throat.

"Bill Terrell," the man replied. "Does the name ring a
bell?"

"Should it?"

"I've been in a military prison for three months."

"Yeah?"

The voice became angrier. "When you had me arrested
you called me a lying thief. You said I was helling around
and had no business in the United States Army. Remember?"

"What do you want?"

Unable to see him, Clay wasn't prepared when, without
warning, Terrell smashed Clay in the ribs with the toe of

his boot. Trying to ignore the pain, Clay sucked in his breath and exhaled slowly.

"D'you remember me now?"

"No," he gasped.

Again he kicked Clay in the ribs, harder this time. Clay grunted against the pain. Sweat, already beaded on his face, rolled down his temples and into his hair. "I have no money," he said, "or anything else of value."

"I know," Terrell answered. "I checked your saddle-bags. You'd think a man of consequence would be more accommodating."

"Sorry to disappoint you."

"Hell, it's not your money I want."

"What is it, then?" Clay was confused, partly from pain but mostly because he didn't remember this character.

"I want your damn hide. I want you to suffer the way you made me suffer for three long months."

So that was his game. Clay shook his head to clear it but his head still swam. He tried to recall the past, but he simply couldn't think clearly. He was dog-tired, and sick and feverish, all of which would make it more difficult to free himself. Still, he had to keep trying.

"Remember how you had me thrown in jail?"

Clay didn't reply. He honestly didn't remember the man.

With anger thickening his voice, Terrell continued. "When they let me out, they bumped me down from corporal to private, and humiliated me in front of men I considered friends. Now they won't even talk to me."

Anger at being attacked by a man who'd only gotten what he likely deserved overcame Clay. "That's the way it goes, boy."

"I left without leave. Just cleared out right then and there." The man spit, and Clay heard it strike near his head. Wetness sprayed the side of his face. "I had nothing. Nothing, I tell you. No food, no money. I had to steal

172

an old nag not worth the oats it took to feed her."

"I expect you got what you earned."

Terrell swore viciously. Clay tensed, knowing what would come next. He didn't have long to wait. With a booted foot, his captor viciously struck Clay repeatedly in the hip. White-hot pain shot down Clay's leg. He bit back a groan—refusing to acknowledge that his enemy had hurt him. He breathed deeply and struggled to stay conscious.

"I got the last laugh, though. I stole the sergeant's rifle and saddlebags."

Clay didn't answer, and in a few moments he heard Terrell walk away. Clay released a slow sigh of relief, even though his reprieve was likely only temporary. Soon he heard nothing but the quiet afternoon chorus of birds and the accompaniment of the tall prairie grass swaying in the wind. Perhaps now he could find a means to get away.

When he next came to, Clay had no idea how much time had passed.

"You really don't remember me, do you?" Terrell's voice sounded nearby. His voice was filled with disgust.

Clay felt his chest lighten. Maybe this man could be reasoned with. He answered honestly, "No."

There was a pause. "It don't matter. I'm gonna pay you back anyway. And right now I got me an idea of how to do it. The schoolmarm should be a start. That should give you something to chaw on while I'm gone, eh, Sullivan?"

Clay strained angrily against his bonds, but to no avail. He passed out.

The sun had reached its zenith overhead. Clay couldn't see it, but he could feel it sear his bared flesh. His sweat only made it sting more. Worse, his body raged with fever.

He shifted in and out of consciousness, but Terrell pestered him no more. In one rare moment of lucidity, he knew he was alone. He struggled again with his leather bonds, but as they dried in the sun they tightened even further on his wrists and ankles. His struggles only made him lightheaded. He cursed. He swore. He prayed to God, then sank into raving delirium.

When next he awoke, his mind, for the time being clear and coherent, thrummed with possibilities. Was Terrell still searching for Nora-Leigh? He cursed himself. Why had he left her alone? What had he been thinking?

If anyone knew about the dangers lurking on the trail, he did. Foul weather. Accidents. Animals. Not only the four-legged variety, but worse, the two-legged variety. Desperate men. Reckless men. Violent men. Men on the dodge from the law, men with no principles, men with vengeance on their minds. Men with no conscience. Men like Bill Terrell. Where was his captor?

Clay wondered where he himself was. Terrell had to have taken him off the beaten track, away from discovery by unwary travelers. Even if he could have screamed, no one would hear. He was doomed. He couldn't escape. He had little hope of being found. Would Terrell leave him there to die a slow, agonizing death, or would he return to do worse? And where was Nora-Leigh?

Clay pulled against his bonds, kicking and struggling, swearing vengeance against Terrell, expending strength he could ill afford to lose. He battled against his restraints until he lay gulping air, his throat raw, his sides heaving. His ribs throbbed dully. Fresh blood dripped from his wrists and ankles.

But he fought to no avail.

"He's not coming back, is he?" Nora-Leigh said, dejection coloring her weary voice.

"Don't know, missy," came Nat's reply.

She sat cross-legged, her blanket wrapped around her

shoulders, staring at the surrounding landscape of rain-spattered tall grasses waving in the light wind, at the mud puddles on the ground. In the bright sunlight tree leaves shimmered with glimmering droplets. In the distance she could hear the newly replenished river as it gurgled over stones and sand. All around, the rough hills and rock out-croppings looked swept clean. Except for herself and Nat, there were no other indications of human life.

Nora-Leigh reflected upon her dire situation as she watched Nat fiddle with something over the morning fire. She leaned over and grabbed her boots from beneath the oilskins. As she pulled one on over her sore, bruised foot, she grimaced in pain. Fortunately, Nat's back was to her and he didn't see.

She'd spent a wakeful night, had only fallen into a fitful sleep a few hours before daybreak. Before that, she had spent the insomniac hours talking with Nat, trying to teach him letters. In turn, he'd regaled her with stories about his adventurous life in the woods and mountains of Montana over the past half-century.

She'd found his stories amusing and entertaining. Under other circumstances, she would have peppered him with questions this morning. But her mind was occupied elsewhere. Every time she heard the slightest sound she glanced up, expecting Clay. It was mid-morning and there was still no sign of him.

She tried not to think about what could have happened. Worse, playing loudly in the back of her mind like a flock of honking geese overhead, she knew he had never wanted her along to begin with. She wasn't even certain that he liked her.

Nat crouched by the fire, pushing the coals around with a short stick. He glanced up at Nora-Leigh, his eyes heavy-lidded, his face gray with fatigue. "It don't look promising, missy. Blue Buffalo said he's a tracker, and a good one. Even though it was raining pitchforks, I reckon he coulda found you. But the fact that he's still not back, well, I jest don't know. . . ."

Nora-Leigh stood up and brushed off the seat of her trousers. She plucked her hat off the ground where she'd tossed it after the rain stopped and plopped it on her head. "I'll just have to find him myself, then."

"Now, that there's a well-greased plan, missy." Nat stood up, shaking his head. "Still, I ain't reckoning yer gonna be talked out of it, and you ain't goin' anywhere in this territory by yore lonesome."

"Nat, you've done enough for me already," she said. "You kept me company and entertained me with your stories when I was feeling a little bit scared during the storm last night. I appreciate all you've done, and it's more than enough. Surely you have plans of your own. Someplace that you need to be?"

"And jist as surely I don't. My life is my own. I go where I want, when I want. Always have. Always will."

Nora-Leigh cocked her head in question. "Have you never had a wife or children?"

"Nope. Never took a wife." He grinned. "I reckon I got no younguns neither. Leastwise, none I was ever told of."

Nora-Leigh felt herself blushing and rushed to change the subject. "Which direction should we go?"

Nat lifted his head and pointed the stick in his hand in a southeasterly direction. "I reckon that's the way Sullivan went. You were following the river, weren't you?"

"Yes."

"I'll do what I can, missy, but my eyesight's not as good as it used to be. And I was never no good at trackin'." He shook his head, setting his braids swinging around his head. "Now, that Blue Buffalo, he's got eyes in the back of his head, I swear."

"We could use him now."

"That's a fact. But ya never know where that Injun is." He gathered up Nora-Leigh's saddle and supplies and started toward Ginger. "I'll saddle your mare for you, missy, but if you don't mind, I reckon I'll just walk along beside you. I never did get a hankering for riding. Too damn hard on my skinny ass. Pardon my French, ma'am, but there's none other lingo I know of to say it."

Nora-Leigh smiled, then patted Nat's wrist. "Don't apologize; I understand completely. I never rode a horse until a few days ago, and my, um . . . that is, my bottom isn't overly happy either."

Nat chortled, his bearded chin bobbing. He tossed Ginger's blanket over her back, then squinted at Stubborn. "Maybe that mule of yours will follow me, if'n I walk him beside me."

"I hope so." Nora-Leigh shook her head. "Much as I'd prefer to leave him to fend for himself, I just can't. He's carrying the foodstuffs and the other supplies, and Gingersnap just can't carry it all."

"I know how to keep a mule in line," Nat said.

"Good. We'll be off, then."

"Right you are, missy." He saluted her with two fingers to his temple. "We'll find that Sullivan, come hell or high water." He paused a moment, then broke into gales of laughter. When Nora-Leigh gave him a questioning glance, he said, "High water. Get it?"

Nora-Leigh grinned. "Of course. High water. Very funny."

Nat sobered a bit. "I hope it isn't too high. That could have been Sullivan's problem: He crossed over the river, then when it filled, he couldn't get back. Still, I reckon he coulda hollered across if he saw us."

Nora-Leigh agreed with his logic. If Clay was within shouting distance, he would have done so. She was worried, and she wouldn't stop worrying until they found Clay. They needed to hurry.

After several hours of searching, the sun beat down directly overhead. Sweat beaded under her hat brim and soaked her hair. Perspiration dripped down her temples and off her chin.

"Damn, it's hot as hell," Nat complained, wiping the sweat from his face with a dirt-encrusted bandanna. "Uncommon for this time of year."

"It certainly is hot."

"You know what else, missy?"

Nora-Leigh met Nat's gaze. "We're lost?"

"Yup." He nodded vigorously, then paused. "Well, not exactly lost. We're just not on the old Indian trail no more."

Apparently, between them Nora-Leigh and Nat weren't very good at following a track, much less a marked trail. Who knew when it happened, but they had wandered off the trail. Looking around now, even Nora-Leigh could tell that. The ground wasn't hard, the grass wasn't chewed down to bare earth, and she could detect no signs of passing livestock. She hoped that didn't mean this area was ruled by wild animals—Clay had warned her that the trails were full of predators at night.

She sighed. It didn't matter. They should have found Clay by now. Nora-Leigh's hopes were all but dashed.

Nat interrupted her thoughts. "Let's refill our water, missy, and take a break. Climb down off that mare." He didn't give her a chance to reply, but simply swung her off Ginger in one fell swoop and set her on her feet. "How's the foot?"

"A little sore, but it's not bad when I don't have to walk on it much."

"Good. I reckon way down that valley there," he said, pointing off to their left, "is the river. We can sit down and palaver about our situation when we get to it."

"All right."

He smiled, his grin sparkling in his eyes. "We'll find him, one way or another. Don't you be frettin'."

They started toward the river, Nat pulling the mule and Ginger along behind him.

"I'm trying not to worry," Nora-Leigh said. "I'm really not a worrier by nature. I tend to be an optimistic person most of the time."

"Optimis-what?"

"Optimistic. It means I look on the bright side of things, rather than the bad."

"I reckon I'm that way, too."

Smiling at him, Nora-Leigh patted Nat's arm. At her touch, Nat pulled her arm through his. "I thought you and I were alike that way."

"A match made in heaven, missy. If I was gonna hitch my wagon to any woman, you'd be the one."

At Nora-Leigh's surprised gasp, Nat threw back his head chortling. "Got you, didn't I?"

Nora-Leigh, only now breathing normally again, nodded but couldn't help grinning up at his bewhiskered face. "You have a wicked sense of humor, Mr. Arbogast."

"Now, who said I was funnin' you?"

Nora-Leigh stopped walking and cocked her head as she gazed at Nat.

"I don't mean to propose to you on bended knee, but if I was a younger man, I might be so inclined. What I meant was that you're an uncommonly pretty little thing . . . and smart and savvy. And sassy. I admire that in a lady."

"I don't know about being savvy. If I was so smart I would have figured out how to get Stubborn to move on my own, now, wouldn't I?"

"Bah, he's a typical mule. Cantankerous as all get out. When they get a notion in their heads, there's no dissuading them." He gave her a stained smile. "What I meant was, you may never been on a horse before, but you don't complain about your aching backside. You just keep going. You do what you got to do. That's the way

179

of things out here in the West. You make do, and you seem to have the bullheadedness for that. And you're optimis . . ."

"An optimist."

"Yeah, that. Me, too." They had reached the creek, and he squatted on the bank. He stuck a blade of grass between his thin lips.

"Thank you for saying those things about me. Though we hardly know each other, I already consider you a good friend."

"You'll make me blush, missy."

"And here I was thinking nothing could embarrass you."

"Ha! When I start getting' compliments from purty young gals, I can turn red with the best of 'em."

Nora-Leigh patted his cheek.

Awkwardly Nat placed his hand on top of hers. "Between us, we'll figure out where Sullivan is. Don't you fret none."

Nora-Leigh blew out a slow breath, then sat down beside him. She stared across the wide expanse of the slow-moving river. It wasn't deep, no more than a few inches even after all the rain, but it was as wide as two freight wagons set end to end.

A flash of movement caught her eye. She stared hard, hoping to see something that lay beyond a tall mulberry tree. She stood up and shaded her eyes. "Look yonder, Nat."

"See somethin'?" Nat stood up beside her and brought his hand to his forehead to block out the sun.

Against the glare, Nora squinted to try to get a better view. "What do you see?"

"Nothing."

"See that mulberry tree?"

"Yep."

"Just beyond it and a little to the left in that square of

180

sunshine, I thought I saw something on the ground. Maybe it's just a squirrel or a rabbit, but it looks like an arm. A man's arm."

Nat spat out the blade of grass and squared his shoulders. He took Nora-Leigh by the hand and walked with her so that they edged closer to the river but stayed hidden behind a boulder. "Missy," he whispered in an urgent tone. "My eyes are poor, but unless I'm mistaken, there *is* a man over there laying on the ground."

"Lying?" Nora-Leigh gasped. She swallowed with difficulty and spoke in a strained voice, "Is he moving? Is he alive?"

"Can't say for certain, but I think he's lashed to the ground." His face held an expression of deep sorrow and deeper anger. He bit his lower lip until Nora-Leigh expected to see a thin trickle of blood ooze from it. "Only a crossbred coward would do such a cold-blooded thing as stake a man down."

She had to know. "Is it Clay?"

He shook his head. "Can't tell from here."

With surprising strength, Nora-Leigh held back the icy fear that rose within her. "He doesn't appear to be moving."

"No, he ain't movin'." Nat pulled his rifle from his pack and checked the load. "You stay here. I'll look the situation over."

With her heart in her throat, Nora-Leigh watched as Nat splashed across the river and climbed the opposite bank. He headed toward the tree line in a crouch, his rifle at the ready. He called Clay's name, but from where she waited, she didn't hear a reply.

Peeking around the boulder, she waited, half in anticipation, half in dread. Part of her wanted it to be Clay, and part of her didn't. Still, she couldn't just sit back and wait.

She scooted around the rock, slid down the embank-

ment, waded across the river in a half crouch, and crawled
up the opposite bank on her stomach. She lifted her head
just high enough over the edge of the bank to see.

Her worst nightmares were realized. She heard the man
tied to the stakes speak in a low, rough voice but couldn't
make out what he said. Whether he spoke a sentence or
merely yelled a warning, she couldn't say, but the words
were barely uttered when a gun blast echoed off the hillside.

To her left, Nat fell in a crumpled heap, unmoving.

Nora-Leigh gasped in horror. Holding her hand over
her mouth to keep from crying out, she watched as a man
stepped out from a wooded area, a long rifle cradled in
his arm. She heard him clearly as he spoke. "So, Sullivan,
did ya think this old geezer was gonna be your savior?
By damn, not this time." His was a hard, ruthless voice.

Oh, my God. Clay! She glanced over at his body, taut
and straining, streaming perspiration into the grass beneath him. She gulped hard against hot tears that threatened to explode from the back of her eyes. *Stop it,* she
cautioned herself. This was no time for swooning, cow-
ering, or cringing. She needed all her wiles, all her savvy,
as Nat had called it.

The gunman walked across the open space to where
Clay Sullivan lay without giving Nat a second look. He
tore away the cloth that bound Clay's eyes. Clay squeezed
his eyes shut, then blinked, slowly opening them. He
squinted against the sun's glare.

"I don't reckon he'll be anyone's savior ever again,"
the gunman stated proudly.

He'd killed Nat! Frantically, Nora-Leigh looked behind
her. Ginger and Stubborn stood on the other side of the
river out of sight, but without much trouble the man
would be able to see them if he walked down to the
river's edge. Then what? Would he think they belonged

to Nat? What could she do? What would her heroine, Hurricane Nell, do?

She took a deep breath, trying to clear her mind. Once again she looked to where Clay lay. She couldn't tell his condition except that he lay still, unable or unwilling to move. She had to rely on herself, because she didn't know if she could count on his help. She doubted it.

She glanced over at Nat. Was he dead? Nora-Leigh knew a little about nursing. One couldn't be a teacher without seeing a number of scrapes and bruises, fractures and burns. But she knew next to nothing about gunshot wounds.

Clay would need help, too. He was likely suffering from sunburn or possibly heat exhaustion. Dehydration. Heaven only knew what else. She tried not to panic, but fear buzzed in the back of her mind like the drone of a hundred hungry locusts.

Nat lay closest to her, with Clay about ten feet beyond. She would concentrate on the gunman first. He might leave and give her an opportunity to see to the others. One thing at a time, she warned herself.

The man with the rifle circled Clay, a sneer playing about the thin line of his mouth. He prodded Sullivan with his foot, producing a grunt. "Got anything to say for yourself?"

"I see you're still alone, Terrell," Clay said in a harsh, raw voice.

"For now," he growled.

"No luck hunting down defenseless women?"

Terrell stood over Clay and pressed the butt of his rifle against his chest. Then he leaned on it, forcing first a mumbled groan from Clay, then a derisive suggestion about where else he could stick his rifle.

The man stared at Clay, a scowl darkening his features. "For all you know," he said, a cold edge in his voice,

"I've got your pretty little schoolmarm staked out naked in the sun. Just like yourself."

Nora-Leigh shivered at the thought.

"Nah," Clay ground out between clenched teeth. "If you had her, you'd be parading her about."

"How would you know what I'd do, you no-'count Indian lover?"

"Is *that* what this is about?"

"I done told you, Sullivan," the man said. "You put me in jail. I'm getting justice by humiliating you the way you did me."

"You think you're humiliating me?" Clay snarled. His voice burned with a savage inner fire. "There's no one to see me except you, and I don't give a damn what you think."

Terrell's eyes narrowed with annoyance. "What if I were to torture you?"

"What of it?"

"Or kill you?"

"I'd be dead. Then I sure as hell wouldn't care, and I damn sure wouldn't be humiliated, now would I?"

Terrell snarled, then tossed back his head and laughed—a sharp-edged, soul-stealing bark of mirth that straightened the hair on the back on Nora-Leigh's neck.

Why did Clay bait him so? She didn't understand his motives. In Clay's voice she heard barely banked anger and frustration, and fierce determination, but oddly enough, no fear whatsoever.

What worried her more than anything was the one thing she could see for herself. Clay wasn't well. The sun had burned his already bronzed skin. His wrists and ankles were covered in dried blood where he'd struggled against his bonds. Beneath the sunburn and the abrasions, his flesh glowed almost incandescently. A sheen of sweat coated his chest and face, and his body shivered uncontrollably. His dry, choked voice quavered when he talked.

His eyes, though focused on Terrell, were glazed and dull. The vitality seemed to be draining from his body.

Nora-Leigh scooted backward down to the river's edge and quickly crossed to where Stubborn stood drinking from the ankle-deep water. She rummaged around in the packs until she found a short-handled shovel. In a low crouch, she scrambled back across the river and up the bank.

She peeked over the rim. At her movement, Clay turned his head in her direction. He swallowed with obvious difficulty, his Adam's apple bobbing. His fixed, pewter-dark eyes caught hers, begging her with an anguished gaze to leave him. With the tips of his fingers he frantically waved her away.

Nora-Leigh edged forward.

Chapter Twelve

The man's contemptuous laughter grated on Clay's tautly stretched nerves. Terrell seemed close to madness, but in his weakened state Clay couldn't judge what the man was capable of.

As he watched Nora-Leigh, a terrible fear erupted in Clay like a geyser. Though he had been exhausted and aching, adrenaline suddenly pumped through his veins; a frantic need to protect her, to shield her, to somehow save her from Terrell consumed him. He desperately wanted to stop her, to spirit her away from here, but he had no way of doing so. Her attention was so focused on Terrell that even had he been able to snare her gaze, he doubted she would abandon her foolish plan.

With his stomach in knots and his hands balled into fists of frustration, he watched her from the corner of his eye. She moved painstakingly slowly, crawling forward on her legs and belly, her forearms pulling her closer. In one hand she held a shovel, in the other, a long-bladed, lethal-looking knife. Her hazel eyes were dark, and stead-fast determination pursed her lips.

He couldn't help a small smile—though it hurt to do so—as he recognized the blade. It was the same one she'd threatened to geld him with. However ill-advised her actions, the woman had a gutsy bravery few men could claim. Of himself he could give no less.

If he had to, he would die diverting Terrell's attention from Nora-Leigh as she stealthily moved toward them.

Clay returned Terrell's grin with a feral smirk. "You're a coward," he spat. By now his voice was a guttural rasp. "Plain and simple."

Terrell's eyes widened and his smile vanished, stripped away by astonishment. A deep flush crept into his unlined face. "What did you say?"

"You heard me."

He jerked the Army-issue Springfield off Clay's chest. He settled it against his shoulder and sighted down the barrel at Clay's face. With a decisive crack, he pulled back the block.

"Got a cartridge in the breech, soldier?" Clay snapped mockingly.

The man stared at Clay, his lip curled in disgust. "What d'you think, scout?" His gaze never left Clay as he pressed his index finger against the trigger.

Clay held his breath.

"I know how to use this weapon," he warned. "Don't think I don't."

Ten feet away, Nora-Leigh crept closer.

"Reckon you do," Clay admitted. He only wanted to get the man's attention, not bring about his own death. "You look like you mean business."

"Damned right I do," Terrell said, his face tight and pinched with resentment. "And I aim to blow your brains out."

"What?" Clay jeered. He had to stall him. "No torture

187

first? I figured you for one of those lily-livered fellas who enjoys seeing a man suffer slowly, inch by inch."

"I ain't lily-livered."

"I say you are," Clay said, baiting him further. How far could he push him before the man actually blew his brains out? Suddenly Clay's gaze wavered. Three men stood over him, sweating in the hot sun. Three men threatened him with a primed rifle. In a fatalistic meandering of his numbed brain, Clay idly wondered where his own weapon was.

"What do you know, anyway?" Terrell taunted. "You're the one with a rifle pointed at your damn nose." He bent closer, his eyes flashing with contempt. "You don't look so good, neither."

"I feel great!"

"I could change that," Terrell said defiantly.

"Yeah? Then do it."

Terrell didn't answer. The rifle barrel tipped marginally and brushed against Clay's nose. Clay squeezed his eyes shut, sweat burning the underside of their lids. He then opened them to find Terrell studying him. The man stared at Clay, his face a mixture of confusion and frustration.

For the first time, Clay saw how really young Terrell was, no more than seventeen or eighteen. Just a boy. He was scared and unsure of himself. A lethal combination.

Nora-Leigh was now six feet behind Terrell. So close that Clay smelled the purple-flower soap she used. He prayed that Terrell wouldn't get a whiff of her.

He promised himself that when this was over and done with, he was going to throw that damn cake of soap of hers off the nearest bluff. Then he was going to tan her hide. Then he was going to kiss her senseless.

Damn the woman. He caught another trace of her flowery scent. He turned his head a mere fraction of an inch to watch her. She was close enough so he could see her furrowed brow, her chalky face. She blinked sweat out of her eyes.

His feisty schoolmarm showed no outward sign of fear, but he knew that in her place, his heart would be pounding like mad. With his eyes, he tried to give her courage.

Good girl. Keep coming. Steady now.

The boy's head lifted, and his gaze narrowed in suspicion. He started to look around when Clay spoke up. "Terrell, you don't need to do this."

Four feet away.

His gaze shifted back to Clay. "Yeah I do. I got no choice."

"You always have a choice. You're free now, but if you kill me in cold blood like you're thinking of doing, you'll be a wanted man for the rest of your days. Your life will never be yours again."

Two feet away.

Nora-Leigh rose to her feet. Clay forced himself to watch. He feared that when the shovel connected with Terrell's back, the boy's itchy trigger finger would find its mark and he would be blown to kingdom come. He clenched his teeth and waited for the blast.

Instead, Nora-Leigh raised the shovel above her head and with what sounded like the squawk of an angry mouse, brought it down hard on Terrell's skull. His eyes rolled to the back of his head and he dropped to the ground like a rock. His hand fell away. The carbine toppled across Clay's chest, the barrel's end lodging in the grass beside him. Clay closed his eyes and released a ragged sigh.

"About time you showed up, Nellie," he whispered, his throat so raw it felt like he was chewing glass. "How was *that* for adventure?"

He wanted to throttle her for putting herself in danger. But even more, he wanted to hug her close and kiss her senseless, to thank her with every fiber of his being. But all he could suddenly think about was rolling over into a tight ball and sleeping for a long, long time.

Nora-Leigh tossed away the rifle and threw herself across his fevered body, her arms around his neck. Satiny ribbons of sun-warmed honey-colored curls tickled his chin. Her ragged breath left a soothing path along his ear and neck and brought gooseflesh to his parched skin. She attempted, without success, to string together a coherent sentence. "That man. He was about to . . . he was going to . . . he wanted to—"

"Shh," he interrupted, consoling her, his breath tight, his rigid control nearly gone. "It's over. Because of you. He didn't do more than scare the living bejeezus out of me. You saved my sorry butt, Nellie."

She released her tight hold on him and sat back on her heels, her expression shy. "I did, didn't I?"

"You damn sure did."

"*You* were scared?"

"I was," he admitted.

Her mouth curved into a smile. She leaned forward and placed a kiss on his fevered brow. An errant strand of hair brushed his temple. She slid her cool flushed cheek against his heated one. When she lifted her head, he noted an endearing smudge of dirt on the tip of her nose and purple-dark circles beneath her eyes. Didn't look like either of them had gotten much sleep last night.

He tried lifting his hands to caress her sweet face, momentarily forgetting that they were tied down, but finally he gave up and they dropped futilely to his sides.

"Can you cut me loose?"

"Oh, what was I thinking?" she muttered. With trembling fingers, she struggled against the tightened strips of leather, mumbling about the blood, the gashes, and his overall pitiful condition.

After what seemed an eternity, he was free of the hellish bonds. He tried to sit up and fell back to the ground. His arms wobbled like the gawky legs of a newborn calf. His head spun, and his vision darkened. What was left of his strength collapsed. And with it, his will to stay awake.

"Clay?" Nora-Leigh whispered, concern etching her voice. As if it came from a far distance, Nora-Leigh's troubled voice beckoned him, but he couldn't reply.

She placed one of his hands in hers and clutched it to her chest. The bold beat of her heart calmed his fears, steadying his spirit. Her tender touch soothed his soul, but nothing short of a miracle could keep him conscious.

Slowly he slid into dark welcome oblivion.

Clay had swooned. No, that was wrong. Women swooned. Men fainted. It didn't really matter, thought Nora-Leigh, shaking her head. Her mind simply couldn't grasp her profoundly strange situation or the events of the last fifteen minutes.

Still, it was no wonder Clay had fainted. He looked terrible. Black and blue bruises marred the skin over his ribs. A purplish marble-sized lump marred his sunburned forehead. His face was as hot as the oven after a long day of baking. Waves of heat rose from his flesh. Nora-Leigh sat back on her heels and stared at Clay, then turned to look at Terrell, then over her shoulder at Nat. The man appeared dead.

Though unconscious for the time being, Terrell still presented a threat to her. She checked his pulse. It beat as steady as the ticking of a clock, and although he bore a good-sized goose egg on his head, it didn't look as if she'd broken his skull. She couldn't decide if that was good or bad.

She tied his ankles together with the leather strips she'd cut from Clay. Grabbing both his ankles and huffing like a steam engine, she dragged his inert body to the nearby mulberry tree. She propped him into a sitting position, then tied him to the trunk. For good measure, she secured a bandanna around his mouth so she wouldn't have to listen to him when he came to. She had a feeling he would be expressing his displeasure about her ill treatment of him in no uncertain terms.

She brought Ginger and Stubborn across the river, but only with Ginger's help was she able to coerce the mule to climb the bank. She took what she needed from the animal's pack and left them to munch on the endlessly abundant supply of prairie grass. Then, her steps hesitant, she walked to where Clay lay and squatted beside him.

He needed to be moved from the sun, but more than that, he needed water. She dribbled it from her canteen and soaked a handkerchief. She lay the square on his heated forehead, then untied his neckerchief from around his throat and soaked it, too.

Prying his jaw open, she squeezed water into his mouth, trying to coax him to swallow. When it trickled down his chin, she placed her other hand to his throat and stroked it as she dribbled water into his mouth. This time he swallowed. She repeated the procedure several times more until the neckerchief held no water.

Nora-Leigh lowered Clay's head into her lap and stared at his sunburned face, shiny with perspiration and fever. She wiped his face with the damp cloth and prayed, willing him to be all right.

Finally his eyes twitched, then opened. He stared at her with a bemused expression; then his mouth curved into a smile of recognition. "I've died, haven't I? And you must be an angel, an angel of mercy," he whispered. "Where are your wings, honey?"

Nora-Leigh knew for sure that Clay was not well. He'd called her a bushel basket full of names, but never once had he called her an angel.

"You haven't died," Nora-Leigh stated, not sure what else to say. She wasn't even certain if Clay recognized her, or if he thought she really was an angel. Either way, she needed to move him. "Can you get up?" she asked. "We need to get you out of the sun."

She didn't think she could lift him. Terrell had been a struggle for her to drag, and Clay was much taller and more muscular. She needed him to be marginally awake so he could help her move him.

His unfocused eyes, glazed with fever, traveled over her face and settled on her mouth. His cracked lips turned up in a feeble attempt at a flirtatious grin. "You sure are pretty."

Pretty? Did he say pretty? She stared at him, for the moment tongue-tied, then found her voice. "Why, thank you, Mr. Sullivan." The fact that it was such a nice compliment at such an improper time made her oddly happy. She bit her lip to keep from grinning. In his confused state, Clay Sullivan was attempting to flirt with her! She only wished he meant it. All she'd gotten from this man were sarcastic kisses and delirious compliments.

"Your eyes are pretty," he continued. "So are your ears. They're like teeny-tiny little shells, all soft and pink and sorta pearl-colored. Pearls form in oysters in the ocean. Bet you didn't know that." He grinned at her, goggle-eyed—or was that just an addled expression?

Rambling and nearly incoherent, Nora-Leigh scarcely recognized Clay. She hadn't known he had a soft, vulnerable side. She could grow used to the lovely compliments, though. Still, the man was babbling like a lovesick schoolboy. Nora-Leigh wished she had pen and paper. She'd relish relating to him what he said in his delirium. She couldn't resist grinning back at him.

"And you have nice breasts, too."

Nora-Leigh almost choked. "Thank you," she murmured. "I think."

He tipped his head and gave her a lopsided, idiotic grin. Nora-Leigh shook her head. "Can you walk?"

"I've been walking all my life," he stated, sounding deeply offended.

"Yes, I know you can walk, but can you walk right now? We need to get you out of the sun."

"Where we going?"

Nora-Leigh rolled her eyes. She put her arm around his shoulder and helped him to a sitting position. He sat up and seemed steady, so she helped him to stand. She kept her arm around his bare waist as his feet fought for purchase. His legs wavered a moment; then he caught his balance. He looked around in surprise, then down at his bare feet. "Where are we? Where are my boots? Where's Jolly?"

"We'll find them later," she promised. "First we need to get you out of the sun."

He touched his bare chest, then tore his hand away, his eyes wide. "My shirt's gone missing."

"I know, Clay. I'll find it, but first we're going to lie down."

"All right." Like a lamb following its mama, he walked with her to a shaded spot near the river. He stood still and avidly watched her as she laid out her bedroll beneath the low-hanging branches of a cottonwood tree.

She helped him lie down, then pulled the blanket to his chest, tucking it beneath his arms. He sighed and closed his eyes.

When she had him comfortably settled, she sat back on her heels. He looked up at her and smiled. His eyes were soft, silvery, and glazed with fever. "Are you going to lie down here with me?"

"Uh, no," she stammered. "I don't believe that would be a good idea."

"Then come here, pretty lady," he said in a whispery voice. She couldn't resist his plea. She placed her hands on his chest and looked down into his sparkling eyes.

He lifted his head and brushed a soft kiss across her

lips. "Thank you," he croaked. His head dropped back against the blankets as his eyes rolled back in his head; he was unconscious once again.

"You're welcome, Clay," she said. She stroked his heated cheek, then placed the wet kerchief again over his forehead. Reluctantly she stood up and left him to get some needed sleep.

With hesitant steps she walked over to where Nat lay motionless on the ground. She leaned over him and stared at his wan face. She'd never seen a dead man before. He merely looked like he'd fallen asleep. His relaxed features still appeared vibrantly alive.

Oddly enough, she saw no sign of blood. She was certain she'd seen Terrell's rifle pointed at his chest. She'd heard the gun discharge and seen Nat fall. Squatting beside him, she placed an ear to his chest. A steady thump-thump-thump greeted her ear. Tears blinded her eyes. Thank God, he wasn't dead! But where had he been shot?

She glanced at his legs, his arms, his head. No blood anywhere. She undid the buttons on his shirt, feeling along his narrow chest and ribs. Moving down his stained, buckskin leggings, she passed her fingers hesitantly along his flanks and thighs. Her fingers wavered over his breechclout, but she refused to examine what lay beneath. If he was shot *there*, she wouldn't know what to do anyway, she told herself, her face heating with embarrassment.

She moved past his skinny calves and was at the top of his moccasins when he moaned.

Nora-Leigh reeled back in astonishment. She stared at his bearded face, no longer wan and pale but flushed a bright dusky pink.

His eyes fluttered, then opened, and he gave her an impish grin. "Whoo-ee!"

"What?"

"Do you know how many years it's been since I've felt

a woman's hands on my body, missy?" he asked, his voice full of laughter. He sat up, shaking his head.

"N-no," Nora-Leigh stammered, embarrassed by his admission.

"A very long time. So long, in fact, that when your hands touched me I hardly recognized what my body was trying to say."

"What do you mean?"

His jaw dropped, then he snapped it shut and puzzled Nora-Leigh with an incredulous grin. "You don't know what I . . . You haven't . . . ? That is, you and Sullivan ain't . . . ?" His voice fell away in a deep chuckle. "I'll be hornswoggled! I reckon you ain't."

"Mr. Arbogast, what in heaven's name are you talking about?"

"It's Nat, missy," he reminded her. "I'm just blabbering away like a damned fool. Musta hit my noggin when I fell. Pay me no never mind." He rubbed his forehead. "How is Sullivan doing?"

"I think he's really sick, maybe with the sun, maybe with something else. I don't know for sure, but he's sleeping now."

"I reckon that's all he needs, a good night's sleep. And that fella what tied him up? The last thing I recall is him shootin' at me. What happened to him?"

"I hit him over the head with a shovel."

Nat's bushy brows rose nearly to his hairline and his eyes widened. "You don't say. I knew you had savvy."

Nora-Leigh cocked her head to the side. "I hope I didn't injure him permanently."

"I'd say it's too durn bad if you didn't," Nat muttered. "The worthless buzzard was askin' to be put to bed with a pick and shovel! Where's he now? He didn't get away, did he?"

Nora-Leigh motioned to the tree where she had tied the unconscious Terrell. His head lolled on his chest.

Nat turned around to look, then whooped with delight and slapped Nora-Leigh on the shoulder, nearly knocking her over. "You're a game one, you are."

"I take it that's a good thing."

"Damned right."

"But how are you?" Nora-Leigh asked. "Are you all right?"

With his hand curled into a fist, he pounded his chest. His eyes crinkled with mirth. "Never better."

"You scared me to death."

"Scared myself," he admitted with a sheepish grin.

"I thought you were shot."

"I was, missy. He hit me dead center." He drew aside his shirt and reached beneath the placket of his long johns. Around his neck, tied on a leather thong, he wore a small pouch decorated with beads and feathers. "My medicine bundle," he said, pulling it out from beneath his shirt to show her.

"Medicine bundle?"

He sat up, then pulled the bag from his neck and handed it to her. "I heard tell that a Sioux warrior's most prized possession is his medicine bundle. He puts in religious herbs, talismans and sech, dream-vision objects that he considers sacred. He brings it out on the eve of a big battle for the battle ceremony to help ward off harm."

Nora-Leigh turned the bag over and over in her hands. There was a tear in it, but otherwise it was in good condition. Stitched from the hide of some dark-skinned animal, it was beautifully made, sewn with colorful beadwork and painted quills. "What's this skin you used?"

"Beaver. I used to trap beaver in my younger days."

"Oh?"

"Yep. Long time ago."

"You'll have to tell me about it sometime."

"Sure will, missy. Anyway, back to the medicine bundle. An Indian's life is guided by his medicine. For some tribes it's a warrior's shield or a weapon, maybe a religious headpiece or some other object they consider sacred. Don't matter much. All things go back to his medicine. It's not medicine like you and me know about, though. Medicaments and sech. More like religious things that an Indian values."

"I see. So you put objects in the pouch that you consider important to you, not necessarily what an Indian might put in his."

" 'Xactly so. Pour it out in your hand and take a gander at what I've collected over the years."

Nora-Leigh untied the string and tipped the bag into her palm. Out fell a bird's claw and a jagged animal tooth, a tiny blue feather the color of the Montana sky, two acorns, a smooth brown buckeye, a small piece of metal about the size of a silver dollar, and another sack.

"What's in the smaller pouch?"

"Herbs for healing and sech. From Blue Buffalo I learned how to make a tea for a sore throat or to lower a fever, and how to make a poultice."

"We might need those for Mr. Sullivan."

"I'd be obliged to help."

"Thank you." She held up the rounded piece of metal. "And what's this?"

He plucked it off her hand and held it up to his eye. "This, my darling girl, is what saved my life. It used to be flat as a flapjack."

The disc did indeed have an indentation on it, and a flattened bullet was embedded in its center.

"It's off a Newhouse beaver trap. This part," he said, pointing to the disc he held in his hand, "is what the beaver stepped on, snapping the jaws shut on him and locking him in the trap. To remind me of my trappin' days, I saved this piece from one that rusted out and broke on me."

Nora-Leigh stared in awe. "My goodness."

"That goldarned little hunk of steel done saved my life today. And this?" He pointed to the flattened rifle bullet. "This didn't kill me because of it."

Nora-Leigh smiled. "I believe God was looking after you, Nat."

"Reckon so, missy. He was lookin' after all of us today, lessen I miss my guess," Nat answered, his eyes misty. He dashed away the unshed tears with the back of his hand and spat on the ground. "Even that egg-suckin' varmint what tried to kill Sullivan."

"I believe you're right," Nora-Leigh said, nodding in agreement. She glanced over at Clay, huddled on his side facing away from her. Through the branches of the cottonwood the sun cast irregular shadows over his bare back. She could see that he'd kicked off his blanket. "I'll have to remember to say an extra special thank you in my prayers tonight."

"Reckon I will, too." Nat stood up and brushed off the seat of his pants, then offered Nora-Leigh a hand up. He reached beneath his long yellow beard and rubbed his hand against his chest. "I'm a mite sore. Gonna have me a colorful bruise. Still, I reckon it's a damn sight better than having a hole in my chest, and a permanent home in heaven."

Nora-Leigh nodded in agreement, giving him a tired smile. "I would have to agree with you there. It's been quite the busy day."

He shot her a conspiratorial wink. "An adventure."

Despite her fatigue and the overwhelming events of the day, Nora-Leigh laughed outright. "Yes, Nat. An adventure."

Chapter Thirteen

Clay woke slowly, light-headed, and muddle-brained. With a groan he rolled over onto his back and blinked open his eyes. In the night sky, the moon and stars sparkled above him. He smelled the enticing aroma of hot coffee and fried bacon.

His stomach growled. He swallowed hard, then winced. His throat felt like raw meat. The inside of his dry mouth tasted like buffalo chips. His ribs ached like a bull had kicked him. But he was most definitely alive.

And alive had never felt so good.

As he sat up, a scratchy wool blanket fell from his bare chest. It wasn't his, and it smelled like Nora-Leigh's damnable flowery soap. In irritation, he pushed the fabric aside. He stretched his arms above his head and wiggled his chilled bare toes. No longer tied up, he sighed, relishing the freedom of movement.

The last thing he remembered was Nora-Leigh crawling toward Terrell with a shovel in one hand, a knife in the other, and a determined look in her stubborn hazel eyes.

What had happened after that?

He rubbed his naked chest as gooseflesh broke out on his skin. Even in springtime, Montana nights could freeze a man to the bone. Where the hell were his shirt and boots?

His eyes watered as a wave of dizziness crept over him. He squeezed them shut, then opened them and tried to adjust his vision to the darkness. A campfire burned not ten feet away, and the sound of whispering voices echoed in his ears.

"Hey," he called out, surprised by the rasp of his voice. He sounded like a bull moose in mating season. He plucked the blanket from the ground and pulled it around his shoulders. Struggling to his feet, he padded toward the comforting glow of the campfire and the sound of human voices.

He recognized Nora-Leigh as she jumped to her feet and scurried toward him. A smile played about her lips. "Mr. Sullivan," she admonished. "You shouldn't be up and about."

He waved her off. "Dammit, Nellie," he bellowed. Sorry that he'd raised his voice, irritating his sore-enough-already throat, he lowered it to a stifled rumble. "Quit calling me Mr. Sullivan."

She came to an abrupt halt several feet away. Her smile diminished, and surprise wreathed her face. "You shouldn't be up," she repeated. She extended her hand. "Are you still feverish?"

"Leave me be," he grumbled. He batted her hand away from his face, then stumbled back and stepped hard on a jagged rock. He uttered an obscenity, which brought a startled gasp to Nora-Leigh's lips. "And for gosh sakes, stop treating me like one of your damn students," he rasped through gritted teeth. "I'm hungry, cold, and my damned throat hurts like hell."

"Yer damned cranky, too," Nat added. "Where's your eye patch, pirate?"

Clay glanced over at him.

"And what happened to your soup strainer?" The old trapper tipped his battered hat and grinned.

Clay scowled at him. "You, too?"

His bushy white brows rose in surprise. "What do you mean, 'you, too'?"

Clay limped over to the fire and sat down. He rubbed his sore toe, then held his hands over the low flames. He glared at Nat. "I mean, what are you doing here, and do I have to take mollycoddling from you, too?"

Nat grinned, then handed him a canteen. "He recovers fast, don't he?"

"I noticed," Nora-Leigh answered as she returned and sat down on the opposite side of the campfire from Clay. She glanced at him, her gaze shuttered, her expression wary. The shadows cast by the blaze and the sweep of her lashes obscured her eyes.

For some reason, it irritated him that he couldn't read her expression. He glared at her over the rim of the canteen as he chugged its contents, then wiped the back of his hand across his mouth. "Stop looking at me as if I've grown horns."

"I wasn't." Her voice sounded thin and tired. Concerned, Clay studied her. A gray cast had colored her face, and there was a tightness around her mouth. Her shoulders slumped, and her usually protruding chin drooped almost to her chest. Damn. Why did he always speak without thinking? Feeling contrite, he glanced away.

"Sullivan, if'n I were you, I'd step lightly around our Nora-Leigh," Nat warned.

"I don't need advice from an old shoe like you." Clay turned back toward the young woman. He waited until she looked up and then gave her an appraising glance. "What's wrong with you?"

In a characteristic gesture, her stubborn chin thrust forward. "Nothing."

He gave her a you-don't-expect-me-to-believe-that look, then waited patiently for her reply.

"Nothing," she repeated with an elaborate wave of her hand. "Honestly."

"You look like hell."

"Thank you, Mr. Sullivan," she said in a huff. "So do you."

"I have a legitimate excuse. I was kinda tied up for a while," he said, hoping to get a grin out of her.

If she gave any indication that she thought he was funny, it was in a slight twitch of her mouth. That was all.

Clay glanced at Nat, who shrugged his shoulders. "You're on your own."

"Thanks," Clay snapped. To Nora, he said, "You look like you're the one who needs rest. Go to bed."

She shook her head, then studied his face. "You might need something."

Clay groaned. Why was she always trying to help him? After all he'd done? "Dammit, Nellie, I can take care of myself. Now go." He waved her off, but she sat still, her gaze unsure.

"Arbogast can catch me up on what's been happening." Clay glanced around the camp looking for the horses. "By the way, has anyone seen Jolly?"

"Like he'd been out for a stroll, he wandered into camp just before dusk," Nora-Leigh said. She pointed to a spot beyond the circle of light. "He's with Ginger and that confounded male, er, I mean mule."

She yawned, then covered her mouth with the back of her hand. "I guess I will turn in."

"Good," Clay and Nat said simultaneously. Clay turned

to the other man, who returned his glance with a good-natured smile.

"Pull your bedroll closer to the fire so you'll stay warm," Clay said.

"Now who's moddlycoddling whom?" she asked. Her chin lifted a notch more. He caught her glance at his bare chest, barely covered by the blanket; she quickly glanced away. She leaned behind her and picked up his shirt and boots where they'd been hidden from his view in the shadowy brush. She handed them over. "You might want these."

Clay took them from her proffered hand. "Thanks. Now, scoot." As he shrugged into his shirt, he watched her. She stood up, her movements slow and stiff. With shuffling feet and head bent low, she left the camp. When she returned with her blankets, she silently arranged them by the fire and lay down. Within minutes he heard her steady breathing. Clay released a ragged breath he hardly realized he'd been holding.

"Plumb tuckered out," Nat said softly.

Clay pulled on his boots. "Long day."

"Reckon so," Nat agreed.

"Tell me, Arbogast, what happened to Terrell?"

"That's the varmint's name?"

Clay nodded.

Nat pointed behind Clay. "Look yonder for yourself."

Clay glanced over his shoulder. Terrell sat on the ground tied to a tree, far enough from the fire to be cold, but close enough for Clay to recognize. With his back to the tree and his arms tied to his body, he fisted his hands tightly at his sides. His bright blue eyes were open and filled with overwhelming anger. His mouth was covered with a neckerchief. Otherwise, Clay had a feeling the bastard would be turning the air blue. He turned back to Nat.

"How did you—"

Nat interrupted. "It was Miss Nora-Leigh, that's who."

"What?" Clay wasn't sure he believed it. "She brought down Terrell? By herself?"

"Yep. She conked him on the head and knocked him out cold. Then had enough wits about her to drag him to the nearest tree and tie him to it."

"That little bit of calico dragged him there by herself?" Clay remarked, flabbergasted. "Where the hell were you?"

Nat shot him a wounded glare. "By damn, I'd a done something if I were conscious, but Terrell shot me. I was laid out cold for a time. Don't you recollect nothing?"

Clay shook his head. "Not much. I must have been half out of my head. At one point I remember thinking I was dying. That was when I was staked out in the sun baking like a coiled rattlesnake. After that, things are fuzzy. I vaguely recall Nora-Leigh coming after Terrell, but I didn't know if that was real or if I dreamt it."

"It were real, all right. That there woman would fight till hell freezes over—"

Clay interrupted. "And then skate with ya on the ice. Yeah, I've heard that expression."

With a slight reprimand in his voice, Nat said, "She took care of you, me, and that cantankerous thorn in the short ribs."

Clay shook his head in disbelief. "I just can't fancy that. Hell, a week ago she was teaching ABC's to a passel of snot-nosed brats."

"I reckon anyone who can corral kids could handle *us* with no problem whatsoever."

Clay bristled at the insult. "No woman 'handles' me."

"That right? Mighty proud of yerself, are ya?"

Clay frowned. "You mistake my meaning. I just meant that she can't—oh hell, I don't know what I meant."

"You just don't cotton to the idea of a woman taking care of you, 'stead of the other way around."

"I guess that's it."

"Well, she did, and did a right fine job of it, too. I'm

thinking she means more to you than you let on."

"I'm thinking you talk too much."

"Maybe so."

"All right, old-timer, give me the whole story."

"I can only tell ya what I know."

"I'll piece together the rest."

Nat shot a glance at their tied-up companion. "What's this Terrell character got against you anyways?"

"He claims I had him arrested while we were both at Fort Keogh." Clay turned to look at him. "I honest to God don't remember the incident, but the boy seems to think I owe him my life for the three months he spent in jail."

The young man in question—eyes narrowed in contempt, face pinched tight—snarled.

"I'd say you're right." Nat gave Clay a questioning glance. "Why didn't he just shoot you?"

"Because he's a yellow-bellied coward, that's why."

Terrell growled. The words, though indecipherable, left little of his feelings to the imagination.

"Guess he don't like being called a coward," Nat commented.

"Guess not," Clay agreed.

Turning their backs to their once-attacker, they stared into the fire in companionable silence.

Nat tossed a couple more sticks and one fat log onto the flames. Sparks shot up into the night sky and disappeared. "Whatcha aim to do with him?" he asked.

"Don't know," Clay answered in all honesty. "Any suggestions?"

"Oh, I got some all right. None that include seeing his sorry ass alive and kickin' come tomorrow, though."

"I oughta return him to Fort Keogh—or Fort Custer, since it's closer—but I haven't got the time or the inclination." He shook his head. "I doubt they'd take him anyway."

"Would the Army pay for his return?" Nat asked.

Clay shrugged his shoulders. "Except for taking off without leave, he's not wanted, far as I know."

"What would happen if you just let him go?"

Clay glanced at Terrell. The boy's eyes were closed and he appeared to have fallen into a light slumber. "With a little persistence, he might be persuaded to leave me be."

Nat's eyes twinkled. "It'd have to be purty damn good persuadin'."

Clay chuckled. "We'll work on him together."

"Sounds good."

"Not that he deserves any, but did he get supper?"

Nat harrumphed, then frowned. "I didn't want to, but your little missy harped about it so long I gave in."

"Sounds just like the little harridan."

"I wouldn't let him loose, so she fed him herself. They even chatted a bit. I kept a keen eye on him, but at that point he sounded purty calm."

"A woman's touch."

"Maybe *she* should do the persuadin'."

Clay grinned. He didn't like the idea of hurting anyone anyway. That was one of the reasons he'd be so happy to leave the Army. "Maybe so. Say, have you got more water? I feel like I could drink the river dry."

Nat tossed Clay his canteen. Clay screwed off the cap and slugged it down. "Can't seem to get enough. Did Terrell get all the grub, or is there any left?"

Nat reached beside the fire where a skillet lay upside down. He lifted it. On the ground beneath it was a tin pie plate, covered with a lacy white handkerchief embroidered with the initials NLD. Nat handed the plate and a fork with bent tines to Clay.

Clay didn't need to ask but he did so anyway. "This Nora-Leigh's doing?"

Nat nodded.

"Did she cook it?" Clay asked.

"Nah, I did."

"Good. She's a lousy cook, I hear."

"She insisted we fix up a plate for you. Filled it herself."

Clay lifted the lacy scrap of fabric and sniffed. "Smells great."

Shaking his head, Nat continued. "I done tried to tell her you wouldn't wake 'til morning, but she said if'n you did come to, she wanted you to have something to eat."

Clay dug in. "Still warm, too."

"She's thoughtful. I reckon she'd make someone a right fine wife."

Clay stopping forking food into his mouth long enough to glance up. Now, where had that comment come from? Seeming to ignore the frank gaze Clay gave him, Nat stoked the fire.

"Go ahead," Clay mumbled, crunching into a slice of bacon. "Far as I know, she's not spoken for."

The other man's head snapped up and he snorted derisively. "I wasn't talking 'bout fer myself. I was talkin' 'bout you. I'm too old fer a young gal like that."

"I've heard tell of men older than you marrying up with young wives," Clay said. "If you still get a stiff one every morning, I expect you could please a wife all right."

"Sullivan!" Nat said, and Clay was amused to see that he had shocked the older man. "I never took you for a man who couldn't pour piss out of a boot."

Clay stopped with a forkful of beans halfway to his mouth. "Shows what little you know about me. I just may be that stupid."

Nat's lip curled in disgust, and he spat in the dirt at his feet. "If you let her get away, you are."

Clay stopped eating long enough to take a good, hard

look at his adviser. The man returned his gaze with a withering glare.

"You might be right about Nora-Leigh. I don't rightly know. But for now I've got a job to do for the Army— an important job. I can't be thinking about marriage or courting a pretty woman or anything else. Just doing what I'm getting paid to do is keeping me as busy as a bath-house on Saturday night, and tangling with Terrell has put me way past my schedule."

"Still, I bet you can't stop thinking about her, can ya?"

"No, I can't," Clay admitted. "She drives me crazy."

"She sure do smell good."

"Don't I know it."

"And purty as a picture." Nat slapped his knee with his hat. "Whoo-ee!"

That did it. He could stand no more nonsense from this randy old man. Nora-Leigh, whether Clay wanted her or not, was better than such comments. And he didn't like anyone smelling her . . . aside from himself, of course. "She snores," he lied.

"Loud?"

"Yep, like a train."

Nat leaned forward as though he was going to give Clay a wanted piece of advice. "The secret is to keep 'em awake," he said with a twinkle in his eye. "I 'xpect you'd know forty-eleven ways how to go about that."

He did know. Just thinking about Nora-Leigh and what they could be doing together instead of sleeping had kept him awake half the night since they'd set out, but he wasn't about to discuss that with some old trapper he scarcely knew. "She's a nag and a shrew to boot."

"When you're kissin' her, she can't nag at ya."

"You don't need much encouragement, do you, old-timer?" Clay set aside his empty plate. He'd reached the end of his string. He couldn't take any of Nat's sugges-tions on how to handle a woman. And if he expected to get any sleep, he didn't need any more discussion on the subject. He opened his jaw and pretended to give a loud yawn.

"Arbogast, I've had a ton of friendly advice from you for one night. Aren't you tired?"

"Nah, I've got a lot more stored up in this ole body. I hardly ever get the chance to chaw with another human. I'm kinda enjoyin' myself."

"Well, you're barking up the wrong tree." Clay yawned for real this time, stretching his arms behind his back. "I'm dog tired."

Nat chortled. "Is that a joke? Barking? Dog tired?"

Clay couldn't hide a grin. "Not on purpose, it wasn't. Simply a man too tired to make head or tail of what he's saying."

"Ha! Another joke! Head or tail. You're a funny one, mister."

"Shut up, Arbogast, and let me get some sleep." *That is, if I can sleep after all we've talked about.*

He glanced across the fire at Nora-Leigh. *She saved my life.* He still had trouble wrapping his ego around the fact. If he wasn't careful, he'd find himself beholden to her, and that he couldn't afford to do. He had a schedule, a timetable, and a plan for his future. No woman was going to get in his way. Even one as foolishly brave and courageously stubborn as Nora-Leigh Dillon.

Without hesitation, his gaze drew back to where she slept. As she lay on her side, her face gleamed, beautiful and relaxed, in the glow from the campfire. She held her clasped hands beneath her head in an angelic pose. Her mouth open, she exhaled a softly feminine snore. Clay smiled. Apparently she snored all right, but in a completely sweet way.

He looked over at Nat. The old man had fallen asleep, too, his knees drawn up with his chin resting atop them. His scraggly beard came nearly to his ankles, and his white braids lay across his shoulders. Clay shook his head. The man's back was going to feel like five miles of bad road by morning.

He glanced once again at Nora-Leigh, and his good-humor disappeared. Her breath rhythmically rose and fell, pushing her breasts in an enticing manner against the worn flannel of her shirt. Just below her collarbone, one button was undone and he could make out a scrap of white lace. He couldn't help thinking about what lay beneath. She slept on, undisturbed by his lustful gaze.

Fervently hoping he'd be able to do the same when he lay his head down, Clay rose to his feet to cover her completely. As he did, he leaned down and caught a glimpse beneath the folds of her shirt. He sucked in his breath when she exhaled, exposing the pink curves of the tops of both breasts, full and ripe, and a tantalizing glimpse of the dark pink peaks his touch craved.

Clay's groin tightened. He jerked the blanket to her chin and lurched back. On stiff legs he walked away, feeling like a lecherous old man. He could have done just fine without seeing her breasts. But now, in all likelihood he would dream about the plump feel of them in the palms of his hands and the soft texture of them against his fingers. All night long.

Clay found his bedroll and started to spread it out across from Nora-Leigh, then thought better of it. If he were lying close—to be safe—with his back to her, at least he wouldn't see her.

He spread the blanket out alongside Nora-Leigh, being especially careful to keep any part of his heated body from touching her. He lay down, tossing and turning, his eyes on the starry sky but her image firmly entrenched in his mind.

A heavy weight enveloped Nora-Leigh and a soft movement of air tickled her nose. Drowsy, though not quite awake, she rubbed it, rolled over, and snuggled her back-side against the comforting warmth. A wisp of breath and a pair of lips nuzzled the back of her neck; then a long arm encased in soft buckskin wrapped around her waist. A brawny thigh fell over hers, effectively trapping her.

Clay?

Nora-Leigh's eyes flew open.

The scout's hand inched upward and slid easily beneath the thin fabric of her chemise. A wide, warm hand cupped the underside of her breast. It instantly pebbled against the feel of his callused touch. Nora-Leigh sucked in her breath at the intimate contact.

"Clay?" she whispered.

"Umm," came the sleepy reply.

She reached up to move his hand, but he rolled her sensitive nipple between his thumb and index finger, causing it to harden. She almost jumped out of her skin. *Oh. My. God.* Heat and unbearable pleasure like none other she'd ever experienced danced along Nora-Leigh's nerve endings. A delightful shiver radiated outward from where his hand performed a potent magic. Her heart hammered in her chest, and a strange tingling began at the juncture between her legs.

For just a heady moment, Clay fondled her breast again, then released it. His breathing resumed to a deep, sleepy rhythm. Nora-Leigh slipped his hand from inside her chemise and scooted away. She released a ragged breath, then swallowed. Her heart continued its erratic pattern. Slowly her body's response to his gentle, know-ing touch dissipated, leaving her empty and wanting. Not wanting to, she craved Clay's hands on her again. She squeezed her eyes shut, striving for a normal balance.

She sat up and pulled her blanket tight around her quiv-ering flesh. Even though it was a cool night, she knew she wasn't shaking from the cold night air. She hugged her knees and looked up at the wide sky, filled with twinkling stars and a silvery slice of moon. Slowly her heart calmed and her breathing resumed its normal pattern. The quivering ceased.

Her awareness heightened, the now familiar sounds of the woods resounded in the darkness around her: the chirping of a cricket, the lonely howl of a wolf, the wind in the branches of the trees overhead.

Then an unfamiliar deep rumble met her ears from across the dying embers of the fire. She looked up. Nat's snores rattled like the tracks beneath a fast-moving train. She'd never heard the like. He appeared to have toppled over and fallen asleep where he sat, his legs and arms flung out, his hat still clinging to his head. He was lucky he didn't fall face first into the fire.

Then she looked over at Clay. She bit her lip, her heart skittering. He lay facing away from her, his dark hair fluttering against the back of his neck in the evening breeze. She studied the broad expanse of his back, his firm, rounded backside encased in soft, supple buckskin. He had no idea the effect he had on her. If he did, he'd probably laugh. All the things he'd said, trying to make her uncomfortable . . . they had affected her so differently than he'd ever dreamed. She could never let him know.

This was her big adventure. Her one opportunity to see the country, to travel, to explore, to learn. She'd known that.

But when she'd left Steamboat Bend, she'd had no idea it would be to fall in love, to feel another's pain so much she hurt with it, to worry endlessly about him. To love him in spite of his faults.

And worse than the surprise of her emotions was that she'd fallen for a man who thought she was an aggravation, a clumsy, too-smart-for-her-grandfather's-britches schoolmarm. No, she'd done something stupid by falling for Clay. No man could ever fall in love with her, especially him—who the hell did she think she was kidding?

Terrell woke from a restless, uneasy sleep. The back of his head throbbed where he'd been clobbered with the shovel. Brought down by a woman, for the love of Pete! A scrapper of a woman, to be sure, but still just a woman. And one not much older than himself, by his reckoning.

He longed to be back at Fort Keogh. Surely jail would be better than what Sullivan had in mind for him. And perhaps he deserved it.

His stiff body complained as he arched his back and stretched his legs as much as he could, then blinked the sleepy grit from his eyes. Across the way, the woman slept. The two men squatted in front of the campfire, talking and warming their hands around steaming mugs. His stomach growled from the smell of frying bacon and brewing coffee.

Last night's supper was the best he'd had since before he joined the Army, just like his mama used to make. In the service, he'd been eating hardtack that could easily chip a tooth and drinking coffee thick enough to float a rock; honest-to-God food tasted heaven-sent. Right now, he thought dismally, his future was looking mighty dim.

The dawn sunshine wrapped the clearing in a radiant pink glow. Terrell glowered. It should have been overcast or raining.

"Well, looky yonder, Sullivan, our young miscreant is woke up."

Terrell glanced at his captors. Both of them were staring at him and grinning like jackasses. Under their scrutiny, he became increasingly uneasy.

"Must be time for a little gentle persuasion," Sullivan said.

"Must be," agreed the old man.

Persuasion?

They rose to their feet and started his way.

The short hair on the back of Terrell's neck stood up.

.

Chapter Fourteen

Persuasion. Coercion. Intimidation. Call it what you would. Throughout his life, Clay had witnessed men of all kinds struggling to control the actions of others. In the West, punishment often came quickly at the end of a rope, the eruption of gunfire, or the hurling of a war lance. And he had grown sick of such violence.

From what he'd seen, the United States Army was an accomplice in that violence. To discipline a soldier, they would fine a man a month's pay, or march him all day with an eighty-pound load strapped to his back. No wonder the men deserted at high rates. He didn't approve of Terrell's *misdirected* anger, but he understood it. The boy wasn't bright, and he had been maltreated for a long time.

A straightforward man, Clay disliked games. He prided himself on self-discipline and logical thinking, but lately his thoughts had been anything but clear. They were muddy and emotional. That had to change.

Right now he had two problems to sort through, and

neither seemed to have a reasonable answer.

Terrell was more trouble than he was worth. Clay wanted him removed from the situation, but he didn't want him dead. He was just a kid who needed to grow up. Guidance and discipline were what he lacked, not the kind of *persuasion* he figured Arbogast had in mind for him. He needed a new start, not an end.

Then there was Nora-Leigh. Simply put, the woman scared Clay to death. Most women did, simply because he didn't understand them. They pretended one thing and said another. They cried. Clay hated their games.

Still, Nora-Leigh was different. Special. She didn't play those games. She was as straightforward as he was, and maybe that was what scared him the most. She didn't need him. She didn't want him. She'd made it plain. She never planned on marrying. Hell, she didn't even like him. She could never lose her heart to a man like him. One who'd been alone so long he didn't even know how to go about courting a woman. After all, he reminded himself, he still had a job to do, and caring about anyone would only muck things up.

So why did it matter that she said she'd never marry? What the hell was wrong with him? He wasn't falling in love with her, for God's sake. He wasn't. So why couldn't he shake her from his thoughts?

Just last night he'd had a startlingly realistic dream about her; when he woke he was still haunted by the imagined texture and feel of her skin against his own.

He'd dreamed he wrapped his arms around her pliant body and she'd cuddled next to him, welcoming him, wanting him. He'd inhaled her scent and buried his nose in her neck. He'd found his way beneath her chemise. He'd clasped her breast, weighing a ripe handful in his palm, and caressed its smooth velvety underside. He'd fondled the firm flesh until it blossomed against his palm. As he'd rolled her nipple between his fingers, the satin skin responded to his deliberate touch and hardened . . .

He'd awakened with a start, aching, and rigid as a fence post. Nora-Leigh lay beside him, close enough to touch, but he didn't dare. She lay curled on her side, lightly snoring and completely unaware of how he ached for her. He'd taken one last lingering look, then left his warm bedding, his body stiff, sore, and wanting.

No, *persuasion* wasn't what he needed with Nora-Leigh. What he needed was distance—about a hundred miserable miles might do the trick. At least that might be far enough so he couldn't smell that *persuasive* lavender soap she wore. He'd convinced himself that she used it just to drive him crazy.

"Well, Sullivan, what you waitin' for?"

"Huh?"

"Sullivan." Nat snapped his fingers in front of Clay. "You with me?"

Jarred from his reverie, Clay shook his head. "Uh, yeah."

"We need to talk to the boy."

They walked to where Terrell sat and squatted down on either side of him. Nat warily untied the cloth from his mouth. "You're not gonna do nothin' stupid, now, are ya?"

Terrell worked his jaw and scowled at the two men. "What? With my mouth?"

Clay lifted a cup of water to his lips. The boy swallowed it in one gulp, so Clay gestured for more. With a growl, Nat snatched the cup from Clay and went to the river to refill it, leaving him and Terrell alone.

Clay waited until the old man was out of earshot before he asked, "It's Bill, isn't it?"

Terrell nodded, his expression hard and resentful.

"Did you get a court-martial, Bill?"

His face flushed with indignation. "I was found guilty

and sentenced to three months without pay. They stripped me of my rank, booted me to private."

"You served your time?"

A muscle in his jaw twitched angrily. "You know I did."

Clay rocked back on his heels, his hands spread wide. "What's your complaint with me, then?"

"You put me there."

"You put yourself there."

"I was just hungry," he said in a dull, whining voice.

"I'm sure you got the same rations every other soldier got."

"Yeah, hardtack for breakfast, hardtack for lunch, and hardtack for dinner. I didn't deserve jail time," he said, his voice rising, his blue eyes blazing. "Maybe a fine or some other kind of punishment, but not that awful damned cold cell."

"Keep your voice down," Clay warned. "Nora-Leigh's still sleeping."

"Aw, hell," Terrell muttered.

"And quit your kickin'. You sound like a sniveling snot-nosed kid, certainly not a soldier."

With Clay's harsh reprimand, the fight seemed to leave Terrell. His body sagged against his ropes and he hung his head on his chest. Looking up, he stared at Clay with a belligerent expression on his young face. But there was fear and a little bit of shame in his eyes.

"You're still young, Terrell, but it's high time you grew up." Clay sat down, legs drawn up, and draped his wrists over his knees. "What are you, eighteen, nineteen?"

"Seventeen last January."

"Damn." Clay blew out a slow breath. Shaking his head, he untied Terrell's bindings. He found himself surprised by the expertise of Nora-Leigh's knots. He reminded himself to say something to her about them later. "Nat offered to take you back to the custody of the Army.

219

Since Fort Custer is closer, you might as well return there. I'll send a note along explaining the circumstances. I know the commander, and he's a fair man. I don't know that it'll help—you're going to be in trouble for going AWOL—but what the hell. You'll have to be punished again. You know that, don't you? The Army won't just forget."

"I reckon," the boy said, his voice contrite. "But why are you letting me go? Why would you do this for me? I tried to kill you."

"But you didn't."

Confusion clouded Terrell's face. "You ain't the man I thought you were."

"No?" Clay asked. He gave the rope one last tug that freed the boy, then began winding it into a coil. "What kind of man did you think I was?"

"Well, damn, Sullivan." The kid wiggled his fingers, and stretched his arms out in front of him.

Clay saw him wince as his blood began circulating once more.

"When you were at the fort, you spent your time with them other scouts . . . and they're mostly Indians. When you were out scouting, they were the only ones you talked with, other than the officers."

"Yeah. I was doing my job."

"Okay, but around the fort the fellas called you an Indian-lover."

Clay shrugged his shoulders. "I got nothin' against the Indians. Most of them are darn good trackers, and they know every watering hole between here and the Rockies."

"I guess."

"Those same Indian scouts have saved many a soldier's sorry butt."

Terrell gave him a scared look. "They kill the whites."

Clay found himself wondering about the boy's past. What had made him so unhappy, so full of hate? "Not the scouts, Bill. They're just doing their job, same as me, same as you. And I reckon the Crow are in worse straits than even you, herded up on reservation land like they are. They must be feeling purely penned in."

Terrell waved his hand in an encompassing gesture. "We're on reservation land right now."

"Probably so."

"Still, I betcha if the Crow objected to you being here"—he glanced with admiration at Clay—"you could talk your way out of it."

"Maybe."

"No, I betcha you could," he insisted. He frowned, obviously confused by some emotional turmoil. "Even before, I didn't want to, but I respected you. Until you had me arrested."

"You respected me?" Clay exclaimed. "Is that why you tied me up and left me to bake in the sun? Because you respected me? You have a mighty strange way of showing it."

"I wanted to prove to myself that you weren't so tough as everybody said you was, that you didn't deserve any respect. I wanted to best you."

"You did."

"I nearly killed you," he said, his eyes wide with self-loathing. "I even shot an old man. Speaking of that, how the hell did I miss him?"

Clay grinned. "You didn't. You hit him square in the chest. He had a piece of steel in a pouch around his neck. You hit that."

"Lucky for me."

"Lucky for both of you, I'd say." Clay stood up and hauled Terrell to his feet. "Terrell, it's not what people say about you that makes you a man, it's what you do. Are you willing to act like a man and take your chances at Fort Custer?"

"I reckon I ain't got much choice."

"You always have a choice."

The boy paused, then he decided. "I'll go."

Clay felt relief wash over him. "Good. I'll write that note."

"Thank you." Terrell stuck out his hand.

Clay shook it, then stared at the boy. He grinned. "I doubt they'll hang you."

Terrell looked scared, but then a grim expression overcame his features. "I need to face up to what I done . . . but I don't want to die."

"Don't sleep on guard duty," Clay said. "They will hang you for that." Then he smiled and gave the kid a clap on the shoulder. Maybe Terrell would turn out all right in the end.

"Thanks for the warning."

Clay wrote the note while the prisoner ate breakfast and worked the stiffness from his bones. When Nat, who had seen their conversation and wisely stayed away, returned, Clay explained the situation to him. Clay even gave him some money for the journey, then warned him to keep an eye on his charge, though he doubted the boy had any spit left in him. The older trapper took his prisoner and set off at once, pausing only to say, "Tell that sweet girl o' yours where I went, and I hope I'll meet up with you again."

"You will," Clay said. After the pair had gone, he walked back to the fire and poured himself a cup of coffee, then sat down and leaned back against his saddle, several feet from where Nora-Leigh slept. He glanced over the rim of his mug and regarded her. Secretly glad that they were alone, he watched her without worry.

It was so nice to watch her sleep. That was the only time he didn't fret about her welfare. The rest of the time, he fretted. Night and day. Day and night. About her falling from her horse and breaking her neck, about her stumbling down a river embankment and drowning, about snakebites, about bear attacks. Oh, hell, he could fabricate scenarios in which she got hurt out of anything or nothing at all.

He needed to sort out his feelings about her. He'd spent endless hours in the saddle beside her; he'd eaten with her and slept next to her side. He'd witnessed countless acts of clumsiness. On the trail, he'd seen her at her best and he'd seen her at her worst. Still, he hadn't seen her as he truly wanted to: flat on her back beneath him, in all her naked glory, as he made love to her. Though it defied common sense, he could finally admit that to himself. He wanted her. It was high time he quit denying it.

He loved Nora-Leigh's spunk, her vitality, and her spit-fire stubbornness. If he weren't on a mission for the Army, he'd ask her to marry him right now. Of course, that mission would eventually end. And he wanted to settle down. But would the stubborn woman turn him down flat? He thought so. She claimed she didn't want to marry, and said she didn't like children. And she'd said she wasn't all that fond of him—not that he believed her.

He'd have to work on convincing her that she couldn't live without him. It wouldn't be hard. He'd seen the sparkle in her gaze when she glanced at him out of the corner of her dancing hazel eyes. She wanted him as badly as he wanted her; she was just doing her damnedest to deny it. As he had. The hell with it. When he found the gold, he'd ask her to marry him.

Standing, he was hit by a wave of dizziness. Disorientation still plagued him, and his sense of balance seemed a mite off, but he was free of chills and fever. He sat back down and looked at Nora-Leigh. For now, he would just sit and watch her sleep.

He also wondered where in the hell they were. He didn't have the faintest notion. Being unconscious and beaten had robbed him of his sense of direction. The great Army scout Clay Sullivan was undeniably lost.

*   *   *

"Clay?"

"I'm here."

His whispered reply came from close by, and she felt his breath brush her cheek. Nora-Leigh's eyes snapped open. He lay on his side, his arm resting on an elbow with his head in the palm of his hand.

"Are you all right?" she asked.

"Yep. You?" He smiled at her. It was a warm, enticing smile that meant . . . what? Clay Sullivan was asking about her welfare? That was a nice change.

Nora-Leigh tossed off her blanket and sat up. She blinked the sleep from her eyes and stared at him. Bleary, bloodshot eyes stared back at her. The scout needed a shave, and his hair stuck out from his head like quills on a porcupine. He'd never looked more irresistible to her. But that was his plan, wasn't it?

Clay was up to something, all right, and Nora-Leigh knew exactly what it was.

"You were trying to scare me again last night," she said. "Do you still want so badly for me to leave you?"

"Last night?" He frowned, rubbing the skin above his upper lip in contemplation as he'd done before he shaved his mustache. He looked truly confused. "What do you mean? I didn't do anything."

Nora-Leigh wasn't falling for his innocent act, but she'd play along for a while to see how far he'd take it. "You touched me—quite intimately, I might add."

"No, I didn't, I . . ." he trailed off, then gazed at her in confusion. Drawing his lip in thoughtfully, he looked at her for the longest time. "That really happened?"

"Really happened?" My goodness, he was a good actor. Well, she could act, too. In a voice that she hoped sounded nonchalant, and praying that she wouldn't blush, she asked, "Are you talking about fondling my breast? Because that was real, all right."

His grey eyes darkened and smoldered; then he spoke in a quietly reverent voice. "I thought it was all a dream."

He was good, all right, but Nora-Leigh was better. She had more practice. After all, she dealt with schoolchildren all day. They could be devious little monsters when so inclined. He was trying to play it all off as a dream, but she knew she could get the truth. She decided to initiate a few fancy maneuvers of her own. She reached across the scant space between them and ran her thumb along his beard-roughened cheek.

He jumped back as if a rattler had just crawled into his bedroll. A muscle twitched in his jaw. "What'd you do that for?"

"What do you think?" she replied in her best imitation of a seductive whisper. It came out much more unsteadily than she might have wished. Fiddlesticks. This wasn't going to work. Straightforward was her best bet. What was it Gramps always said?

Honey is dear bought if licked off thorns.

She was going to attempt to lick the honey from Clay's thorns. She placed her hands on his broad shoulders and looked him square in the eye. "Remember when you said to stay away from you?"

"Yeah. So?"

"I can't do it anymore."

He stared at her, obviously flabbergasted. The stare at last gave way to a quizzical frown, and she clasped her hands behind his neck. She would go for broke; she pulled him closer. His warm breath, redolent of fresh coffee, sped up and tickled the loose curls of her hair. His pupils dilated, darkening his eyes to discs of pewter. "What are you up to, Nellie?" he asked.

Her mind flickered with the image of what she was about to do, igniting her body like kindling. She gulped before she could answer. "I'm going to kiss you."

She meant to do so, but before she could he gave her a questioning look. "The hell you say. What for?"

"Why am I going to kiss you?"

He sat still as a stone. "Yeah."

"Because I want to."

"What if I don't want you to?"

But there was no denying the sizzling desire in his face. "You do," Nora-Leigh said.

"You're right," Clay answered, his voice a husky whisper that sent a shaft of pure delight through Nora-Leigh's heated blood. "I damn sure do."

Savoring the moment, she closed her eyes and breathed in his masculine scent. Beneath the sensitive tips of her fingers, she felt warmth under the soft fabric of his shirt, his muscles flexing and stretching. She listened to his rapid breath. She opened her eyes to find him smiling at her.

He lifted his hands to her waist and held her loosely. A flash of impatience sparkled in his shadowed eyes. "I'm no monk, Nellie," he whispered. "If you're gonna kiss me, please get on with it."

He slanted his head to align his mouth with hers, and his eyes drifted shut.

She lowered her mouth to his, his lips parted, and she kissed him. And what began as a sweetly innocent kiss on her part soon became his kiss—hot, wet, and overwhelming. His tongue swept inside her mouth to caress the underside of her lips with strokes of pure pleasure. He pulled her tongue deep into his mouth, and nipped it with his teeth.

A small moan of pleasure escaped her.

Without stopping, he pulled her forward, tight to his chest, until she was pressed next to him, their hearts beating rapidly against one another. With one quick movement he rolled her over and pressed her against the ground, his lips never leaving hers. Low and hard, his hips moved against hers, grinding in a circular motion.

Nora-Leigh felt no thorns, only tasted the honey of Clay's kiss and the heat of his body. In fact, she felt like honey inside—warm, gooey, sweet, heated. And just like when she tasted honey, she wanted more.

He lifted his lips from hers and took a deep breath. "God," he whispered. Leaning his forehead against hers, he drew in a deep breath and said in a voice thick with emotion, "Nellie, my returning of your kiss wasn't meant to scare you or teach you a lesson or drive you away."

"No?"

"No. Nor was it a thank-you for saving my life."

Why was he telling her this? Nora-Leigh's heart sank to her feet. Were these lies? Didn't he find her attractive or desirable? Was she like Billy Seth Torrence, in love with someone who only felt pity for her? He wasn't in love with her, not with Steamboat Bend's eccentric schoolmarm. He could never love her the way she loved him. This was just about what people expected from each other, not what they wanted. Or worse, was he just taking what he could where he could? Was this only about physical gratification?

Honey is dear bought if licked off thorns.

Gramps, Nora-Leigh thought miserably, *I'm finding that out the hard way—and it hurts deep down inside.* Dear bought? She had paid with her pride. She squeezed her eyes shut to hold back the tears building inside. To hide her agony, she joked with him. "No? That's not why you were kissing me?" Her voice cracked. She cleared her throat before she spoke again. "And here I thought *I* was kissing *you*."

He chuckled. "You started. I finished."

"We're finished?" she asked, her voice barely above a whisper. Somehow, that even seemed worse. She refused to cry like a prudish maiden.

His words made her heart beat crazily. "Not by a long shot."

Chapter Fifteen

Clay pinned Nora-Leigh to the ground with his hips. She moaned, but to his dismay, it wasn't a moan of pleasure. He held himself still, despite the overwhelming need to thrust his hips against hers, to place his hardness against her softness, his strength against her weakness. This was the oldest instinct known to man. Yet, obviously he wasn't operating on instinct alone. He sensed a change in Nora-Leigh. And though he didn't know if it was something he'd said or done, he couldn't continue. Not like this.

"Nellie?"

Was that a sob? He lifted his head. Nora-Leigh's eyes were closed, but fat tears clung to the lashes. His gut wrenched. His heart stopped. He felt like an uncaring, stupid ass. She was obviously a virgin, for God's sake. Had he just expected her to fall into spasms of erotic joy when he ground himself against her?

"Is something wrong?" Dumb question. Of course something was wrong.

"No."

"Did I hurt you?"

"No."

"Then what is it?"

A loud whoosh near Clay's ear brought him up short. His eyes flew open.

Calico Jack flew down out of the sky and with a flap of wings landed at Clay's elbow. The crow blinked his inky black eyes, then cawed loud enough to wake a man dead and buried.

Not having seen the bird before it screeched, Nora-Leigh let out a shriek. She dislodged Clay from atop her body by arching her back, and with arms outstretched pushed him away. He fell off her and onto his back, startling Jack, who cawed raucously again. His ears ringing from the resounding squawk, Clay batted at the damned bird. The crow seemed to glower, then flapped its wings, flew a few feet away, and landed on a rock. He gave Clay another earful before settling his ruffled feathers.

"Damn your feathered hide," Clay grumbled. He turned to Nora-Leigh. "Are you all right?"

"Yes."

"I seem to recall a rhyme from my childhood that sounds damn good right now."

"Oh?" She asked, sounding much more composed and sure of herself.

"Yeah. Four and twenty blackbirds baked in a pie."

"Calico Jack isn't a blackbird."

"Close enough. He's black and he's a bird. He might make a tasty pie."

"It would have to be one very big pie."

"Instead of twenty-four blackbirds, it would just be one large annoying crow."

Insulted, Jack screeched loudly and flapped his wings. Several iridescent feathers flew into the air; then the bird began preening himself, ignoring Clay and Nora-Leigh altogether.

"What is he doing?" Nora-Leigh asked. Tears still clung to her lashes, but the sudden appearance of the disagreeable bird seemed to have dispelled whatever had caused them.

"Believe it or not, this is Jack's way of talking. Who the hell knows what he's trying to say, though?" Clay rose to his feet, his hand near his gun, but he stayed in a crouched position near Nora-Leigh. He darted a glance around the periphery of the campsite. He saw movement and drew his gun. Beside a shoulder-high boulder stood Blue Buffalo.

An enigmatic smile lit the Indian's dark eyes. "Is this a bad time to come across your camp, Sullivan?"

Clay gave him an annoyed look, then said, "No." He stood and holstered his pistol.

"I did not think so." Blue Buffalo chuckled as he stepped into the clearing. "You should save your love play for the night, Sullivan, unless you wish to find a knife between your shoulder blades."

Clay snorted. "If you're planning something, I'm not too worried. You can't see six feet in front of your face."

Blue Buffalo nodded sagely, the feather in his hair bobbing. "And yet I got this close without you knowing."

Nora-Leigh, eyes round as saucers, tore her gaze from Calico Jack long enough to stare at Blue Buffalo. Seeing the kindly Indian, she gave him a smile. Clay, glad to see her returned to her former good spirits, heaved a sigh of relief. He was almost grateful for Blue Buffalo's untimely—or had it been timely?—interruption.

"Come on over and have a cup of coffee." Clay gestured to the pot nestled in the coals of the morning cook-fire. "Still hot."

Blue Buffalo ambled over and sat down next to Clay, accepting a cup. He stared into it. "Sugar?" he asked.

"Not this trip," Clay answered.

"Too bad." He looked up with a sincere expression of dismay. "I like sugar."

"Sorry we can't be more obliging," Clay retorted. "Next chance I'll be sure to buy some." He turned to Nora-Leigh, who had been avidly listening to their exchange. "How about you? Coffee?"

"No. Thank you anyway," she answered in a formal tone of voice. She stood up, dusting off the seat of her trousers, and glanced around the camp. Her eyes settled on her satchel. When she spotted it, she grabbed it off the ground and started toward the river. "I believe I'll wash up and . . . well, you know."

Clay did know. He tried to hide his grin but not very hard. She hated him knowing that she had normal body functions. He guessed he'd been too long among the company of men to be worried about such things. He'd spent most of his time in places just like this. And soldiers didn't worry about relieving themselves in front of each other. "Don't wander off," he said watching her delectable retreating backside.

She glanced over her shoulder. "I'll try not to, Mr. Sullivan," she said, glaring at him. He smiled back.

"Clay," he hollered. Hell, when was that stubborn woman going to start calling him by his given name?

"Twit," came her answering reply.

Clay laughed.

At his reaction, Blue Buffalo, who had been watching Nora-Leigh, turned back to Clay. "What did she call you?"

"A twit," Clay said, still chuckling.

"What is this twit? A bird?"

"Uh, no." Clay chuckled. "A twit is a . . . well, it's an

insult. Not the same as a coward or a bully, more like an obnoxious child."

"She called you a child?" Blue Buffalo sounded affronted.

"Not exactly. It's kinda hard to explain. I can't think of a Crow word that means the same thing. Maybe someone who does something foolish."

"A fool?"

"Yeah, that pretty much covers it."

"You and she were acting like fools when I came across your camp. It is dangerous to be unaware of who approaches your camp."

Clay nodded, remembering. "I lost my head."

Blue Buffalo nodded. "A woman can make a man act the fool."

"Don't I know it."

"She is a beautiful woman. It is understandable."

Somewhat irritated about what seemed to be everyone's considerable notice of Nora-Leigh, Clay said, "I believe you said that the last time we crossed paths."

"Yes. And you are beginning to believe me. You have changed."

"How so?"

"Before today, I do not believe you truly cared for her. Now you do."

"I cared what happened to her," Clay answered in his own defense, sounding a little cranky even to his own ears. "But she's like a sliver under my skin. One I can't remove. She just keeps working herself deeper and deeper."

Blue Buffalo nodded. "Maybe you don't want to remove her."

"Maybe not."

Clay reached for the coffee pot, shook it to ascertain the contents, and refilled his cup. He gestured to Blue Buffalo, but the Indian declined more.

"Not good without sugar."

"Not as good," Clay agreed. "So, old man, what brings you out of the hills and onto the reservation?"

He shot Clay a look of surprise. "Are we on the reservation? I did not know."

"The hell you didn't. You always know exactly where you are." Clay leaned in closer and whispered, "Though I don't. Where are we?"

"Hmmmm. Sullivan, the great white scout for the Army soldiers." Blue Buffalo gaped at Clay in mock astonishment; then his bronzed, lined face broke into a wicked grin. "He really does not know?"

"I've been sick," Clay groused. A flush of humiliation stole up his neck, infusing his face with heat.

"That is why you know not where you are?"

"That's what I'm saying. Now, can you help me out here or not?"

"I do not know."

"What? You don't know where we are, or you don't know if you can tell me?"

"Both."

"I'll give you this much, you stubborn old coot, you'll never be confused with one of the *friendly* Crow Indians."

Blue Buffalo sat back on his heels and snickered.

"And you have an awful sense of humor."

Blue Buffalo snorted with laughter.

Both men glanced up as they heard Nora-Leigh approach. She walked back into their field of vision with her satchel under one arm, and waved with the other. She'd washed her honey-blond hair; it was slick and smooth as an otter's fur, wet and darkened to the shade of molasses. Clay's fingers itched to touch the glistening mass. She'd combed it straight back off her scrubbed pink, smiling face. A towel was slung casually over one shoulder, and she moved into camp unaware of the enticing swing of her hips or the temptation of her leggy limbs. Beneath the thin flannel of her worn shirt, her high-perched breasts swayed ever so slightly. Clay drew in a sharp breath, then let it out slowly.

"She is a beautiful woman," Blue Buffalo reiterated. He shook his head. "It is too bad she has eyes only for you—a man who doesn't know where he is or where he's going."

"Shh," Clay warned, scowling. "I don't want Nora-Leigh to know any of that."

"I do not blame you," Blue Buffalo whispered conspiratorially. "I would not want my woman to know my shame and disgrace."

"Shame? Disgrace? What are you talking about, Blue Buffalo?"

"As you are now, you are useless in guiding her. Maybe *I* should be her guide."

"Dammit, Blue Buffalo," Clay complained in a stifled whisper. "I'm not useless. Just lost."

"If you say so." Still, the grin remained firmly planted on his knowing, humor-filled face.

Nora-Leigh entered the clearing. "I feel much better."

And you look good enough to eat, thought Clay. However, he refrained from saying so.

"Blue Buffalo was just telling me we're definitely on the Crow reservation," Clay said, and then, fishing for more information, he continued, "on the banks of the Little Bighorn, didn't you say?"

Blue Buffalo didn't say. His eyes followed Clay intently as Clay stood up and crossed to the opposite side of the campfire away from the beguiling fragrance of Nora-Leigh's lavender-scented soap. The Indian's lips twitched, giving away his amusement.

Clay paced, hoping against hope to dispel the turmoil spinning inside his gut. Whether the agitation was caused by his close proximity to Nora-Leigh or his continued bewilderment about being lost, he couldn't say. Either way, his anxiety was beginning to affect him. He couldn't sit still.

"Is that so? The reservation?" Nora-Leigh plopped down beside Blue Buffalo and crossed her legs. She grabbed the towel from her shoulder, then shook her hair forward and began drying it, her head bent. "So what does that mean exactly?" she asked, her words muffled beneath the damp cloth.

"Nothing," barked Clay.

Nora-Leigh's head bobbed up beneath the frayed end of the towel in surprise.

He stopped his pacing and threw up his arms. "What I meant," Clay said, retreating like a fool who had spoken without thinking, "was that we're not in any danger. The Crows are generally friendly toward the whites."

"Generally speaking, that is so," Blue Buffalo added. His eyes crinkled. Clay suspected the old warrior was getting way too much fun out of this conversation. "Yet you never know when they might become hostile. That is the right word, is it not, Sullivan?"

"Hostile. Interesting choice, but, yeah, that'll do." He turned to Nora-Leigh, who looked a mite edgy. "Don't worry. They won't."

"They do not like life on the reservation."

"And you don't either," Nora-Leigh said. She finished towel-drying her hair, then draped her towel across a clump of sagebrush and dug into her satchel for a comb. When she pulled it out, she began dragging it through her hair, head cocked, her gaze on Blue Buffalo.

Mesmerized by the wholly feminine way Nora-Leigh's small hands moved through her hair, Clay watched with avid fascination. She didn't notice, though, her concentration focused on Blue Buffalo. She seemed enchanted by his clothes, his stoic, though at times humor-filled, demeanor, even the cadence of his voice as he slowly picked and chose his English words.

Their exchange gave Clay the opportunity to study her without her awareness. He knew he acted like a nonsensical fool where she was concerned, but he didn't care. He simply wanted to look at her, to memorize every detail of her demeanor, to remember them all and relate them to his grandchildren when the time came. And the time would come. They would have children together. Many of them. And they would have ample—sultry and satisfying—opportunities to conceive those children.

That is, if he ever found that confounded missing gold shipment. No, he amended. *When* he found that confounded missing gold shipment. That reward was what he was basing his future on.

Clay stopped pacing. "Nora-Leigh."

She glanced at him, her head tilted, the comb in her hand held motionless.

"It's past time to pack up and head out."

At her words, she tossed her comb and towel into her satchel and picked up the coffeepot. Then she tossed the dregs into the fire, which had burned down to a mere pile of ash. It hissed and crackled.

Blue Buffalo rose to his feet. He politely handed Nora-Leigh his coffee cup. "I am pleased to have looked upon your face today."

Realizing he was gaping at Blue Buffalo with his mouth as wide as a pickle barrel, Clay snapped his jaw shut. The old Crow knew and used the English language well, though he often liked to hide the fact. He knew full well what he was saying to Nora-Leigh, and he had said it to get under Clay's skin.

"Why, thank you," she said, blushing prettily. Her hair had begun to dry, and dark blond curls danced around her face. Color rose high along the ridge of her cheekbones as she gifted him with one of her contagious smiles.

The old warrior smiled back. Was he actually flirting with her? No doubt about it, thought Clay as Blue Buffalo plucked an eagle feather from his headband and handed it to Nora-Leigh.

"For you, for good luck," the Indian said solemnly. With a nod in Clay's direction, he added, "You will need it."

Nora-Leigh grasped the feather in both hands, staring at it in wonder. She glanced over at Clay, then back to Blue Buffalo. Her smile was radiant. "Thank you."

Clay found himself wishing she would smile at him like that.

She threw her arms around Blue Buffalo's neck and hugged him. Then she stepped back as if embarrassed. "I'm sure we will see you again."

"Perhaps," he replied. "You watch your back, Sullivan," he said, stepping toward Clay and speaking in low tones. "And don't make love to your woman in daylight. Better to wait until dark when you can have her beneath the blankets, out of sight of watchful eyes."

"Thanks for the advice. Now, are you going to tell me where we are?"

"No." He sauntered off. "You will find your way soon enough, scout."

"You're lost, aren't you?" From the corner of one questioning hazel eye, Nora-Leigh glanced at him. Her lips quirked in a small smile that even after five days in her company drove him crazy. If it wasn't her lavender scent, it was that grin. No one, especially a tinhorn woman, had the right to be so cheerful in light of all the things that had gone wrong on this trip.

Hell, yes, he was lost—but he'd be strapped on his horse, toes down, before he'd admit it. The heat of humiliation singed the tips of his ears. What kind of scout worth his salt got lost?

237

"If I had that confounded map of yours, I wouldn't be," he grumbled.

The grin lingered on her face as she cocked her head in his direction. "So you *are* lost?"

"No," he replied through clenched teeth. "I'm not lost."

Her chin lifted. Then she asked in that stubborn tone he recognized—it was beginning to exasperate him all out of proportion to what it should—"Where are we, then?"

It was a damned good question. "We're riding southwest."

"And?"

"And what? What more do you need to know?" He was unable to keep the irritation from his voice.

Her voice lightened. "I see you remember one of the three B's your teacher taught you when you were in school," she said. "You were in school way back when, weren't you?"

Clay scowled at the insult. "Yeah, I went to school. Which B you referring to?"

"Be yourself."

"I try."

"You don't have to try very hard, do you? It's pretty easy to be rude."

"Ha-ha." He gave her a hard stare. "Besides, I thought it was the three R's you teach. What are the other two B's?"

"*Be* thoughtful and *be* kind."

"I don't subscribe to those—"

"So I've noticed."

He snorted, annoyed that she hadn't let him finish. "One out of three isn't bad."

"Hmphh." Pointing at the shallow yet wide ribbon of water off to their left, she asked, "Do you know what river that is?"

He'd never admit it, but he wasn't sure if it was the Bighorn or the Little Bighorn. For all he knew, they could

238

well be back on Rosebud Creek, or some lesser known watercourse, for that matter.

Right now he felt about as disoriented as he'd ever felt in his misbegotten life. His balance was shot, his perception was fuzzy, and there were times since his illness when he saw double. He still experienced dizzy spells. Once when Jolly misstepped, he'd almost toppled off his horse's back. He'd hidden that from Nora-Leigh by blaming his poor horse for stumbling.

It was all getting worse, too. He had trouble estimating distance. Time seemed to make no sense. The only thing he knew for certain was that if the sun was directly overhead it was midday, but they'd been plagued with overcast days and intermittent showers. Half the time he didn't know if it was morning or afternoon. Oh, well. What the hell. Half the time he was right.

"Sure, I know what river that is," he lied.

"Which is it?"

"How about you give me that map?" he asked, changing the subject.

Nora-Leigh surprised him by reaching inside her shirt and pulling it out. It was yellowed with age and wrapped in opaque waxed paper. When she handed it to him, he didn't want to seem too anxious. He tucked it inside his jacket. "We'll go over it the next time we rest."

"All right."

As if on the wings of a giant goose, a norther bearing stormy weather swung down out of Canada. Within an hour, the wind swirled with a cold, slashing, breath-stealing force all its own. Icy rain mixed with pellets of sleet battered Nora-Leigh's back.

She pulled the collar of her jacket up around her neck and pulled her grandfather's slouch hat low on her forehead, securing the string beneath her chin. She glanced at Clay riding beside her. Even beneath the heavy twill fabric of his jacket, he shivered. His attention centered on controlling Gingersnap, he didn't see her as she watched him. He muttered something beneath his breath. His blue lips quivered, and his nose was red with cold.

Nora-Leigh flexed her gloved hands on the reins. She figured that if they were as cold as Clay's, his fingers were tingling and painful just as hers were.

Though normally well mannered and gentlemanly, Jolly had been testy all day, and at times difficult even for Clay to control. Nora-Leigh, though she knew little about these things, suspected that Gingersnap was coming into heat and Jolly was simply acting like a male. Between the weather and the horses, they needed to find shelter, and a lean-to just wouldn't do.

When Jolly began nosing Gingersnap, the mare answered with a squeal and a kick of her hind legs. Nora-Leigh grappled with the reins in an effort to handle the peevish mare. Gingersnap nipped at Jolly's neck, and the two of them pranced, sidestepped, and warily circled each other. Nora-Leigh felt helpless.

"Nora-Leigh!" Clay hollered. She glanced up. His arm shot out and grabbed Gingersnap's bridle. He held the mare still until she settled. Clay pointed ahead, then raised his voice against the rising wind and driving rain. "Look."

She lifted her eyes to where he pointed. Sheltered with a high butte behind it and a copse of cottonwood trees adjacent, an indistinct small wooden structure stood in the misty distance.

"Let's see if we can raise a welcome," he yelled. He motioned at the reins in her hands. "Hand me those. If we stay out in this miserable weather much longer with Jolly acting like a lovesick cowboy, you'll never keep your seat."

Nora-Leigh happily gave Clay control. With him leading, the skittish mare had no recourse but to follow along placidly. Also, with the stallion in front, it no longer could harass her. Both Nora-Leigh and Gingersnap were as happy as the icy rain allowed.

As they came closer to the building, it became evident that it was a home, and unoccupied. No light shone through the single window. No livestock stood in the pens or corrals or even the collapsing lean-to. Clay stopped in front of the homestead. He handed the reins of the two horses to Nora-Leigh. "I'll knock on the door and see if anyone's about."

He held Gingersnap still as Nora-Leigh kicked free of the stirrups and jumped down. She stood between the two horses, shivering with cold.

Clay rapped on the wooden door and waited, huddled inside his jacket, shivering. He received no answer. He tried again, then glanced at Nora-Leigh. Rain dripped off the lowered brim of his hat and fell soundlessly to the ground.

"Guess no one's home." He pulled his gun, checked it, and said, "I'm going inside just to make sure it's safe."

He pushed open the unlocked door and stepped inside, and came out a minute later. "Go on in, no one's home. I'll stable the horses and the mule."

He tossed her his saddlebags. She caught them with both hands, held them to her chest, and squinted up at him through the downpour.

"See if you can get a fire started," he said. "Try to make sure that the chimney's not blocked and will draw good. Don't want to burn down the only shelter I've seen in miles."

She nodded. He rode away leading Gingersnap and Stubborn and disappeared around the corner of the house.

Nora-Leigh gingerly nudged the door with her gloved hand. It opened with a creaky hollow sound. She stepped inside, then pushed the door closed behind her and stood in the entrance waiting for her eyes to adjust to the semidarkness. It smelled musty from lack of use. She shrugged out of her wet coat and hung it and Clay's saddlebags on the back of a slat-back chair near the door.

She looked around, feeling guilty for invading another person's privacy. What would she herself think if she returned to her own house to find strangers making themselves at home and warming themselves in front of the fireplace? She didn't know. She supposed that on the frontier it might be considered differently, but she'd lived in town all her life. While friends and family in Steamboat Bend often walked in with just a knock and a hello, without an invitation, it seemed so different here—and they were hardly kin. This was far from town, from civilization, from forts even. This was the Crow reservation. And who wanted strangers tromping around their home? Then she found herself thinking that if they'd gotten in, so could someone else. And they might not be good people. When Clay returned, Nora would throw the bar across the door. That would keep out any dangerous drifters.

It was only a single room, but it was large. It looked to be completely stocked, as if it were just waiting for its owners to return.

The cross-beamed ceiling and the walls all seemed to be made of cottonwood, and it even had a plank floor. Two simple wooden benches and a crudely constructed table were pushed against the wall beneath the unadorned window.

A china cupboard, with newsprint instead of glass inserts, stood against the left wall beside a counter filled with stacks of bowls, plates, and pans of every shape and size. Above the counter a shelf had been nailed to the wall, which held a flour sifter, assorted tins of spices, and jars of fruit. An upended wooden crate held canned goods. A skillet, a washboard, and a washtub hung on nails hammered to the wall. To her surprise, a four-legged wood stove had been vented through the roof.

Against the right wall, a smallish rope bed made up with a lumpy mattress and a patchwork quilt looked too inviting to ignore. Nora-Leigh sat down. The feather mattress gave way beneath her weight, and she lay on her back. Her battered hat pushed forward and covered her face. She removed the soggy hat and tossed it across the room, then closed her eyes and groaned. Softness cocooned her.

If not for Clay's imminent return, she would have allowed herself the luxury of badly needed sleep. Instead, she yanked off her boots and walked stocking-footed across the floor to inspect the fireplace. A stack of split wood had been placed next to it, and a wooden box of kindling waited to start a blaze.

She got down on her hands and knees, craned her neck, and looked up the chimney. Four sheer walls of blackness greeted her gaze, and the smell of wood smoke lingered in her nostrils. She fiddled with the damper several times until she was certain she had it in the open position.

Though she was still uneasy about making herself at home, she placed the kindling in a neat stack and, retrieving Clay's saddlebags, took one of his precious store of matches from its waterproof tin. Soon she had a fire blazing up. When it didn't fill the room with smoke, she added several good-sized logs and sat down to wait for Clay to return from stabling the animals.

She stretched her legs in front of her and leaned back on her arms. Watching the flames build, she waited for the warmth to seep into her frozen limbs. Soon her stocking-covered toes tingled with heat. She listened to the sleet-driven wind pound on the roof. Thankful that she was out of the weather, her thoughts inevitably returned to Clay, as they always seemed wont to do.

Nora-Leigh didn't have time to contemplate him for long.

The door flew inward, followed by a sheet of pelting

rain and the flap of wings. Startled, Nora-Leigh's head shot up and she glanced over her shoulder. With a resounding thud, the door crashed against the wall, and Clay stepped inside. Right behind him, Jack flew in and landed on the wooden table.

"Sorry," Clay murmured. "The wind caught the door and Jack followed me. For a crow, he's such a coward."

Clay reached for the door and slammed it shut. Then he barred the door. At Nora-Leigh's look, he said, "You can never be too careful."

"What about the owners?"

"Any sign of them?" he asked. He sat down and removed his boots, then stood up, removed his Stetson, shook the rain off, and placed the hat on the chair where Nora-Leigh had left her jacket.

"No sign of anyone," Nora-Leigh said. "But the place is well stocked as if they will be returning anytime."

"That's a possibility," he agreed. He glanced around the room. "Pretty nice place. Leastways it's clean. Thank God you got a fire going." He sat down cross-legged beside Nora-Leigh and rubbed his toes. "I feel like I'm frozen solid."

"The fire's warm. You'll thaw out quickly."

He nodded, then pulled his buckskin shirt off over his head. At her questioning gaze, he said, "It's soaked." He draped it on the stack of logs. Steam rose from its brown folds.

Nora-Leigh stared at Clay's bared chest, and her breath caught in her throat. He was so beautifully masculine, bronzed and hard. As he had caressed her breasts in the night, she wanted to feel his cool flesh, knead the muscled wall of his chest, and know the texture of the dark curling hair that grew in swirling patterns and feathered down his taut belly. She wanted to squeeze the brown nubbins of his nipples and see if they hardened as hers did when she stared at him.

244

She tore her gaze away before he could guess what she was thinking. "What did you do with the horses and Stubborn?" she asked, staring into the fire and hoping he didn't notice that she sounded out of breath.

He chuckled. "I tied Stubborn between Gingersnap and Jolly, and gave them the few oats I thought to bring along. Hopefully, between the grub and the mule, they will leave each other alone. I know it won't last, but we can pray for a peaceful night. If we wake up to the sounds of horses snorting and kicking up a ruckus, I might have to bring one of them inside."

"Surely it won't come to that."

"You don't know horses very well, do you?"

"No."

"When a stallion wants a mare in heat, not much can stand in his way."

"Would it be so awful if he were to . . . well, you know . . ." Nora-Leigh trailed off, embarrassed and unsure of the word she was searching for. It was undoubtedly a word not used in the company of women. Not that it would stop Clay from speaking it aloud, for he, despite certain behavior that belied it, claimed he was no gentleman.

"Probably not," he answered, humor tinting his voice. "At least we'd get a foal out of the fracas."

Nora-Leigh looked up from the blazing fire and caught Clay glancing at her out of the corner of his eye. Firelight flickered across his features, and the humor fled his face. His expression grew still and serious, and he gazed at her with such tenderness that Nora-Leigh fought to keep from wrapping her arms around his neck and hugging him close to her. There were times when he nearly stole her breath away.

Nora-Leigh dropped her gaze to his chest and released a ragged breath.

"Would you rather I put on a dry shirt?"

"No," she whispered, her head bent, her voice muffled.

"Is something else on your mind, Nellie?" he asked, his voice uncompromising yet gentle. "I may be wrong, but that look on your face, I know it. I know what you want because I want it, too."

Her pulse raced, and she asked breathlessly. "What do I want?"

She glanced up then and their eyes locked. With the tips of his fingers, he tilted her chin. His gaze searched her face intently, the smoldering flame in his silvery eyes startling and guileless.

"You look half starved."

She raised her brow in question.

"Not for food," he said in a husky, velvet murmur. He picked her hand up and placed it palm down on his chest where she felt the warmth of his soft skin, the hard muscles beneath, and the thundering beat of his heart. It matched her own.

"Touch me, Nellie," he whispered. "Can you feel my heart pounding? I want to kiss you as bad as you want me to."

Chapter Sixteen

"I want to touch you," Nora-Leigh said, easily disarming Clay with her timid smile.

The words thrilled him, yet were frightening. His mind told him he shouldn't even be considering this, but his body said something else altogether. Maybe an inexperienced girl like Nora-Leigh didn't know, but he sure as hell knew where kissing led. He promised her grandfather he'd bring her back a virgin. Well, maybe he hadn't said so in so many words, but that was their unspoken agreement.

"Mr. Sullivan," she began, her voice cracking.

"Clay," he reminded her with a frown.

She began again in a tremulous, sensuous whisper that sent Clay's senses soaring. "I mean Clay. I've wanted to touch you ever since I saw you washing up in the creek. Even then I wanted to know that you weren't cold and hard like a marble statue, but a warm, flesh and blood man."

"God." Clay released a long, shuddering gasp. He was never so glad to hear Nora-Leigh's honesty than at that precise moment. No woman had ever made him want her more. No woman had made him love her more. Yet he was not worthy. He should be running headlong in the opposite direction. Instead, he caught her hand and kissed the cool tips of her fingers, then placed both of her tiny palms flat on his chest so she could caress his touch-starved flesh. "Explore, Nellie, to your heart's content."

Clay felt feverish, and his body shook with need. He vibrated inside like a plucked fiddle string. The scent of her, the blatant yearning in her eyes, her tender touch upon his sensitized skin, all sent a shaft of desire straight through him.

He took her face in his hands. "This is what I've waited for. You, Nora-Leigh, are who I've been waiting for."

He showered her face with short-lived, hot, wet kisses. His lips never left her skin. He kissed her forehead and her brows, her nose and her cheeks, her jaw and her chin. His lips drifted toward her mouth, and there he lingered, inhaling her gasping breath, stealing it for his own.

All the while, her fingers slid against his chest and his shoulders, exploring, wandering, tantalizing him, moving lower, probing his ribs, scraping against the taut expanse of his belly, ever closer to the waistband of his trousers and the hot, swollen evidence of his desire.

He feared he might climax before they ever consummated the act of love. Though embarrassing and humiliating beyond measure, he would console himself with one sure thing. At least Nora-Leigh would then still be intact. He could return her to her grandfather with his conscience clear. Well, dammit, almost clear.

"Oh, Clay," she whispered into his mouth. She spoke his name on a gentle sigh. He swallowed her words and disguised the lust-filled moan that he couldn't contain.

Lifting her hands, she threaded them through his hair,

then allowed the strands to fall back through her fingers, grazing his scalp with her fingernails. Although he was seated, the delicious sensation made Clay nearly jump out of his skin.

"Kiss me like you mean it, Nellie," he cajoled. He kissed the corner of her sweet mouth. "Open up for me. And don't you dare call me Mr. Sullivan."

Her eyes widened with surprise. "All right," she said. Her lips parted in invitation.

Then his mouth was on hers again, tasting her, teasing her, kissing her hard. Stroking her tongue with his, he delved deep and thrust deeper. She moaned, and Clay was lost, mindless to everything around him but Nora-Leigh.

He released his slight grasp on her face and moved his mouth lower, breathing in her fragrance, absorbing the taste of her. Straying to the open collar of her flannel shirt, he ran his knuckles along the long column of her neck and felt her shiver. He followed his fingers with his lips, slowly unbuttoning her shirt and pulling it off and over her narrow shoulders.

Beneath the masculine shirt, she wore a thin linen chemise, a female frippery held together with bits of lace, pink ribbons, and satin roses. With shaking hands he hoped she wouldn't notice, he undid the ties holding it closed and bared her breasts. He couldn't contain the gasp that burst from his gaping mouth.

My God.

He had touched Nora-Leigh's smooth skin—in the dark and half asleep. But he'd never envisioned that she would look like this. Bathed in the low light of the fire, her skin shimmered and glowed like pearls, snow-white and almost iridescent. Her full, ripe breasts, delectably round and pertly upturned, waited for his mouth. He leaned forward and licked a pink pebbled tip, then blew on the wetness. He glanced up at Nora-Leigh to gauge her reaction. She gasped as the tip hardened, begging for more.

Then she surprised him by lifting both breasts and offering them to him. He needed no more inducement. Like a starving man, he tasted, teased, and cherished each in turn until she squirmed, moaning his name and clasping his hair. He moved his mouth lower and ran his tongue across her warm, soft belly, then darted inside the curve of her navel. She sucked in her belly as he ran his tongue along the waist of her trousers. When he slid the top button free from the buttonhole, she gasped his name in a hoarse whisper.

Clay released a long, slow breath, his fingers poised on the second button. He felt light-headed and woozy, as if he'd drunk way too much tanglefoot whiskey on a Saturday night. "Nellie?"

"What are you doing?" she asked, her tone quizzical, her voice raspy.

He looked up from her naked belly. She was looking down at him, her eyebrows arched, her radiant face uncertain.

Clay laughed. He kept forgetting that she was new to lovemaking. He lifted his head from her lap, then sat up and stared into hazel eyes shimmering with confusion and, yes, desire. Desire for him. He gulped. She'd be his undoing yet . . . and they'd only just begun.

He slipped the straps of her chemise up and over her shoulders. He couldn't talk to her rationally with her bared breasts calling for his touch. He placed his hand over hers and set both of them against the flap of his trousers. His aching arousal throbbed against her fingers. He held her still as, embarrassed, she tried to jerk her hand away. A flush already covered her cheeks, and it darkened to a dusky shade of rose at the movement beneath her hand. He heard her swallow.

"You feel this, don't you?"

"Yes," she said hesitantly. Her gaze sought his for reassurance. He smiled.

"You know what it means." He purposely didn't word it as a question. He needed to know that she knew. "When I kiss your breasts, you feel something strong and powerful, a wanting, a need that you don't know how to satisfy, don't you?"

She nodded. "Yes."

"This, the way I am right now, is the same thing."

She vigorously shook her head. "It's not the same thing."

"It is."

"No, it's not, because you . . . well, you . . . grow."

He burst out with laughter. This blatant conversation was making him *grow* even more. If he *grew* much more, he'd burst the buttons clean off his trousers.

"What's so funny?"

"Nellie, darlin', it's not that it's funny, it's just the way you put it."

"I don't know how else to say it," she admitted.

"It's a darn good thing." At the look of surprise on her reddened cheeks, he explained. "It just seems that nice girls such as yourself shouldn't know any words for this, even if they are schoolteachers."

Her chin lifted in that stubborn way she had. "I'll just look it up in one of my schoolbooks."

Clay choked back a bark of laughter. "I hope to hell you don't have any book like that." Then he winked and, leaning close, kissed her cheek. "But on the off chance you do, can I read it, too?"

She grinned, realizing that he was teasing her. Then she became serious. "Clay?"

"Hmm?"

"I want to make love with you."

"Well, then, we're agreed on that."

"But I don't want any baby to come from it."

He knew he shouldn't feel wounded by her admission, but he did. She'd told him she didn't like, much less want, children. And he'd never mentioned marriage, even though he'd given it some serious thought, but he had no intention of proposing until he had the gold safely in his clutches. Still, she wanted him. "All right."

"I've heard that some of the women in town say there are ways to prevent it."

"I know of two ways." But one was abstinence, and that was out of the question. "Don't worry. There will be no baby."

Clay picked Nora-Leigh up and carried her to the bed. He undressed her slowly, and with each piece of clothing he removed, he kissed the bared skin beneath until she was panting with desire.

He tore off his trousers and stood naked and vulnerable before her. He would not join her until she invited him into her bed. He just hoped he met her expectations, and could satisfy them.

Nora-Leigh stared at him with a wild intensity in her wide hazel eyes. Her gaze moved from his face, then slowly down his torso. When she stopped at the blatant expression of his desire, she inhaled a sharp gasp. "My goodness."

Clay held his breath.

"You don't look like that picture of the statue now."

Clay laughed, releasing a small measure of the tension building inside him. His arousal, much to Nora-Leigh's discomfiture, grew.

She gave a huff of irritation. "Clay Sullivan, are you getting into this bed with me?" she asked, her tone light, yet sensuous and urgent. "Or are you just going to stand there all night?"

It was the invitation he was waiting for. He pulled the quilt back and joined Nora-Leigh beneath the coverlet. Her warmth and eager welcome were everything he'd dreamed.

He kissed her and touched her everywhere, readying

her for their joining. She kissed him back and watched him with such a look of love on her face that a lump formed in the back of his throat.

He nudged the folds of her womanhood with the tip of his aroused flesh, his eyes on her face. She was flushed pink, her curly hair mussed. A slight sheen of perspiration dotted her forehead. He waited for permission.

"I'm ready, Clay."

"It might hurt at first."

"I know, but it doesn't matter." She gently touched his cheek. "I love you."

Clay bit the inside of his cheek and pushed his way inside. He nestled his head in the space between her shoulder and neck so she wouldn't see the tears forming in his eyes. He knew not where they came from. He felt vulnerable and completely at a loss. He knew only one thing to do. He thrust. Slowly at first, allowing Nora-Leigh to adjust to the feel of him inside her; then they found a rhythm together.

When he felt Nora-Leigh pulse around his shaft, followed by her quivering gasps of release, he waited a moment for her to calm; then he began again. Taking his time, he built to the culmination of his own fulfillment, then pulled free and spilled his seed onto Nora-Leigh's belly.

Their breathing slowed. Within minutes, Nora-Leigh fell asleep, in spite of Clay's weight upon her. In spite of her lost virginity. In spite of everything, she felt safe in his embrace.

Clay rolled to his side, taking her sweet, pliant body into his arms. He kissed the moisture from her brow; then, wiping the tears from his eyes, he closed them.

He took a long, ragged breath. The love he felt for Nora-Leigh overwhelmed him. He didn't know what to think, and he didn't feel comfortable with the strong emotions she evoked in him.

She had such power over him. He didn't like that idea at all. Still, falling asleep with the love of his life safely ensconced in his embrace was wonderful, even if he had the weight of the world on his shoulders.

Nora-Leigh woke up smiling, a dream of Clay resonating sweetly in her head. Slowly she blinked open her eyes to the pink dawn as it crept into the tiny window. The room was quiet but for the crackle of a fire, and faintly lit, bathed only in the dim glow of firelight. A steady dripping sounded just outside the window, perhaps water trickling off the roof and into a rain barrel.

The bed's rumpled quilt was tucked up childlike beneath her chin. Acutely aware of her nudity, she snuggled deep beneath the covers. She ran her tongue over sensitive, bruised lips that still tasted of Clay. She gingerly brushed her fingertips across her tender, achy breasts. A stiffness and soreness penetrated her body in places better left unmentioned. Still, she smiled. The night had been remarkable.

With Clay, she experienced something she'd never even known existed. And she thought she'd discovered a new and different meaning for the word *satisfied*. Although he never *said* the word—his actions spoke louder than words—Nora-Leigh felt thoroughly and completely loved, as only a woman must feel at a time like this. Bright promises and lifelong dreams all seemed possible in the wondrous light of a new day.

She rolled over and reached for Clay, but found herself alone in the warm bed. Fantasies of marriage and children fell by the wayside as a premonition of disaster jarred away her drowsy thoughts.

Behind her, someone swore. It was Clay. His fuming voice confirmed her worst fears. She rolled over and looked across the room. Clay sat on one of the benches, hunched over the table, his face in profile. A sputtering candle cast flickering shadows across his stony features. Jack sat at his elbow preening his wing feathers.

Shirtless, his hair falling into his eyes, his trousers donned but undone, Clay sat still. He bent his head over a piece of paper, studying it intently. A pensive frown furrowed his brow. Then both his hands clenched into fists. He pounded the tabletop and swore again.

The map.

Nora-Leigh bit her lip. A wave of apprehension swept over her.

As casually as she could manage, she said, "Morning."

He raked his fingers through his hair and slowly lifted his head. He turned his head sideways and beneath lowered brows shot her a distrustful, vengeful scowl. His tone was thick with insinuation when he said, "You *knew*."

Nora-Leigh nodded and swallowed hard. Suddenly feeling self-conscious about her nudity beneath the covers, she clutched the quilt to her breast.

"Have you seen it?" he asked. His voice was taut with repressed anger. Nora-Leigh guessed he was doing his best to rein in the worst of it. She was a little afraid of this side of him, never before having seen him truly angry.

Still, she refused to lie to the man she loved—regardless of the consequences. "Yes."

"Why didn't you say something?" He threw both legs over the bench and faced her directly. He pounded one fist against his thigh. "Before we left."

Nora-Leigh flinched. "I hoped you had an inkling of where you were going."

"I had no idea," he shouted. "Whatsoever. I trusted your family to know more than I did. Obviously, my trust was misplaced."

"No." Pushing the quilt from her shoulders, Nora-Leigh started to get out of bed.

"Don't," he ordered. "If you are within a foot of me, I swear I don't know what I might do."

The anger in his voice chilled her. She sat back in bed and yanked the covers to her chin. "You don't mean that."

"The hell I don't," he said, his voice rising. "You were so darn set on this little adventure of yours that you didn't care whether I was wasting my time flying off on some wild goose chase, did you?"

"No, Clay, I cared. I still care," she amended. "I will always care."

"You weren't thinking about anyone but poor Miss Dillon. Yourself!"

"No."

He continued as if she hadn't spoken, his voice a mocking parody of her own. "Poor Miss Dillon, the spinster schoolmarm. She'll never marry because she's an eccentric know-it-all. She could use a little vacation. An adventure."

"That isn't the way it was."

"This changes everything."

"How?"

"What's the point of going on?"

"I thought . . . well, I thought things would be different between us."

"Between *us?* There can be nothing between us now. I have no future. This map tells me nothing. I'd have to be a damned fortune teller to decipher it. Dammit, Nora-Leigh, you tricked me. You and your grandfather."

"But last night—"

"Last night meant nothing."

She stared at him, appalled.

"I made no promises."

"But—"

"You knew my single-minded preoccupation was finding that gold."

"I know that you are a scout for the Army, that you're

256

probably on an assignment for them. Nat told me that much."

"Then you knew what I have to do."

"I didn't know—"

"You didn't know what?" He slapped the table in misery. "That this meant more to me than anything else has in my entire misbegotten life? That finding that gold was the ticket to my own future? To starting my own spread? To living my own life?

"You kept telling me I am no gentleman. Well, dammit, I'm not. I've lived a rough, crude life with plain ol' hard work and my own sense of honesty for companions."

"I don't understand."

"You will never understand me, so don't even try."

Her lower lip quivered.

"And don't go crying on me, either."

Uneasy with the remembrance, she recalled how during the night she'd blurted out her feelings of love. Clay had said nothing. She'd told him of her hopes, her dreams. He'd never said a word. It was true. The worst of her fears was realized. He'd wanted her, but what they'd done together meant nothing to him.

Her throat closed and her eyes burned with unshed tears. She would not let him see her cry. She thrust out her chin and glared at him. He glared back.

Then he swore loudly, a vicious invective directed at Nora-Leigh. She swore right back at him. He looked at her with surprise. "Ladies don't swear," he said.

"Ladies don't do a lot of things that I've done lately. But after what we did together last night," she said with a hitch in her breath, "I don't believe I have the right to be called a lady anymore."

"Nellie," he said with a warning tone. "Don't . . . aw, hell." He stared at her a moment. Was that regret she saw on his features? Or guilt? No, not the mighty Clay Sullivan.

Nora-Leigh wrapped the bed's quilt around her body and stood up, holding her head high. She stalked to where he sat on the bench, his back resting against the table. He looked up and stiffened, surprised to see her standing so near.

She fisted her right hand, hauled back her arm, and with a wide swing hit him with all her might.

"Damn." He staggered back, knocking the table against the wall. Jack cawed. The sound rang in her ears. With a flap of wings and feathers drifting down like black rain, he flew up into the rafters.

Fingering his chin, Clay said, "You pack quite the wallop, Nellie." He looked as if her attack had cooled him down, although it had only riled her further.

"Don't call me Nellie," she ordered as she sucked on her knuckles. "You don't know me well enough."

Clay stared at her a moment. "Reckon I don't."

"I'm sorry I ever met you," she lied. "And despite what else you think of me, I am sorry I messed up your plans. I'm sorry I came."

He stared at her without speaking, his eyes narrowed. Then he carefully folded the map and stuck it in his pocket. Without another word, he stomped from the house, working his chin back and forth and grumbling something about the most stubborn, hell-raisingest woman he'd ever known.

Nora-Leigh waited until the door slammed shut behind him. Then she grabbed the nearest object, the burning candle, and threw it at the door. It sputtered out and fell to the floor with a soft thud. Then and only then, did she burst into tears.

"Well, boy, I've muddied up the waters damn good this time."

Jolly snorted in reply.

Guilt gnawed at Clay's conscience. He'd trampled on

Nora-Leigh's pride, stolen her virginity, and pretty much made an ass of himself. It was a great way to start the day. Of course, just to brighten things up, he could always add to that column of misdemeanors: bad behavior, ill humor, blundering missteps too numerous to count.

After spending the night in the warm embrace of Nora-Leigh's love, he felt he had nothing to offer her. Yes, he loved her. Desperately. Wildly. Even now thinking about her, he wanted to make love with her again. But he had no future, no money, and no home to call his own.

She was a fine woman, but he had *absolutely nothing* to offer her.

He stood beneath the eaves of the lean-to that was more of a lean-over, hungry and cold, barefoot and barechested, talking to his damned horse. Even the belligerent stallion wasn't interested in hearing his complaints, though, and he wasn't offering any advice. He was a whole helluva lot more interested in Gingersnap. He kept snorting and pawing, trying to find a way to get to her. The mare kept her distance.

"Females, Jolly. They'll only cause you headaches, pal." Clay worked his jaw. It didn't appear to be broken, but it was sore as hell.

And so was Nora-Leigh. She'd woke up expecting love-talk and sweet nothings. What she'd got was a tongue-lashing. Even as dumb as he was, Clay could have found something better to do with his tongue. Now she was riled up and on the prod, and wouldn't take any more of his horse puckey. Like a cornered rattler, he'd do well to fight shy of her.

Still, her deception angered him. He deserved better. So did she.

He was even angrier with Devin Spooner. The wily old boatman had pulled the wool over both their eyes. He'd known the map was useless; he'd likely only done this to get Clay in a compromising position. Or had he been so blinded by the lure of gold that he'd ignored the clues the old guy had given him? In retrospect, he thought he had. Yet there was one thing he'd overlooked.

A niggling suspicion penetrated his thoughts. For Nora-Leigh's sake, he knew what he had to do. He saddled the horses.

Chapter Seventeen

An hour later without ever having spoken another word to each other, Clay and Nora-Leigh cantered out. Clay kept to a southerly course following the meandering river. Since he'd claimed he didn't know where they were headed, Nora-Leigh wondered what he was up to. She couldn't bring herself to question him.

She honestly didn't care where they went or what they did, now. As far as she was concerned, the adventure had ended. It was time to get back to practical matters. She was nothing more than an eccentric spinster schoolmarm on holiday. Nothing would change that.

Nora-Leigh rode with her head high, her shoulders back. It didn't matter what happened now, but she couldn't let Clay see how he'd broken her heart when he told her there was nothing between them. She refused to let any man, particularly the one she loved, see her with her pride ravaged, trampled beneath his boot heels like he would stomp out a still-warm campfire.

Her ruined adventure left an aftertaste like dry sawdust in her mouth. She only hoped she could make it back to Steamboat Bend without shedding any weepy tears in front of Clay.

She caught his occasional glances. He started to say something once, but after stammering and stuttering, he swore and gave up.

After what seemed like endless hours in the saddle, they stopped and made camp. They stripped down the animals, started a campfire, and ate a simple meal in deafening silence. Dusk began settling around them, and still they had only exchanged a few desultory words of necessary conversation. The distance between them widened with each passing, soundless, agonizing moment.

Clay sat on a fallen log, cradling his coffee cup between his hands, his elbows on his knees. His dark brown hair fell into his eyes, hiding his expression from Nora-Leigh. Staring into the campfire, he seemed deep in thought and perhaps he was, but Nora-Leigh suspected he was simply ignoring her.

She sat across from him, desperately wanting to talk but not knowing how to begin.

"—Clay."

"—Nora-Leigh." They spoke simultaneously.

"You go first," Clay offered.

"All right, but let me finish before you say anything or else I'll lose my"—Nora-Leigh paused, searching for a suitable word—"gumption."

Clay shot her a look of disbelief.

"Believe it or not, I'm not as sure of myself as you think."

Clay started to speak, but Nora-Leigh held up her hand to forestall him. "Please."

He nodded, his mouth grim, his gray eyes remote.

"I know I can be difficult at times."

His brows shot up and he cocked his head to the side

in mock surprise, but much to Nora-Leigh's relief, he said nothing.

"I'd like to tell you the story that Gramps told me about his days on the steamboat. In June of 1876, the *Far West*, the boat Gramps was working on at the time, got lost. It was supposed to hook up with the Seventh Cavalry's General Terry to drop off supplies at the junction of the Bighorn and the Little Bighorn rivers, but Captain Marsh, who had never piloted the Little Bighorn before, missed the rendezvous point and traveled fifteen or so miles too far north. When he realized what he'd done, he tied up for the night and decided to backtrack in the morning.

"At the same time, a freight wagon driver named Longworth was hauling a consignment of gold from Bozeman to Bismarck to supplement the Seventh Cavalry's Army payrolls.

"When Longworth saw the *Far West* tied at anchor, he stopped to warn the captain that he'd seen clear signs the area was alive with Indians—lots of them. Since he was worried that he'd be attacked before he got the gold to Bismarck, he asked the captain if he could leave the gold with him."

"Why?" questioned Clay, leaning forward. "Indians have no interest in gold."

Nora-Leigh shook her head. "I don't know. Gramps didn't say." She thought about it a moment. "Maybe the freight hauler was so afraid of being attacked he wasn't thinking clearly."

"Maybe."

"Anyway, the boat's crew didn't know Custer's troops had been killed the day before, but that night they saw the Indian fires on the opposite side of the river. They panicked and decided the best thing to do was bury the gold."

Clay shook his head. "This part I knew about, though I never understood why."

263

"Gramps thought that if the Indians attacked, the gold would still be safe if it was buried. The gold wouldn't be lost on the bottom of the river with the boat."

"Yeah, but if no one lived, who would know what happened to the gold?"

"Good question. They probably didn't even think about that possibility. The freight-wagon driver left before they decided, so he didn't know what they did with it. But he was right to be concerned. The Indians attacked, and he was killed along with two other men.

"Under cover of darkness, they buried the gold in a cave in a sandstone ridge not far from the river."

"Did your grandfather help move the gold?"

"No, but he spoke to one of the men when he returned. Gramps had the foresight to draw up a map. I didn't know anything about the map until you questioned him about being on the *Far West*. Now I know how they relate."

"Your grandfather is no cartographer." Clay nodded in thought. "So in all the ruckus, no one thought to go back for it?"

"No, I guess not. The next morning, when the steamboat captain traveled downstream and finally met up with General Terry, he learned the truth about Custer. Now Captain Marsh had to ferry casualties downriver to be taken care of."

"This is where I picked up the story. Heard most of it from a Crow scout who claimed he was at the battle," Clay said. "Anyway, the captain, the first mate, Thompson, and the pilot continued working on riverboats the rest of their lives. They didn't live extravagantly like rich men, so the Army knows they didn't go back later to retrieve the gold. Or they couldn't find it."

Clay looked at her pointedly. "For a long time, no one could figure out what really happened to the shipment. As you said, only days after Longworth transferred the gold to Marsh, another freighter found the burned-out wagon and the bodies of Longworth and his two guards, but no sign of the cargo. The freighter company, apparently suffering too many losses, went out of business shortly afterward. It was just a lucky rumor that led me to your grandfather and this map."

He gave Nora-Leigh a considering glance. "So why are we going through all of this now? It's a good story, but how does it help?"

Nora-Leigh hesitated, then found her courage. "You're too far south. We're on the Little Bighorn. Unless I'm reading the map wrong, the gold is buried along the banks of the Bighorn River."

"What?" Clay jumped to his feet, dropping his cup and spilling coffee into the fire. He reached down and jerked the cup out of the embers, then stood above her looking like the wrath of God. His eyes glowed like silver balls of flame.

"I think you made the same mistake that Captain Marsh made."

He shook his head. "I got lost. I thought we were still *on* the Bighorn. When I was sick I got all turned around." Clay sat down, his body slumping forward. He lowered his head into his hands. "How long have you known?"

"I wasn't certain."

"Why didn't you tell me sooner?"

"I don't know."

"I should be mad as hell at you."

"I know," she admitted. She had withheld the map and information for far too long.

"But I can't."

"Why?" She felt her heart flutter.

"I wish I knew." He lifted his head and looked across at her, frustration in his level gaze. "You drive me crazy. You know that, don't you?"

"I came to that conclusion some time ago."

"But I can't stay mad at you, no matter how hard I try.

I didn't mean what I said this morning. None of it." He gave her a slightly put-upon grin. "Still, you could have told me this story the first day that we set out."

"I suppose so."

"Any reason why you didn't?"

"None that comes to mind." *Because you might have ditched me.*

"You mean none that make any reasonable sense." He heaved a sigh. "Like saving us time? Or not setting off on a wild goose chase?"

She didn't bring up the way he'd treated her at the onset of the quest—the lies, the pretenses. "I still think we can find the stash of gold using the map."

"Then you're a better map reader than I am." He reached inside his pocket, unfolded the heavily creased paper, then laid it flat on the dirt in front of him. "These symbols?" He pointed at a row of upside-down vee-shaped marks. "What are they supposed to mean?"

"That's the ridge, I think." Nora-Leigh stepped around the fire and crouched beside Clay. "See here?" She pointed to a spot midway along the ridgeline.

"Yeah?"

"This is the cave."

"Yeah, but what are those crazy-shaped things in front of it?"

"Pine trees."

"Pines? Hell, they look like feathers. Figured it was an Indian sign of some kind."

"Gramps said there were a few scrubby pines that hid the cave opening. And this?" she said, pointing to a short wiggly line. "This is a wagon trail that led to the river."

"Hmmm," Clay murmured as he nodded, tracing the line with his finger. "From the river, that makes sense. But distance; how are you supposed to measure distance on this confounded thing?"

Nora-Leigh gave a sigh of resignation. "That, I believe,

is the problem. I don't think Gramps knew exact distances. Since he didn't go with the other men, he was just guessing. But before we left, he gave me approximate distances."

"Like what?"

"Oh, from the river, he thought it was about a mile."

"And we're just supposed to stop wherever there is a similar ridge and take a look around?"

"I suppose so."

"Do you know how many ridges there are just like that one around here?"

She shook her head.

"Neither do I," he said, sarcasm heavy in his voice, " 'cause there's too damn many to count. Almost one at every turn in the river."

"I know."

Clay blew out a slow breath. "Oh well, we've come this far. What the hell."

Nora-Leigh and Clay spent an awkward, tension-filled night. She waited for Clay to turn to her—hoping he wouldn't for her pride's sake, and yet fearing she wouldn't be able to turn him away if he did. Although she heard him tossing and turning, getting little sleep either, he did nothing. She couldn't decide if she was relieved or disappointed.

The next morning, instead of continuing south, they rode north. At each promising sight of a ridge or rock outcropping, they stopped the horses and went exploring for caves. They spent as much time on their feet as on horseback, all without any luck. Since Nora-Leigh was smaller, she crawled inside the caves after Clay made sure no animals occupied them. By the end of the day, sticky cobwebs covered her from head to toe and dirt clung to her face and hair. Her scalp itched like mad.

But she had regained her enthusiasm. This was the adventure she wanted. She tried to put aside her feelings for Clay—not an easy thing to do—and concentrate on enjoying herself. Even though they hadn't found the gold yet, she was having fun. And just being with Clay was exciting, and tormenting at the same time.

After they made camp that evening, Nora-Leigh rummaged through her bag for a towel and washrag, and the ball of lavender soap she cherished. When Clay gave her a quizzical look, she said, "It was bad enough that I had to worry every time I stuck my head inside the dark of a cave that a cranky bear just waking from hibernation was going to bite me. There were times I was afraid I'd back out minus my head. That might have been better, because my hair feels like glue. I can't stand it a minute longer. I'm going down to the river to wash up and give my hair a good scrubbing."

He bent to retrieve their supper dishes. "I'll follow along and clean these up." As he stood, he gave her a mischievous grin. "Don't want any of those ferocious bears attacking you when you aren't watching."

"Why, thank you, Mr. Sullivan. Don't forget to take along your bear-shooting rifle."

Clay laughed as he sauntered along behind her.

Nora-Leigh stayed within his sight but moved upstream from Clay to a shallow area with a rocky bottom. She stripped off her flannel shirt. What little modesty she possessed at the beginning of this trip had long since vanished. Besides, Clay had seen her wearing nothing at all. He wouldn't even notice her in her chemise.

Clay noticed.

While his fingers rubbed sand onto a tin plate, his avid gaze was on Nora-Leigh. His groin tightened at the sight of her. She sat on her knees, her head bent over the edge of the river, the sweet curve of her neck exposed. She washed her face, and then with cupped hands she dribbled water over her head. It dripped down her back and over her shoulders, quickly soaking the thin fabric of her chemise. Then she sat up and looked around her for the soap.

He inhaled sharply. The fragile material clung to her like a second skin. As if she wore nothing at all, it displayed the roundness of her firm breasts, the dark pebbled tips, and even the shadowy indentation of her navel.

Clay dropped the plate he was washing and moved to Nora-Leigh's side. Sinking down next to her, he ignored the sharp stones and cool water that soaked the knees of his buckskins.

She glanced sideways at him, water dripping down her face and back into the river from which it had come. "Did you see a bear?"

Clay chuckled a little hoarsely. "No." He picked up her soap and, holding it to his nose, sniffed the heady fragrance. "But I would like to wash your hair for you."

"Why?"

Because I want one last chance to touch you. Because I can't keep my hands off you. Because despite everything I've said and done, I love you.

Clay, of course, said none of these things. He smiled as he tossed the bar back and forth in his hands. "So you don't have to keep one eye peeled for any cantankerous bears."

"I thought that was your job." He heard the amusement in her voice.

"It is, and I'm good at washing hair with one eye peeled."

Nora-Leigh burst out laughing, then brushed water from her temple. "Go ahead."

Without a moment's hesitation, Clay worked the soap into sudsy foam. Then, he leaned over Nora-Leigh and slowly worked it into her hair, pulling it through the thick golden strands, relishing the slippery feel and the tingling sensation in his fingertips. He massaged her scalp with small circular motions until he heard a groan of pleasure spring from her lips.

"That feels wonderful."

"Not worrying about bears?"

"No, Mr. Sullivan," she said in a muffled voice. "I'm completely in your capable hands."

Don't I wish.

Clay kept his fingers on her head, barely enduring the sweet temptation of her nearness. To just be so close to her made his head dizzy. He allowed himself to drown in the moment, closing his eyes, inhaling the flowery fragrance, and imagining the unimaginable. The unthinkable.

"I think you can rinse it now," Nora-Leigh said, interrupting his thoughts. "It feels deliciously sinful to have someone else wash my hair."

Sinful. She knew nothing about feeling sinful. The tightness in his buckskins, that was the true expression of sinfulness.

Suddenly he made a decision. Ducking his head under the water, he came up sputtering—only that could have effectively cooled his ardor. He glanced at her out of the corner of his eye and casually began scrubbing his own hair.

"You could have rinsed me off," Nora-Leigh complained. She eyed him critically before she reached for the cup she'd brought with her.

"I'll do it," Clay said, taking it from her hand. His eyes stung as soap slipped into them. Blinking like an owl and feeling as stupid as a fence post, he said, "I just thought it would be easier to do two heads at the same time." The excuse sounded lame even as he said it.

Quickly he filled the cup and gently tilted the back of Nora-Leigh's neck forward, then poured clear water over her head. After doing that several times, he handed her the towel, then began rinsing his own hair. By the time he finished, she had donned her flannel shirt again. He was about to release a sigh of relief when he noted that she hadn't yet buttoned it up. Just a glimpse of the upper curve of breast and the pearl-white skin beneath the damp fabric ignited his desire all over. Their eyes locked.

Clay reached his hand out to her face. She backed away, shaking her head.

"I don't think so, Clay. We . . . It just . . ."

Nora-Leigh rose to her feet and walked away, her back ramrod straight, her head high, and her steps measured. He shook his head. Although he wanted her so badly, how could he not admire her strength of will? She had a strength he himself did not. Because he knew she wanted him, too.

He took several deep breaths, then rinsed out his burning eyes. After wiping his face, he draped his towel around his neck and gathered up their dishes. Plucking her forgotten, sweet-smelling soap from the ground, he followed Nora-Leigh back to camp.

Over the next two days the pair rode north along the bank of the Little Bighorn, skirted Fort Custer, and resumed travel north along the Bighorn River, each day with a similar routine and similar results. No gold.

Although Nora-Leigh was unaware of the fact, and Clay was reluctant to tell her, they had circled about to within a day's ride of Steamboat Bend. After so many hours in the saddle, Clay had finally regained his bearings. All his dizziness and light-headedness had dissipated and he finally felt like himself again.

Because Nora-Leigh seemed to be enjoying herself exploring so much, Clay put off telling her he was giving up the search after today. They could search every cavern along this river, and Clay was beginning to think more and more that they would never ever find any sign of that last shipment of gold. And with his acknowledgment of defeat came a worse fear: what was he going to do for the future? He'd put so much stock in finding it, and now that his best lead had failed . . .

When they stopped, early in the afternoon, he forced himself to tell her that he was taking her home. For an instant a nearly imperceptible wistfulness stole into her expression, but then disappeared. What was she thinking?

After an early supper and cleanup, they sat across from each other pretending that nothing was different, pretending they didn't mean anything to each other.

"What will you do now?" Nora-Leigh asked. Her gaze settled on Clay's face.

A clear black velvety night sky hung high over the two of them. The stars twinkled above, a half-moon hovered there, too. And except for the occasional howl of a wolf, they seemed alone on the prairie. The campfire had dwindled down to red-hot embers and occasional sparks. Clay leaned back against his saddle, his hands behind his head. He stared at his traveling companion, his eccentric schoolmarm, his woman. The woman he loved. Within hours, the woman he would leave forever. He could offer her nothing without having found the gold, nothing. Grief tore through him, but he sought hard to keep it at bay.

Looking back, he saw that there was nothing either of them could have done to change things. From the day he'd ridden into Steamboat Bend, they had been on a collision course. And it had ended as it had to end.

Determined to allow her joy in her last few hours, Clay braved a smile. He doubted its effectiveness, for Nora glanced away, her expression so sad it tore at his heart.

"I have to figure out what to do next," Clay said. "There are several options since we didn't find the gold." Robbing banks and holding up trains were just a few thoughts that had occurred to him. His measly savings weren't nearly enough to start a ranch. He'd been so counting on the gold. "I have to report back to Fort Keogh."

"Of course."

"I can always go back to scouting. I'd like to move farther west. Maybe someday . . ."

"Maybe someday you'll find a wife and settle down." He heard her swallow, but as he glanced at her, her eyes were downcast, her lips compressed. "Have children."

Only if I can have them with you, Nora-Leigh. Only with you. "Maybe someday."

"That would be nice."

How polite she was being. Where was the feisty, independent schoolmarm that had won his heart? If they kept up this depressing, confounding conversation much longer, both of them would soon be weeping like babes.

"You reckon Nat got that boy, Terrell, to the fort without any problems?" Clay asked.

"Why wouldn't he?" She gave him a questioning look.

He snapped, "Dammit, Nora-Leigh, I'm just trying to converse a little here. You could at least give me some convincing help."

She shot him a hurt look. "I wasn't aware I wasn't contributing. What do you want me to say? Thank you for this delightful adventure? Thank you for putting up with me?"

"No. God, no. Why is it you misconstrue everything I say?"

"Misconstrue?" she said somewhat peevishly. "Why, Mr. Sullivan, what a big word for you."

"Dammit, Nellie, don't talk that way."

"What way?" With the suddenness of a gust of wind, her bitterness disappeared. Her shoulders slumped and her voice dropped to a weary whisper. "I'm sorry, Clay. I have had a wonderful time. Honestly. This has been an adventure unlike anything I could have imagined. Better than I could have imagined. It's just that—"

Clay interrupted her. "I know."

"I guess you do."

"If I could change things back to the way they were, I would."

She gave him a hurt look. "I wouldn't."

He paused, then shook his head. "Dammit, Nellie. Neither would I." Clay stood up and walked around to where Nora-Leigh sat huddled by the fire. He could see her shaking even though it was a relatively warm evening. He took her in his arms and held her close. She snuggled her head beneath his chin. The fresh scent of her hair tickled his nose.

"God, you smell good."

"Funny," she said, a trace of humor in her soft voice. "I was going to say the same thing about you."

She had no idea what just the sound of her voice did to him. But he was so enjoying their light banter, he wasn't about to let on. He laughed. "Well, I did use your flowery-smelling soap."

"Lavender. And I have to tell you, Mr. Sullivan, it smells lovely on you."

"Lovely?" he muttered. "You win. That's the last damn time I use your soap."

"I don't mind sharing."

Clay kissed the top of her head. "Thank you kindly, but I reckon I'll return to my own lye soap."

"If you insist."

"I do. But now *I* insist it's time for us to get some shut-eye. Tomorrow's going to be a long day."

Nora-Leigh lifted her head from his shoulder and stared up with round hazel eyes moist with unshed tears. He immediately regretted his words.

She stood up, then turned her back to him and walked a ways away. "Good night, Clay."

"Good night, Nellie. Sleep well."

He hoped she would, but he knew there wasn't a chance in hell that *he* would.

Chapter Eighteen

Devin Spooner considered himself a reasonably intelligent man. He didn't pick fights with drunks, fools, or his wife. And no intelligent man deliberately provoked a wolf in his den. But he was about to do just that. He was going to confront Clay Sullivan.

When Clay and Nora-Leigh returned, Devin had known immediately that something had happened. He had nearly caught fire from the sparks flashing between them. Was it anger or sexual tension? Most likely both. The two emotions were closely related. That also explained why Nora-Leigh was locked in her room.

Setting out, he figured he'd find Clay at the livery. When he reached the building, he walked inside and stood in the high opening, waiting for his eyes to adjust to the light. The distinctive odor of horse manure and old hay assailed his nose. Once his eyes were fine, he ambled down the aisle until he spotted the top of Clay's dark Stetson.

The man stood beside his dapple-gray stallion, inspecting the horse's left front fetlock. Apparently happy with what he saw, the man lowered the horse's leg to the straw-covered dirt floor, then patted the stallion's sleek neck and turned to leave. Devin wished he could gauge Clay's mood before he spoke to him, but the hat he wore low over his brow shaded his features.

Clay lifted his gaze and spotted Devin. He came forward, giving him a grim smile.

Devin decided to take things lightly. "Good to be able to see with both eyes again, eh?"

Clay grunted.

Apparently humor was not going to help, so Devin got right to the point. "Be leaving soon?"

"Tomorrow. No reason to stay any longer." He leaned back against a stall door, his hands stuck in the front pockets of his britches.

Devin raised his eyebrows. "My granddaughter isn't a good enough reason? I expect she thinks you are."

"You about to give me a going-over?"

"Is there a reason to? I saw Nora-Leigh. She's not her usual chatty self."

"It was a long trip. Besides, we had a . . ." Clay paused. "Well, we had a misunderstanding. Several. I reckon you know what one of them was about."

"The map?"

"How'd you guess?" Clay's voice held both bitterness and anger.

"Why didn't you just give *me* the damn map? You could have saved me a boatload of trouble—and stopped me from getting my hopes up."

"Because then you wouldn't have fallen in love with Nora-Leigh."

Clay's jaw clenched. "You're mistaken."

"I saw when you arrived that you two were right for each other. Are you sayin' it ain't so?"

Clay folded his arms over his chest. "What I'm saying, sir, is that it's none of your damn business."

Devin felt himself grow angry. "It will be my business if she turns up with your babe in her belly."

His expression hardened. "That won't happen."

"Dammit, Sullivan, I didn't come here lookin' to argue."

"What *did* you come here for?"

"I came to find out your intentions."

"And if my intentions don't match your own? Would you then come back with a shotgun?"

Devin couldn't restrain a smile, but he wiped his hand across his mouth to disguise it. Sullivan would make a perfect partner for his Nora-Leigh—feisty, moody, and not about to take any guff. "I don't cotton to violence."

"Glad to hear it."

"Have you got a weapon on you?"

A momentary look of surprise crossed Clay's face. "I've got a knife in my boot, but my rifle and pistol are stashed with my saddlebags. Why?"

"Promise not to use that knife on an old man?"

"Hurt you? Of course not," he said with a slight scowl. "Nora-Leigh would have my hide if I touched even one of those white hairs on your head."

"It's just that I've got something to say you're not gonna like."

"I don't think there's anything you could say that would shock me."

"Well, you ain't gonna like this."

"Just spit it out, Spooner."

"*I* have the gold you're looking for."

Clay's mouth sagged open. "You . . ."

"Had it all along."

The scout's gray eyes widened to the size of dinner plates. "You . . ."

"Yep."

277

Clay was all but gasping like a fish out of water. He doubled over, his hands on his knees. His back shook. Devin watched, unsure if he was reaching for his knife, laughing, or crying. He waited uncertainly.

The scout suddenly straightened to his full height. Tears of laughter streamed down his face. "God, I should have known. It figures! After all that time . . ."

Devin released a huge sigh of relief.

As Clay struggled to take a breath, he asked, "Nora-Leigh know?"

"No."

"She probably would have said something to me, I reckon, if she had known." His eyes were still wide with amazement as he lowered himself to a bale of hay. With the tip of his index finger, he wiped the last of the moisture from his eyes, then tilted his Stetson to the back of his head. He glanced at Devin. "How much have you got left?"

Devin plopped himself down on a hay bale across the aisle and looked back. "All of it."

"What? How come you never spent any?"

"Plain old-fashioned guilt. And I knew someone would wonder where I got it."

"Well, I guess that solves the mystery, and you don't have to worry about anyone else coming after it. Not after I make my report. What'll you do now?"

"Give it to you."

"Me?" Clay seemed surprised. "Why?"

"You're the answer to my prayers. Nellie told me who you're working for. . . . Well, you found that gold right where it was supposed to be."

Clay threw back his head and laughed, then rubbed his forehead. A smile turned up the corners of his mouth. "This is pure craziness."

"Yep," Devin agreed, nodding. "Say, Sullivan, I just now noticed that sorry-lookin' mustache of yours is missing. What happened? Did you get tired of it?"

"Sorry-looking?" Clay answered, sounding offended. With his thumb and forefinger, he absentmindedly rubbed the skin above his upper lip. "I liked that mustache. You'll have to ask your granddaughter why it's gone."

"She have a hand in your decision to shave it off?"

Devin got a good-natured grin from that. "You could say that."

He clapped his hands together. "Well, now, what are you gonna do about her?"

Clay immediately sobered. "She's pretty mad at me right now."

"If there's one thing I know, Sullivan, it's women. They get hot quick and take a long time to cool down. If I were you, I'd give her a few days."

"I haven't got a few days," Clay stated. "I've got to get back to Fort Keogh, and if I'm hauling that gold, it's going to take me more than a few days."

"She's not going anywhere. I expect she'll be here when you come back." Devin found himself thinking that might be for the best, anyway.

That evening just before dusk Clay found himself walking the boardwalks of Steamboat Bend, his thoughts on Nora-Leigh. He was torn as to what to do. As he started toward the livery to pack his saddlebags, Clay heard Nora's name spoken from across the street.

Three men stood outside the livery. One was the owner, Slim Jim Walken; the other two Clay didn't recognize. A lanky redhead of no more than eighteen years leaned against the door frame, a straw in the corner of his mouth. The other, a short fellow with a stocky build and a full black beard, seemed to be doing most of the talking, and none of it was to Clay's liking.

"Say, Whitey, what makes you think she'll have aught to do with you, anyways?" Walken asked, grinning. "As

I recollect, she's been ignoring your ugly mug since she was thirteen years old and showed up in this town. You tried to steal a kiss from her in the schoolyard and she wrangled you to the ground and nearly tore all your hair out."

"She was just a kid then. And no one's tried courtin' her since, have they? Besides, after spending a few weeks with that there pirate fella, she's had a *taste* of men now." Whitey sniggered. "And with him leaving, I reckon she'll still want to sit down to *dinner* regular-like. And I'm the man that knows what to feed her."

"And what would that be?" the redheaded kid asked.

"Meat." Whitey answered, puffing out his broad chest. "Nothin' but meat, and I got plenty of it."

The liveryman, Walken, hooted with laughter. He punched the redhead on the shoulder, nearly knocking him over. "Say, Roy, would you even know what to do with a lady if'n you had one?"

"I ain't talkin' 'bout no lady," Whitey said before the boy could reply. "I'm talkin' 'bout Nellie Dillon."

"Boys," Clay called, stepping off the boardwalk where he'd stood hidden in the shadows. He sauntered forward. "I wouldn't say things about a lady that aren't true."

Walken smiled as he recognized him. Clay stepped in front of Whitey and, a head taller, towered over him. The young man, Roy, and Walken, their smiles disappearing, retreated.

"Yeah?" Whitey retorted. "Who are you to say what's true?"

"I'm a friend of Miss Dillon's."

"She ain't got no friends."

"Not you, that's for certain."

"Well, from what I hear tell, she's been mighty friendly with that pirate, Sullivan. They been sharing the same blanket."

"Now, Whitey," Walken cautioned, flapping his arms

in an attempt to calm him down. "You don't know what you're yammering about."

"The hell I don't." Above the black of his beard, Whitey's cheeks flushed. His eyes darkened.

"You'd better watch where you're taking this conversation, pal," Clay warned. Close to the boiling point, Clay tamped down hard on his rage. He wanted to strike the arrogant smirk off this man's face, but that would hardly help Nora's reputation.

"Sullivan'll be moving on," Whitey continued. "And when he does, I'll take over his territory."

"I don't think so," Clay snarled before he could think.

Whitey stepped forward, then stabbed a finger into Clay's chest. The man had been drinking. "*You* gonna stop me?"

With a not-so-gentle shove, Clay pushed the loudmouth away. "If I have to."

The man's thick black brows rose almost to his hairline. "You're Sullivan."

"And if I am? What of it?"

Whitey sneered, then winked at his pal. The redhead glanced uncertainly between him and Clay, then stepped backward another pace, as did the liveryman.

"Was she good, Sullivan? I'd bet my last dollar she was as sweet as honey—jest like the color of her hair."

"Stop now," Clay snapped.

Whitey lowered his voice to a licentious whisper. "What'd she taste like . . . down there?"

"Shut up," Clay growled. He grabbed Whitey's collar and yanked him off his feet. The surprised drunk squawked and reached for his gun, but Clay slapped his hand aside. He hauled him up against the side of the livery, his feet dangling mere inches from the ground. "I don't want to hear another word from your filthy mouth."

"He don't mean n-nothin'," Roy stammered, his face

turning as red as his hair. "Please, just let him go, and we'll move on."

"That's right," Walken added. "Whitey's just got a leaky mouth."

None too gently, Clay released him, but his anger was still raging. Clenching his fists at his sides, he turned to go. As he did, a sharp blow caught Clay in the kidney. He doubled over, reaching for his side.

Clay fell to his knees and turned to see Whitey jerk his pistol from the holster slung low on his hip. The man thumbed the hammer back and jammed the barrel against Clay's temple.

Clay slowly rose to his feet, lifting his arms away from his body.

"Now, what did you go and do a dang fool thing like that for?" Walken asked his friend anxiously. "He was just looking out for Miss Nora-Leigh's reputation."

Whitey was apparently past reason. "I don't like being meddled with. He ain't gonna do it again, now, is he?" Whitey inched the pistol away from Clay's head.

As Clay started to turn, the man cocked his arm and struck him in the temple with the butt of his gun. Everything went black.

As Devin, taking his nightly constitutional around town with the sheriff, came around the corner of Main, he saw three men standing over a man on the ground. Nearing, he was shocked to see it was Clay who lay face down in the dirt. Blood was oozing from a nasty gash on his head.

Rushing forward, Devin rolled him over onto his back and inspected his pale face. Pulling a kerchief from his back pocket, he held it to the cut to stanch the flow of blood.

The sheriff, Augustine Temple, hurried forward. "What's going on here?"

"Whitey and Sullivan had a bit of a disagreement, Augie," Walken said. He glanced guiltily at Devin, then back to the sheriff. "Whitey was saying some things that Sullivan didn't cotton to."

"About what? My granddaughter?" Devin snapped.

"It's none of your concern, old man," Whitey answered belligerently. He wiped the back of his sleeve across his mouth. " 'Twas between him and me."

Devin felt a mixture of pride that Clay Sullivan had stood up for Nellie and anger at the man who had struck him. "If it's about my Nellie, then it damn sure is my concern."

Dismay in his voice, Roy spoke up. "Are you gonna arrest Whitey, Sheriff?"

"For fighting over a woman?" the lawman asked. There was a touch of humor in his voice. "If I arrested men every time they argued over a bit of calico, I'd run out of room in the jail. Is he gonna be all right, Devin?"

"Far as I can tell," Spooner said. "Looks like a nasty cut over his eye, but otherwise he seems all right. Bring over a dipper of water, Roy. That oughta bring him around."

"You best have the doc check his innards," Walken warned. "Whitey punched him from behind when he turned to go."

Devin graced Whitey with an expression of disgust. "You're a sniveling coward! Always have been, always will be. Get on with you before I decide to do somethin' I wouldn't like."

"You let him do that, Sheriff?" Roy asked as he handed Devin the dipper of water.

"Expect I would, were he so inclined."

Clay came to with a spluttering cough. They sat him up, his eyes glazed with pain. Holding him upright between them, Devin and the sheriff managed to get him to the Spooner house. There, despite what had happened between them earlier, Devin knew Nora-Leigh would give Clay her undivided and loving attention.

Nora-Leigh cried out when she saw the two men bring Clay, unconscious, onto the porch. Her heart in her throat, she rushed to his side. Her grandpa and the sheriff shooed her aside, claiming he wasn't badly hurt, but she didn't believe them.

Finally, after moving him from the porch to Nora-Leigh's bed, Devin left her alone with Clay and went for the doctor. She kept pressure on his head wound until the bleeding stopped, all the time swearing that the doctor was taking too long.

The town doc and her grandfather arrived back at the house together. Again they shooed her outside the room until Clay had been examined.

Afterward, the doc came out of the room and closed the door behind him. "Well, your friend has a bruised kidney, but it won't cause any permanent damage. I stitched and bandaged up his head, and he'll be back to himself in no time. I'm not sure how long it will be, though."

As Nora let herself feel relief, she noticed the doc whisper a few terse words to her grandfather. What had he said?

Granny evidently noticed, too, for she spoke up. "Just what is all this secrecy about?"

The doctor blushed. "I was just saying that he needs to rest and not get agitated. Still, I guess we shouldn't worry about that just yet." And with those words, he left. Her grandparents followed.

Nora-Leigh pulled a chair up to Clay's bedside. She caressed his cheek, scratchy with several days' growth of dark beard. With his face relaxed in sleep, he looked younger and less complicated than the man she'd grown to love. With a sigh, she realized she really knew very little about him. She didn't even know his age. He'd spent his life as an Army scout, but did he have family or friends? Surely he must.

Still, she didn't particularly care about what she didn't know. What mattered was what she did know: For all his male posturing and claims of ungentlemanly behavior, Clay was a caring, tender, generous man. He possessed a wonderful sense of humor. And today, at risk to his own well-being, he had defended her honor. What more could a woman ask of a man? She pulled her chair closer to the bed and kissed his beard-roughened cheek.

Opening a book but not reading it, she kept vigil throughout the night. Clay slipped in and out of consciousness, occasionally mumbling only two words she recognized: "soap" and "home."

Near dawn, with the tip of a finger she stroked the soft curve of his black lashes as they swept below his closed eyes. Surprising her, they fluttered half open.

"Nellie's soap," he murmured. His unfocused gaze seemed to settle on her face.

She picked up his hand and held it to her cheek. "Clay," she whispered. "Can you hear me?"

"We're going home."

"Who's going home?"

"We are." His eyes were open and he spoke clearly, but his words made no sense. She doubted he knew what he was saying. "Nellie's soap," he repeated.

Nora-Leigh shook her head. Should she try to talk with him? Would that help him regain consciousness? She wanted to heal him, to protect him, to share her love.

"Nellie?"

"What, dear?"

"Soap. I want to . . . soap. Go home. With you. Nellie."

She smiled, fighting tears. She could almost hear in his disconnected phrases a marriage proposal. "I want to go home with you, too."

285

"Good." His thumb caressed her jaw. "I love you."

"I love you, too, Clay Sullivan," she whispered around the lump in her throat. Filled with resignation, she watched as his eyes drifted shut again.

If only he meant it.

His hand fell away from her face, and she tucked his arm beneath the sheet. She folded her arms on the bed and lay her head down. Her body slumped in despair, and her eyes closed. Soon she fell into a restless sleep.

Clay didn't recognize the room where he lay, but he damn sure recognized the fragrance. He smelled it in the feather pillow beneath his head, in the sheet covering his body. If this weren't Nora-Leigh's room, he'd bed down in the stable and share oats with Jolly.

He couldn't recall how he got here. The last thing he remembered was Whitey holding a pistol to his head. He touched his throbbing temple and was surprised to find a bandage covering it. Now, how had that happened?

He glanced around. Beside him, Nora-Leigh sat in a chair—or at least the lower half of her body was in a chair. She lay draped on his bed with her head cradled on her folded arms. Her soft breath whispered against his hip with her every exhalation. He came to full wakefulness, realizing he was covered with a thin sheet and nothing else. He touched her sleep-tousled hair. Soft as silk, the honey-colored strands slipped through his fingers.

He glanced up and saw Devin standing in the open doorway, a tender smile on his weathered features. Clay brought a finger to his lips and pointed at Nora-Leigh.

Devin nodded and tiptoed into the room. "How ya feeling?"

"Not bad, considering."

"Woozy?"

"No."

"Any pain in your back?"

"No. What happened?"

"Whitey Jackson punched you in the kidney, then cold-cocked you with the butt of his gun."

"Ah." Clay gingerly fingered his head. "That explains this lump on my head. What time is it anyway?"

"Around six."

"I was out all night?"

Devin nodded.

"Did I say anything . . . stupid?"

Devin gave Clay a quizzical stare but didn't question his meaning. "You were in and out of consciousness most all night. Can't say what you said when I weren't in the room, but a coupla times when I looked in on you, you were spouting nonsense, something about soap and going home. Nothing that made any sense to me. But Nellie stayed by your side all night long."

Clay glanced at her, sleeping beside him, warming his body as well as his heart. "Hmm."

"She's a peach, ain't she?"

"She is."

He stole a glance at Nora-Leigh. She slept on undisturbed, obviously exhausted from her all-night vigil.

"Do you have something to say to me besides how wonderful your granddaughter is? Because I already know that."

"Nah. Just that when you feel up to leaving town, let me know. We'll make our exchange on the outskirts of Steamboat Bend. I know a place no one will see." He turned to leave the room. "Get some sleep while you can."

"Thanks, I will."

When next Clay woke, Nora-Leigh was no longer beside him, but the scent of lavender lingered on.

Chapter Nineteen

Clay found Nora-Leigh near the river with a book opened in her lap. She sat beneath the leafy branches of a tree covered with pink flowers. Though he knew she wasn't happy—how could she be if she felt anything like what he did for her?—she looked more content and peaceful than she had since their return to Steamboat Bend. The adventure had been good for her.

She wore a dress the exact shade of her hair—a dark gold and yellow pattern with an endless row of tiny brown buttons all the way from below her waist up to her slim neck. At the throat she wore a carved ivory cameo pin. As if mocking the prim and proper style of her dress, beside her lay a pair of discarded high-top button boots. She sat with her feet tucked beneath her.

Clay smiled. He'd seen her just once before in a dress. He'd forgotten how feminine she could look. It was amazing how a dress, even one buttoned-up and modest, showed off her lush curves and delicate bone structure.

She bent her head to look closer at something on the pages of her book, her golden hair swinging forward to hide the expression on her face. She didn't look up as he neared, so engrossed was she in reading.

How he loved her. A lump lodged in Clay's throat. He ducked behind a tree to collect himself. He didn't want to leave her behind. It tore him apart to think about going away, leaving her smile, her laughter, her love of life, her love for him. He took a long, ragged breath. He wanted to tell her he'd be back for her—but what would she say to that? And he would not make any promises he wasn't sure he could keep. Besides, she probably wouldn't believe him. Why should she?

He'd ridiculed her, berated her, and generally made her miserable from the day he'd first arrived, deceived her from the first day they met. He'd lied about his profession and his reason for coming to Steamboat Bend. And his biggest lie was one of omission. He'd never told her he loved her. How could she believe a word he said?

He rubbed a trembling hand down his beard-roughened face, then pasted on a smile. If it killed him, he'd get through this good-bye without tears from either of them. With any luck at all, he'd be back in no time to claim her as his bride—with the money for their ranch.

He stepped around the tree, then sauntered forward, his hands crammed into the front pockets of his denim trousers. "Hi."

Nora-Leigh looked up and gifted him with a warm smile. "Hello, yourself." The love she bore him shone through her eyes like a lighthouse beacon, beckoning him to take her in his arms.

He jammed his hands farther down in his pockets.

"How are you feeling?" she asked. A tiny line of worry furrowed her brow.

"Fine."

"Good." She closed her book. "How did you know where to find me?"

"Your ma told me I might look for you out here."

"Ah."

Glancing around, he said, "It's a nice spot."

She nodded, looking around herself as if seeing it through his eyes. "I come here often when I want to get away."

Clay drew his hands from his pockets and sat down beside her, his knees bent, his hands clasped around his legs. He had to ask. "Did you need to get away from me?"

Nora-Leigh glanced at him, her eyes large and liquid; then she looked away. "No."

He didn't believe her, but there was little point in arguing. "You're not digging to China today?"

She looked up and smiled. "No, I think I've outgrown my days of digging holes."

"That's too bad."

An expression of surprise crossed her face, but she said nothing.

He took a deep breath. "I came to say good-bye."

"You're leaving," she stated. Her voice was oddly warm.

He understood. She was trying to distance herself from him emotionally, as if by doing so she could keep her pain at bay. He wished he could do the same. "I have to report back to Fort Keogh."

Clay watched the words sink in and Nora-Leigh compose herself. She swallowed hard, and then finger-combed her hair. As she gazed at his face, a thin smile tugged at the corners of her mouth. "I miss your mustache. You looked so different when you first got here."

He laughed, absentmindedly stroking the shaved flesh where his bushy mustache once flourished. "I reckon I miss it, too. But what about that dashing black eye patch? Ethan thought it was the crowning touch."

"Who's Ethan?"

"My little brother. The pirate getup was his brilliant idea."

"Well, sir, it certainly caught my attention."

"Yeah, but I couldn't see worth a damn with that darned eye patch on. Have you ever tried to see with one eye? It's like trying to find hair on a frog." He shook his head. "And I never could recollect which eye I was supposed to have lost."

Nora-Leigh's mouth twitched with ill-concealed humor. "I thought so."

"What do you mean?"

"The first time I saw you, I thought it was on your right eye. Then the next time, it was on your left. I assumed I just hadn't been paying close enough attention, but now I understand."

A comfortable silence settled between them, with nothing but the twitter of the jays and the calling of the crows breaking the stillness. A light breeze whispered through the overhead branches. It seemed as if they were the only two people for miles around.

Clay straightened out one leg, then leaned toward Nora-Leigh and draped his arm around her. She lowered her head onto his shoulder. He closed his eyes and inhaled her scent. Smothering a groan, he asked, "What's the name of that soap you always use?"

"Lavender."

"Lavender," he repeated. "I may forget the name but I'll always think of you when I smell it."

He heard a slight hitch in her breath. "I'm going to miss you, Clay."

He deflected her heart-stopping words by answering in a teasing tone, "At least you're not calling me Mr. Sullivan anymore."

Laughter floated up from her throat.

He caressed the hair at her temple, pushing it off her forehead as he stroked her face. "I'll miss you, too, Nora-Leigh."

"Could we . . ." He heard the hesitation in her voice as if she were drumming up the courage to say more. "Could we make love once more before you leave?"

"Oh, honey."

She lifted her head from his shoulder and looked Clay in the eye. Her honest, direct gaze almost destroyed him. "You don't want to?"

"I do, very much."

"But . . ."

"But do you think it's a smart thing to do, what with me leaving and all?"

She sat up straight and placed one hand on her hip. "Clay, you should know me well enough by now. I'm not a smart woman."

He snorted in disagreement. "Don't you be saying that about yourself, Nora-Leigh! You may be a tad innocent, but you're as smart as anyone I know. Man or woman. In fact, I reckon you're more savvy than most of the men I know."

Nora-Leigh sighed. She dropped her head to his shoulder again. Plucking nervously at a loose thread on the lace cuff of her dress, she asked, "Are you saying no?"

"No." He entwined his fingers with hers. "It's just that I don't know what to say. This just doesn't seem right somehow."

"It seems right to me," she whispered.

His head fell back against the tree trunk and he squeezed his eyes shut. She could undo all his good intentions with one simple sentence. "I'm trying to do the right thing here."

"Trying to be a gentleman?"

Clay chuckled. "Yeah, you could say that."

"But you've told me you can't be something you're not. So stop trying."

Aw, hell. He drew her into his arms and rolled her over to lie beneath him in the grass. Leaning on his elbows, he pressed his hands to either side of her face, and smiled.

She looked up at him, a warm, entrancing smile that turned up the corners of her lips. Her eyes twinkled. "I've never liked gentlemen."

He grinned back. "Me, either."

Nora-Leigh stood at the parlor window as she reminisced over the last few days. She clutched the curtain and fought back tears. This was where she'd been the second time she'd seen Clay. It seemed like a lifetime ago. And now he was leaving.

She recalled standing beside Granny as together they watched the men riding up and down the main thoroughfare of Steamboat Bend. Granny was the first to point out the stranger in town. He sat his horse well, confidence exuding from his stance. He'd looked so captivating and intriguing—the way he absentmindedly fingered his mustache as he spoke with the liveryman. His smile had interested her even then. Even Granny, who had trouble with her vision, pointed out his handsome face and easy assurance.

But more so, she remembered their first meeting outside of town. He'd laughed mischievously, dimples creasing his cheeks as he pulled her from the muddy hole she'd fallen into. What a different person she'd been then.

She and Clay had spent today, the whole glorious afternoon, making love. They'd laughed, talked, and teased each other, while studiously avoiding discussion of the future. She placed her hand over her flat belly. They'd made love more than once, but Clay hadn't withdrawn early as he had before. Was his seed even now taking hold? She was surprised to realize that she hoped it was, regardless of the scandal it would surely cause. If she wanted nothing else, she wanted to have Clay's baby.

Her heart in her throat, her hands clenched into fists of frustration, Nora-Leigh watched as Clay rode out of town. Tears streamed down her face.

He glanced at the house, his expression hidden beneath the brim of his hat. Nora-Leigh dropped the faded blue curtains and stepped back where he couldn't witness her misery. She clutched at the back of a chair to keep from rushing out to the street and throwing herself at his feet. She heaved a sigh and glanced heavenward. How melodramatic she sounded. Straightening her back, she wiped the tears from her cheeks and sniffled one last time.

"He'll be back."

Nora-Leigh swung around. Gramps stood at the front door. He wasn't watching her but Clay as he disappeared down the dusty street.

She desperately wanted to believe him. "How do you know that?"

"We chatted a bit before he left."

"Did he say he'd be back?"

"Not in so many words," he said enigmatically.

She sank into a horsehair-stuffed parlor chair and stared at her grandfather's stooped back. The sweet cherry scent of his pipe smoke wafted her way, comforting in its familiarity. She closed her eyes and took a deep breath.

Why, she thought morosely, did she keep reminding herself that this was her life? Here with her mother, with Gramps and Granny. Teaching. Riding her bicycle around town scandalizing the citizenry with her eccentricities—wearing trousers, flaunting her shorn locks. Being herself. Alone.

She glanced up to find Gramps staring at her, a contemplative expression on his weathered, lined face. She dropped her gaze to her clasped hands.

"He didn't talk with you about it?"

She couldn't reply, just shook her head.

Gramps ambled over to where Nora-Leigh sat slumped in her chair. He patted her head. "He's a fool."

"No, he's not. I was the fool . . . for even thinking he could love me. I fantasized about a future that was never meant for someone like me."

"Oh, Nellie." Gramps patted her awkwardly. "What did you want from him?"

"Just an adventure at first."

"He made you want more."

"*I* made me want more, Gramps. It was my silly imagination. It had me thinking about a husband, about a life away from teaching, away from Steamboat Bend."

Gramps lifted his hand. "You don't want to stay here? Would living here be so bad?"

Nora-Leigh jumped to her feet. She hugged her grandfather close. "Don't be silly! That's not what I mean."

He harrumphed, then stepped back and gave Nora-Leigh a mock scowl. "Nellie, honey, men don't cotton to being called silly, especially men of my age."

She grinned, then kissed his grizzled cheek. "Forgive me, Gramps."

"You don't sound like you mean it," he muttered, sounding affronted. "I'm going to find my wife. She treats me with respect."

"Granny?" Nora-Leigh questioned. She broke into a chuckle of honestly provoked mirth. "Are we talking about the same woman? My grandmother treats you with respect?"

"All right, I lied," he admitted, then shuffled away. "But she was putting together the makings for a gooseberry pie earlier—my favorite. Maybe she'll take pity on me and feed her old husband. That's enough respect for this gentleman."

With a smile on her face, Nora-Leigh watched him walk away.

Just before he left the room, he turned to her. "Mind me, Nellie. Sullivan may not have said it—he's stubborn like you—but he'll be back."

"I hope so."

"I wish I could tell you why, but I know so."

On the outskirts of Steamboat Bend, Clay passed beneath a sign that read:

Undertaker/Carpenter/Tooth Puller
S. Wright

He shook his head. Undertaking and carpentry made sense, but tooth-pulling? Maybe the good man's patients needed an undertaker after enjoying the dentistry skills of S. Wright. Obviously, Nora-Leigh Dillon wasn't the only eccentric in town. He was surprised that Mr. S. Wright and she hadn't hooked up. He was glad they hadn't.

He was just kicking Jolly into a canter when he heard his name called out. He glanced over his shoulder and saw Devin driving a team of oxen and a tarp-covered wagon. He slowed to a walk, then stopped. He nodded his head. "Mr. Spooner."

"Sullivan."

He waited until Devin pulled up alongside. "Thought maybe you'd changed your mind, sir."

Devin chuckled. "Had to stop and have me a piece of my wife's gooseberry pie. It's my favorite." With his pipe clenched between his teeth, he squinted against the late-day slanting rays of sunshine. "This gold has been tempting me too long. I'm mighty glad to be getting rid of it."

"Since you've had it this long, I reckon a few more days wouldn't matter much." Clay studied the loaded wagon. "Couldn't have been easy keeping *that* a secret."

Devin grimaced. "The first couple of years I hid it in the barn. Believe you me, I laid awake many a night fretting over it. That was when I was still arguing with myself about keeping it. Then I got smart and buried it in the backyard one Saturday afternoon when the ladies were shopping."

"Well, it worked for the captain of the *Far West*."

"Yep, sure 'nuff. But then, he didn't have guilt nipping at his butt all those years."

Clay dismounted. He walked Jolly to the back of the wagon and tied the dapple to the back of the wagon bed. He lifted the corner of the tarp and peeked inside. "Whoa. With all this, I could sure use someone riding shotgun." He climbed onto the buckboard, and Devin handed him the reins.

"These old bones can't abide a wagon seat that long," he said. "You can handle it just fine. Besides, how would I explain my absence to my girls?"

"The real question is, how would you have explained it if they'd found it earlier?"

He shook his head. "Don't rightly know."

"Knowing Nora-Leigh, she would have had you arrested and tossed in jail."

Devin laughed, a sharp bark that emanated from deep in his throat. "She might've at that. She's got a clear-cut notion of what's right and wrong."

"I used to think that I did, too," Clay muttered. "If it weren't for her, I might have had you arrested myself, you devious old codger."

"What's got you so riled?"

Leaving your granddaughter behind. "I believe we crossed that bridge before."

"I'm not a man to be giving advice, but—"

Clay interrupted. "I always know I'm in trouble when someone starts a sentence like that."

Devin grinned. "That's the truth. Still, I know you think what you're doing is the right thing."

Clay raised his brows. "I'd like to think so."

"You don't want to make a promise to my granddaughter and not be able to keep it. Am I right?"

"Yes, sir. I can't say what'll happen tomorrow, much less a month from now."

"Son, none of us can."

He didn't know what to say to that.

"Do you love her?"

When Clay didn't immediately answer, Devin continued, "I think you do, but I reckon you're afraid to tell her."

"Now, wait one damned minute—"

"I'm not saying but one thing more. You're doing what you think is right, and that's fine—but it's my granddaughter's happiness we're discussin' here. And I want her happy. What's more, I'd like to see some little ones kickin' up the dust at my feet. If not yours, then someone else's."

Clay's stomach clenched. "Can't say I'm partial to the idea of her having anyone else's younguns but mine. Still, I understand your concern. What is it you want me to do?"

"If you find you can't come back, for whatever reason, promise me you'll write to her, you'll explain your situation so she won't be pining for you. So she can get on with her life."

Clay couldn't stand the thought of that. "I can't see Nora-Leigh pining over anyone, especially not me."

"Mr. Sullivan, let's not kid each other, shall we?"

"All right, if I can't come back, I promise to write her."

Devin gingerly climbed off the wagon. "I'll walk back to town. No need for you to go back."

"How you going to explain the missing wagon and oxen?"

"I'll think of something."

"I can sell them and send you the money if you want."

"That'll do. We never use 'em anyway."

"All right. Thank you for your hospitality. Give your wife and daughter my best."

"And Nora-Leigh?"

"We said our good-byes already."

Clay snapped the reins, called to the oxen, and left Steamboat Bend without a backward glance. He ignored the lump in his throat and wiped the moisture from his eyes. Blaming the dust in the air, he pulled the brim of his hat lower and settled more comfortably on the hard wooden seat. It was going to be a long ride.

Two weeks after Clay left, Nora found that things had returned to normal—everywhere but in her heart. She was in the kitchen when she heard her mother's voice.

"There's someone here to see you, Nora-Leigh."

Glancing up from the carrots she'd been slicing for dinner, Nora saw her mother in the kitchen doorway, a quizzical expression on her face.

Nora-Leigh's heart jumped in her chest. Clay? "Who is it?" she asked, striving for calm as she wiped her hands on her apron.

"I'm sorry, Nora-Leigh, it's not Mr. Sullivan."

"Oh." She couldn't keep anything from her mother. "You know me so well." She hugged her, then took her arm and began walking with her to the front door.

"He said he was a friend of yours," Elsa continued, "but I don't know him."

"Well, if he's a friend, we'd best invite him inside, shouldn't we?"

"I invited him to step into the parlor, but he said he couldn't stay. He said he had a lot of miles to cover yet today."

Nora-Leigh pulled open the front door and gasped. "Why, Mr. Arbogast, what a pleasant surprise."

The man's back was to her, but she recognized him before he twirled around and yanked his battered hat from his head. Holding it to his chest, Nat grinned. "My pleasure, missy."

"I didn't expect to see you again so soon, and certainly not here in Steamboat Bend." Nora-Leigh touched her mother's arm. "Mother, this is Mr. Arbogast. He's a friend of Clay's whom I met when we were . . . um, gone."

Her mother nodded and smiled. "Mr. Arbogast, how nice to meet you. How are you?"

"Right as rain." The man's smile deepened. "Why, ma'am, you're just as purty as your daughter."

"How kind of you to say." Elsa patted Nora-Leigh's shoulder, then turned from the doorway. "I'll leave you two to catch up. Have a nice chat."

Nora-Leigh gestured toward the porch swing. "Nat, come sit with me and tell me what you're doing in Steamboat Bend."

Nat sauntered over and sat gingerly in the swing. Nora-Leigh sat down beside him.

"I just stopped by to say howdy." He thumbed his chest. "I'm on my way west. Got me a real job."

Nora-Leigh patted his arm. "How wonderful. What will you be doing?"

"You ain't gonna believe it. You remember Bill Terrell?"

"How could I forget him?"

"Ain't that the truth." Nat shook his shaggy head. "That boy may have tried to kill me and Sullivan, but it turns out he's not a bad sort. Mostly he's just bluff and bluster."

Nora was surprised, but she had noticed a change in the boy. "He did seem to do some growing up after you and Clay spoke with him."

"Just so. Anyway, Sullivan got him mustered out of the army."

Nora-Leigh's heart sped up at the mention of Clay's name. "Oh?"

"Yep. Turns out he was a lousy soldier, but he's a fair carpenter."

"Good for him. I didn't think he was too happy in the army, anyway."

"Anyway, me and him are going to work for Sullivan. Clay bought himself some land up on the Powder River."

"That's quite a ways away." Nora-Leigh swallowed the lump in her throat that formed at the thought of Clay living so far away. Apparently he'd be starting a new life without her. She tried to smile, but it felt strained. She hoped Nat wouldn't notice.

"That's why I can only stay a minute. Got to meet up with Terrell and get out there so we can get started."

"Started?"

Nat's eyes twinkled. "On a cabin for Sullivan and his new bride." After that, Nora didn't hear much of anything the man had to say.

Chapter Twenty

It was a sunny summer day when Clay returned to Steamboat Bend, a land deed in his saddlebags and the home he'd always dreamt about halfway built.

Boldly dressed in his pirate attire, he wore a black patch over his right eye, a loose white blouse, and indecently snug trousers tucked into knee-high polished black boots. He'd grown back his mustache and hadn't trimmed his hair. He wore it tied at the back of his head with a strip of leather.

On a whim, Clay had even added a red sash around his waist with a pistol tucked into his belt. As an added touch, he wore a knife in a jeweled scabbard attached to his belt. He thought he looked disgustingly piratical. He couldn't help but grin.

He hoped Nora-Leigh would find his clothing amusing enough to deflect some of her anger. And he had no doubt that she was going to be furious with him.

So here he was riding into town on Jolly since pirate

ships were scarce in Montana. He held his head high. His spirits soared.

Clay had a wife to acquire—an eccentric, beautiful, hazel-eyed schoolmarm. But he had yet to convince her that she was the woman with whom he wanted to spend the rest of his life.

The first man Clay saw when he rode into town was its pompous mayor. He called out, slowing his horse to a walk, and then stopped alongside the man.

Mayor Hannibal Boardman, his face red and dripping with perspiration, waddled off the boardwalk and over to Clay. He stared at him, taking him in from eye patch to jeweled knife scabbard. He stepped back a pace, heaving like a steam engine. "I see you're back."

Clay nodded. "All of a piece, too." He dug in his pocket, found a five-dollar gold coin, and tossed it at the mayor.

The fat man fumbled for it before dropping the coin into the dusty street; then he leaned down and picked it up. "What's this for?"

"Place an advertisement in a newspaper back East, Mr. Mayor. You're gonna need a new schoolmarm."

The mayor gaped at him as he trotted off down the street.

Nora-Leigh held the tiny, fragile gown she'd been stitching up to the light. It was a gift for one of her former students who was expecting her first child, and it was Nora-Leigh's first attempt at anything more than embroidering a handkerchief. She dropped it back to her lap and jabbed the needle into the fabric and pulled it out again. In and out. In and out. She sighed, biting her lip, and attempted another stitch. Poorly done, as usual. She hated needlework.

Glancing enviously out the window, she took her eyes off the gown and pricked her finger. She stuck the bleeding digit in her mouth and glanced out the window again. The bright sunshine and the endless sky of blue beckoned. She sighed. She'd rather be riding her bicycle. For that matter, she'd rather be *anywhere* else, doing *anything* else.

As they had for the last six weeks, every single day, several times an hour, her thoughts turned to Clay. She missed his mischievous grin. She missed his teasing. She missed him, period. She stroked the soft cotton garment in her hands. How Clay would laugh to see her sewing, sitting quietly, acting almost normal. Almost domesticated.

Since he left town, she'd tried to deflect the scandalous gossip by staying home, but she found out she didn't cook well and she couldn't sew a straight stitch to save her soul. And she disliked both. She'd read every book she owned and every book in the lending library. Twice. She was bored to tears. She craved another adventure, but sadly, all of her adventuring was behind her. She almost looked forward to school starting. Well, sort of.

Just whom did she think she was fooling by staying home and not acting the way she'd used to? She was sick to death of it.

Making a decision out of the blue, Nora-Leigh tossed the baby garment onto a chair. She ran into her bedroom and changed from her dress into Gramps's borrowed worn shirt and trousers, then tucked her hair, grown almost to her shoulders, up inside an old beat-up hat.

She found her bicycle stashed haphazardly under the back porch. Pulling it out and dusting it off, Nora wheeled it around to the street in front of the house. She climbed on, began pedaling, and set off down the dirt road.

The breeze tumbled her hat from her head and sent her hair streaming behind her like a Fourth of July banner. She laughed aloud for the first time since Clay had left her broken-hearted and alone. Free again at last, she bubbled over with the joy and freedom of being herself.

She waved as she wheeled past Slim Jim Walken, who stood outside the livery holding the reins of a dapple gray that closely resembled Clay's horse, Jolly. Nora-Leigh glanced over her shoulder for a second look, but the horse wasn't as big as Clay's stallion.

On a slight decline in the road, she stretched out her legs and let the momentum carry her downhill, laughing all the way. For a few minutes she forgot about Clay, but as soon as she evened out and began pedaling again, her thoughts returned to him.

And his new bride. Damn him. God, how it hurt.

She couldn't believe she'd been so gullible. She'd practically begged him to make love to her that last day they were together. How humiliated she felt. How silly and stupid. She'd given him her love, and he'd given her heartache.

But unless she was reading her body wrong, he had left her one last precious gift. The promise of his baby come this winter. Although she was sorry about many things she'd said and done, she refused to be sorry about his child.

She had to smile about the prospect. All these years, she'd said she didn't want children. She'd claimed she didn't even like them. Now she shook her head and grinned. She had a feeling she would love this one.

No one knew about her condition yet, not even her mother or Granny. When the citizens of Steamboat Bend found out, she'd be driven out of town on a rail. But it seemed worth it. Besides, she knew she could count on her family to support and defend her.

With her thoughts on Clay and the baby, she didn't see the hole in the road until it was too late. The front wheel dipped, Nora-Leigh's feet slipped off the pedals, and she careened out of control. She looked up in time to see a sapling looming ahead of her. She closed her eyes as she crashed into it. She flew forward and struck her head against the slender trunk. Tumbling off, she rolled to the side of the road.

From his position inside the door of the mercantile where he'd just purchased a gift for Nora-Leigh, Clay watched as she pedaled her silly bicycle down the street. Her cheeks gleamed with a healthy pink glow. Her thick golden hair sailed out free and loose around her head. She'd never looked lovelier.

Whistling, Clay left the mercantile and followed. The road up ahead curved, and he lost sight of her. With long strides, he rounded the corner and looked around. He didn't see her or her bicycle. He glanced left, then right, and even looked behind him. She was nowhere to be seen. Frowning, he continued walking, searching for her bright head of hair.

When he spotted her lying against the base of a tree, her bicycle overturned, he ran to her side, his heart thundering. He dropped to his knees and gently rolled her onto her back cradling her in his arms. Her eyes opened. She blinked several times, a frown wrinkling her brow.

He knew when she recognized his face. She gasped aloud. Her face lit up, and she threw her arms around his neck. Clay couldn't have been more surprised. This wasn't the reception he'd been expecting.

But almost as suddenly as she threw her arms around him, she released her grip on his neck and pushed him away. Her eyes slanted into a grimace. Anger simmered beneath the surface of her expressive features. "*You!*"

That was more the reception Clay figured he'd receive. He grinned. "Hi there, Nellie. How are you?" He reached out to help her up, but she slapped his hand away.

She scooted back and sat up. She rubbed her forehead with her thumb and forefinger where a pebble-sized lump was just forming. "How do you think I am?"

"Does it hurt?"

"Of course it hurts, you fool." She frowned at him, her eyes as belligerent and stubborn as he fondly remembered.

"You should stay off that darn bicycle. You seem to have trouble staying seated."

She glared at him. "What are you doing here, anyway? And why are you dressed like that again?"

"Looking for my new wife," he drawled, deliberately baiting her.

"She ran off already?"

"Ran off?" Confused, Clay squinted at Nora-Leigh. He pushed his eye patch to the top of his head. "What are you talking about?"

"Nat stopped by a few weeks back. He told me that he and Bill Terrell were building a house for you and your new bride."

"Ah-ha," Clay said, finally understanding. "Well, he is."

"Ah-ha," she mimicked. She started to get to her feet, but her face paled and she plopped back down onto her sweet bottom. "I think I might be sick."

Clay tenderly brushed the hair from her face and cradled the back of her head in his palm. "Take a deep breath. Several."

She brushed aside his hand, but her voice wasn't as brusque as before when she said in a low whisper, "Don't coddle me, Mr. Sullivan."

"I wouldn't dream of it, Miss Dillon. Just breathe. I don't want you puking all over me."

She sat a moment, breathing deeply. Soon color returned to her face. High on her cheekbones, pink splotches bloomed like tiny rosebuds. When she looked at Clay, her eyes flashed angrily and her chin rose a notch. He heaved a sigh of relief. He hadn't realized how worried he'd been.

"You didn't answer. What are you doing in that preposterous pirate getup again, anyway?"

Clay pushed his eye patch back into place. He stood, bent his knee, and bowed low before her. "Don't you like it?"

"No," she said.

"I thought I needed to look as daring as any swashbuckler you'd see around here."

"Ha."

"I needed to look handsome."

"For what?" She waved her hand toward town. "Don't you have someplace to go? Like looking for your runaway wife?"

Clay squatted beside her. He thought about taking her hand, but doubted she'd have anything to do with that. "Have you ever seen the Powder River valley, Nellie?"

She looked at him quizzically, her lower lip caught between her teeth, a touch of sadness in her expressive eyes. "No."

"Wouldn't you like to?" Clay asked. "It's beautiful country."

"Why are you asking me these things? Shouldn't you be out looking for your wife?"

"I *am* looking for my wife."

"Not sitting here, you're not. Besides, what's she doing in Steamboat Bend?" She cocked her head in thought. "No one comes here unless . . ."

"Unless what, Nellie?"

Comprehension dawned in her gaze. "Unless they really want to."

"And this, my darling girl, is where I want to be."

"I don't understand."

"You didn't up and marry that fool Billy Seth Torrance while I was gone, did you?" he asked.

"Of course not. Besides, Granny told me that we'd no more than left town when he started courting the undertaker, Sissy Wright. Within days they ran off and got married."

"The undertaker, carpenter *and* tooth-puller is a woman? The folks in this town let a person named Sissy yank out their teeth?"

"Yes."

"Damn." He frowned a moment then turned his attention back to her. He stared into her eyes a moment. A slight smile turned up the corners of his mouth.

Clay clasped both her hands in his and took a deep breath. He released it slowly, keeping his gaze on hers. "*You* are the wife I'm looking for."

For a long interminable moment, she stared at him. Then she blinked several times, and her lashes flew up as she realized what he was asking. Clay smiled.

Nora-Leigh couldn't believe what she was hearing. After all he'd put her through. After all this time. Now he offered for her? Anger seethed inside her. She yanked her hands free of his. Furious, she clenched her fists, drew one back, and with all the rage stored inside her, socked him in the face as hard as she could.

He tumbled onto his back, his feet flying out from under him. Next, rubbing his jaw and running his tongue along the inside of his mouth, he cried, "What the hell was that for?"

She crawled over him. Crouched on all fours and with her hands planted on either side of his head, she stared down at his surprised face. "Everything, you bumbling, foolish idiot of a man."

"And here I thought I was being romantic," he mumbled. "What did I do wrong?"

"For starters, you never once told me you loved me."

"Ah, Nellie, I just didn't want to make promises I couldn't keep."

"Saying you loved me? That isn't a promise."

"I guess not," he admitted. "Are you going to let me up now?"

As if he couldn't toss her off him as easily as an apple falls from a tree. "No."

"All right." He grinned, dimples creasing his cheeks. He clasped his hands together and folded his arms behind his head. He leisurely crossed his ankles. "I kind of like this position anyway."

"Do you?"

He gave her a gleeful grin. "I sure do."

She pinched his cheek. Hard.

"Ouch," he grumbled.

"Say it."

He captured her gaze with his. "I love you."

"Say it again."

"I love you, Nora-Leigh Dillon. Is that good enough?"

"I don't know."

"Hell, woman, what more do you want?"

"Why did you come back?"

"I came back to ask you to marry me."

"Are you going to?"

"Dammit, Nellie, I'm trying."

She waited expectantly.

"Nora-Leigh Dillon, will you have my hand in marriage? I promise to give you lots more adventures."

"But you didn't find the gold you were looking for. I thought that was the reason you had to return. . . ."

"It was. But something wonderful happened. I got an unexpected windfall. I don't want to keep any secrets from you, but I have to get someone's permission to tell you the whole story. It's a long, interesting one, though. And I think you'll get a kick out of it. But now I'm able to start up my ranch—and I want you there with me. If you'll come."

Nora-Leigh sat down on Clay's legs. "Let me see if I understand this. You loved me but didn't say anything.

You wanted to marry me but didn't think you had enough money."

"That's about the gist of it." His eyes twinkled. "Are you going to say yes, now?"

Money. How could men be so stupid? "Yes, Clay Sullivan," she said, her heart overflowing with love. "I'll marry you."

"Can I kiss you now?"

She gave him a feisty look, daring him to try. "Not until we're married."

Casually he unfolded his arms and placed them around her, then pulled her forward until she was lying on top of him. "I'm going to kiss you anyway."

"Oh?" she whispered. His breath was warm against her cheek. Her heart raced. She wanted him to kiss her, and she wanted him to go on kissing her the rest of the day. Right there by the road for everyone to see.

"I've wanted to kiss you since I first set eyes on you, Nellie, and I promise that nothing short of a bolt of lightning shot straight out of the sky is going to keep me from it."

Nora smiled at him and pulled away. "I have something I should tell you first."

"Whatever it is, it'll keep. Nothing you could tell me will do anything but make me want you more."

Like a whisper of velvet, his lips pressed against hers. As she opened her mouth, his gently covered it. Her eyes drifted shut, and she savored the taste of him.

Suddenly, a loud caw startled her. Clay's crow, Calico Jack, flew out of the bright summer sky and landed at Clay's side, wings flapping, feathers flying. Clay let out a series of choice cusses.

It wasn't a bolt of lightning but it had been just as effective. Clay swatted at the bird, which finally, with a squawk and a flap of its wings, flew off, leaving them alone at last.

Clay grinned. Nora-Leigh grinned back.

And then as he promised, he kissed her again.

As their lips met, Nora-Leigh thought that life was perfect. Loving Clay, and living with him as his wife—wherever that might be—her life would be filled with adventure. And there would be enough to last for the rest of their lives.

AUTHOR'S NOTE

Dear Reader,

I hope you enjoyed *Fortune's Treasure*. Like many of you, I've often dreamed of finding treasure—a pirate's chest of coins and jewels, a lost gold mine, or that distant pot of gold at the end of the rainbow. That hope is what prompted the earliest settlers to leave their homes and travel west in search of gold in the 1800s. And it's what prompts men today to travel to the depths of the ocean to rediscover such things as the mysteries of the *Titanic*.

That dream is what compelled me to start this book. I wanted to take a legendary tale of the Old West—one that has always fascinated me—and intertwine it with fictional characters. Then, of course, to wrap the actual history around a thrilling romance made it all the more fun. I've had a great time writing this, and if you've enjoyed reading it, please look for more of my books in the future.

The mystery of Custer's missing payroll continues to this day. Do you suppose the gold is still buried in a cave somewhere along the Bighorn River?

All the best,
Carol Carson
1/30/00

BAD COMPANY

CAROL CARSON

Trixianna Lawless is furious when the ruggedly handsome sheriff arrests her for bank robbery. But when she finds herself in Chance's house instead of jail, she begins to wish that he would look at her with his piercing blue eyes . . . and take her into his well-muscled arms.

___4448-X $4.99 US/$5.99 CAN

Dorchester Publishing Co., Inc.
P.O. Box 6640
Wayne, PA 19087-8640

Please add $1.75 for shipping and handling for the first book and $.50 for each book thereafter. NY, NYC, and PA residents, please add appropriate sales tax. No cash, stamps, or C.O.D.s. All orders shipped within 6 weeks via postal service book rate. Canadian orders require $2.00 extra postage and must be paid in U.S. dollars through a U.S. banking facility.

Name_____
Address_____
City_____ State_____ Zip_____
I have enclosed $_____ in payment for the checked book(s).
Payment <u>must</u> accompany all orders. ❑ Please send a free catalog.

WANTED. FAMILY MAN. MUST LOVE CHILDREN. PAYMENT NEGOTIABLE.

Rider Magrane knows what "wanted" means; he's spent time running from the law. Those days are over now, and he's come back to Drover to make amends. But the man he's wronged is no longer in town. Instead he finds the most appealing woman he's ever met—Jane Warner—and she thinks that he's come about the ad he now holds in his hand. To be near her is tempting, but what does a cattle rustler know about children—or love? Jane posts the ad to lure a capable male into caring for her nephews—she herself has never been part of the deal. But examining the hunk that appears at her homestead, all she can think of are the good aspects of having a man in her life. The payment is negotiable; she's said so herself. No price is too dear for this handsome stranger's heart.

___4625-3 $4.99 US/$5.99 CAN

Robin Lee Hatcher
Midnight Rose

Adored and protected by her father and nine older brothers, the high-spirited beauty Leona has always chafed beneath their loving domination. An arranged marriage with a total stranger is the last thing she will tolerate now, even if that stranger is the most handsome man she's ever seen. Diego has come to California to honor his father's pledge to an old friend, but he doesn't plan to make good on a marriage contract written before he was born. But then, he never expects to find violet-eyed Leona awaiting him at Rancho del Sol.

___4504-4 $5.99 US/$6.99 CAN

Forever, Rose
Robin Lee Hatcher

With a drunk for a father, and ne'er-do-well for a brother, Rose Townsend needs more than generous neighbors—she needs a knight in shining armor to rescue her from a life of drudgery. And the dangerously desirable stranger staying at her mother's boardinghouse seems to fit the role. Rose never guesses that she'll be forced into a shotgun wedding with Michael Rafferty and that he believes her a deceitful schemer who wants his money. Trapped in a marriage neither of them wants, Rose can't deny the irresistible attraction she feels for Michael—or her hope that one day they will forge a love as pure and passionate as the promise of her heart.

___4629-6 $5.99 US/$6.99 CAN

Remember When

ROBIN LEE HATCHER

Homestead—1898. It is the kind of place where life seems to change very little, where a man can find a home and a good woman to share it, where childhood wishes come true in the most unexpected manner.

Certain that her destiny doesn't lie in dull little Homestead, Sarah McLeod wants to shake off the town's dust and see distant lands. But as long as her ailing grandfather needs her, her fantasies of exotic cities and dashing noblemen have to wait. Then Jeremiah Wesley returns from years of wandering about the world. He is the last man Sarah thinks she'll ever love. Yet as she gets to know Jeremiah, she finds herself dreaming less of a far-off prince—and more of a virile lover only a heartbeat away.

___4709-8 $5.99 US/$6.99 CAN

Dorchester Publishing Co., Inc.
P.O. Box 6640
Wayne, PA 19087-8640